Graham Lord has published several novels, most notably *The Spider and the Fly* and *Time Out of Mind*. He is the author of the bestselling biography *James Herriot: the Life of a Country Vet*, and is also the biographer of Jeffrey Bernard in *Just the One*.

He was for many years Literary Editor of the *Sunday Express*, where he interviewed a wide variety of writers including P.G. Wodehouse, Graham Greene and Jackie Collins.

He is now working on his next novel and a new biography.

D1634442

BOOKS BY GRAHAM LORD

Novels

Marshmallow Pie

A Roof Under Your Feet

The Spider and the Fly

God and All His Angels

The Nostradamus Horoscope

Time Out of Mind

Autobiography

Ghosts of King Solomon's Mines

Biography

Just the One: The Wives and Times of Jeffrey Bernard

James Herriot: The Life of a Country Vet

A PARTY TO DIE FOR

Graham Lord

WARNER BOOKS

A *Warner* Book

First published in Great Britain in 1997
by Little, Brown and Company

This edition published by Warner Books in 1997
Reprinted 1998

Copyright © Graham Lord 1997

Playback by Raymond Chandler,
first published by Hamish Hamilton in 1958,
reproduced by permission of Penguin Books Ltd,
Copyright © Raymond Chandler 1958

A CIP catalogue record for this book
is available from the British Library.

ISBN 0 7515 2027 6

Typeset by Solidus (Bristol) Limited
Printed and bound in Great Britain by Clays Ltd, St Ives plc

Warner Books
A Division of
Little, Brown and Company (UK)
Brettenham House
Lancaster Place
London WC2E 7EN

For Juliet

CONTENTS

PART
ONE

CHAPTER 1

The Editor came down the first class steps off the overnight Air France flight from New York as cool as always, slim, uncreased, unjetlagged. She slipped through the echoing caverns of Nice airport, past the scrum at the baggage carousels and towards the palms beside the glass doors, trailing behind her a little bald porter with a besotted smile, a squeaky trolley and three pieces of matching luggage.

The porter trotted at her heels like a lap-dog. Ugo Legrandu grinned. He would not have been at all surprised if the porter had suddenly bounded away to sniff all the other porters. Still, Ugo sympathised with him: you had only to glance at The Editor to want to sniff her. Yet she also always carried that whiff of untouchability that is worn like scent by the truly stylish. Whenever she stepped off a plane in Paris or LA or Tokyo the airport paparazzi always snapped her photograph, just in case. You would never have guessed that in fact she was only a journalist, like them. She looked exactly like a Celebrity.

Even the way she walked towards him weakened him: the way her girlish summer skirt flirted with her long bare legs, the shy little toenails glistening like seashells, the boyish figure, the *gamine* haircut, the frilly blouse, the delicacy of her fingers. He dreamed of being touched by those exquisite little fingers: he knew exactly how they would feel. She was so unlike his wife and the other swarthy, stocky women he knew – so pale, so elegant, so feminine, so English. Even her pert little nose looked Anglo-Saxon. She looked about thirty-two but she had to be quite a bit older. It was amazing how these Anglo-Saxon women kept their looks. And she was always so fragrant: she smelt faintly of herbs; she smelt like home, like Corsica. How could Peppu say as he always did that Vietnamese women are the most beautiful in the world? Peppu had lived in Saigon for far too long. Peppu had forgotten the pale shimmer of the Anglo-Saxons. They said she was divorced. Her husband must have been mad to let her go.

Ugo clicked his heels and fingered the shiny peak of his cap. He smiled. '*Bonjour, madame*,' he said. 'Welcome back.'

Her sunglasses gazed at him with silver reflections. In their lenses he saw himself duplicated and diminished. Was he really as short as that? He looked stunted in her lenses. He pulled his shoulders back and held his head high. He wished she would take the glasses off: her eyes were green.

'Step on it,' she said. 'The autoroute. We're late.'

The airport's glass doors slid open and the warmth of the Côte d'Azur wrapped them like a towel. The porter scurried towards the back of the Mercedes, grunting. Ugo opened the rear door for her, releasing a cool metallic whiff of air-conditioning and relishing a glimpse of creamy thigh as she climbed in and her legs parted slightly, caressing gold leather.

She frowned and wrinkled her nose. 'Have you been smoking in here?'

'Me, *madame*? I do not smoke. Never.'

'I have told you before: I will not tolerate smoking.'

'I do not smoke for eight year, *madame*. I terminate.'

'I can distinctly smell smoke in here.'

She peered into both ashtrays. They were empty. She sniffed suspiciously. Ugo bent his head and sniffed inside the car as well. His nose was close to her knees. He sniffed again.

'That's enough,' she said. She tugged at her skirt.

Ugo straightened. 'Is I think the fires, *madame*, the incendiaries. They have burn much of the coast this summer. They are setting fire to many hectares of Provence and Côte d'Azur.'

The silver sunglasses flickered at him.

'They say it is Mafia,' he said. 'They say the burnings make cheaper the land for them to buy.'

'I can't stand cigarette smoke,' she said. 'Do you hear? I shall not tolerate it.'

'*Non, madame.*'

'Now move.'

'*Weh, madame.*'

'*Oui!*'

'*Weh, madame.*'

'Step on it.'

He tipped the porter, slid behind the wheel, pulled on his thin black driving gloves and already she was speaking on the telephone, organising their lives. He eased the Merc out of the airport and into the northbound traffic, despising the careering lanes of vehicles racing blind beside the seaside through the ozone haze towards Nice. He headed inland instead, towards St Laurent-du-Var and the A8 *péage* autoroute, soaring high on the three-lane northern flyover above the city's smoky industrial suburbs, past the salmon-pink and blue apartment blocks stacked on the scarred hillside on the left, up into the clean air of the jutting granite foothills of the Alps. Far down below on the right the Baie des Anges glittered blue and silver in the sunlight and a distant Corsican ferry, bound perhaps for Ajaccio or Bastia, lay paralysed on the sea like a tiny flaw in a mirror.

'Kelly?' she was saying on the telephone.'Yes. Fine. OK. Not bad. All right, Kelly, that's enough social chit-chat, thank you. We've got loads of work to do. Now listen ...'

She always had loads of work to do, thought Ugo, as they hummed across the Viaduct St Isadore. In the old days, when she had had more time to spare, she had sometimes told him to take the slow, winding coastal road to Monaco along the broad sweep of the Promenade des Anglais and through the old ochre fishing port of Nice towards Villefranche. When they took that route Ugo used to imagine as they cruised past the lush gardens of Cap-Ferrat and the boats bobbing at Beaulieu how different it must have been here in the twenties and thirties, how much more stylish and languid, in the heydays of Yves Montand and Simone Signoret and Brigitte Bardot, before the bulldozers and trippers moved in and ruined it all. On those rare seaside drives he had been able to slow down and take his time and she had seemed to slip into a lower gear herself, settling back to watch the expensive villas and views slide past and sometimes humming gently to herself as though remembering some long forgotten happiness. He had wanted then to tear her clothes off, throw her onto the back seat and ravish her.

But they rarely took the single-lane coast road any more: she was far too busy nowadays and the road had become sticky with traffic jams. Sometimes in the summer it could take a couple of hours to get from the airport to Monte Carlo on the coast road and nowadays she was always in a rush to get to the *Celebrity* offices in Monaco, to meetings or lunches in Cannes or Antibes, to the airport, or to her villa up in the hills at St Paul de Vence. For months now she had been working non-stop on *Celebrity* magazine's biggest promotion ever, a glamorous celebrity party to end all celebrity parties: a huge New Year's Eve ball to be held on 31 December 1999 to welcome the new millennium. It left her with little time to dawdle on the coastal road to Monte Carlo.

They cleared the grubby outskirts of Nice and sped east

high in the hills along the deserted autoroute towards Eze and La Turbie. Wisps of cloud clamoured about the mountain tops like groupies and if he had switched off the air-conditioning and opened the windows he would have been able to savour the smell of heaven: the heady perfume of the *maquis*, that wilderness scent of lavender, myrtle, rosemary and thyme which always reminded him of her. He glanced at her in his rearview mirror. She had left the glass partition open as usual as she spoke on the telephone. She never seemed to care whether he overheard her conversations or not: it was almost as though she considered him to be of no account, but instead of feeling insulted he found her dismissive attitude strangely arousing. A woman's contempt was always oddly exciting. In the rearview mirror her lips teased the telephone. Her voice oozed into it like honey. He wanted to lick the corners of her mouth.

'Christ, Kelly,' she was saying, 'why the hell didn't you think of that before? What? Don't give me that bog-Irish blarney, you should have realised – what's that? What balls! Plus you failed to get me on that TV show in New York – what? That's no excuse – I hear what you're saying, Kelly, but I don't take it on board: you're an idiot, Kelly. I don't know why I bother to keep you on.'

Ugo grinned secretly behind his lips: she treated Kelly like *merde*, which always made Ugo happy. He had no time for the Irish: they complained too much. They whined.

'I want that millennium file on my desk in thirty minutes,' she was saying, 'with a complete update on the venues for the ball and what we can do to sort it out. Plus I want all the CDs and videos that have been sent in for review since I've been away. Yes, Kelly, all of them. Plus call conference for midday, on the dot. Plus I want to see Campbell at twelve thirty, Ferré at twelve forty-five, Murdoch at twelve fifty, Langoustier at twelve fifty-five and Merlot at one. And book a table for four at Roquebrune for one thirty sharp. Plus I have to be in London by six thirty for dinner and a power breakfast tomorrow, so I'll need to meet François at the airport at about three thirty. And book me on a morning flight on Wednesday from London to Hong Kong, coming back the next Monday via LA and Washington with a two-day stopover at each of them. Tell BA they owe me a favour: the Ottawa piece we did. Plus I want you to get me on at least one TV chat show while I'm in London and at least one in Hong Kong and no mistakes this time, or else. That's a must-have, Kelly, do you hear? Right. Now get on with it. *Capeesh*? I'll be with you in fifteen minutes.'

Ugo slipped the Merc into the fast left-hand lane of the autoroute, taking the car up to 180kph. It barely trembled. 180kph was illegal, of course, but the *flics* would never stop a speeding Merc on the A8. Everything went much too fast on the A8, with Mercs and little Peugeots alike racing each other at lethal speeds like dodgems through the tunnels and over the viaducts. The *flics* knew that if they did try to stop a hurtling Merc they might find themselves peering down the barrel of a Mafia shooter since most of the Mercs on this road were part of the daily Italian invasion of France that poured over the border just up the road. Italian gangsters and hoodlums descended every day on the Côte d'Azur to feed like locusts off the casinos, brothels and property developments of the entire coast from Menton to Toulon. Mussolini would have been proud of them. And the French, of course, did nothing about it, nothing to defend themselves from this invasion of the *macaroni*; not the *flics*, not the local politicians. The French never did. The French were pathetic. They should take a few lessons from Corsica, thought Ugo, where the local bandits and FLNC guerrillas had sent the Mafia scurrying back to Sicily with bombs and bullets up their neat little Italian *derrières*. You didn't see many of the *macaroni* nowadays screaming into their mobile phones on the beach at Palombaggia.

The Editor killed the telephone connection with a stab of her finger and made several more calls: to Tony Murdoch, to the libel lawyer, to someone in Athens, the marchesa in Venice, her secretary in London, to Iain Campbell. Ugo had no time for Iain Campbell, either. Campbell was her new deputy editor, but he spoke a strange English dialect and the other evening Ugo had seen him wearing a skirt as he went off to a party after work. True, Campbell had also been wearing a dagger in his sock, but what kind of a man is it who goes out at night in a skirt? The previous deputy editor, the American, did at least wear trousers but then she had sacked him for his drinking and had hired Campbell instead. Ugo suspected that Campbell probably came from Greece – some of them wore skirts too – and he had no time for the Greeks, either. He had met a few in Cargese. Shifty, the Greeks.

It was cosy in the quiet cocoon of the car, thought Ugo, just the two of them together, with the engine and the air-conditioning whispering together like lovers and the glass partition open and her voice melting the telephone receiver. Then the telephone crackled and died as the Merc hurtled into one of the tunnels, plunging deep into the hot darkness of the mountains, the engine throbbing as the sound echoed against the walls. He thought of touching her in the dark. He wanted to nuzzle her tiny breasts.

They shot out of the blackness of the tunnel into the blinding sunlight again and she switched her telephone off, leaned forward, closed the partition and removed her sunglasses. At times he was convinced that she could read his mind. She began to flick through her pile of magazines: *Hello!*, *OK!*, *Tatler*, *Vanity Fair*, *Marie Claire*, *The New Yorker*.

He hunched over the wheel, fingered it with the tips of his gloves and slid the Merc into the slow lane and down off the autoroute through the Tunnel de Monaco towards the bustling upper reaches of Monte Carlo. A gap in the hills offered a rare glimpse of the Mediterranean at Cap d'Ail and the air-conditioning suddenly smelled of rubber, hot metal, petrol fumes. Down by the sea the skyscrapers huddled too close together around the bay, like Italian sunbathers. He hated it when she read her magazines in the car. It separated them much more effectively than any glass partition.

Strange, he thought: why does she close the partition only after making her telephone calls? Perhaps it was only in silence that she felt she needed protection from him, when she had taken her sunglasses off and her eyes were naked. She looked up and caught his glance in the rearview mirror. Her naked eyes were as green as traffic lights.

He licked his lips. His voice was hoarse. 'It is good to have you back, *madame*,' he said.

She shivered. Something slimy seemed to crawl across her spine.

Patrick Kelly slammed his telephone receiver into its cradle in his tiny office high in the *Celebrity* building in Monte Carlo. 'Bitch!' he said. 'Ugly Brit bitch!' What was it about these arrogant English women? Kelly had met plenty of feminist ball-breakers when he had worked in the States, God knows, with their padded shoulders and multiple orgasms, but this English hag was something else. She didn't just break your balls: she tied fancy knots in them and draped them round her neck. When she had sacked Bill Warren a month ago for drinking at lunchtime she had called him in to her office, made him stand beside her desk and sniffed his breath. 'I will not tolerate alcoholics in this office,' she had told him. 'You know very well that I have forbidden midday drinking.' Bill had had one glass of wine with his lunch – and he had been the deputy editor.

Kelly opened the top drawer of his metal cabinet and retrieved the millennium file. It was already two inches thick. And that was another thing: why did she always insist that everything had to be printed out on paper before she would consider it? Why did she refuse even to look at a computer, let alone learn how to work one? Paper reassured her. She turned pages with confidence, as though they were promises.

He carried the millennium file through to her office and dropped it onto her desk. He wished he had never heard of the millennium file or, come to that, of the shite millennium itself. He wished he had never heard of the New Millennium's Eve *Celebrity* Ball. He wished he could suddenly wake up in Kilkenny in the year 2001.

At first it had seemed a brilliant idea when she had suggested a *Celebrity* magazine New Year's Eve party on 31 December 1999 with two thousand guests to welcome the year 2000. And not just any two thousand guests but two thousand mega-celebrities, with invitations going out to the biggest A-list ever, from the Queen of England and the US President to Madonna, Maradona and Mother Maria of Calcutta. They would hold the party somewhere stunningly exotic, she had announced with confidence, somewhere like the Seychelles or the Taj Mahal, and when *Celebrity* published page after page of exclusive pictures after the ball the circulation would quadruple around the world. What was more, she had pointed out that the ball would cost *Celebrity* nothing since every airline, caterer, hotel and entertainer in the world would be fighting for the chance to be associated for free with the ball of the millennium. It could even make a huge profit for the magazine when they came to sell exclusive TV, movie, book and other subsidiary rights. It would be the biggest money-spinning PR stunt since the moon landings. Even Tony Murdoch, *Celebrity*'s one-eyed Australian production editor, had been sufficiently impressed to deliver himself of a traditional, quaint old Australian oath.

'Shit a brick!' Murdoch had said, winking his good eye. 'That's fucking brilliant.'

But Kelly had soon discovered that finding an exotic venue was not as easy as the Hag From Hell seemed to think. The Seychelles refused permission for environmental reasons, the Taj Mahal declined on religious grounds, and for months Kelly had been searching with increasing desperation for some stunning venue that had not already been taken by somebody else. The world's tallest building, in Kuala Lumpur, had been booked years ago. So had Central Park, the best sites at the

Grand Canyon, the beach at Rio, the lower slopes of Mount Everest, the Victoria Falls, the Egyptian pyramids, Stonehenge, the Kremlin, the Palace of Versailles in Paris, the Colosseum in Rome and the National People's Congress building in Beijing. So too had the Sears Tower in Chicago and the Rainbow Room at Radio City in New York and every hotel in the Western world from Paris to Johannesburg to Buenos Aires, not to mention the Excalibur in Nevada, the Rossiya in Moscow, the Westin Stamford in Singapore, the Tump Nak in Bangkok, the Mathäser in Munich and the Sydney Opera House. Even the Royal Albert Hall in London had been booked as long ago as 1975 by some clever PR guy called Roger Haywood. It seemed to Kelly as though everyone in the world – all 6,000 billion people – were going to be out partying on 31 December 1999. Who the hell was going to do the babysitting that night? Perhaps that was where the real money was going to be made: by setting up a worldwide New Millennium's Eve babysitting company. Kelly felt as though he had tried everywhere. Time was trickling away and the Hag From Hell was becoming increasingly heated. He knew now what he wanted to do on 31 December 1999: the really stylish thing would be to stay at home, crack a couple of cans of Guinness, watch TV and go to bed early.

And then two weeks ago, in the last editorial conference before the Hag From Hell had flown off to the States on yet another of her globe-trotting freebies, Tony Murdoch had come up with a wonderful solution.

'Well, bugger me,' Murdoch had said, 'I've just had a beaut idea. OK, so we can't get the very best venues but we can still make sure that we throw the very first New Year's Eve party. We can scoop the rest of the world.'

The Hag From Hell had considered him with the keen expression of an Apache squaw out hunting for paleface scalps. 'How?' she said.

'Easy,' said Murdoch. 'No worries. We have the ball on a Pacific island, the one nearest to the international date line.

That way we get to celebrate midnight on New Year's Eve before anywhere else. We'd be the first in all the world to reach the year 2000.'

The Editor gazed at him with disbelief, as she always did when one of her staff came up with a decent idea.

'I used to go there for bonzer holidays when I was a kid in Oz,' Murdoch announced. 'It's a beaut little island called Vava'u, in the Tonga group, and it's only forty miles this side of the date line, so it gets each new dawn before anywhere else in the world. It's even an hour ahead of Fiji and New Zealand because there's a bend in the date line just there so that the line doesn't go right through the middle of them.'

They had all gazed at him for a moment.

'Fantastic,' said Caroline Ponsonby.

'Brilliant,' said Kelly.

The Hag From Hell had snapped her fingers – 'An atlas!' – and Kelly had come running, opening the vast, unwieldy book at the South Pacific as he ran. Her scarlet fingernail slid down the map like a drop of blood, tracing the international date line. Murdoch was right: there, packed as close to the date line as a packet of figs, was a scatter of Tongan islands and the closest of all was Vava'u.

She had given Murdoch a brief nod. It was very nearly a thank-you. 'Right!' she had said. 'I don't have any difficulty with that. OK, Kelly, go for it. I want that island for the ball.'

But Kelly had failed so far to deliver. Vava'u had been taken already, bought up entirely in 1995 by a foreign company that had already sold hundreds of tickets for New Year's Eve 1999 to customers who had paid £20,000 each. The entire island had been sold – lock, stock and Paradise International Hotel, and even the Ocean Breeze restaurant.

Kelly had begun to panic. 'She'll like crucify me!' he had wailed. 'Jaysus, Tony, what do I do?'

Murdoch had tried to comfort him in traditional Australian fashion. 'Strewth, Paddy, don't shit your strides, mate. You're not completely fucked yet.'

'But what do I do? She'll crucify me. I'm that harassed, I tell you. That harassed. I'm just a blur.'

'Get a grip, mate. We'll think of something, no worries. No probs. Don't get yourself into a paddy.' Murdoch blinked his good eye. 'Let's just try another of the Tongan islands. They can't all have been flogged already.'

But they had. Every speck of Tongan soil, from Tafahi to Namuka, was going to be packed out on 31 December 1999. Planeloads of tourists had booked every flight into the place. One British travel company, First Dawn Celebrations, had even arranged as far back as 1994 that six hundred of their customers would celebrate the arrival of the new millennium not just once but twice: first with a musical laser show on the biggest of all the Tongan islands, Tongatapu, then all over again twenty-four hours later just across the international date line in Western Samoa, where it would still be 31 December 1999.

'Well, poke out me eye with a burnt stick!' said Murdoch.

'Oh God,' whimpered Kelly. 'She's like back again next week. Oh God.'

'No worries, mate.' Murdoch had focused his concentration by scratching his scrotum. 'There are two more little islands much further south, Chatham and Pitt, that belong to New Zealand. Their pozzie's a bit further from the date line than Tonga, but because Chatham and Pitt are that much further south than Tonga, they'll get the first daylight on the first day of January even before the Tongans.'

'Brilliant!' said Kelly. He had thrown his arms around Murdoch and had kissed him on both cheeks. 'I love you I love you,' he had warbled.

'Strewth, Paddy, rack off, you bloody great poof. They'll think we're a couple of shirt-lifters.'

But Kelly soon learned in despair that both Chatham and Pitt, too, had already been booked – in 1994 by a company called First Light Promotions that was planning its own big celebrity party there. They even had a letter from the Royal Observatory at Greenwich which said: 'We can confirm that we believe the first populated area to encounter sunrise on the first day of the new millennium to be the Chatham Islands.'

'The ratbags,' said Murdoch. 'Drongo bastards. Jeez, mate, that's crook.'

Kelly had slumped into his chair and curled up in a foetal position. 'She'll like kill me for sure,' he said. He nodded for reassurance. 'That's right. That's it. She'll do for me.'

'That's rougher than an outback wallaby's bum.'

'She'll like chew my balls off.'

'You still got some left?'

'Help me, Tony. Help me!'

'Wish I could, mate, but you're stuffed. You're as stuffed as Ned Kelly's auntie's parrot.'

'Mammy,' said Kelly. 'Oh, mammy.'

They were all there, waiting for her in the conference room on the eighteenth floor with the huge picture windows overlooking the tall sailing ships and the top-heavy gin palaces parked like fat tarts in the harbour in Monte Carlo. Far up on the right Rainier's silly little palace, with its toytown battlements and clock and toytown turrets, perched high on the hill like a child's fantasy. They were all there: Iain Campbell, Tony Murdoch, Pascale Merlot, Caroline Ponsonby, Jean-Paul Ferré, Nat Wakonde, Michèle Langoustier, Kevin Thomas, Mary Rogers, Pauline Chang. All waiting for her, all needing her to make them necessary. They looked up as she passed, a couple of them half-smiling, but she strode on, camouflaged by her sunglasses, ignoring them, heading for her own office.

'Well, get Lady Muck,' said Murdoch, picking his teeth with the cap of his biro.

'Shh, Tony, be quiet!' muttered Pauline Chang.

'Stand by for another episode of *Malice in Wonderland*.'

'She'll hear you.'

'I don't give a dingo's fart,' said Murdoch. 'No probs.'

Kelly was hovering just outside her office. He gave her his winning Celtic smile, the one that made his eyes twinkle and then disappear. 'Welcome back, ma'am,' he said, 'to be sure.'

She strode past him, trailing a whiff of *Poison*.

'The file's in your tray, so it is.'

'It had better be.'

She shed her briefcase and sat at her desk. 'Sack the chauffeur,' she said.

'Ugo?'

'Whatever his name is.'

'Ugo Legrandu.'

'Legrandu? The Big?' She laughed unpleasantly. 'That's rich. The man's practically a dwarf. Sack him. Now.'

Kelly hesitated. Poor little Ugo. First Bill Warren, now Ugo Legrandu. For a moment the ancient blood of the Kellys rose in his breast. He had to say something. The Kellys had always resisted injustice, ever since Cromwell, though most of them it is true were dead because of their courage.

'He's been with us like for three years,' said Kelly. 'He has a wife and kids back in Corsica.'

'So do them a favour and send their little daddy back to them.'

'With no payoff?'

'Why should he have a payoff? I don't have any difficulty with that.'

'But he's like –'

'Oh, for God's sake, Kelly! All right: give him a week's pay. Then sack him.'

'Do I not give him some sort of explanation?'

'What for?'

'Well, people do like to know why …'

A merry vase of flowers smiled at her from the corner of her desk, from beside the silver-framed portrait of Dirk Molloy, *Celebrity*'s proprietor. She ran her fingers lightly over the gleaming surface of the desk. They were elegant fingers, delicate: her men had always liked the way she touched them. Even David had liked the way she touched him, even after he left her and took Geoffrey with him. For a year after the divorce David had still tried to go to bed with her whenever they met to collect or return Geoffrey. She had always refused. The bastard. Who did he think he was? No one had ever left her before. She had never forgiven him for the humiliation.

She stroked the wood, enjoying its hardness. She remembered the little chauffeur's strutting walk as he met her at the airport, as though he owned her, and his leer in the rearview mirror and the tufts of coarse black hair peeping out of the back of his black leather driving gloves as he gripped the steering wheel. His gloves would leave no fingerprints. She touched her throat. The stack of documents in her IN tray towered above the polished desk like a miniature paper skyscraper. On each of its levels whole lives awaited her judgement and each decision would take her no more than a sudden few seconds. Perhaps God was also a woman. She looked up at Kelly. Her sunglasses glittered. They made her look blind.

The little Corsican pig had touched her as he had helped her out of the car, she was sure of it. His fingers had lingered on her buttock, the dirty little goat. How dare he?

'Tell him he smells,' she said.

'Smells?'

'Tell him he stinks. Like a rutting camel.'

'I'll think of something,' said Kelly.

'You'll tell him precisely that or you're out yourself. Do you hear?'

He stared at her. He could feel his blood rush up his neck. His face glowed like a Grafton Street drunk on a Saturday night. Arrogant Brit bitch!

'I said, do you understand?'

He nodded. His face was burning.

'Say it.'

'Yes.'

She pointed a finger at him. 'Say it!'

'I understand.'

'You'd better,' she said. 'Plus don't stare at the floor when I'm shouting at you. Now sod off.'

They all stood up when she joined them in the conference room: the men, the women, the two who were in between. It was a polite gesture that always irritated Caroline Ponsonby. 'Why should we always stand up for the bitch?' she had asked Tony Murdoch.

'Because she's a sheila,' said Murdoch, 'and also The Editor.'

'She's a slut. She never washes her hands when she's been to the loo. And why do we always call her The Editor? As though she was the Madonna, the Virgin Mary?'

'Old-fashioned good manners,' said Murdoch, 'and fear.'

The Editor took the empty seat at the head of the table beside Iain Campbell, her new deputy, who looked genially at them over the half-moon lenses of his spectacles.

Stone me, marvelled Murdoch, what does she think she looks like? That girly skirt is ridiculous at her age, and that frilly blouse. And bare legs! White sandals! Peek-a-boo toenails! My God, thought Murdoch, she looks like a flat-chested teenage tart. Worse: she looks like a titless teenage tart from Tasmania. No wonder she hasn't got a man, the poor old slapper.

'G'day,' he said. 'Good to have you back, Stella.'

She sniffed and frowned. 'Someone's been smoking in here,' she said.

'No,' said Campbell.

She sniffed again. 'Who's been smoking?'

'No one, Stella,' they said together, like a kindergarten chorus.

She looked at them with contempt. 'Bloody liars,' she said. 'If I catch anyone smoking in this office, they're out. Understand? I will not tolerate smoking. OK, let's get to it.' She glanced around the table. Her eyes were unimpressed. 'Quite frankly,' she said, 'most of next month's schedule is crap. There's not nearly enough glamour. Plus there's not enough glitz. I want new ideas. From all of you.'

She looked at her favourite victims. They were always the same victims: Caroline Ponsonby, Pauline Chang, Mary Rogers. She always picked on the most vulnerable ones, and she always picked on women. What a cow, thought Murdoch: why did she always bully other women?

'Ponsonby?' she said.

Caroline Ponsonby swallowed nervously. She cleared her throat. 'Yes, well, we're getting some nice pics of Prince William and his new girlfriend.'

'Nice pics?' said The Editor quietly. 'Since when did we start going in for nice pics, Ponsonby?'

'Well, they're very ... romantic.'

'I'm so bored of the royals,' said The Editor. 'Nobody gives a damn about them any more, let alone about Prince William. They're just not glamorous any more. God, Ponsonby, how many times do I have to drum this into you? Glamour is what we're about. Fame. Sparkle. Style. The royals nowadays have about as much style as Clacton on a wet Wednesday. This is *Celebrity*, for God's sake. We need glitz. It's a must-have.'

Caroline hesitated and then took another dangerous plunge. 'We're also negotiating for some pics of the Pope in his bath.'

The Editor raised an eyebrow. 'That's better.'

Caroline smiled with relief. 'Yes,' she babbled. 'He's actually soaping –'

'His cock?'

'His ... ?'

'Cock, dear. C, O, C, K. You know? The dangly thingy that men tend to have between their legs?'

'I ...'

'He is a man, you know, Ponsonby. The Pope. Don't be fooled by his fancy frock. He comes fully equipped.'

'But only in his sleep,' said Murdoch.

'What was that, Murdoch?'

'Nothing.'

The Editor tapped the table with her silver biro. 'So what's the point of the pics then, Ponsonby, unless you can see how big his tool is? Otherwise he's just another flabby old man with hairy tits.'

'Yes –'

'What we all really want to know, Ponsonby, is whether the old fart's hung like a donkey.'

'I –'

'We want to be able to show the picture to all our girlfriends and say "My God, look at that! Would you believe it? It's huge! The Pope! God, what a waste!" '

'I thought you sheilas don't mind about a bloke's size,' said Murdoch.

'Come off it,' said The Editor.

'I thought you just fancied our brains.'

'That would be really bad news for you, Murdoch.'

He grinned. 'No, seriously: are donkeys really all that big? Or is it just another of those urban myths, like the one about the couple who were screwing in the back of a Mini –'

'Murdoch …'

'– and had to be rescued by the fire brigade. Remember when there was all that fuss a few years ago about Princess Diana and that army chap? Hughes, Hewell …'

'Hewitt.'

'Hewitt! John Hewitt.'

'James.'

'James Hewitt, of course. *Major* James Hewitt.'

'Captain.'

'Whatever. Well, they said at the time that Di fell for Hewitt because he was hung like an orang-utan. Then some clever dick pointed out that an orang-utan's todger is only two inches long.'

'All right, Murdoch, that's enough,' said The Editor. 'I think you'll find that donkeys are in fact quite substantial in the nether regions. Right, Ponsonby: send the snapper back to the Vatican and tell him to try again. Plus tell him we need to see His Holiness's dong.'

'Merrily on high,' said Murdoch.

The Editor frowned. 'Grow up, Murdoch,' she said.

'OK. No worries.'

'And shut up.'

'No probs.'

She ran her pen down the schedule, shaking her head, deleting most of the items.

'This just isn't good enough,' she said eventually, looking up from the schedule. 'The Mick Jagger stuff is just OK, I suppose, plus the piece about the Yorkshire Ripper's hobbies, but the rest is crap. I mean, all this dreary stuff about computers and that Internet thing. I mean, yawn.'

Iain Campbell, sitting beside her, cleared his throat and adopted his deputy editor's face. Loyal but brave, it was the wary yet eager expression of the faithful Scottish retainer addressing the chief of the clan. 'It's not really about computers,' ventured Campbell in his carefully modulated Edinburgh Morningside voice. 'It's mainly about Bill Gates.'

'So?'

'The computer tycoon.'

'I know very well who he is, Campbell, but my God, we don't want to fill the mag with computer nerds.'

'He's not a nerd, Stella, he's a genius. And very rich.'

'He's as rich as Greece is,' said Kelly.

'What did you say, Kelly?'

'Bill Gates is as rich as Greece is.'

'Croesus, you moron.'

'Who was Greek,' said Murdoch.

The Editor gave Murdoch a look perfected by another old Greek, Medusa. 'I don't want computers,' she snapped. 'Right? Computers are dull. I'm bored of computers. We don't have computers in *Celebrity*. OK?'

Campbell shrugged. 'You're The Editor.'

'Yes, I bloody well am and don't you forget it. So no computers and no nerds. And what's all this stuff about comets and outer space?'

'It's a profile of Stephen Hawking.'

'The cripple?'

'The brilliant mathematician.'

'The one in the wheelchair?'

'*A Brief History of Time.*'

'Good God, Campbell, I don't want cripples in the mag. Not spastics. We're meant to be all about glamour, for God's sake. You think cripples and wheelchairs are glamorous?'

'He is a celeb, Stella. The most famous scientist in the world.'

'That's another thing: no scientists. What's glitzy about them? All those test tubes and smells.'

Campbell adopted his loyal-but-long-suffering-Highland-clansman expression again. 'They've found a mysterious new comet in outer space.'

'I don't care if they've discovered the original great-great-grandfather of Einstein's theory of relatives flushed down the lav,' she said. 'I still don't want scientists in *Celebrity*, thank you very much.' She jabbed her finger at the schedule. 'Plus who wants to read this piece about Euro-politicians' wives on a trip to Euro Disney? All politics is Disneyland, anyway, especially Euro-politics. All politicians are related to Mickey Mouse.'

'Is that Einstein's theory of relatives?' said Murdoch, winking his good eye.

'What was that?'

'Nothing.'

She glowered at him. 'As far as *Celebrity* is concerned, all politicians are out, zilch, *finito*, for ever. Nobody gives a damn about any of them. They're just boring. Plus that goes for every president and prime minister you care to mention. Grey people. Mogadon. We've got to find much sexier subjects: TV stars, models, sports personalities, in-your-face comedians, people who really do things. People who touch all our lives. The real movers and shakers. Right, so let's do a spread on all the most famous astrologers with pics, backgrounds, tips, quirks, forecasts. Langoustier, you can handle that. Plus an interview with that new weather girl on CNN: you, Ferré. Plus that Albanian hairdresser who's wowing them all in Moscow. Right, Rogers? Plus a big picture number on the new Italian couturier, Antonio Verucci. They say he's even better than Versace. One for you, Chang. Plus there's a fabulous new chef in Paris who comes from Brazzaville. One for you, Merlot. They say he's a pigmy.'

'Small portions, then,' said Murdoch.

The Editor looked at him.

How does he get away with it? Caroline Ponsonby felt a twinge of envy. *Anyone else would be savaged. He must have some hold over her. He must know where the bodies are buried. Or – my God! – maybe he's sleeping with her!*

'Sorry,' said Murdoch. 'Small joke.'

'Small brain,' said The Editor. 'Right, what else? Ah, yes: Fritz Gröning's seventeen-year-old daughter has run off with some geriatric hippy and is living with him in a New Age caravan in Wales. Get after her, Wakonde. Find her. It's no good offering her money – her father's loaded, multi-millions – but they say she despises his money and success so she'll probably talk for nothing. And let's get pics of Larry Dzerzinski. They say he's dying of Aids. Get a snapper to take a series of shots at monthly intervals and then after six months we can run them in sequence to show how quickly he's wasting away.'

'We could call it KILLER SERIAL,' said Murdoch.

'And let's get after Salman Rushdie. Find out what he's doing for sex in captivity. Are any of his minders women? Is he screwing them? Or has he gone off women altogether? Perhaps he's gone gay.'

'Perhaps his cock has been converted to Christianity,' said Murdoch. 'Like the Pope's.'

The Editor sighed. 'Get a life, Murdoch,' she said.

'No probs.'

She looked at her notes and ran down her list again. There was a long, uncomfortable silence. Eventually she looked up and stared at Murdoch. Her eyes were as cold as emeralds. 'OK, Murdoch,' she said. 'You're so full of witty ideas, so let's have some for the magazine. Now.'

People shuffled their feet, chewed their biros, looked away, frowned with concentration.

'Why don't we get Arnie Schwarzenegger to write us a novel?' suggested Murdoch jovially. 'Well, a short story, anyway. He could probably manage that.'

'Actually, Murdoch, that's not a bad idea. Look at it, Campbell.'

'Right.'

'Or O. J. Simpson could write us a cookery column,' said Murdoch.

'Hmm. Possible.'

'Or what about Charles Manson on religion?' suggested Michèle Langoustier.

'Or Hillary Clinton on marriage guidance?' said Pauline Chang.

Ideas spilled around the table like a Mexican Wave.

'Mickey Rourke on gardening.'

'Cindy Crawford reviewing books.'

'Maggie Thatcher on films.'

'Pelé on chess.'

'We could get Elton John to do an agony aunt page.'

'Brilliant,' said Jean-Paul Ferré.

'Mega,' said Nat Wakonde.

The Editor held up a hand. 'OK, OK: I hear where you're coming from.' She looked at her watch. 'It's a start. And I want at least two more brilliant ideas on paper from each of you as soon as I get back from lunch at three o'clock. I want a list of ideas to die for. Right, Langoustier, here's what you do in the next couple of days: get out the celeb B-list and start sounding out some of their agents. Tell them we don't actually want any of the celebs to write anything, of course. God forbid! We'll do it for them ourselves. All we want is their names on the cover and the top of the page.'

'Why don't we actually hire some people who can write?' said Murdoch. 'I mean, like writers. Updike. Easton Ellis. Amis. Maybe dear old Salman himself.'

'Don't be so bloody stupid, Murdoch,' said The Editor, gathering her notes and rising from her chair. 'We don't want writers in *Celebrity*. Where's the glamour in writers? Where's the glitz? They all sit at home all day feeling sorry for themselves and drinking too much. They're even more boring than the royals.'

'Even Rushdie?'

'Rushdie's the one exception. He's even quite sexy if you're into the sleeping-pill look. Those bedroom eyelids. But he's only sexy because of the *fatwa*. Nobody actually wants to read him. Not his books.'

The Editor made for the door. 'Right, Kelly,' she said ominously. 'In my office. Now. Come!'

She left the conference room and they rose from the table.

'Forget Euro Disney,' said Murdoch. 'This is *Neuro* Disney: bring on Goofy and the Seven Dancing Dwarves. D'you know what her latest move is? She told Kelly she wants all the CDs and videos that are sent in for review. All the freebies.'

'The ones we sell for the Widows' and Orphans' Fund?' said Caroline Ponsonby.

'Yep. She wants them all herself.'

'My God, she's a greedy cow.'

'Hey, man,' said Nat Wakonde. 'What was that story about the couple in the back of a Mini?'

'It was in the *Daily Mirror*,' said Murdoch. He chuckled. 'An English couple. They were screwing in the back of this Mini down a quiet country lane one night but the bloke had a bad back and it gave way at the critical moment; they got jammed together and couldn't move and had to be released by the fire brigade. The firemen could only get them out of the back of the Mini by cutting into the roof, peeling it back and winching them out. The bloke was rushed to hospital for his back to be fixed. But the sheila wouldn't stop crying: she was sobbing her heart out, inconsolable. "Come on, love, he's going to be fine," said one of the firemen. "Sod that!" she wailed. "What the hell am I going to tell my husband happened to the car?" '

Wakonde lifted his head and howled.

'How do you get away with it, Tone?' said Caroline Ponsonby. 'All those terrible jokes and interruptions? She'd sack anyone else.'

Murdoch grinned. 'Not me,' he said. 'She'll never fire me. No worries.'

'She fired Bill Warren and he was deputy editor.'

'He was also a sitting target: male, middle-aged, hetero, and a White Anglo-Saxon Protestant as well. Jeez, how politically incorrect can you get? It's almost illegal these days to be a middle-aged WASP bloke who likes ladies. She could sack him whenever she liked. He hadn't a hope. But what can she do about me, eh, mate?'

A big white milkstain grin spilt across Murdoch's big black face. 'How's she ever going to be able to sack a black, one-eyed, crippled, culturally deprived, Australian abo? I'm a persecuted minority six times over. I'm a one-man Heritage Conservation Area.'

'You're no more crippled than I am.'

'You should see inside my head.'

Murdoch leaned back in the chair, closed his good eye and pretended to read the inside of his eyelid.

'Shit a brick!' he said suddenly, sitting up. 'I've cracked it!'

He jumped out of the chair and headed for Kelly's office.

'Paddy, I've cracked it!' he bellowed. 'The New Year's Eve ball! I've got it! We don't need an island at all! What do we want a bloody island for? Complete waste of time. We just hire a liner instead. That's all: a sodding great liner.'

Kelly appeared in The Editor's doorway. 'A liner?' he said.

'A liner,' hooted Murdoch. 'Of course. It's obvious. The *QE2*! The *Oriana*! The *Ile de France*! The *Southern Cross*! A liner! Any liner that will take two thousand passengers! And we park it right there in the middle of the ocean, slap-bang on the international date line itself.'

'Brilliant!' said Kelly. 'Brilliant!'

A tear crept out of the corner of Kelly's eye and slid down his cheek. 'I love you very much,' he said, 'to be sure.'

CHAPTER 2

Steve Marlowe distrusted daylight. It made shadows. He loved working at night, especially that stillness after midnight, the lights twinkling beyond the safety of his window, the yellow headlamps on the freeway slicing the silence, the howl of an ambulance siren tearing the darkness apart, the smell of loneliness. Sitting alone in his room with his computer, Chandler, in the early hours, he felt a great sense of power as Chandler glowed, hummed, flickered and obeyed every tap of his fingers. Marlowe could not imagine what he would do without Chandler. Chandler was every man's dream. Chandler carried out every order and never answered back.

Marlowe yawned, stretched, swung his legs out of bed and rubbed his eyes. He scratched the full curve of his belly and gazed out of his bedroom window towards the sea. Chandler had automatically opened the curtains for him and turned the radio on as usual. Dusk was spreading like smog across Los Angeles, drifting in across the city from Palm Springs and Pasadena and chasing the last lingering rays of sunlight away across the Channel Islands towards Hawaii and Tokyo. A guitar solo drifted from the radio, waking him gently. He was starving this morning. He was always starving after sex. He reached for the plate of cookies he always left beside the bed and ate three of them before rolling off the bed and lurching towards the bathroom. Chandler was humming quietly at his workstation in the next room, brewing the coffee, sorting and scanning the newspapers. Marlowe heaved himself into the bathroom, scratching his anus, and by the time he had showered, Chandler had printed out for him his personalised newspaper tailored from journals published all over the world: an article from the *New York Times* about mugging on the Internet; a profile of Bill Gates in *Newsweek*; a piece from the London *Daily Telegraph* about the big grisly British murder trial; a feature from *Space* magazine about the discovery of a giant comet; a report about an international convention of Trekkies; a news story from Japan about a software programme that would allow driverless automobiles to slalom down winding mountain roads at 80mph while the passengers sit in the back and watch TV; the *LA Times*'s astrology forecast for Virgo; the latest ballgame results; some Hollywood gossip; a full-colour pin-up of a very young, very black boy from Mozambique; and as always, tucked away in a corner of page three, Marlowe's regular small ad from the local newspaper's personal column:

MEANSTREETS DETECTIVE AGENCY
Private Eye Marlowe
Fully Computerized
Delicate Matters A Specialty
Confidentiality Guaranty.

Chandler knew Marlowe's reading tastes exactly – computers, the Internet, food, crime, science, science fiction, sport, showbiz celebrities, astrology, gay pictures – and never wasted his time by selecting articles on politics, diplomacy, fashion or foreign affairs. Most of the electronic newspapers were leading their bulletins with a story about the threat of a new war between China and Vietnam in the South China Sea but Marlowe did not give a damn about politics or foreign affairs. He cared hardly at all what happened beyond his computer screen and what he could pick up surfing the Infobahn. At school they had called him a fat nerd, which was ridiculous: everyone knows that nerds are skinny and wear glasses. Later it had gotten worse as fattism had started to spread across America: they had called him gutbuster, grossbelly and flab-faggot, especially after he changed his name to Marlowe for business reasons. Well, fuck 'em, the dickheads. Marlowe was just the right name for a private eye in LA. It was certainly better than Markczwicz. Clients had a problem with Markczwicz and Marlowe was respected in the gumshoe business. As for being called a nerd, he saw more of the world on his computer screen than most of those dorks ever would in their dreary dead-end lives in their high-rise offices and low-price supermarts. Thanks to the miracles of cyberspace, the Internet and a virtual reality headset, Chandler's screen was a magic window on the universe. Nowadays there was nothing – nothing at all – that you could not experience in your own room at the tap of a few keys or the click of a mouse. Last night, for instance, using the VR headset, Marlowe had gone down on Rock Hudson on a Caribbean beach and – jeez! – that Rock had been hung like a mule. Marlowe sniggered. They hadn't called him Rock for nothing, no sir. Before he got Aids, of course. Marlowe wouldn't have gone down on anyone with Aids, not even Rock Hudson, not even in VR.

He picked the newspaper out of Chandler's printer basket and glanced through it while he ate the usual brupper that Chandler had rustled up for him: a thick underdone steak, three eggs over easy, a plate of french fries, two cream buns, some pecan pie, ice cream. He watched the sun drown far out to sea in a wild western blaze of scarlet fire. The night came down like sequinned velvet. Marlowe belched and wiped his mouth on the back of his sleeve. He heaved himself over to

Chandler's dishwasher and stacked the dirty plates in the racks, chose a two-pound bar of chocolate from the cupboard, tore the paper off, and waddled munching to his workstation to read his e-mail.

He settled in front of Chandler's pale blue screen and pressed a key. Letters flashed across the screen.

<hi> said Chandler <have a nice day>

Marlowe grunted.

<42 messages today> said Chandler.

The first e-mail message flashed up on the screen. Junk mail. Some crap about life insurance. Why insure your life? It was death you had to worry about. Marlowe chewed his chocolate, excavating his gums with a juicy brown finger and punching Chandler's keyboard with his other hand. More junk mail: unsolicited electronic crap from fashion wholesalers, furniture-makers, health stores, supermarkets and banks. There were disgusting unhealthy ads for cigarettes, a dating agency, even a funeral parlour. 'Invest in Your Future NOW!' suggested the funeral parlour. One message was selling Christmas decorations and it was still only June. Only three of the forty-two messages were of any use to him. The first was from a woman in Long Beach who wanted him to find evidence of her husband's adultery. A Mrs Schweitzer. Marlowe sighed and knuckled his eye. Not adultery again, for Chrissake. Adultery was so old-fashioned. Why did anyone mind any more if their husband or wife was humping other people? Who cares? Still, he'd better call her. He needed the money.

He clicked onto the second significant e-mail message. It was from a businessman in Vladivostok who wanted him to do a computer search number on a business rival in Seoul. Routine stuff. The third message was from a guy in Santa Barbara, a Bill Warren, who had been recommended by another client and wanted some discreet enquiries made in Monaco. Monaco! Wasn't that someplace near Monte Carlo? Someplace in Italy, anyway – or was it Spain? Probably Spain if it ended in *o*, like San Francisco was Spanish; like Ohio, like

Idaho. Spanish. Marlowe liked the Spaniards, the Latinos. They had neat little asses. Marlowe liked that. He and Chandler often went cruising down the Internet to Mexico and South America and had even learned some of the lingo. There was another *o* – lingo. He licked the last chocolate stain off his fingers. Spain sounded much more fun than Long Beach or Vladivostok. He tapped at the keyboard and Chandler logged on to the Santa Barbara guy's computer. Downline the two computers interfaced for a couple of seconds in a quick little dance of electronic foreplay before the one in Santa Barbara confessed that Warren was out but agreed to accept a message.

After leaving a message Chandler logged on to the Vladivostok businessman's computer, an old Soviet model so ancient that even across thousands of miles of Pacific Ocean cable you could hear it thinking. Chandler sat patiently humming while the distant geriatric Siberian machine cranked itself up to some sort of Mongol response. There was a clanking noise and a hollow echo that sounded like whales moaning in the depths of the Pacific. What the hell was going on? Marlowe wondered. It sounded like the guy in Vladivostok was still using twin drives, perhaps even $5\frac{1}{4}$-inch floppy disks! It was like something out of the Middle Ages! Either that, or the Siberian machine was seriously into the vodka. It gasped, clattered and eventually announced that the Russian was out too.

Marlowe was disgruntled. Why did these jerks always leave their screens unattended and go out so often? What was the point of owning a computer if you were never there to enjoy it? What was it about the outside world that drew people away from their workstations? Out there the air was polluted, the freeways a nightmare, the city crowded, the people violent and diseased. He remembered with a shudder the last trip he had taken abroad, five years ago; the junkie in Amsterdam with Aids, the angry sailor in that public john in London, the cold air foul with curses, the smell of urine, the disgusting stench of cigarette smoke. He shivered. He would

never take those risks again. Here in his cosy room with
Chandler, in front of his own screen, he was safe and
comfortable. Here he was protected from the filth of life
outside as he and Chandler cruised the global electronic
highways of the world of cyberspace and knocked silently on
distant unknown doors and flirted across thousands of miles
with strangers he would never meet. Here no one called him
a nerd or a fat pervert. Here in the private silence of his room
he could surf the Internet across oceans and continents, from
Buenos Aires to New York, from London to Melbourne, from
Moscow to Tokyo. Anything here was possible and everything was safe.

He left a message for the Russian and called the Long Beach
woman's Internet number. Chandler logged on to her
computer, coupling with it swiftly, and his screen suddenly
blossomed gold and green to a triumphant fanfare of trumpets
as a cute little pink kitten in a top hat danced across the screen.

<*kitty schweitzer*> said the screen in fancy italics <*hi
there*>

The kitten waved its paw and bowed, Chandler gave a
miaow that must have terrified the mouse crouched on the
desk, and the kitten's grin faded like the Cheshire cat, leaving
the screen pale blue again.

Marlowe tapped his keyboard and white letters stuttered
across the screen: <hi maam this is meanstreets detective
agency returning yore call>

<sure howre ya doin>

<grate + u>

<not so good>

<im sorry 2 here that>

<its my husband the bastard>

<misbehaving>

<miss behaving and missus behaving the bastard>

<thats funny>

<thank you>

<im glad to see u havnt lost yore sens of humor>

\<you might as well die\>
\<so who r these broads\>
\<3 i know about\>
\<3!!!\>
\<yeah\>
\<wow\>
\<right\>
\<all at the same time\>
\<i wouldnt be surprised THE BASTARD\>
\<yore flamin at me maam\>
\<IM SORRY\>
\<dont flame at me maam it aint my folt\>
\<SORRY\>
\<yore still FLAMIN\>
\<I MEAN sorry\>
\<thats better now id better hav some details maam whats his name\>
\<micky schweitzer\>
\<has he ever used any other names\>
\<not that i know\>
\<adress\>
\<2386 sunrise\>
\<biznis\>
\<the bastards a realtor\>
\<rich\>
\<stinking\>

Marlowe grinned. Things were looking up. He hated it when the wronged wives were poor: you never started any job without a deposit upfront, but even so they could take forever to pay the rest and sometimes it could get messy. Sometimes Marlowe had had to hire heavies to collect a debt and he hated having to do that. They always wanted twenty per cent. Debt collectors were greedier than even lawyers or agents. But he wouldn't have that sort of problem with Mrs Schweitzer. Her husband was loaded and cheated wives like Mrs Schweitzer just love spending their loaded husbands' money.

<good hotels then> suggested Marlowe.

<the best for those bitches the mean bastard>

<u no ware hes taken them>

<new york miami paris france rome athens the bastard>

<jenrus guy hey hes not gay is he by any lucky chans>

<whats that>

<just jokin maam>

<gay>

<just jokin wen was he in these places>

<new york and miami in feb france march rome athens may>

<u no the girls names>

<there not girls there just old hores>

<rite>

<ones called joanne>

<rite wot evidens do u want photos witnisses or will copies of checks credit statemens bookin receets be enuf>

<theyll do I just need to stick them to my lawyer>

<ok maam now my fees r $200 per hour>

<sure>

<+ expences>

<ok>

<i just need a deposit>

<yeah>

<1000>

<you got it>

He tapped a macro and Chandler flashed the regular payment instruction onto the screen automatically: <please make immediate electronic deposit in bank of california la branch a/c meanstreets agency 93864793947>

<just give me a minute> she said.

The cursor sat blinking in the middle of the screen, a flashing white hyphen bobbing on blue like a seagull riding the ocean. After thirty-two seconds a purple window opened in the bottom right-hand corner of the screen with the bank's confirmation that $1,000 had just been deposited electronically in Marlowe's bank account.

<grate> said Marlowe.

<your welcome>

<thanx>

<dont mention it>

<now ware do i start>

<well i do believe hes with one of them now>

<jeez maam wares that>

<who knows>

<can u try to think ware>

<some motel on the coast i guess THE BASTARD>

<yore doin it agen>

<SORRY>

<like that>

<well i just get so mad>

<sure rite im onto it maam ill be in tutch>

<screw the bastard> she said.

<slong then>

<so long>

<hav a nice nite> he said.

His screen burst gold and green again with an explosion of colour as she signed off and their computers uncoupled and withdrew from each other. Her pink pussy pranced across the screen, swishing its tail and winking.

Chandler uttered a fetching little miaow that sounded like *goodbye*.

<missing you already> said the screen.

Nice lady, thought Marlowe. For a woman.

He lumbered through to the kitchen to fix himself a hotdog and a litre of Coke, and then spent an hour with Chandler hacking into all the more likely computers in the more upmarket hotels and motels along the length of coastal California. A guy like Schweitzer was hardly going to take his latest doxy to some flea-bitten dive in Monterey and the better joints were easy enough to find since they were all listed there on the Internet hotel directory with all their telephone and fax numbers. It couldn't be easier. Mrs Schweitzer could almost have done the job herself and saved a thousand bucks.

A couple of the computers were not all that easy to break into and it took him and Chandler ten minutes or more to work out the right passwords. They ran at random through all the more likely combinations of words and letters that security conscious organisations used these days, but most of the hotels didn't bother too much with computer firewalls and electronic security. Those that did have some sort of security code had chosen passwords that were so obvious they were almost insulting to an old pro like Marlowe. The Sunset Motel in Monterey, for instance, was using the password *twilite*. Pathetic. The Reagan in Redwood City had chosen *ronnie*. The Churchill Hotel in Salinas was *V*. Sure, just that: *V*. I mean, can u believe it? They might just as well have left all their doors and windows open.

It took just under the hour to locate a Mr and Mrs Mickey Schweitzer who had checked that evening into the $900-a-night Suite 593 in the Royal Majesty Hotel in San Luis Obispo. Marlowe examined their running check on-screen. They had ordered a bottle of champagne to be sent up to their room and had then spent $258.36 on dinner in the hotel restaurant. Just reading their menu made Marlowe feel peckish again: they had eaten quail's eggs, lobster, partridge and *crêpes suzettes* and had sluiced them down with a bottle of *Pouilly Fuissé* and a bottle of *Gevrey-Chambertin*. Afterwards they had had another bottle of champagne sent up to the suite. Mrs Schweitzer had been right: her husband was loaded, all right, in more ways than one. How in hell's name did he still get it up after all that booze? And with a woman at that? Marlowe was impressed. He programmed Chandler to record the suite and reference numbers in order to make it easy to download a full copy of Schweitzer's final check when he paid it in the morning. Then he called his tame San Luis Obispo gumshoe, José Diaz, and programmed him to get over to the hotel and bribe a night porter to photograph Schweitzer and his bimbo together before they left in the morning. Marlowe was well content: $1,000 plus Diaz's fee; not bad for an hour's work.

He took a break for a while, pouring himself another jug of Coke. He watched a couple of old episodes of *Star Trek,* played a video game and a couple of hands of poker with Chandler, and then they did a quick job that had been waiting for forty-eight hours – a cheap library scan for a low-grade client in Mexico. He browsed for a while through the on-screen shopping catalogues and had Chandler order for him a hamper of goodies from the new delicatessen in Burbank and some monogrammed silk underwear from Hong Kong. Together they trawled the Internet, sending the cursor searching through the international menus, the thousands of lists of news and information services, university libraries, bulletin boards, commercial on-line networks, discussion groups, problem centres and sex forums. There was nothing much new. Marlowe was bored. Should he watch *2001* again? Or *Meteor*? No. He felt sexy. He called up the movie menu to see the latest films on offer and Chandler scanned the list of titles for him, picking out those that had had the best reviews in the gay press and running a couple of trailer clips for him across the screen. Marlowe chose one from South America called *Manacled Macho Male Madonna* and Chandler located it in Uruguay, in the Montevideo cinematic archive, in thirty seconds and downloaded the entire film onto hard disk in fifteen seconds. Chandler debited Marlowe's bank account $10, credited $10 to the Montevideo archive's account in Uruguay and stored the film in a hard-disk videofile until Marlowe decided to watch it.

Later, much later, when it was nearly dawn in LA but still early evening on the other side of the Pacific, he and Chandler would go cruising in cyberspace, loitering on screens in Manila, Hanoi, Beijing. He had always had a yen for Asians: their golden skin, their glittering black eyes, their perfect smallness. But not yet. He liked to wait until he was tired and nearly ready for bed, until that dark still hour just before dawn when the moon itself was asleep and the whole world seemed to be waiting for something and even the leaves of the trees beyond his window were motionless. The mystery of that expectant silence always excited him. What if one day the sun simply failed to rise? What if it got lost on the other side of the world and left LA in total darkness for ever? Eternal night. Just dark, and a flickering screen. The idea excited Marlowe. Just thinking about it gave him a small erection.

At midnight in Los Angeles it was 9 a.m. in Monte Carlo and The Editor's secretary was sprawled in The Editor's swivel chair in The Editor's office, his feet crossed nonchalantly up there on The Editor's polished desk. Patrick Kelly was smoking a cigarette, as he always did in her office when she was away, and he was pretending yet again that one day he would be The Editor and she would be his gofer and dogsbody. It was a fantasy he indulged whenever she was away. He blew a smoke ring and narrowed his eyes and imagined her face in his lap right there in her own seat of power as he lolled back and swivelled to the rhythm of her attentions. This particular fantasy never seemed entirely credible.

He swivelled the chair and reached for her telephone to call her in London before she left the Savoy for Heathrow airport. She was due to catch her flight for Hong Kong where she would have dinner with Pak chung-ho. It seemed a hell of a long way to fly just for dinner but distance had never been a deterrent when The Editor sniffed a freebie. Her deputy editor before Campbell, Bill Warren, had once told Kelly that she had even been known to fly to Rio just for a free weekend. For this Hong Kong trip Kelly had eventually managed to persuade one of the Far Eastern airlines to give The Editor a first class ticket in exchange for a plug in a future *Celebrity* feature – but he had had to beg. The Kellys were a proud people and it did not come easily for one of them to beg but this one was learning fast.

'Does she ever pay for anything herself, Mr Kelly?' the airline's publicity director had asked.

'She like buys her own toothpaste.'

'That's nice. Who squeezes it onto the brush?'

Kelly stubbed out his cigarette, dialled London and braced himself. What should he give her first? The good news or the bad? His mouth was dry. Whenever he spoke to her on the telephone his brain turned to jelly.

The Savoy switchboard put him through to her suite.

'Yes?'

His buttocks tightened. 'Top o' the mornin'. 'Tis Kelly in the office.'

'Kelly.'

'So it is. Is everything like hunky-dory now?'

'Get on with it, Kelly. What is it?'

'Brilliant. I thought I would wish you a safe journey, *bon voyage*, dah-dee-dah.'

'I'm hardly going to the moon. Now look here, Kelly: that TV show you fixed. The other guests were nobodies. Ring Hong Kong and see who's on the show with me there and fax their names and CVs to me at the Mandarin. Plus in future when I go on television I want to know in advance who the other guests are.'

'Right you are, sure enough. Brilliant.'

'Now I have a plane to catch.'

'I must also update you on the situation regarding the – uh – QE2, like.'

'Have you booked it?'

'With great regret I must confess I have not.'

'And why's that?'

'It's already been booked.'

'You're an incompetent nincompoop, Kelly.'

'Something called the Millennium Society of New York booked it ages ago for a ten-day New Year cruise to the Mediterranean, Egypt, pyramids, blah-blah-blah.'

'So offer to pay Cunard more for the ship. Gazump them.'

'I have so but they refused.'

'Christ, you're useless.'

'No, see, they're like "We can't do that, Mr Kelly, it would be unethical." '

'Unethical? Bloody cheek! Who do they think they are, Saint Teresa of Calcutta? What about the *Oriana*?'

'Booked as well.'

'The *Southern Cross*?'

'That too.'

'My God, Kelly, what are we going to do about you? What's the unemployment rate in Ireland nowadays?'

His throat was dry. He swallowed. 'I've found an alternative,' he croaked. He cleared his throat and tried again. ''Tis a brand new cruise liner that's being built in Finland for a cruise company registered in the Philippines. 'Tis due to be delivered next year and they're looking for something special to celebrate on the maiden voyage, so they are. They would be willing to sail it from Manila to Tonga for us and to park it on the date line on New Year's Eve. And they'll let us like have it for nothing if we can guarantee at least five hundred celebs on board.'

He pressed the telephone receiver against his ear. He thought he could hear a TV or radio droning away in the background. He could hear her breathing six hundred miles away.

'What sort of liner?' she said.

'Couldn't be better.'

'Yes it could. It could be the *QE2*.'

'Well there is that of course, to be sure, but this Philippines boat is going to be a real luxury job. It's going to be a five-star-rated ship with plush cabins for two thousand five hundred passengers and every mod con: gourmet restaurants, theatre, casino, dah-dee-dah. I checked with Lloyd's: they say it's going to be the last word in luxury.'

'What's it called?'

Kelly wriggled his buttocks. He took a deep breath. This

was the good news: even she could hardly fault him this time. 'This is the best of all,' he said.

'I'll be the judge of that.'

'They like haven't decided yet on a name for the ship.'

'So?'

'They'll call the ship the *Celebrity* if we want them to.'

The telephone line hummed with anticipation. He could hear a tug hooting faintly on the Thames outside her window and one of the London churches' bells striking a muffled hour.

'I hear what you're saying,' she said slowly.

'Shall I go for it then?'

'I hear where you're coming from.'

'Do I book it?'

The line sounded hollow as silence echoed off a telecom satellite high up in space. How strange it is, thought Kelly, that even silence nowadays is sent into space, like prayers.

'Tell them we're interested,' she said, 'but don't fix anything yet. I'll need to see the ship's plans. Plus photographs. Every detail they can let us have.'

'Right. Brilliant.'

'Fax them all to me in Hong Kong. Plus tell Campbell that I want a full list of three thousand possible A-list, in-your-face celebrity guests on my desk the minute I return from Washington next week. That's a must-have. Tell him I want every member of staff to come up with names: Murdoch, Langoustier, Wakonde, all of them.'

'Wakonde's gone off to Wales on that story you gave him: the Gröning girl, the New Age dropout.'

'Well, all the others. I want a list to die for.'

'Right. Brilliant.'

She hesitated a moment. 'And Kelly...'

'Yes?'

She stalled. There was silence. 'No, nothing,' she said. 'It's nothing.'

'Brilliant,' he said.

She replaced the receiver.

For one heady moment he had imagined that she was actually about to thank him.

In Los Angeles Marlowe was munching a Hershey bar at a quarter after midnight when Chandler flashed up on the screen a message that someone was calling him from Santa Barbara and wanted to interface directly. It was the guy who wanted a job done in Monaco. Bill Warren. He came on screen without any preamble.

<Jerry Saunders says I can trust you>

Jeez, thought Marlowe: this guy uses capital letters! No one used capital letters on-line nowadays. Warren had to be new on the Internet and probably middle-aged. No young cyberpunk would dream of using capitals. This guy was a cybercrumbly. Marlowe grinned. *call me sherlok homes.*

<sure u can trust me> said Marlowe.

<You've acted for Jerry before in confidence?>

He even uses question marks, thought Marlowe. No one had used punctuation on the Internet in years! He must be a teacher, some sort of professor maybe. Marlowe tapped a quick instruction for Chandler to download Warren's computer's code number, which would allow them to track down Warren's address and identity. Chandler flashed up the code immediately in a yellow window in the top right-hand corner of the screen. It was like a sudden ejaculation, thought Marlowe: as though the two connected computers had shared a quick orgasm. Marlowe grinned: Internet intercourse.

<You've acted for him before in confidence?>

<thats confidenshul>

Warren was amused. He typed a horizontal smiley, :-)

<Nice> he said <I like it>

<my lips r always seald mr warren sir>

<I'm glad to hear it because this is seriously confidential. I mean really seriously private>

<u have my word>

<I'd like that in writing>

<u got it onscreen now>

<Right. OK. Copy. OK. Now I want for you to investigate a magazine that operates out of Monaco. It's called Celebrity>

<is that the 1 about celebs>

<I can see you have the makings of a great detective>

<thank u>

<I want for you specially to investigate the editor. Her name is Stella Barrett>

<wot do u wanna no about her>

<Everything. Every weakness, every peccadillo>

<pecca-wot>

<dillo. I want to destroy her> said Warren <and then I'm going to kill her>

CHAPTER 3

In her office in the history faculty building at Tây Ninh University in Vietnam, fifty-three miles north-west of Ho Chi Minh City, the senior lecturer in European Studies, Nguyen Thi Chu, pressed the SAVE button on her computer and switched the machine off. It sighed and fell asleep.

She stretched her arms above her head, linked her fingers, bent her neck and rotated her head, flexing her muscles to ease the stiffness in her shoulders. A small headache lurked like a bandit behind her eyes. Still, at least she had earned her headache. The book was coming along well – *The Old Barbarians: The End of the Western Millennium* – thanks to the miracles of the computer and Internet. Thanks to the Internet and the World Wide Web it had taken her only two days to raid the university libraries of Oxford, Oslo, Copenhagen and Yale and to download into her computer thousands of megabytes of background information about Anglo-Saxon England at the end of the first millennium, taking in the years from 990 to 999. She still found it amazing that she could do all her research for a chapter about tenth-century Britain without moving from her office near the Cambodian border. For that she was grateful. She never wanted to go to Britain again.

Twenty years ago she had spent a year at Cambridge as a mature exchange student and she had never felt so cold, wet and friendless. She had hated Cambridge, all those grey buildings, the gloomy colleges, their dank passages, the sinister alleyways echoing with medieval melancholy, the rain glistening on the cobblestones, the river wetter than any in the world. There had been about Cambridge and England an oppressive sense of history at a dead end, of something having gone wrong. She had hated huddling over thin gas fires and scuttling in the gloom from one damp building smelling of cabbage to another damp building smelling of rot. Even the British summer had been spoilt for her by the feeling of decay and disillusionment everywhere: the black plastic bags spilling garbage across the streets day and night every day of the week, the vandalised telephone kiosks, the smashed public seats, the litter sweating in the gutters like broken promises, the chewing gum stuck to the pavements and the soles of her shoes, the dogshit, the graffiti. Then there were the slogans sprayed across walls: FUCK OFF YOU CUNT or BAZ WOZ ERE. Why were the British so dirty? Why did they allow their dogs to shit on the pavements? Why did they not eat them instead, like civilised people? Why did English women wear ugly leggings and athletes' shoes as though they were running away from themselves? And why did English students bother to go to university if they did not want to learn anything? They took drugs and insulted their teachers and believed in nothing. To teach history at Oxford or Cambridge must be close to teaching in hell. How was it possible that these people had once ruled the world? Her book would become their epitaph – *The Old Barbarians: The End of the Western Millennium.* The British smiled with their teeth, like animals. They were still Anglo-Saxons at heart: they carried their grudges like bludgeons and wore their prejudices like shields.

Still, for all Nguyen Thi Chu's dislike of England, the university library at Oxford was now proving to be invaluable for her research into the decline of Britain, America and their global Anglo-Saxon culture and the contrasting rise in the power of the Asian nations. In seconds the Tây Ninh University computer had downloaded from the other side of the world into its own files the entire texts of Stenton's *Oxford History of Anglo-Saxon England*, Garmonsway's translation of *The Anglo-Saxon Chronicle*, Hunter Blair's *Introduction to Anglo-Saxon England* and Loyn's *Anglo-Saxon England and the Norman Conquest*. Within minutes it had then read every page of all of them and had picked out and printed only those pages that would be of direct use for her thesis. Even more miraculous, whenever she stumbled over some difficult passage in English she had only to tap the computer's HELP key and it would flash onto her screen an instant rough translation from English into Vietnamese.

Her students took such miracles entirely for granted. Some of them, indeed, had never read right through a whole book. But then why should they nowadays? Books had become old-fashioned and soon would be obsolete. It was not only the end of the western millennium, it was also the end of the age of the book. Thanks to the speed of modern computers no one would need to read an entire book ever again. Chu was only forty-five but sometimes, when she looked at those bright-eyed, computer-nonchalant young students of hers, she felt as old as the Mekong Delta itself. She was so old that she could even remember when people used to write books on typewriters. And how had those old authors ever written whole books by hand? All those Anglo-Saxon monks slaving over their illuminated manuscripts. All those steel-wristed writers like Li Ju-chen, Sunthon Phu, Nguyen Du, Bankimchandra Chatterji, Charles Dickens, Leo Tolstoy, all churning out thousands of pages tirelessly by hand. Just thinking of their huge handwritten volumes was enough to ache the bones.

She picked up her notes and a couple of books that she would need during her Comparative Politics lecture and smiled at the silver-framed photograph of Quang Linh that stood on her desk beside the computer. He looked so proud and young in his naval uniform, his tufty hair as always sticking up uncontrollably, his big ears flapping like a baby elephant's. She was so afraid for him. She wished she could make him safe. She touched the frame tenderly, her fingers as gentle as a blessing. 'Be safe, my child,' she said. Apart from her love of history he was all that she had.

She allowed herself a smear of lipstick and a squirt of perfume and left her office. She crossed the sunny central square of the campus towards the lecture hall, counting the twenty-five cracked, grassy flagstones as she crossed the square. She always did this for no other reason that she could think of except that they matched her strides. She tried to dismiss her fears by relishing instead the warmth of the balmy afternoon and the splash of colour in the flower bed beneath the statue of Ho Chi Minh and the breeze rustling the palms. But the peace of the campus seemed false. How long would it be allowed to last, she wondered, this blessed peace? How long would they be left to enjoy it, to stroll in the sunshine without the fear of sudden deadly shadows hurtling out of the clouds, to sleep without being woken in the night by howling sirens and crashing anti-aircraft guns? Vietnam had been deafened by war for as long as she could remember and yet already they were all in danger again. The Chinese dragon was once more breathing its raucous fire and hundreds of thousands of young men and women like Quang Linh might be burned by it: Quang Linh, so full of vitality, so eager, so determined never to shame his ancestors. Please no, she prayed: he is only eighteen. His uncle had been only eighteen, too, when he died at Chau Doc.

Outside the lecture hall a smiling student stepped back and held the door open for her. She nodded at him. How polite they were, this fresh young generation. So much nicer than we were at their age, she thought, much more considerate, much gentler. She was glad that the years of drab equality had gone, that men were once again treating women with gallantry. She could never understand the grumblers who complained about the young. They were only jealous.

The students stood as she entered the hall, nearly three hundred of them stacked in tiers that rose to the back of the auditorium, and clapped politely as she mounted the platform. She walked to the lectern and arranged her books and notes before her and gestured at them to sit. As they clattered and coughed and scuffed their feet she scanned the back of the hall. He was there as usual, high up on the furthest tier, the government spy, the smooth-faced northern man with the flat, polished hair and eyes like pebbles; those hard eyes sometimes haunted her dreams. He looked at her without recognition, as though they were strangers, yet they shared a silent intimacy closer than any she had had with any man since Tran Xuan Kai had died. Late at night, she knew, in the privacy of his room, the informer would caress the memory of her voice on the tapes he recorded at the back of the hall with a miniature Japanese recorder and sometimes, she knew, he and his superiors would linger over her words together and lick their lips like customers in an afternoon dance hall. Once she had thought that he looked at her like that, like a lizard, because he wanted her but now he frightened her, with his sulky face and pointy ears, for she knew that one day he would expose her and leave her naked. She suspected that he too dreamed of her, of the one mistake she would make that would bring her down and raise him up, like children together on a playground see-saw. What had he been like as a child? She looked at his pointed ears and knew exactly: even as a child he had been an informer.

She pushed a stray wisp of hair behind her ear and rapped on the lectern. A hush spread across the auditorium like a game of Chinese whispers. She raised her voice.

'Good afternoon, comrade students,' she began. 'In previous

lectures we have already discussed the parallels between ancient Greece and modern Australia, between Rome and Japan, between eighteenth-century France and Indonesia, and the historical and political lessons to be learned from those parallels. Today I want you to consider another remarkable similarity: the parallels between Anglo-Saxon Britain in the year 999 and our own dear nation today, a thousand years later. It is a lesson rich with significance for us all, for all the Pacific nations, as we go into the third millennium, into our own Pacific age. It is also a lesson of vital importance as we face the threat to our sovereignty from the Chinese invaders in the Spratly Islands.'

A murmur lapped like a gentle wave across the hall. Nguyen Thi Chu's lectures were famous for bringing history alive and for drawing parallels between ancient history and modern problems, but China's invasion of the Spratly Islands was so topical that it was still today's headlines. The spy sat up at the back of the hall like a buddha.

'As you all know, the Chinese enslaved and colonised Vietnam for a thousand years until the great warrior Ngo Quyen threw them out in 939,' said Chu, 'but ever since then the Chinese have resented our independence, and now they want to steal the Spratly Islands from us.

'For centuries we have owned the Spratlys, the Quan Dao Thruong Xa, a group of about sixty tiny islands and hundreds of little rocky outcrops, reefs and sandbanks that are scattered across the South China Sea. Most of them are uninhabited and have no fresh water. Some are often covered completely by the sea at high tide. Yet now the Chinese want to steal them from us because the islands control the important shipping lanes between the Pacific and Indian oceans and also because geologists suspect that there might be rich deposits of oil and gas beneath the islands even though the Spratlys are nearly fourteen hundred kilometres from the nearest Chinese shore and are only three hundred and fifty kilometres from Vietnam. In 1973 and 1979 Chinese military garrisons occupied some of the Spratlys and in 1988 they invaded Fiery Cross Reef and like pirates they sank two of our ships and butchered seventy-seven of our gallant sailors in a bloody war which some of you are old enough to remember.

'Since then our troops have occupied islands too and we have built lighthouses but now even the most ridiculous countries are claiming sovereignty too: Malaysia, Brunei, the Philippines, even Taiwan. Even so, in 1992 the Chinese claimed complete sovereignty over all the islands and have even had the cheek to sell oil concessions to an American company even though we have already sold concessions to another American company. And now the Chinese navy is blockading our oil rigs just north of Spratly Island itself, between Cu Lao Hon and Fiery Cross Reef. They are trying to bully us by threatening to use their most terrible nuclear weapons, and some of their astrologers are trying to frighten us by prophesying the end of the world.'

The hall was so silent that she could hear the clock ticking softly on the wall behind her head. At the back of the auditorium the informer stared at her, his expression never flickering. A student coughed gently. The sound rumbled around the hall like monsoon thunder.

'So what has all this to do with Anglo-Saxon Britain a thousand years ago?' she said. 'I will tell you. A very great deal. Like us, the Anglo-Saxons have good reason to remember the year 939. By then their Saxon leader Alfred the Great had long ago driven out the Viking invaders and bandits who had enslaved and terrorised his people, and for decades the Anglo-Saxons had lived in comparative peace, security and freedom. Alfred the Great's grandson, Athelstan, even became the first king of all England and ruled the entire land in harmony and prosperity. But in 939 King Athelstan died and once again the Viking bandits and pirates returned, like the Chinese bandits and pirates in Vietnam in the very same year, to cause bloodshed and misery all over again. Like the Chinese, the Vikings came under the banner of the dragon, with the bronze heads of dragons snarling on the prows of their longboats. For more than fifty years, just like Vietnam, right up to the end of the first millennium, Anglo-Saxon England was again a turmoil of war and instability. By the year 999 the Vikings were treating the feeble Anglo-Saxon king, Ethelred the Unready, with complete contempt. Their pirates even sailed right up the river Thames to London that year and they kept demanding that he should pay them huge ransoms, which they called Danegeld, to go away. Ethelred was a weakling who thought that the way to deal with the Vikings was to appease them by paying them all the Danegeld they demanded. But blackmailers never go away, they just become greedier. Ethelred's appeasement policy never succeeded in pacifying the Vikings or driving them out of his country. By 999 the Anglo-Saxons were completely enslaved again and the victims of unspeakable brutality and horror.'

She picked up one of the books on the lectern before her and found the quotation she wanted.

'As the Anglo-Saxon poet Kipling wrote a thousand years later – and I translate loosely:

> *And that is called paying the Dane-geld;*
> *But we've proved it again and again,*
> *That if once you have paid him the Dane-geld*
> *You never get rid of the Dane.'*

Chu shut the book with a crack as loud as a rifle shot. Her eyes patrolled the hall. The students sat in absolute silence. She sensed that many of them were afraid. Of course they were. She was afraid too. Even the spy was probably afraid. She glanced at him. He was studying his fingernails.

'As the first millennium bled to death in 999,' she said, 'Anglo-Saxon history had become again a brutal nightmare: terrified women were tortured and raped, babies butchered, men slaughtered, treasures seized, buildings burned and the whole land was afflicted with misery, famine and pestilence. Superstition replaced true religion, as it has again in the West today. And the *Anglo-Saxon Chronicle* described portents as terrible as the fiery dragons that were seen flying through the air when theVikings sacked the ancient Holy Island monastery of Lindisfarne; omens like "the long-haired star called *comet*" which the *Chronicle* reported in 995. Many people, like the Anglo-Saxon holy man Augustine, like the Chinese astrologers today, believed that the end of the world was near.'

In the silence she could hear in the distance a factory siren hooting a warning across the city. The second shift was ending. They had used the same siren to warn of American air raids.

'But the world did not end,' she said. 'After Ethelred's death the Anglo-Saxons resisted the Vikings so successfully that, gradually over the next millennium, they overwhelmed not only the Danes but half of the whole world. They founded the fat devil dragon, America, which you will notice is an anagram of the old Anglo-Saxon kingdom of Mercia, and they seeded their culture in every corner of the globe – Australia, Asia, Africa. They built the greatest empire the world has ever seen, so great that even our Spratly Islands themselves were named in 1867 after a British whaling captain. The second millennium gradually became the Anglo-Saxon millennium as their power, influence and language spread across the whole globe like a virus, as devastating as Aids.

'The power of the Round Eyes now is waning and our own Pacific millennium is about to dawn. All around the Pacific Rim this century the Anglo-Saxon empires have withdrawn: from Vietnam itself, Hong Kong, Malaysia, Singapore, the Philippines. The Long Noses have all gone home.

'But there are still lessons that we can learn from the Anglo-Saxons, powerful yet simple lessons: above all, that with courage and determination victims can become victors and aggressors can be overcome. For where are the Danes today? Where are the descendants of those brutal Vikings? Peddling pornography in Copenhagen. That is the Anglo-Saxon lesson, and they've proved it again and again: "if once you have paid him the Dane-geld you never get rid of the Dane." It was a lesson we learned well ourselves in Vietnam when the Anglo-Saxons invaded us in the south in the 1960s; we refused to surrender and drove them out. Appeasement never works, student comrades. It never has: not in Anglo-Saxon England in 999, not in Europe in 1939, not in Vietnam in the 1960s, not in the Spratly Islands in 1998.'

She hesitated. She could see in some of their eyes disbelief as well as fear. It was easy enough for her to say, a middle-aged woman now too old to fight.

She raised her chin in a gesture of defiance. 'I speak as one who fought for three years with the Viet Cong against the Americans when I was younger than any of you, when I was no more than a child. I remember the black silence of the jungle at night, and the sweat and mud of the underground warrens at Cu Chi where we hid for months at a time, and the black pyjamas we wore, and the terror of the napalm bombs.'

How could she ever forget? In a box under her bed she still kept the black pyjamas, the black-and-white checked scarf, the conical peasant straw hat she had worn in the fields. And sometimes when she went out alone she still carried, strapped around her leg, the knife she had used to kill the black American GI. How could she ever forget those days in the heroic Iron Land of Cu Chi, in the legendary Land of Fire?

'And my brother was killed in battle at Chau Doc during the Tet Offensive of 1968,' she said. 'And my son is now in the navy. He is serving today in the South China Sea, in the waters around the Spratlys.'

She gazed across the hall and caught the eye of the government informer. She nodded, bowed, collected her books and papers and turned to leave the platform. The informer stood and began to applaud and several young men stood too and started clapping. Others joined them until it seemed as if every student was standing and the ovation had become a dull roar like the crash of the ocean. It swept her all the way to the door and out into the corridor and began to ebb only when she left the building.

As she crossed the square towards the history faculty, her head down, counting the flagstones as always, towards the statue of Ho Chi Minh and the blaze of colour in the flowerbeds, the sun was too bright. Her headache confronted her openly now like a burglar and close behind came her conscience like a detective.

All those fine words, all the soiled old arguments. How could she still go on spouting the government line so effectively that even her enemy led the applause? How could she betray the trust of those fresh young faces by urging them to gamble with their lives?

Because she was afraid, that was why: she was middle-aged and tired and afraid of the government informer and of losing her job, and afraid of admitting even to herself that so much of what she had once believed no longer seemed to be true. Was Vietnam any happier now than it had been under the French or the Americans? There was still hunger, poverty, cruelty, injustice. Spies still sat at the back of university auditoriums. And who gave a *xu* who owned the Spratly Islands? Why should her students waste their youths as she had wasted hers in the jungle in black pyjamas and the underground hell-holes of the Viet Cong? But how could she ever admit it? To confess her doubts now would be to lose the respect of her son. Quang Linh would never forgive her.

Back in her study, twenty-five flagstones later, she dabbed at her eyes and picked up the framed photograph of Quang Linh. Behind his proud smile she could still see the eager little boy with the skinny legs and shorts too long and baggy for his bony knees, and later the serious, gawky teenager who had tried to protect her from the world when his father had left her for the American woman. Chu pressed the glass to her lips, leaving a misty kiss on Quang Linh's forehead. She wished so much that Tran Xuan Kai were still alive. They had had such happy times together just before the war: the tranquil evenings beside the river, the books they shared, the way he looked at her with adoration, the first sweet clumsy fumblings; they were both so young, so ardent.

She wiped her eyes. She wished that she had a man again to lean on. She had always needed a man; his strength, his warmth. But nowadays men seemed to be afraid of her. They thought she was too clever. She wanted to tell them they were wrong, that behind the steel-rimmed spectacles and greying hair there was still a romantic girl who dreamed of love, who had so much love to give.

And she wished that she could bring herself again to believe that history really could teach you something worthwhile, that there were indeed modern lessons to be learned from what happened in Anglo-Saxon England a thousand years ago. But she doubted it. She had lost her faith. She still loved history as an eternal melody but that was all it was; just a jaunty, unfinished tune. She feared that the Chinese astrologers were right, that the tune was about to come to an end, and she knew that if Quang Linh were killed in a war over the Spratly Islands she would never forgive herself.

The editorial staff of *Celebrity* magazine – all but The Editor, who was asleep on the eighteenth floor of the Mandarin Hotel in Hong Kong, and Nat Wakonde, who was drunk in a basement club in London – sat smoking around the conference table in Monaco. Around them was a scattering of reference books and scribbled lists of the names of all the mega-celebrities they had ever written about, starting with Gerry Adams, the Aga Khan and André Agassi and ending with Franco Zeffirelli, Fred Zinnemann and Zsa Zsa Gabor. The room was thick with cigarette smoke. As each name was suggested – and then approved by Iain Campbell – Caroline Ponsonby dangled her cigarette from the corner of her mouth and clacked the name into the *Celebrity* computer: every A-list actor, TV personality, singer, model, hairdresser, billionaire, footballer, chef and a few really major royals. They had listed all the society lawyers, psychiatrists and astrologers, the fashionable hookers and homos, the high-profile Aids victims, a few of the very biggest bestselling authors, a notorious child-molester who had just published his autobiography *I Put Away Childish Things*, and all those 'starlets' who had never made a movie but were famous for Being Famous. Campbell even approved the murderers: Charles Manson, Ian Brady, Myra Hindley, Reggie Kray, Sirhan Sirhan. Why not? They might all be released by the end of the century – what about a nice millennial amnesty? – and The Editor had always had a weakness for glossy spreads about celebrity criminals. Any one of them might win her annual Celebrity Monster of the Year Award.

Now Caroline Ponsonby was inputting names from the B-list and even dredging the C-list, and still they did not have the three thousand names that The Editor had demanded. Campbell removed his half-moon spectacles and gazed out hopelessly across Monte Carlo harbour. Once he had been chief features sub on a proper Scottish newspaper. Why had he ever taken on this Mickey Mouse job? Money. The promise of sunshine. Stella Barrett's ankles. How could he ever have fancied her? He must have been mad. The big white yachts slurped quietly at their expensive berths in the harbour far below. Their serenity seemed to mock him. What was it that Somerset Maugham had called Monaco? 'A sunny place for shady people.' A large, off-white seagull swooped past the big picture window, turned on its side like a fighter plane and shat on the glass just in front of Campbell's nose.

'Was that The Editor?' said Murdoch, looking startled.

Campbell sighed. 'How many names do we have now?'

Caroline Ponsonby tapped on the computer keyboard. The screen fizzed suddenly like a stir-fry meal. A number skittered across the bottom of the screen: *2642 words*, replied the computer.

'Holy Moses, another three hundred and fifty-eight to go, then,' said Campbell.

'No, it's much more than that, I'm afraid' said Caroline. 'We actually need another sixteen hundred and seventy-nine. The computer is counting words, you see, not names, and each name has two words in it so we have to halve the total.'

'Shit a brick, mate,' said Murdoch, blinking his good eye disconcertingly. 'We'll be here for a month. Why do we need three thousand? I thought we were inviting two?'

'She wants to have the pleasure of eventually dumping people off the list,' said Campbell.

'So why don't we make her day by deliberately including a few we know she'll dump?'

'Good idea, laddie. Very well, insert Princess Michael.'

'Rather you than me, sport,' said Murdoch.

Caroline giggled.

'And Fergie.'

'I thought The Editor said no royals.'

'Quite.'

Caroline giggled again.

'And insert Jeffrey Archer too.'

'But she said no writers,' said Caroline.

Campbell gazed at her over his half-moon spectacles.

She chortled. 'OK, OK, I'll put him in.'

'In that case, what about Maggie Thatcher?' said Mary Rogers.

'Or David Frost,' said Pascale Merlot.

'Sir David, please.'

'Barbara Cartland,' said Michèle Langoustier.

'Tina Brown.'

'Ruby Wax.'

'OK, OK, that's enough of those,' said Campbell. 'Joke's over. Now let's start again seriously, right at the beginning, with the A's. Are there any A's we've forgotten? Pauline, have a look in that *Who's Who*, will you, lassie? Let's trawl through the A's first and see what we've missed.'

Pauline Chang reached for the big red volume and flicked through its pages.

'Right, let's start at the very beginning.'

'Graham Aaronson,' she said. 'Claudio Abbado. Sir Albert Abbott. Diane Abbott. James Abbott.'

'Who in all creation are they?' said Campbell.

Pauline Chang studied the entries. 'Aaronson's an English lawyer. He says his recreations are photography, sitting in the sun and staring at the sea.'

'He'd be great on this cruise, then,' said Murdoch. 'Just the job. He could sit in a deckchair and take all the snaps.'

'Next.'

'Claudio Abbado. He's artistic director of the Berlin Philharmonic Orchestra. He won the Sergei Koussewitzky Prize in 1958.'

'Come again?'

'And the Dimitri Mitropoulos Prize in 1963.'

'Fuck me,' said Murdoch.

'Next.'

'Sir Albert Francis Abbott. Mayor of Mackay from 1970 to 1988.'

'Mackay?' said Campbell. 'Where's that? Not Scotland.'

'It's in Oz,' said Murdoch. 'Queensland. Huge port on the Pioneer River. Lots of sugar.'

'How sweet. Next.'

'Diane Abbott. Brit politician. Member of Parliament.'

'We don't want any of them. Come on, Pauline, give us the book, lassie. Let's have a look. We'll be here for weeks unless we get a move on.'

Pauline Chang slid *Who's Who* towards Campbell. He lit another cigarette for inspiration and scanned the fat columns of names, dates, schools, wives, children and achievements. Who the hell were all these so-called famous people? He'd heard of none of them. Here was a retired Shell Oil researcher, there a Eurocrat, yonder an accountant. Who on earth was Abdelwaheb Abdallah and what was he doing in *Who's Who*? And Mahmood Abdul Aziz? And why was the chairman of the Penang Port Commission included, or Henriette Alice Abel Smith, an 'Extra Lady-in-Waiting' to the Queen of England.

What was an *Extra* Lady-in-Waiting? And what was she waiting for?

Glumly Campbell turned page after page, past Egil Abrahamsen (chairman of Norwegian Telecommunications) and Professor Iya Abubakar (the Wali of Mubi) and Sayed El-Rashid Abushama Abdel Mahmoud Abushama (author of *Matrimonial Relations in both Sudanese Islamic and Czechoslovak Family Laws*) and Chief Simeon Olaosebikan Adebo (the Okanlomo of Itoko and Egbaland).

'Kathryn Adie,' he said eventually with relief. 'Put her on the list.'

'Who?'

'Kate Adie.'

'Who's she when she's at home?'

'You know: the broadcaster. Television.'

'Never heard of her.'

'Come on, Caroline, for Pete's sake, lassie. Don't you remember? Every night on TV? "This is Kate Adie, BBC, Kuwait." She practically won the Gulf War single-handed. She won the Monte Carlo TV News Award.'

'Before my time.'

'Stick her on the list,' said Campbell.

'What about Saddam Hussein?' said Murdoch.

'We are not inviting Saddam Hussein.'

'Ah, well, no worries. He'll probably invite himself, like he did in Kuwait. Stormin' Norman, then. Co-lin Powell. George Bush.'

'OK, put them down.' Campbell ran his finger down the page. 'Here's another: Larry Adler.'

'Who?'

'Larry Adler. Plays the mouth organ.'

'The what?'

'Mouth organ.'

Caroline Ponsonby snickered.

'Don't be dirty, lassie. Put him down. He won the Maryland Harmonica Championship in 1927. And he wrote a book called *Jokes and How to Tell Them*.'

'Sounds like a right galah, if you ask me,' said Murdoch.

'Put him down.'

Campbell read further. 'Ah, yes, of course. Now we're getting somewhere. We've forgotten the second Aga Khan.'

'The second? There are two?'

'The first one's uncle. Prince Sadruddin. Works for the UN. Stick him on the list, lassie.'

'She doesn't want royals.'

'He's a big cheese at the UN, for God's sake. He's done a hell of a lot for refugees and human rights. He's got a *château* in Switzerland. He married Nina Dyer.'

'Ah well, that's different. Nina Dyer, eh? I'll put him down, then.'

'This is great,' said Murdoch. 'Only sixteen hundred and seventy more names to go. No probs. No worries. This is easier than riding a croc bareback in a dried-up billabong.'

'And Jenny Agutter!' cried Campbell, running his finger down the page. 'How in tarnation did we forget wee Jenny Agutter?'

'Who?'

'*The Railway Children*, remember?'

'Never heard of them.'

'And Maria Aitken! Holy Moses – and Akihito!'

'Eh?'

'The Emperor of Japan! Akihito!'

'Ah *so*!' said Murdoch, blowing a smoke ring. 'And I know something else that begins with an A, too, mate, and it isn't at all polite. Here, why did the cassowary cross the road?'

Campbell sighed.

'Because it wasn't chicken.'

'Dear God,' said Campbell. He put his head in his hands.

'Good, eh?' said Murdoch. 'I made that one up myself.'

In Los Angeles it was the darkest hour before dawn. Marlowe had not hesitated before taking on the *Celebrity* magazine job.

So the client, Bill Warren, had threatened to kill the editor of *Celebrity*. So what? Maybe she deserved to be dead. And anyway, millions of guys threatened to kill people every day and they didn't do it. You couldn't live your life as though everyone meant what they said: that way you'd go nuts.

Marlowe and Chandler had taken just a quarter of an hour on the Internet to break into the *Celebrity* magazine computer in Monaco, which turned out not to be in Spain or Italy after all but somewhere in France. Well, you learn something new every day, thought Marlowe. Just because Monaco ended in *o* he had thought it had to be Latino but then he remembered that lots of French names end in *o* too: Bridget Bardo, Hercule Poiro, wine from Bordo. Even the French word for water was just that: *o*.

Marlowe managed to hack into the *Celebrity* computer so quickly because the client, Bill Warren, had once worked there and knew the six security passwords that they changed every couple of months. What sort of security is there in changing your password every two months but always using the same six over and over again? And *Celebrity* had such feeble passwords, too: *f@m0u5neS5, n0ta8il1ty, 5t@rD0m, n0t0r1etY, r3n0wn, 1lluStr10u5*. They were an insult to any decent hacker.

Marlowe activated Chandler's anti-virus software to check that none of the Monaco files was corrupted – you never knew what sort of nasty virus you might pick up off one of these foreign computers – and then swiftly and silently he raped the *Celebrity* files, downloading dozens of them for proper browsing later. At first sight they all looked pretty boring: lifestyle articles, interviews with actors, magazine stuff. One file, catchlined *mileniam*, was just a long list of hundreds of names, starting with someone called Gerry Adams and ending with Zsa Zsa Gabor. He had heard of Zsa Zsa Gabor, of course, and he knew most of the famous showbiz names, but who were all the others? Who was Jeffrey Archer? Kate Adie? Larry Adler? The names meant nothing to him. Marlowe activated Chandler's word-count facility which showed that there were

1,397 names on the list. What sort of idiot would sit at a computer just making a list of hundreds of names?

Marlowe began to feel weary. He had done enough for one day. He disengaged Chandler from the Monaco computer, carefully wiping off any electronic stains or fingerprints that they might have left on the files there, and tiptoed back across the Atlantic to LA. He licked his lips. He loved this time of night, when he and Chandler went out cruising on the World Wide Web not knowing who they might meet, sidling up to strangers in the dark, computers interfacing, whispered messages on screen.

Marlowe was breathing heavily. His thighs were cramped and sweaty. He eased them apart and scratched his scrotum.

The snack could wait a while.

He pulled on the VR headset and the sensitive body connections and plugged them into Chandler's VR port with a grunt.

Marlowe's fingers reached for Chandler's keys. He stroked them gently, checking Chandler's protective anti-virus software. It was firmly in place: Chandler was safe.

He selected a macro.

<gay.net.pacific.search>

He pressed the ENTER button and Chandler swaggered off into cyberspace, cruising for partners in the dark.

CHAPTER 4

Nat Wakonde had never been to North Wales and he was
astonished by the luscious green of the countryside when he
and the freelance photographer, Charlie Potter, stepped off the
London train at the little wayside railway station at Oswestry.
All the way from London Potter had been as bored as all
photographers are always bored. Potter wore chinos, an olive
fisherman's jacket and was humping a rucksack bulging with
equipment. 'How much further is it, squire?' he had asked
every twenty minutes as the train sped through Reading,
Oxford, Banbury, Birmingham, Shrewsbury. 'Is there a buffet
car on the train? How far is it from the station when we get
there? God, I hate the country. All those fucking views. And
sheep. God, I hate sheep. Shit all over their arses. Will we be
back in London before dark? I hate overnight jobs. I hate
staying in hotels. Do you think there's a vegetarian restaurant
in North Wales? Shit, I bet there isn't. I'm allergic. God, I hate
out-of-town jobs like this.'

On the forecourt outside the station at Oswestry a battered

old Cortina was parked under a sign that said TACSI.

'TACSI!' said Potter. 'Fucking Welsh! I mean, look at it, squire: TACSI. I mean, Christ.'

Nat Wakonde had never seen any green as vivid as this Welsh green. There was certainly nothing to match it on the Côte d'Azur. As a boy in South Africa he had grown up in the ochre lowveld wilds of the Eastern Transvaal and although the highveld and the valley of the Crocodile River turned green in winter it was just a pale smudge compared with this green. A thin mist hung over the lush Welsh hills and the whole wet world looked ripe and bursting with fertility. Everything seemed to be pregnant: the wheezing sheep waddling in every field, the tubby cattle, the chubby clouds, the swollen river. Even the fat Welsh taxi driver appeared to be about to give birth. He sat wedged behind the wheel with his hands folded fondly across his belly like a woman expecting twins.

'Pennant Melangell,' said Wakonde.

The driver looked at him sideways, suspiciously. It was a very Welsh face. It was not the sort of face that would buy a second-hand car from an Englishman. 'Is that the writers at Trefechan you're wanting?'

'No …'

'The hospice, then?'

'No, the –'

The driver sucked air through his teeth with a whistling sound. 'Not the gypsies? Not the hippies?'

'Well, yar, the New Age travellers, man.'

'That's them. The Crusties. I don't take no one out there, not nohow for nothing. Them are dirty buggers.'

'Bigoted old sod,' said Potter. 'Bloody fascist. Let's take another cab.'

'Fascist, is it? I'll have you know I've voted socialist all my life.'

'So did the Nazis.'

The driver looked them up and down like an undertaker.

'I can't say I think much of your friend,' he said to Wakonde, 'but you look clean enough. OK. Hop in. I'll take you to Pennant but only for twenty pound, paid in advance, see.'

'Let's get another taxi, Nat.'

The driver grinned a crusty grin of his own. 'There's not another taxi for fifty mile,' he leered. 'Twenty pound up front or you walk.'

'Get in, man,' said Wakonde.

'Shit,' said Potter.

'And no swearing like that and no drugs, no smoking, no syringes, and if you're sick in the back you're out, see.'

'Welcome to Wales,' said Potter, 'where men are men and the sheep are called Blodwen darling.'

They drove in silence for several miles, the driver with a pious expression, Potter sullen in the back seat, Wakonde admiring the silence and sweep of the countryside as it jolted past. But silence is not a taxi driver's natural habitat.

'First time here in Welsh Wales then, is it, boy?'

Potter snorted. 'Boy?' he said. 'Why not just have done with it and call him Sambo?'

'Shut it, Charlie,' said Wakonde. He had never understood why photographers were always so aggressively politically correct, especially photographers who wore chinos and sighed a lot. Wakonde could not have cared less about being called 'boy'. He had been called much worse things in South Africa. As a kid that old Afrikaans bastard Hendrik van der Merwe had always called him *hey you kaffir* or *black baboon* or *skellum piccanin*. Who cared? Van der Merwe and his kind were dinosaurs and would soon be extinct. As for the Welsh taxi driver, how could you expect him to have caught up yet with the twentieth century? Up here in North Wales he was still living in the Middle Ages: the ancient dry-stone walls still imprisoned the fields as they had for centuries; the valley was still as silent and deserted as it had been a thousand years ago; the primitive tracks meandered still up the hillsides following the ancient tracks of Celtic goats, and falcons stooped as of old high above the granite peaks. The taxi itself was so decrepit that it rattled like an ancient tumbril. The driver's eyes had the cunning glint of a medieval prelate.

'Yar, first time,' said Wakonde. 'It's beautiful. *Lekker*, man. What a pleasure. So green.'

'You think this is green, boy?' The driver chortled. 'You should see my granny's teeth.'

'Oh God,' said Potter. 'A comedian.'

'Come far then, is it?'

'London.'

The driver cleared his throat and spat out of his window. 'I been to London. You can keep your London. This is the place for me.'

'Fucking views,' said Potter.

They drove west into Clwyd towards Lake Bala and the Cambrian Mountains. THANK YOU FOR NOT SMOKING, said a faded notice that swayed and danced as it dangled from the central rearview mirror. Nat lowered his window, struggling with the stiff handle that clicked and groaned like an old arthritic wrist. The mountain air tasted of chilled silk. A stream sparkled beside the road. On the hillside a lamb bleated. No wonder Helga Gröning had stayed here for so long. For someone in hiding from the world this place was paradise.

It had taken Nat only three days to pick up her trail after flying to London from Nice. Her father, Fritz Gröning, was too rich and famous for her ever to be able to hide from the media for long. Celebrity was hereditary nowadays.

'She's in a caravan in North Wales with some old hippy who calls himself Arthur Lancelot,' said the *Daily Herald*'s gossip columnist. 'I ask you: Arthur Lancelot!'

The *Herald* man had that superior but seedy expense-account look that English journalists so often wear like cheap cologne. He wore a carnation in his lapel but there was dandruff on his collar. Nat was surprised by the dandruff. He had always thought of gossip columnists, with their precious ways and petty feuds, as being the hairdressers of journalism.

'He's probably got a dog called Merlin,' said the *Herald* man. 'I'll bet his real name's Reg Boggitt.' He laughed like a woodpecker. 'I can't imagine why you're wasting your time on this stale old story, old boy. Everyone's done it to death already, months ago, even the dear old *Express*.'

'Our bloody editor doesn't give a damn about what's in the newspapers, man,' said Nat. 'She only cares about the other glossies.'

The *Herald* man grinned. 'Is it true that she hires young gigolos when she's in town?'

'Stella Barrett?'

'Yeah.'

'Gigolos?'

'That's the whisper.'

'Hell, man: first I've heard of it. Where did you get that?'

The *Herald* man tapped the side of his nose. 'Little bird.'

'Gigolos? Stella? That's crazy, man. She wouldn't have to pay for a bloke to slip her a length. Yar, she's a bit flat-chested and skinny but she wouldn't have to pay for it. No way. She's not that ugly.'

The *Herald* man winked. 'They say she likes them under-age. Fourteen or fifteen. And black.' He sniggered. 'You ought to have a crack at her yourself. Sleep your way to the top. She might even give you a rise.'

The *Herald*'s electronic library was stuffed with dozens of old stories about Helga Gröning. They described how she had run away from her billionaire parents and her home in West Saxony six months ago, when she was seventeen, to live in Britain in a caravan in East Anglia with a fifty-five-year-old English hippy who claimed he had once played guitar in a sixties rock band and who now wore ethnic Celtic clothes –

cloak, jerkin, leather leggings – and a soulful expression. The hippy was said to scratch a living making 'authentic' Celtic trinkets for gullible tourists: rings, bangles, illuminated manuscripts. In the photographs Arthur Lancelot looked like a deadbeat sixties has-been with spaced-out eyes and a nose that appeared to be held together by a safety pin. Nat gazed at Helga's photograph. She looked stunning. Real tasty. Long blonde hair, blue eyes, trim tits; a triumph of Aryan Saxon genes. A real babe. What the hell did she see in a broken-down old fart like Arthur Lancelot? 'I am loving my Arthur more than any man,' she had told one reporter. 'He is teaching me what is really mattering in life. We are both Aquarius, under the sign of the air, and he is making his own clothe, weaving the wool himself for his tunic, dyeing the clothe himself with nettles and madder, curing the hide himself for his jerkin and sandals, hammering bronze trinkets for jewellery, whirling the wheel to shape the clay for pottery. He has made for me also a silver brooch and a necklace of amber beads. Arthur is a good man, good in his head and especial good in bed. *Ja*. This is so.'

Nat stared at the photographs. Good in bed? What? This shambling old sixties wreck? Poor old Fritz Gröning back at the family mansion in Saxony must be going spare at the thought of his gorgeous seventeen-year-old daughter being humped by a drug-shagged Englander crumblie with rings in his ears and a safety pin through his hooter.

'My Arthur is an holy man,' she had told another journalist. 'Not like my father, who wants only for money and power. We family money was make in the Hitler War when my Nazi grandfather is an SS officer who is torturing Jews and also owning a factory that uses slaves labour, *ja*. He is dead now, my Nazi monster grandfather, but I hate him still. I am hoping he is in hell with Hitler. *Hell Hitler! Ja*. This is a joke I am making.'

Her best friend among the travellers was Jewish, she said: a single mother called Rachel.

What a silly little rich girl, thought Nat, just another spoilt brat playing games. In a year or two she'll be back at home, married to another millionaire's blue-eyed son and about to make perfect Aryan Saxon babies to gladden the heart of Hitler's ghost.

'Already we have went in the caravans and tents from East Anglia to Anglesey,' Helga Gröning had told one of the colour supplements. 'We have went to all the holy places like Glastonbury for the burials of St Patrick and St Joseph of Arimathea and King Arthur, called like my Arthur and Queen Guinevere. And we have went to Winchester, Canterbury, Bury Saint Edmunds and Lincoln City with its cold cathedral and now we are halt in a beautiful valley near Lake Bala in the north of Wales, where the real Old English still live and name themselves Celts. This is beautiful country here, with the mountains blue in the mist and the dripping leaves and the streams so clean for washing away all the dirt. There is here no polluting, no evil, no meat or vehicles, no cruelty, and my Arthur has learned me - taught me - how to understand astrology and the tarot cards and Nostradamus, who is saying ago four hundred years that the world is ending in 1999 with fire and brimstone from the sky. Later we are travelling south in the caravans for Stonehenge, the ancient holy place where my Arthur he says we must be camping when the world should be coming to an end and we will be welcome to the Age of Aquarius, the age of peace. The big stones at Stonehenge, he is saying, are prayers. They will pray for us at the end of the world. I am liking that, *ja*. It is comforting me. I am wishing to hear the old stones whisper for me at the dawn.'

Oh dear, thought Nat. Oh dear oh dear oh dear.

'You West Indian, boy?' enquired the taxi driver.

'Eh?'

'You really must stop calling him that,' snapped Potter. 'He's South African, for Christ's sake.'

'No swearing. Not in this cab, see. No smoking, no swearing.'

'How would you like it if he kept calling you Taffy?'

'So what, boyo? All my friends do.'

'Lay off it, Charlie,' said Nat. 'It doesn't matter. Really.'

The driver glanced at him sideways. 'South African, eh? Things all right there now, then?'

'All right?'

'All the racial stuff, like. All that unpleasantness.'

'Unpleasantness!' said Potter. 'Christ!'

'That's enough of that. No blasphemy. Not in my cab. This is a God-fearing cab, so it is.'

THANK YOU FOR NOT BLASPHEMING. THANK YOU FOR NOT TALKING, thought Nat. Why do taxi drivers, all over the world, always talk so much? They chatter almost as much as their meters.

'Bollocks,' said Potter.

In the Tanat Valley near Llangynog, in a field near the hamlet of Pennant Melangell, Helga Gröning sat in the bright blue caravan that Arthur Lancelot had painted with golden sunflowers and unicorns and put the finishing touches to her latest illuminated vellum manuscript. This one would surely sell to some American tourist for at least £100. Arthur had carefully aged the parchment and had written the legend down for her, and she had spent nearly a week inscribing the text onto it in deep black Gothic script and decorating the borders with colourful interlocking designs: flowers, tendrils, Celtic shields, Welsh dragons. American tourists could never resist that sort of thing. It looked so historic. It looked so ethnic. And the legend was so beautiful it made her tremble.

Before the dawn of history, in the ancient mists of Celtic legend, near Llangynog in the silent Tanat Valley of northern Wales, there was once a handsome Celtic prince named Brochwell who galloped one day into the head of the peaceful valley with his hounds, at a magic place called Pennant, in pursuit of a terrified hare, which took refuge in a thicket.

As the barking hounds surrounded their prey, Prince Brochwell followed the hare into the thicket and found it cowering there beneath the skirts of a young virgin who was kneeling in prayer.

The virgin's name was Melangell and she told the Prince that she had fled to Wales from Ireland, across the savage Hibernian winter sea in a fragile little coracle, after defying her father by refusing to marry the husband he had chosen for her.

Now she lived in the thicket, sleeping in a fissure in the rock.

The Prince was so awed by her holiness that he let the hare run free and named the virgin Sanctes Melangell and gave her the valley as a place of perpetual refuge, which is why it is now called Pennant Melangell.

And there she founded a convent and tended the sick, and built a church where eventually her own body was buried.

For centuries afterwards sick pilgrims have come to the church to pray for healing at the carved stone tomb of Saint Melangell and the sick still come to the valley to find sanctuary and solace at the modern holistic cancer centre there.

And even the stones themselves pray too for the soul of the hare whose simple faith inspired their own eternal destiny.

Amen. Amen. Amen.

Helga smiled, pleased with her work. She liked all those *Ands* at the end and the three *Amens*: they were so authentic. And there was something so special about the English language. She loved all those resounding English words: *ancient, legend, sanctuary, tomb, eternal, destiny.* And the British had saved the world from Hitler. How could you ever repay them for doing that? She had relished the job of applying carefully onto the illuminations and borders of the parchment the bold, rich colours that the grey-faced medieval monks had loved so much: the gold of Prince Brochwell's crown, the scarlet of his tunic, the azure of his cloak, the flash of silver in the eye of the terrified hare. The legend made her shiver: a girl like her, escaping just like her from her father and finding sanctuary here in this very valley where it had happened so long ago.

They said that the hare and the saint had been found by the hunters just up there on the hillside, on a hidden ledge beside the old stone farmhouse, Trefechan, with the smoke wisping up from its chimney like an offering to the ancient gods. They said that Trefechan was haunted. Helga was glad. It seemed right. Whenever she climbed the hillside and sat to look across the valley she thought of the lonely farmhouse ghost as she listened to the gurgling of the glistening streams tumbling down the hillside, the bleating of pregnant ewes fat on the meadows lush with the promise of spring, and the holy quiet of the towering wooded mountains. She savoured the sense that there was also another haunting presence here, as though something momentous were about to happen. There was in this magical valley a silence greater than mere noiselessness, she thought, as though God Herself were lost in deepest thought.

She dusted the manuscript with fine sand, let it dry, blew the sand off and laid it to rest in its narrow wooden coffin. Somewhere nearby she could hear Arthur playing an ancient melody on the lyre.

Beyond the field of caravans the taxi drew up at the side of the road by the five-bar gate and sat there clattering like a dustbin factory.

Potter emerged from the back seat, dragging his cameras and rucksack behind him. 'Well, you can fuck off for a start,' he said. 'Welsh cunt.'

'For Christ's sake, Charlie, shut up,' said Nat Wakonde.

The driver's teeth gleamed. 'Cunt, is it? I tell you this, boyo, if I'm a Welsh cunt then an Englishman's home is his arsehole.'

'Please wait, driver,' said Nat. 'We'll need to get back.'

The driver crunched the Cortina savagely into gear. 'Wait? There's optimistic, boyo. I wouldn't wait for that ignorant prat even if he was the Prince of Wales bollock-naked in a hurricane playing "Land of My Fathers" on the spoons.'

The taxi reversed with a brutal roar, its wheels spinning on the grass verge. It shunted forward with a crunch, reversed again, scattering gravel, and clattered back along the empty lane towards civilisation.

'Now you've dropped us in the manure,' said Nat. 'That was bloody stupid.'

'Good riddance.'

'How the hell are we going to get back now?'

Potter shrugged. 'One of the crusties'll give us a lift.'

'A lift! It's fifteen miles back into town.'

'We'll think of something, squire. The man was a wanker.'

'Do you want to know something, Charlie? So are you.'

There were six dingy caravans parked in the muddy field beside an old truck, one of them painted bright blue and decorated with golden sunflowers and unicorns. Even at this distance the little settlement was stained with the sour smell of poverty. In the middle of the field two young women with straggling hair and long spattered skirts were tending a steaming pot on a smoky fire. Four ragged children were standing in the mud staring at the gate. Pitched nearby were three tents and sitting outside one of them a squat, dark-skinned young woman was perched on the edge of a broken-down old sofa breast-feeding a baby, her stubby legs spread wide under a long, black skirt that was spotted with food and milk stains. Hair sprouted from her armpits and her huge, creamy breast was swollen fat with milk. The baby sprawled naked across her lap, its fat little legs pumping up and down as it knuckled her breast.

Nat opened the gate and walked into the field. Potter followed, shouldering his rucksack.

A large, unkempt black mongrel appeared from behind one of the caravans and galloped towards them, barking, scattering a couple of squawking chickens as it came, followed by a tall, elderly man wearing a cloak, a jerkin, leather leggings, long hair and a sparse silver beard.

'Oh God,' said Potter. 'Dogs. I hate dogs. I'm allergic.'

'Just show it who's the master,' said Nat. He held out his

hand towards the dog as a peace offering. The dog galloped towards him, growling. Its eyes glinted. It leapt for his fingers and bit them.

'Yarra!' cried Nat, sucking his fingers.

'Ah God,' said Potter. 'It's coming.'

'Down, Merlin!' called the man in the cloak. 'Cool it, boy. Heel.'

'It's coming for me.'

The dog leapt for Nat's crotch and sank its teeth into his other hand.

'Yiy!' cried Nat Wakonde. Blood seeped across the back of his hand.

'Blood,' said Potter. 'I'm going to faint.'

'Down, Merlin! Cool dude, baby.'

The dog advanced on Potter, growling and baring yellow teeth. A string of saliva hung from its jaw.

'No, Merlin! Chill out, kiddo.'

'Ah please no,' said Potter.

'Ow!' said Nat. 'Ow ow ow!'

The dog loped towards Potter with menace in its eyes, as though it remembered its wolfish ancestors. It licked its lips and snarled.

'No, Merlin! Sit, baby. Sit! Be nice!'

The dog sniffed Potter's knees suspiciously and then his thighs. Potter stood still, paralysed. He closed his eyes. 'Do something,' he whimpered.

The dog sniffed his ankles. Suddenly it started to wag its tail. It grinned, barked once with delight and without any warning rammed its nose into Potter's groin.

'Oh God, it'll have me balls off.'

The man in the cloak arrived and patted the dog. He was wearing a small gold ring in each ear and a silver safety pin in his nose. 'Groovy, man,' he said. 'He likes you. That's cool.'

The dog rammed its muzzle deeper between Potter's legs.

'Bloody animal!' said Potter. 'Good boy. Lovely boy. Nice doggie.'

'Ouch,' said Wakonde. 'I can't stop the bleeding.'

'Sorry about that,' said the man in the cloak. 'He doesn't like blacks, I'm afraid. Naughty of him.'

'The bloody thing's black itself,' said Nat, sucking his knuckles.

'Yeah. And Hitler was Jewish, but there you go. Funny old world, eh? I'm Arthur, by the way: Arthur Lancelot.'

'Nat Wakonde and that's Charlie Potter.'

'Friend,' said Lancelot to the dog. 'Friend. You OK?'

'I'm bleeding a bit.'

'Soon fix that, man. Come up to the caravan. Groovy. At least Merlin hasn't got rabies – so far as I know.'

'Oh, great.'

'No problem, man. Stay cool.'

He turned away. Nat followed.

'What about me?' cried Potter. 'I can't move an inch. He's got me by the nuts.'

'Thank God he's not a squirrel, then,' said Nat.

Lancelot laughed. It was not a pretty sound. His teeth were as crooked and discoloured as his dog's. He snapped his fingers. 'Drop it, Merlin. Good boy. Leave. Leave!'

The dog removed its muzzle from Potter's crotch, licked its lips, sniffed, circled Potter once and then rammed its nose between Potter's buttocks.

'Oh God, I hate dogs,' said Potter. 'Nice dog. Good doggie. Why do the dirty buggers always go for your arse?'

'They dig the smell, man. He likes you.'

Potter was standing on tiptoe. 'Just get this sodding animal out of my bum, will you, squire?'

Lancelot grabbed the dog's collar and pulled the beast away.

'God, I hate the country,' said Potter.

Lancelot gripped the dog's collar and headed towards the blue caravan. They followed, squelching in mud, past scuttling chickens, past the smoky fire and the unkempt women and dirty, snot-faced children.

'You're looking for Hell, I expect,' said Lancelot.

'Eh?'

'Helga Gröning. You're reporters.'

'How did you guess?'

Lancelot shrugged. 'Two guys turn up in the middle of nowhere and one has three cameras and enough equipment to shoot *Gone With the Wind*. Even I can work it out. I wasn't born yesterday. I'm an old rocker. She won't talk to you, you know. She won't even say hello. She hates the Press. Every piece about her has been full of lies.'

'We're not like that. We're from *Celebrity* magazine.'

'You're all like that, man. All you bastards want is a tasty story, even if it means making up lies.'

'Not me,' protested Nat. 'Do I look like that sort of shit?'

Lancelot glanced at him. 'Yeah,' he said.

The caravan was surprisingly roomy. An old Simon and Garfunkel song was leaking out of the CD player - 'Bridge Over Troubled Water' - and scraps of food littered the table: bread crumbs and crusts, a piece of gristle, a home-made roll-up cigarette stubbed out in a cold pool of grease. The rumpled sheets on the double bed were grey. There were traces of her everywhere: some dresses and a kaftan hanging on an open rail, a pair of dirty knickers thrown in a corner, a smell of woman. The lucky old bastard, thought Nat: how did an old deadbeat like Lancelot pull a gorgeous babe like Helga Gröning? Obvious, really: he was a father figure. Easy pop psychology: she resented her father's millions and values and had replaced her old man with another old man.

Lancelot lifted a stack of unwashed plates out of the basin and gestured for Nat to wash the blood from his hands. He went off in search of a bottle of disinfectant and Potter snatched a couple of quick photographs of the inside of the caravan.

The dog jumped onto the table to savage the gristle. It chewed, swallowed, licked its lips, burped, and rested its chin on Potter's shoes, gazing adoringly at his ankles.

'Could we please get rid of this dog?' asked Potter.

'No,' said Lancelot.

'About this interview,' said Nat. 'We'll pay for it.'

Lancelot laughed unpleasantly. 'Pay? She doesn't need money. Her old man's a zillionaire. And he keeps sending her money.'

'I mean we'll pay *you* to fix it for us. Couple of hundred quid? Three?'

Lancelot snapped his fingers. 'You guys always think you can buy anyone just by bunging them some bread. But that's exactly what Hell's been running away from: all that capitalist shit about money and possessions.'

'So what does she want, then?' said Nat.

Lancelot grinned. His mouth was wet and red. 'She wants me,' he said.

The door opened and Helga Gröning ducked into the caravan, bringing with her a slice of sunlight that glanced across the floor. She was wearing a linen tunic that hung ragged above her knees and was belted at the waist with only a piece of string. She had a metal bottletop-opener on a chain around her neck and on her feet a clumpy pair of Doc Marten boots. She had cut her blonde hair short and spiky, punk style, but still she looked like a goddess. As she came through the doorway she was bending her head but she raised it and looked straight at Nat Wakonde, into his eyes, touching her hair with a delicate flick of her fingers. A small silver stud glinted on her left nostril. A tiny silver ring pierced her left eyebrow. Her skin was as smooth as cream. Nat Wakonde was mesmerised. What a pleasure it was just to gaze at her. What a pleasure. He did not simply want to touch her. He wanted to protect her.

Her eyes were angry. 'Who are these people being, please, Arthur? *Ja?* I am seeing them arriving from Rachel's tent.'

'No sweat, Hellish. This is Nat; this is Charlie. From London.'

Nat held out his hand to her. He wanted so much to feel her fingers. He could smell her from here.

She ignored him.

'Why are you bringing these peoples in my caravan? Please? I am wanting an answer for this. These are being reporters, I think, *ja*. This man is being a photographer. He is having a camera now.'

'Don't worry, darling,' said Potter, smiling horribly. 'It's German too: a Leica.'

'Merlin bit Nat, baby,' said Lancelot. 'Drew blood. Had to come in here to disinfect them.'

Helga glanced at Wakonde's hands without sympathy. 'This he has done now, I think, so now he can go.' She stood aside and motioned them towards the door with both hands. Her breasts trembled naked under her shift. Her eyes were as blue and white as the ocean.

'They wanna talk to you, too, babe.'

She clenched her lips. 'You know I am never talking again with reporters, Arthur. Send them away.'

Nat gazed at her. He smiled gently. No no no, he thought, you've got it all wrong. I'd never do anything to hurt you.

'We'll pay you, doll,' said Potter. He tapped the side of his nose and leered. 'We'll see you all right, sweetheart. Trust your Uncle Charlie.'

Nat looked at her hair. It was like silk. Her mouth was a magic promise.

'Get out,' she said. 'Out! Now!'

'Just a few pics, darling,' said Potter. He winked. 'Couple of nice leggy shots. Hitch the skirt up a bit. Flash some thigh. Show a bit of knicker.'

So much for the politically correct photographer, thought Nat. Give a snapper a pretty girl and he's as bad as the rest of us.

'Right, that does it,' said Lancelot, standing up. 'You heard the lady, now sod off.'

'No, please,' said Nat. 'Let me explain –'

She glared at him. 'I hate you,' she said. There was spittle on her lip. He wanted to kiss it. 'Go away, you filth! Go! *Raus! Raus!*'

The dog stood too. It lowered its tail and growled like distant thunder.

'All right, all right,' said Potter hurriedly, reaching for his rucksack. 'Don't get your knickers in a twist.'

Nat smiled at her.

'Are you never in shame of what you do for money?' she sneered. 'People like you. Churnalists. *Untermenschen. Raus, raus, Untermenschen!*'

'And give my love to Piccadilly Circus,' said Lancelot.

'King Alfred the Great, like another Anglo-Saxon leader a thousand years later, Winston Churchill, was a notable writer and scholar as well as a warrior,' wrote Nguyen Thi Chu. She paused and looked away from the computer screen.

Beyond her window hundreds of students were spilling out of the lecture rooms in the history faculty building and surging across the central square of the Tây Ninh University campus. It was her one free day of the week: no lectures, no tutorials, no seminars, no administrative meetings, no indoctrination group. She treasured these days: they allowed her to write without any distractions. Her book, she knew, would make her reputation at last. It would bolster the pride of the Vietnamese people, their sense of nationhood and destiny, their reading of history and politics, their true Pacific identity, their confidence in the future. It would help them at last to shrug off the shackles of the past, of colonialism and racism, and the exploitation and subservience that had stained so much of their history. She felt in her bones that when her book was published it would come to the attention of the Leader himself. It might even win her awards and honours. If that happened she would be able to demand that the government spy be removed from her lectures, the smooth-faced northern man with the flat, polished hair and pointed ears and eyes like pebbles. She might even be able to arrange for Quang Linh to be posted somewhere safer than the Spratly Islands.

She glanced at his photograph in the silver frame on her desk: he was so young, so happy and smiling, so proud in his naval uniform. At least Quang Linh was still safe. At least there was still no war over the Spratlys in the South China Sea as the Chinese sat back on their haunches like tigers and waited, digesting Hong Kong.

She frowned and chastised herself. Too much undisciplined thinking. Her mind wandered too much, too often these days. The curse of middle age. The book would not write itself. She turned back to the computer and tapped at the keyboard.

'But deep in the Anglo-Saxon soul,' she wrote, 'there is a fiery dragon that incinerates itself from within. The Anglo-Saxons are their own worst enemies. After the death of Alfred the Great the golden age of Anglo-Saxon peace and prosperity was carelessly thrown away by the weakling appeaser Ethelred the Unready at the end of the first millennium, just as the death of Winston Churchill towards the end of the second millennium was also followed by decades of western Anglo-Saxon weakness, incompetence and appeasement.'

Could it happen in Vietnam too? she wondered. Would peace sap the nation's energies after so many years of war? She could not bear the possibility. She and her generation had sacrificed so much to fight for a better world. Tran Xuan Kai had died for it and her hopes of love had all but died with him except for those few weeks with Quang Linh's father. The cynics argued that patriotism and idealism are self-delusions, that humans fight because they need conflict and challenge almost as much as they need food and water. If that were true then life was hopeless. Outside her window the shadow of a cloud moved across the square, briefly blotting the sunlight and dressing the statue of Ho Chi Minh in a grey cloak. If she ever came to believe that man was born to struggle endlessly, to slaughter and be slaughtered, she would have to believe that

Quang Linh's death and the sacrifice of her students' lives in exchange for a few uninhabited islands in the South China Sea were not only inevitable but also right. She would have to accept that all her years of study and teaching had been wasted, that all her work had been in vain, that history was not only pointless but not even a tantalising melody.

If only she had a lover. But he could not be just any man. Not now, not after Tran Xuan Kai and all those years. He had to be a lover.

Work. She turned back to the keyboard. Only work could hold the shadows back and keep you sane, and the book would change her life and give it meaning.

Steve Marlowe woke at dusk, yawned, stretched and heaved himself out of bed. Beyond the window an evening haze was squatting on the city. He grabbed a handful of cookies and lumbered towards the bathroom. Chandler was breathing quietly at the workstation in the next room. It was good to wake each evening and feel Chandler nearby, warm and breathing.

Marlowe stumbled into the bathroom. He was starving again. He sat on the lavatory and grunted. The little Filipino had been exhausting last night. They had sidled up to each other in a dark corner of a World Wide Web bulletin board somewhere off the coast of Vietnam, in the South China Sea. He had noticed at once the cute way the little Filipino was surfing the net, playing his keyboard with a delicate musical sense of humour in his fingertips so that even their computers seemed to smile as they locked on to each other. Later Marlowe and the Filipino had exchanged their images on-screen, injecting them feverishly into each other's computers. Nice eyes, the Filipino, smooth skin, tight little ass: just right. Marlowe scratched his balls. He had enjoyed the Filipino so much that he had nearly exchanged names and e-mail addresses. But that was always a mistake. Exchanging personal details nearly always led to trouble, like the time it had taken him three months to shake off a vicious old South African

queen in Johannesburg. In any case, Marlowe had recorded the
Filipino's performance on the tape in the VR headset: they
could always do it again and again without ever meeting.

Chandler rustled up a snack for him: three eggs on a steak,
french fries, two cream buns, ice cream, pecan pie, a litre of
Coke. Marlowe sat at his workstation just as the sun slipped
over the western horizon to wake the Filipino in the South
China Sea.

Chandler gave him a bright blue flickering smile.

<hi> said Chandler <have a nice day>

Marlowe grunted.

<57 messages today>

The usual crap. Electronic hucksters selling carpets, false
teeth, miracle drugs, religion. They should ban all this garbage
on the Internet. A couple of years ago nobody would have
dreamed of sending unsolicited ads – it was just not netiquette,
and anyone who did was flamed by hundreds of cyberspace
freaks – but now any shyster seemed to think he could clutter
up the cables with unsolicited crap.

Marlowe clicked quickly through the junk. As usual there
were only a couple of messages worth reading. The Siberian
businessman in Vladivostok wanted another industrial espionage
job done on his South Korean rivals. Kitty Schweitzer had called
from Long Beach to say that thanks to his evidence she was
divorcing her husband and would Marlowe like to meet her for
a drink – <im still only 52 and blonde and well-preserved and i
just love men> *Me too*, thought Marlowe. And some guy in
Jerusalem wanted him to track down a missing relative. There
was also a message from the guy in Santa Barbara who wanted a
number done on the magazine editor in Monte Carlo. Bill
Warren: all capital letters and punctuation marks.

Marlowe called Warren downline and found he was at his
computer.

<ive got her check a/c + credit card statemens> said
Marlowe.

<That's great. Anything suspicious?>

<wenever shes away from home she always uses escort agencees>

<Really?>

<+ she pays them $1000 a time>

<My God. What for?>

Marlowe did a smiley. <:-) well i gess shes not payin them that much jus 2 hold her hand>

<We'll need evidence>

<ill get it theres 1 other thing ive found already shes makin a long list of thousans of names some of them famus peepl>

<Right. She's planning a party. Can you get me the list?>

<sure>

<Can you screw the list up? Change some of the names?>

<sure>

<Get me on it? Without them knowing?>

<yeah>

<You're doing a great job, Marlowe.>

<thanx ill keep in touch have a nice day>

Marlowe squirted the *mileniam* file downline to Warren in Santa Barbara and killed the connection. It would be easy to infect the *Celebrity* computer in Monte Carlo with an undetectable virus so that dozens of names on the *mileniam* list were lost or corrupted and replaced by invisible dozens of others, including Warren's. They would be ghost names that would haunt the *Celebrity* file but appear only when Marlowe chose to make them visible.

Marlowe chuckled. His fat fingers danced around the keyboard and Chandler set off east across the North American continent and across the Atlantic Ocean to greet the rising sun and to break the data bank in Monte Carlo.

<f@m0u5neS5> typed Marlowe <mileniam>

'Oh God,' said Iain Campbell, fiddling with his half-moon spectacles and stubbing out another cigarette. 'Have we got Michael Douglas down on the list?'

'Yes,' said Caroline Ponsonby. 'About three times now.'

'Charlie Sheen?'

'Yes.'

'Keanu Reeves?'

'Yep.'

'Mickey Rourke?'

'You've asked four times about Mickey Rourke.'

'Naomi Campbell? Kate Moss?'

'Yeah.'

The editorial staff of *Celebrity* – except for The Editor, who was in a jumbo jet somewhere between Hong Kong and Los Angeles, and Nat Wakonde, who was standing in a trance in a muddy lane in Wales – sat around the smoky conference table in mounting desperation. They still needed 247 names and She was due back in Monte Carlo in three days. The air-conditioning chuckled quietly. Murdoch lit a small cheroot and closed his good eye: the false one glinted beneath a half-shut eyelid. Jean-Paul Ferré tapped his biro against his teeth. 'Jill Vandenberg?' he said.

'Who's she when she's at home?'

'Tony Curtis's girlfriend. Just an idea.' Ferré tapped his teeth again with his biro.

'Don't do that, for Pete's sake,' said Campbell.

They sat in silence again.

'Camille Paglia?' suggested Michèle Langoustier.

'Got her.'

'Germaine Greer?'

'Yeah.'

'Erica Jong?'

'Yup.'

Silence descended again as tangible as the cloud of cigarette smoke that lay grey-blue across the conference room.

'Where's Paddy Kelly?' said Campbell eventually. 'Why shouldn't he suffer too? Kelly!' he bellowed.

Kelly sauntered in from his office.

'We need to pick your brains, laddie,' said Campbell. 'Celebrities. Names.'

'I'm busy. I'm opening Her mail.'

'We need ideas, laddie.'

'There's a pile of stuff and she's back on Thursday.'

'Which is why we need two hundred more names, pronto.'

'I'm that harassed. That harassed. I'm just a blur. If her mail's not done …'

'I'll be right behind you as she fires us both. Now - names.'

Kelly frowned. 'Well, let me see, now. Like do you have Gary Busey at all?'

'Yes,' said Caroline Ponsonby.

'Alice Cooper?'

'Mmm.'

'Linda Evangelista?'

'Yeah.'

'Pierce Brosnan?'

'Yeah yeah.'

'Danny DeVito? Nicole Kidman?'

'Come on, Paddy. Too obvious.'

'Well, then, now, let me see now. Youssou N'Dour?'

'Come again?'

'N'Dour. He's a singer from Senegal. Like brilliant. He had a song called "Seven Seconds".'

'Big?'

'Mega.'

'Put him down.'

'And Johnnie Cochran?'

'Eh?'

'O. J. Simpson's lawyer. The Editor like thinks he's great, blah-blah-blah.'

'Put him down.'

'Annie Leibovitz?'

'Good. Yes.'

'And Heidi Fleiss?'

'Who?'

'The Hollywood madam.'

'Is she still in prison?'

'Who cares?'

'Stick her on the list.'

'Tarts,' said Murdoch, opening his eye and blowing a perfect smoke ring. 'What about Christine Keeler? Mandy Rice-Davies?'

'Who?' said Michèle Langoustier.

'The girls in the Profumo scandal.'

'The what?'

'Profumo scandal.'

'What was that?'

Murdoch shook his head. 'I think I'll go and lie down,' he said. 'Jeez, it was only thirty-five years ago.'

'Before I was born.'

'But it's history,' said Murdoch.

'English history. Who cares about England now?'

'Hear hear,' said Kelly. 'Up the Republic!'

'England is finished,' said Pascale Merlot.

'Poor bloody Poms,' said Murdoch.

'Any more names, Paddy?' said Campbell anxiously.

Kelly thought. 'I'm like all squeezed out,' he said.

'Well, thanks, laddie.'

'Brilliant.'

'Back to the mail.'

Kelly left the room and silence descended again like an invisible stain. They fiddled with biros and toyed with their fingers and avoided each other's eyes. Murdoch chewed his cheroot and made a paper dart. Kevin Thomas assaulted his cuticles. Pascale Merlot lit a fresh cigarette and gazed out of the window. Were there really three thousand famous people in the world? Three thousand real celebrities, known to everyone everywhere?

'Martina Navratilova?'

'Got her.'

'Andrea Dworkin?'

'We're not that desperate,' said Campbell.

There was another silence.

'David Copperfield?' said Pauline Chang.

'We've got him.'

Another silence.

'I know,' said Jean-Paul Ferré. 'That American guy. Bobbitt. The one whose wife cut off his *je ne sais quoi*.'

'You can not be serious,' said Pascale Merlot.

'John McEnroe?' said Murdoch.

'Yes.'

'The Pope?'

'Yes,' said Caroline Ponsonby. 'And Mrs Bobbitt will photograph His Holiness in the bath.'

An explosion thundered across the corridor.

'Holy Moses!' said Campbell. 'Kelly's office. A bomb!'

'Ring security,' yelled Murdoch.

'Jesus!'

'A bomb!'

'Security!'

'For Pete's sake. Pascale! Ring security.'

'We'd better see how he is,' said Murdoch.

'You can't go in there.'

'There might be another.'

'A booby trap.'

'We can't just leave the poor bugger,' said Murdoch. 'I'm going in.'

'I'm with you, laddie.'

They ran towards Kelly's office.

'Paddy? Paddy? You all right, mate?'

Kelly was sitting behind his desk. His face, shirt and hands were blackened. On the desk before him lay a shattered package.

'Holy Moses!' said Campbell. 'We must get you to hospital.'

Kelly sat immobile, looking at his hands.

'You OK, Paddy? You OK, mate?'

Kelly nodded. 'Dah-dee-dah,' he said. 'Brilliant.'

'Shock,' said Campbell. 'We must get him to hospital.'

'Blah-blah,' said Kelly.

'A letter bomb.'

Kelly looked at his hands, turning them both in slow motion as though they belonged to a stranger. He seemed to be counting the fingers.

'No worries, mate. Eight still there and two thumbs.'

'Bomb,' said Kelly. 'Letter bomb. From Corsica.'

CHAPTER 5

Hendrik van der Merwe winced as he knelt in his nightdress beside his bed at dawn to say his prayers in the old family farmhouse far out on the ochre lowveld of the Eastern Transvaal, between Nelspruit and the Kruger National Park, where even the water sometimes smells of dust. The early darkness chilled his skinny shins and calves, and pain stabbed his guts like a lance of fire. He groaned. The pain was getting worse. That was only to be expected – the doctor had warned him that it would – but he wondered how much longer he would be able to kneel when he said his prayers. He would kneel for as long as he could bear it; he would force himself to kneel for the Lord, twice a day, morning and night. But the time would come when he could kneel no more, when the pain in his body would rival the fires of Hell, and what then? Would the Lord forgive him for not kneeling while he said his prayers or would He punish his weakness? Already the pain sometimes made van der Merwe whimper. The doctor had offered him drugs but he had sworn to resist them until the very end, until he whimpered and howled for the mercy of the Lord and the Lord in His mercy called him home. But van der Merwe would never whimper in front of his kaffirs. He promised himself that. His kaffirs had always respected him because he had never allowed them even to glimpse any weakness in him, not even when he had been mauled by the lion, and he was not starting now. They might be running the country now, the kaffirs, but they weren't running him − not now, not ever. Once you let them see you were vulnerable you were finished. That was where that *baster* de Klerk had gone wrong: he had looked into Mandela's eyes and he had flinched, and that had been the end of 350 years of white civilisation. Van der Merwe never flinched, not in front of anyone and especially not in front of a kaffir. When Moses Wakonde and the woman Miriam were working around the house van der Merwe was careful to avoid sudden movements so that the pain retreated glowering; it crawled back into its den, deep and dark within him, and crouched there growling quietly, a hyena, waiting.

Van der Merwe pressed his knuckles into his closed eyes and as the lightning flashed behind his eyelids he prayed as always for Hephzibah's soul and the souls of his father and mother, and for Zechariah, Rebekha, Reuben, Saul and Ruth − even Ruth, the dirty *hoer*. They had all gone away from home now, praise the Lord, to seek their own damnations. And he prayed too for the three infants that had died so young and had faded with sadness the light in Hephzibah's pale blue eyes. He prayed too for the Volksraad, that it would be wise in its counsels, and for the Volksleger and Kommandant-Generaal Bezuidenhout and the Oud Baas and the Afrikaansche Reformed Church, that they might be staunch in their defence of the Lord's people. And he prayed as always that one day the Boere Republiek would come into being again at last; the independent Volksstaat that they had dreamed of for so long, ever since the unbelievers and *Uitlanders* had given this beautiful country all away to the kaffirs. For this he prayed hard, even though he knew that the Volksstaat would come too

late for him. The doctors had given him no more than a year
and each week the pain seemed sharper. When he said his
prayers again last thing every night he sometimes thought he
could hear Hephzibah calling him.

'Amen,' he said.

He washed, pulled on his khaki shorts, khaki bush jacket,
long khaki socks and *velskoene,* and combed his big bushy
beard. How thin his face had become, he thought, with
hollows and gullies and *dongas* as dark and dramatic as those of
the Drakensberg. His face could almost be that of a stranger.
Would Hephzibah recognise him when he joined her in
Heaven? When he and his father met again, who would be the
older? They said that the boy is father to the man: perhaps the
father too is the son of the boy.

Such foolishness! He chided himself and tucked the comb
into the back of his long khaki socks and walked carefully
outside into the brisk morning air. As the sun came up on
another perfect morning he sat on the *stoep* as always to read
the big old family Bible for ten minutes and to contemplate his
soul; he must prepare it for death today, if the Lord so chose.
Dew shimmered on the grass. To the east, beyond the bluegums and cedrilla trees he had planted forty years ago, beyond
the syringa and fever trees and umbrella thorn of the Kruger
and the flat brown sourveld towards Komatipoort and
Mozambique, the sky blazed white with promise. The sun
splashed a pale grey wash across the huge black granite *kopje*
that hunched like a giant tortoise behind the farmhouse. A
Go-Away bird chattered and chuckled beyond the trees like a
gossipy *rooinek* housewife and the smell of the morning
touched his memory as always with longing; it was the smell of
pine and gum, damp grass, dust, animal hides, warm elephant
dung, black sweat; the smell of Africa, the smell of life. It
reminded him of so much: of the days of his youth, of Malachi
and Hephzibah, of *braaivleisaand* on Saturday afternoons with
Piet Viljoen playing 'Sarie Marais' on the mouth organ, of
hunting trips and campfires flickering at night under the Lord's

great sparkling midnight temple, and weeks alone in the bush, and the lion that had attacked him over at Saxonwold.

Van der Merwe sighed in the morning stillness. What a pleasure! He loved this time of day, when the world was fresh and new again and the pain within him still half asleep. This was his inheritance. This was all he had to leave his children. How could he let the blacks steal all this from them?

He unclipped the big brass clasp and opened the old family Bible. Within was the family tree going back to 1783, which included the van der Merwe who first forded van der Merwe's Drift down south on the Vaal River: Jaapie and Martha van der Merwe (thirteen children, ten died in infancy); Hendrik and Hannah (eleven children, ten died); Nathan and Beulah (nine children, two died); Ezra and Hannah (four children, none died); Hendrik and Hephzibah (eight children, three died); Piet and Leah (no children at all but great mourning). Van der Merwe turned to the Book of Revelation for comfort, to Chapter 21, verse 8. He wanted to remind himself of the fearsome promise of the Lord, of His covenant with His people: 'But the fearful, and unbelieving, and the abominable, and murderers, and whoremongers, and sorcerers, and idolaters, and all liars, shall have their part in the lake which burneth with fire and brimstone.'

He smiled. *Ja!* They did not know it, all those heathen abominations filthy in the sight of the Lord, but their time of retribution drew near: all those kaffir politicians, the Mandelas and Tembos and Buthelezis, the Archbishop Tutus and all the other heathen 'Men of God', the Commies like that bastard Joe Slovo, the fellow travellers, the pinko liberals, the fornicators, the queers and all the other perverts. And the Brits: *ja*, especially the Brits, the Anglos, the *rooinek* bastards. *Basters!* The Lord is not mocked. Together they had all destroyed South Africa. They were Satan, Baal, Beelzebub, Moloch. They had corrupted Paradise and turned it into Babylon. 'Vengeance is mine', saith the Lord God of Hosts. And there it was in the

Book of Exodus, Chapter 21, a promise to sanctify the people of the Lord: 'And if any mischief follow, then thou shalt give life for life, eye for eye, tooth for tooth, hand for hand, foot for foot, burning for burning, wound for wound, stripe for stripe.'

Yea, burning for burning, thought van der Merwe: thanks be to God.

Afterwards he closed the Bible reverently and turned it to face away from him while he lit a cigarette. Self-indulgence should never be flaunted before the Word of the Lord. Long ago he had given up trying to give up smoking: he had managed it once for five months but the grief he had suffered then was like mourning for a lost love. The smoke made him cough now and burned his throat and sent pain searing through his lungs but that no longer signified. It was far too late for caution or common sense; he had smoked for fifty years, ever since he was a boy stealing single kaffir cigarettes from the Indian store in Kaapmuiden. Tobacco was an old friend now helping him to die.

The woman Miriam brought him breakfast barefoot on the *stoep* as always. She walked like a dark ghost, averting her eyes as Hephzibah had taught her, for it was not right for a daughter of Ham to look boldly upon a man of the Lord. That way lay uncleanliness and damnation. It was his favourite *skof*; paw-paw, *sadza* porridge, *izimbabi* bread. '*Goeiemôre, baas,*' she mumbled into her shoulder.

'*Goeiemôre, umfazi. Hoe gaan dit met jou?*'

She giggled into her hand. '*Goed, baas, dankie.*'

She was wearing her usual faded floral frock. She turned away. She had good buttocks, the woman Miriam; firm, supple. He bowed his head and begged forgiveness for his impure thought and said grace. In return the Lord blessed him with golden light as the sun rose out of the Indian Ocean and stretched itself warm across the old wooden planks of the *stoep* as van der Merwe ate his breakfast and drank a glass of fresh orange juice squeezed from one of his own trees. How good it was still to be alive despite the pain, he thought, the sun warm and yellow as butter on his knees, the leaves rustling in the slight morning breeze, the long grass stirring. *Lekker.* What a pleasure.

After breakfast he strapped his bushknife belt around his waist, reached for his *sjambok* and olive-green bush hat, tucked his rifle into his elbow and went to look for the old Ford truck where his sister had left it at the side of the house.

Van der Merwe's sister. Leah. Shrivelled and barren and bitter. Sour as the frontier bush of Mozambique. He preferred not to think of Leah, not just now. Leah's husband Piet du Toit had suffered her for thirty-six years and had welcomed death with relief. And now she just sat around all day staring at the television or reading magazines about film stars and famous people: magazines with names like *Hello!*, *OK!*, *Totsiens!* and especially one from Europe called *Celebrity*. 'Sister, that *Celebrity* magazine of yours is an abomination in the sight of the Lord,' he had told her many times. 'I will not have it in my house. It is Babylon, filth. It worships false gods. It represents everything that is foul in the world today. It is the work of Satan.'

'It is my house too,' she had said. She had sniffed her narrow little sniff. 'I like the pictures.'

Van der Merwe laid the *sjambok* and rifle on the passenger seat of the pickup truck, just in case – you never knew these days – and jolted rattling down the stony track to join the tarmac road to White River, Sabie and Lydenburg for the secret monthly midday meeting of the Volksraad. It was a long, tiring drive, especially the winding switchback route over Long Tom Pass up to the highveld, but he never missed a meeting, no matter how exhausted or busy he was or how bad the pain, or whatever the danger. The black police were always on the lookout nowadays for any signs of underground resistance and they liked nothing better than to stop old

Afrikaaners and demand ID, jokingly asking for their pass-books as though any government would dare to introduce passes for whites. Cheeky *tsotsis!* But a few cocky kaffir cops would never stop him attending meetings of the Volksraad. It was his patriotic duty: somebody had to give leadership now in these black godless times; somebody had to make plans and shine a great light in the darkness. If the Boers did not stand firm now there would be nothing left to pass on to their children. The kaffirs would take everything. He had to stand firm, for the sake of Zechariah and Reuben and the grand-children. And today there were three important items on the Volksraad agenda: how to celebrate the centenary of the outbreak of the Anglo-Boer War in 1899; how to deal with the 1999 elections, the first in history that could leave South Africa with a completely black Cabinet; and how to mark the Day of the Vow on 16 December, the anniversary of the Voortrekkers' victory over Dingaan's Zulu warriors at the battle of Blood River in 1838. Mandela had tried to rename the anniversary the Day of Reconciliation but 16 December had nothing to do with multi-racial reconciliation: it was about white victory and Boer power and Afrikaans revenge. *Ons vir jou, Suid-Afrika.*

Van der Merwe found himself wedged into a traffic jam in White River next to a flash pink open-topped sports car that was trembling and shuddering to the pounding beat of African music on the radio. The driver, a young black man wearing large scarlet-framed sunglasses and a small moustache, was chewing gum and drumming his fingers on the steering wheel in time to the music. There were three gold rings on his fat black fingers and his whole car vibrated to the music, which clattered and drummed like Soweto on Saturday night. Pain stabbed at van der Merwe's back. The music pounded at his ears. He could taste bile at the back of his throat, and anger. Why did these bloody munts always play their jungle music so loud even in their cars? You could hear this black *baster*'s stuff four blocks away. Van der Merwe glared at him and wound the window up. The driver looked across at him and winked.

Van der Merwe edged forward in the traffic. His fingers itched for the *sjambok* lying on the seat beside him. Ten years ago it had all been so different. How could a young black buck afford a pink sports car nowadays? Drugs, probably. Prostitution. Crime. No kaffir ever made any money from working, that's for sure. And these were the sort of scum who were being given jobs ahead of much better qualified young Afrikaaners just because they were black. You had to be black these days to get the best jobs. There was terrible, anti-white racist discrimination.

He hated White River. He could remember when it had been a little frontier *dorp* smelling sweetly of orange blossom and cyanide gas from the fumigating machines but now it was just another ugly, sprawling, bustling, foul-smelling dump. It smelled corrupt. It was too full of Anglos, always had been, with its Planters Club and Snob's Alley, ever since the bastards had cheated the Voortrekkers' descendants out of their land after the war and had let in kaffir-loving Brits like those bastards John Buchan and Rider Haggard and Percy Fitzpatrick. Bloody Buchan up at Tzaneen in 1902 or 1903, secretary to that British imperialist bastard Milner, had scribbled some story about a black uprising that had put ideas into the kaffirs' heads. And then there was Haggard coming out to the Transvaal and writing that crap book *She* which idolised the kaffir Rain Queen Modjadji up at her *kraal* in the forest near Duiwelskloof. And what about that bastard Cecil Rhodes's brother Herbert, the Brit gun-runner who ran a pub called The Spotted Dog up at Mac-Mac and supplied the kaffirs with weapons? Come to that, what about Mac-Mac itself, which was called Mac-Mac because it was so full of bloody Scotsmen? And what about Cecil Rhodes himself, that squeaky-voiced homo who had to have his balls chopped off when he was seventeen to stop his tuberculosis spreading. Rhodes a eunuch! The great Brit hero with no bollocks! They never told you *that* in the English history books, did they? And

that big fat shit Winston Churchill, too, the Brit spy the Boers
captured in 1899, who only managed to escape by skulking in
a filthy crap-house, which seemed just right for such a shit. I
don't suppose they tell you that, either, in the English history
books, thought van der Merwe. The Boer Field Cornet who
captured Churchill in 1899 should have shot the bastard there
and then and saved Hitler a lot of trouble later.

Van der Merwe spat out of the window. The black in the
pink sports car wrinkled his nose and shook his head.

Van der Merwe had always hated the Brits, like the old
Voortrekkers who used to joke that the three greatest pests in
Africa were drought, locusts and Englishmen. They thought
they were so superior. They jeered at Afrikaaners, calling them
morons, and told their cruellest anti-Boer jokes about some
made-up character called van der Merwe. Van der Merwe's toes
curled with embarrassment inside his shoes as he remembered
all the van der Merwe 'jokes' they had tormented him with at
school.

*So this kaffir is arrested by Sergeant van der Merwe but he escapes
after persuading van der Merwe to let him go back into the house to
fetch a coat. Six months later Sergeant van der Merwe again arrests the
same kaffir, who tries the same trick. 'Oh, no, you don't,' says van der
Merwe. 'You can't fool me twice. This time you wait here and I'll go
into the house and get the coat.'*

What was so funny about that? Anglo *basters*! Or the one
they used to tell about van der Merwe learning to play golf.

*So the golf pro gives van der Merwe a pack of tees. 'What are these,
then?' says van der Merwe.*

*'They're for playing your first shot,' says the pro. 'You-rest your
balls on them.'*

*'My God,' says van der Merwe. 'They think of everything these
days.'*

The Brits had even allowed that Zulu blasphemer Isaiah
Shembe to set up his so-called Nazarite Church over at
Ekuphakameni and at Mount Nhlangakazi. *Shembe*! A man
who dared to call himself 'The Promised One', 'The Black

Christ'. Who promised his followers that after he died they would find him standing at the gates of Paradise to let them in and to keep the whites out! What was that if it wasn't a filthy, obscene black version of apartheid?

Soutpiels! They were all *soutpiels*, the Brits: one foot in Europe, one foot in Africa and their balls dangling in the Atlantic Ocean.

The lights changed and suddenly the traffic jam eased and the road ahead was clear. The pink sports car erupted, belched and cut in front of van der Merwe's truck as it sped away in a cloud of black fumes. As it went the young black driver held high the middle finger of his right hand. There were times when van der Merwe knew that he might be capable of murder.

He drove away from White River and up towards the escarpment and the cooler air and broad green grasslands of the highveld. He headed past eucalyptus, blue gums and bananas, towards Sabie and Lydenburg, up the winding mountain road to the dizzy heights of Long Tom Pass where a huge replica of the Boers' Long Tom cannon still brooded over the misty mountains and the valley far beneath.

He drove into Lydenburg past the Voortrekker monument and the Burgher monument erected in the memory of the thirty-three men of Lydenburg who died in battle during the war against the British between 1899 and 1902. Heroes. Boer martyrs. Lydenburg meant 'the town of suffering' and the Boers had always suffered, all right. Throughout their history they had been pushed about, shunted from one part of the country to another, discriminated against, attacked, harried and sneered at by the British, but here was one town, praise the Lord, that was still Afrikaans in its clean Boer soul. Even after Mandela and the blacks had come to power Lydenburg had still flown the old Suid-Afrikan flag and all the street signs were still in Afrikaans first and in English second. Good strong old names they were, too: Voortrekker Street, Kantoor,

Lombard and Kerk; Minaar, Potgieter, Lange, De Villiers; Brug, Berg, Burger, Rensburg, J Coetser; Schoeman, Buhrman, Jansen, Viljoen, De Beers. Names like the sound of an ox wagon's wheels churning the Transvaal earth. Names with the harsh outdoor poetry of the baobab tree, horse saddles, bushveld fires, diamond mines. And all the streets of Lydenburg were set out on a proper, tidy grid-plan – not like Tzaneen or Phalaborwa or Pilgrim's Rest, where the streets were all as crooked as kaffir politicians. Square shapes in Lydenburg, firm edges, no nonsense. Like the Boer character, thought van der Merwe, praise be to God.

'Kruger's gold,' said the Oud Baas. 'The millions he buried when he left the Transvaal in 1900 to go into exile in Europe.' He smiled like a crocodile. 'We have new evidence of where to find it.'

They were sitting around the Volksraad conference table in the safe house on De Clerq Street, shielded from the road by the high wall and big garden. Four of Bezuidenhout's Volksleger troopers patrolled outside in plain clothes. The Oud Baas sat at the head of the table, his eyes a translucent grey, his beard a silver jungle. Kommandant-Generaal Bezuidenhout sat at the foot of the table, wearing the banned Volksleger uniform and his medals from when he was a mercenary in the Vietnam War. Ranged between them were van der Merwe from the Lowveld, Strydom from the Cape, Botha from Pretoria, de Wet from Stutterheim, van Zyl from Graaff Reinet, Grobler from Phalaborwa, van Wyk from Griqualand West, Labuschagne from Johannesburg, Pienaar from Bloemfontein, Trigard from Natal, Steyn from Mafikeng, Potgieter from Louis Trichardt, and Cronje from Potchefstroom.

After the Bible reading and the old forbidden anthem *'Die Stem'* – deep voices throaty with pride, emotion and memory – they had re-elected the Oud Baas for another year. He might be frail but he had the heart and balls of a bull elephant and he had seen things that other men had never even imagined.

'When President Kruger finally decided to leave South Africa and make a tactical retreat into Mozambique in September 1900,' said the Oud Baas, 'the Transvaal currency was still in British sterling and he had with him at least five hundred thousand pounds in gold bullion which he planned to use to continue the war against the British. In addition, Kruger was privately a rich man. Throughout the 1890s his salary as President of the Transvaal Republic was seven thousand pounds a year, which was worth fifty times more then than it is now, so he was earning nearly two million rand a year in modern terms.'

Steyn whistled.

'The gold was hidden on the President's special train that took Kruger in slow stages, as the British advanced, from Pretoria to Nelspruit. Eventually, in September, the train passed just south of the Kruger Game Reserve, which Kruger had recently created, before he finally crossed the Mozambique border into exile between Komatipoort and Ressano Garcia. But when he arrived on the coast at Lourenço Marques, just eighty kilometres further down the line, and the train was searched by the Portuguese authorities, they found he had only one hundred and fifty thousand pounds in cash. And when Kruger died in Switzerland four years later he left only twenty-eight thousand, six hundred and ninety pounds.' The Oud Baas looked down at his notes. 'And eight shillings. So what happened to the rest of the gold? Where is the missing three hundred and fifty thousand pounds, which is worth about fifty times as much today – perhaps as much as one hundred and fifty million rand?'

Steyn whistled again.

The Oud Baas touched his beard like a benediction. 'A hundred and fifty million!' he said. 'Think what we could do with that. We could set up our independent state here in the Transvaal. We could arm the Volksleger properly. But where is the gold?' He glanced around the table. 'At last I think we have a real chance of finding it.'

***

The silence around the conference table was oppressive. An African was whistling tunelessly in the street beyond the garden wall and from a distance came the sound of a lawn-mower chortling across a suburban garden.

'We've all heard the rumours that Kruger buried the gold somewhere on the lowveld as he left the country,' said the Oud Baas. 'Somewhere between Kaapmuiden and Komatipoort, just before he crossed the border into Mozambique.'

The Oud Baas scanned their faces. They sat in silence. Several looked sceptical. For nearly a hundred years fortune hunters had been searching for Kruger's secret treasure trove but nothing had ever been found.

The Oud Baas licked his lips. 'I know what some of you are thinking,' he said. 'But it is obvious that Kruger must have told at least one person where the gold was hidden. At least one person must have helped him to bury it. He couldn't have carried all the gold alone secretly or dug the hole himself. He was seventy-four, and tired, and surrounded by officials and guards who feared that the British would assassinate him. So someone else had to know the secret.'

The Oud Baas pulled from the file in front of him a sheaf of photostats that he handed to Cronje to pass on around the table.

'Eight days ago I received this letter,' said the Oud Baas. 'It is not signed. Read it.'

The letter, on two sheets of paper, was computer-printed in Afrikaans:

Gentlemen,

I understand that you are dangerously short of funds to finance your great cause. It is therefore time for me to pass on to you the secret of President Kruger's gold, that you may be able to use it to defend the Boer nation against its enemies.

My grandfather, then a young man, went into exile with Kruger in September 1900. It was he who buried the gold secretly on the President's instructions but he died tragically young before he could return to South Africa. When he died in 1902 he left his diaries to his son, my father, with a letter forbidding him to touch the gold or reveal its whereabouts 'until Boer leaders of Kruger's stature and honesty once more cry out for justice on behalf of the People of the Lord.'

In 1902 my father was a small child, and by the time he came of age in 1919 Smuts had become Prime Minister of South Africa and the Boers were not only under no threat from their enemies but were in fact controlling the Government. So my father kept the secret all his life, and when he died in 1979 he left the diaries to me with a similar letter forbidding me to use the gold except when the Afrikaans nation should face a new crisis.

Since then I have faithfully kept the secret, but over the last year it has become increasingly obvious that our people once again cry out for justice and vengeance against their persecutors and that the time has come when Kruger himself would have wanted his gold to be used for the liberation of our people.

The time my grandfather envisaged has come. Consequently I enclose a photostat of the relevant pages from my grandfather's diary in the sure knowledge that you will faithfully use your new-found riches only in the service of the Lord and His People.

I regret that I cannot sign my name since I am a high-ranking government official.

A Patriot.

'Scheiss!' said Pienaar.

'Praise the Lord,' said van der Merwe.

'Amen.'

The Oud Baas reached again into the file. 'And here are the photostats of the pages from the diary. Cronje, pass them around.'

The diary, also in Afrikaans, had been written in a sprawling hand in black ink on ruled paper:

12 September 1900. Hectorspruit. It must be tonight. Tomorrow we enter Moçambique. K insists that we take only one Kaffir to dig the hole and that I should 'ensure' afterwards that

the Kaffir never reveals the hiding place. I take this to mean that afterwards I must shoot the Kaffir, though of course a man as devout as K cannot be a party to this, even though we know Kaffirs do not have souls or feelings or suffer pain like White Men. In any case his death will be a necessary act of war.

13 September 1900. Ressano Garcia, Moçambique. It is done. At 6 p.m. last night K ordered Kotze to have the train stopped for the night at Malelane, just our side of the Moçambique border, saying that he wished to spend one last night on the sacred soil of his beloved Transvaal. Then at 9 o'clock, after dinner, he suddenly announced that since it was such a clear night he desired one last short trek just across the Krokodil River to sit once more beneath the stars of the great open bushveld of the Animal Sanctuary that he himself ordered to be created here two years ago to preserve for ever the dwindling numbers of wild beasts. He insisted that he would leave the train for an hour or two and ride out into the bush on a donkey accompanied only by me and one Kaffir. This we did at 9.30, with the gold and a short spade hidden in two panniers, despite vehement protests from Kotze, who was loth to allow K to wander into the wild at night with so little protection. 'You will not find lion or leopard in these parts,' said K, 'just hyena and wild dogs.' He chuckled. 'Perhaps you are concerned about the fever? Do not disturb yourself, Kotze. The fever season here does not commence until October.' Thus we went alone into the bush at night, just two men, two rifles, a donkey, a Kaffir, a small spade and £500,000 of gold bullion. I am surprised at how little gold there is to total such a great value. The ingots barely filled each pannier by half.

We crossed the river at Malelane and entered the animal sanctuary at about 10 p.m., disturbing kudu, waterbuck and a herd of impala, their eyes shining reflected in the scrub. I was watchful for lion and leopard in the clear moonlight despite K's assurances that they do not come this far south, and wished that I had allowed the Kaffir to bring his panga after all. K breathed heavy but rode the donkey with a pannier on each side like any

*old-time gold prospector and I and the Kaffir followed on foot,
scanning the bush for danger, until we reached the base of the
great granite mountain where trees and bushes sweep down
from the rocky summit: seringa, bush willow, jackal berry, date
palm, tamboti.*

'Net hier,' *he said.*

*I gestured the Kaffir to dig. K sat beneath a marula tree and
ordered me to make measurements so that we should find and
retrieve again the gold on our return. The gold is buried five
paces from the marula tree, seven paces from the strange-shaped
rock at the foot of the mountain and ten paces from the furthest
western edge of the* donga *beside the dry river bed, where these
measurements intersect.*

*The Kaffir dug deep for half an hour, perhaps three feet deep
to protect the gold from scavengers, and we emptied the panniers
and covered the hole with twigs, soil and stones. No human is
ever likely to find the trove in such a remote spot. By now the
Kaffir was panting with exertion and smelling like a pig (their
sweat alone is quite inhuman, another indication that they
have no souls) and so without further ado I tempted the Kaffir
away to the river bed on a pretext and shot him there once in
the head and returned to K. 'The Kaffir attacked me, Sir,' I
said. 'I have had to shoot him. He was going to murder you.'*

'The British will stoop to any treachery,' *he said.*

*K sat under the marula tree and the stars for another
half-hour, in silence, no doubt remembering too much. I too felt
moved to be leaving our beautiful land but as soon as possible I
shall return to continue the battle against the British invaders.
K plans to take ship to exile in Europe. A banker from Ajaccio,
a Monsieur Lanzi, has offered him refuge in a villa in Corsica
but what would K do there? It is bandit country, remote,
violent, backward, uncivilised.* 'They say that parts of Corsica
are very like the Lowveld,' *said K sadly.* 'And Napoleon
Bonaparte was born in Ajaccio. He beat the British too at first
and then they forced him also into exile.' *K is old. I fear he may
never return.*

We returned to the train soon after midnight but K refused to retire to his cabin until the engine driver had been aroused and the train driven over the border into Moçambique. I fear K could not endure another beautiful Transvaal dawn. As we crossed the border Kotze asked him, 'Shall I blow up the bridge behind you?' K looked back towards the west, back into his past. 'No,' he said, 'there has been destruction enough already.' And so he passed into history.

Not one of the guards seemed to notice that the Kaffir was missing. Kaffirs tend to be invisible in the dark unless they smile.

Van der Merwe chuckled and thumped the table top. '*Ja! Ja! Goed, goed!*'

'It is manna from heaven,' said Potgieter.

'A sign,' said van Wyk.

'Amen.'

The Oud Baas waited for them all to finish reading, until even van Zyl had stopped running his forefinger slowly across the page and moving his lips.

'Are we agreed, then, that we should try to find the gold?' asked the Oud Baas.

'*Ja!*'

'*Natuurlik!*'

'*Sonder twyfel.*'

'Very well. I need volunteers.'

'I.'

'I.'

'I must be one,' said van der Merwe. 'I know the area well. It is no more than a few kilometres from my farm.'

The Oud Baas tugged at his beard. 'Of course, Hendrik, but are you well enough? Your health …'

'Ach, man, it's perfectly good,' said van der Merwe, 'for the time being.'

The Oud Baas nodded. 'In that case …'

'And I,' said Kommandant-Generaal Bezuidenhout, 'with a small troop of soldiers to do the digging.'

'Why not use kaffirs?' said Strydom. 'We can always shoot them afterwards!'

Guffaws of laughter rolled around the table. Only the Oud Baas did not smile. The Oud Baas had never enjoyed jokes about race. You would almost think he was a kaffir-lover if you didn't know better, thought van der Merwe.

'Very well,' said the Oud Baas. 'Bezuidenhout, van der Merwe and six troopers: two to dig and four to keep watch. And it will have to be done at night. To search during the day would attract immediate attention.'

Labuschagne was still sceptical. Perhaps he had spent too many years in Johannesburg. 'Why should we believe this anonymous letter and this diary, *baas*, any more than any of the other rumours about the gold that we have all heard for so many years?' he asked. 'Who is this anonymous writer, this patriot? And why is he telling us where to find the gold when he could dig it up for himself? And if he is such a patriot, what is he doing as a high official in this black government? It could be a hoax. It could be a trap.'

The Oud Baas nodded. 'You are right. But we have been given a chance that we cannot afford to reject. We have barely enough money even to organise a demonstration to mark the Day of the Vow and the centenary of Kruger's War, let alone to set up the Volkstaat and declare independence.'

Labuschagne shrugged. 'It is worth a try, I suppose. But Bezuidenhout and van der Merwe may well be arrested if it's a trap.'

'It would be an honour to suffer for the Cause,' said van der Merwe. And for Zechariah and Reuben, he thought, and the grandchildren, even unto the fourth generation.

'So we are agreed?' said the Oud Baas.

'*Ja!*'

'*Top!*'

'*Afgespreek!*'

'Good,' said the Oud Baas. He looked down at the photostat diary. 'At the foot of a great granite mountain,' he said, reading, 'five paces from the marula tree, seven paces from the strange-shaped rock at the foot of the mountain and ten paces from the furthest western edge of the *donga* beside the dry river bed.' He looked up at van der Merwe and Bezuidenhout and nodded. 'You will need skill and luck,' he said. 'Our hopes are with you both. And before I close the meeting, I would remind you all of one of Kruger's last messages to his troops when the British captured Pretoria in June 1900 and he realised at last that he would have to take refuge in Europe.' The Oud Baas took another sheet of paper from his file and read out Kruger's message: *'Flinch not and fall not into unbelief, for the time is at hand when God's people shall be tried in the fire. And the Beast shall have power to persecute Christ, and those who fall from faith and their Church will know Him not, nor shall they be allowed to enter the kingdom of Heaven. But those who are true to the faith and fight on in the name of the Lord, wearing their glorious crown of victory, they shall be received in the Church of a thousand years.'*

'Amen,' said van der Merwe.

'Amen.'

'Amen.'

Beyond the garden wall a heavy silence lay across the afternoon. The African had stopped whistling.

Ugo Legrandu was sitting at a sunny table in Ajaccio on the pavement outside Le Petit Caporal café in the Place Maréchal Foch, sipping coffee, smoking a Gauloise and reading the *Corse-Matin*, when the police arrested him. He was scanning an article about the discovery by the Nice Observatory of a mysterious new comet deep in outer space and was wearing his thin black driving gloves so as not to smudge his fingers with ink.

The police van, siren howling, drew up outside Le Petit Caporal just a few yards from where the *petit caporal* Napoleon Bonaparte was born in 1769 in a tall old house in the narrow

Rue Saint Charles. It was still the kind of street where creased old women would growl at each other from high windows, shutters would echo on chill dark stone, and laundry could be seen flapping high in the breeze like coloured naval flags from washing lines strung across the ancient alleyway.

The Emperor Napoleon, thought Legrandu: Corsica's greatest son, born just around the corner, small like him but eventually the conqueror of Europe. Napoleon, like all true Corsicans, a bold adventurer, indeed, like so many Corsicans scattered around the world; like Ugo's brother Peppu in Saigon. Yet two centuries later the French army of occupation, the *pinzuti*, the 'pointed helmets', were still arresting patriotic Corsicans as they sat in the sun quietly enjoying a coffee and watching the girls prance by in their twirling skirts. Two centuries later the French Foreign Legion was still headquartered in the castle at Calvi, as though Corsica were Chad or Timbuktu. No wonder the Corsican flag featured the head of a pirate.

Corse-Matin had reported briefly on the letter bomb at the offices of *Celebrity* magazine in Monte Carlo and had printed a picture of the Irishman, The Editor's secretary, the one who had sacked him. Kelly. That was it. Patrick Kelly. The sort of Irish name you might associate with the IRA. Legrandu chuckled: an IRA man blown up by a bomb!

Six *flics* approached him with their right hands resting lightly on their holsters. Two carried truncheons. Six *flics* just for me, he thought! Salvatore would be proud of him. Did they think he was going to pull a gun on them? How stupid they were, the *pinzuti*. Where had they been when the Furiani football stadium in Bastia collapsed in 1992 and seventeen people died and more than two thousand were injured? Playing with their truncheons as usual.

The policemen surrounded his table. Legrandu nodded. One of the *gendarmes* placed his hands on his hips. Legrandu sniffed. A whiff of stale sweat. The café had fallen silent. A small crowd was gathering across the street, muttering. Someone whispered hoarsely.

'Legrandu?' said one of the *gendarmes*.

'*Weh.*'

'Ugo Pasquale Legrandu?'

'*Weh.*'

'*De Sartène?*'

'*Weh.*'

'*Alors.*'

The *gendarme* nodded towards the van. Legrandu shrugged.
He folded the newspaper carefully, tucked it under his arm,
finished the coffee slowly and took a last drag of his cigarette.
He filtered the smoke down his nostrils so that the two thin
plumes enjoyed a sinuous dance together like grey ghosts
before fading into the morning light. The *flics* waited. One
looked at his watch, another tapped his thigh with his
truncheon. They knew the game. This had nothing to do with
contempt. This was simply Corsican style. This came of being
born male in southern bandit country in a shadowy medieval
hilltop village like Sartène where the women had learned to
listen with their eyes.

Inside the café someone was playing one of I Muvrini's
patriotic Corsican songs on the jukebox; the sad, haunting
melody of '*À Voce Rivolta*', the voice of Corsican revolt:

> *L'ore zitelle di libertà,*
>
> *U sole innora e cime quassù,*
>
> *E u mio cantu ti chjama dinù,*
>
> *O terra Corsa di li mio turmenti,*
>
> *O terra Corsa dimmi s'è tù senti.*

They would never pin this one on him, thought Legrandu.
He had not touched the bomb nor the letter. In Corsica there
were plenty of volunteers who would do it for you gladly, so
long as the targets were French. Revenge is not simply about
pride and silence, like the Sicilians, but about pleasure as well;
the fierce joy of bearing grudges. That was why he had insisted
that the letter bomb should be posted in Corsica rather than
the mainland: what was the point of revenge if your victim did
not know where it came from?

Legrandu had certainly had no intention of killing or maiming anyone, least of all La Barrett herself, for the bomb was not merely a gesture of revenge: it was also Legrandu's first bouquet for her; a gift of love. So she had tried to insult him with one week's pay, eh? What a woman! What a come-on! It was obvious that she was testing him: the way she had glanced at him in the rearview mirror when he was driving; the way she flashed her thighs at him whenever she slipped in or out of the back seat. The deliciously cold English way she pretended to ignore him when she was speaking on her mobile telephone, her brusque Anglo-Saxon contempt. The way she had shivered when he had patted her neat little *derrière* as he had helped her step out of the car that last day in Monaco. Legrandu had met such women before, women who liked to be threatened, taken, women who needed it rough. It was good to know that even nowadays there were still women who were excited by masculinity. The bomb was just a start. The bomb was just the first light tickle in a game of Còrsican foreplay.

'*Alors*,' he said, nodding at the *gendarmes* and stubbing out the Gauloise, sending up a wispy blue smoke-signal like an Indian love call. He stood and offered his wrists. '*Allons!*'

They would never be able to pin this one on him. Never.

The handcuffs clicked.

I Muvrini were reaching the end of the song:

> Sò to figlioli e ancu di più,
> Quand'ella hè l'ora, rispondi ancu tù,
> Populu Corsu, pè l'ultima volta,
> Dilli chè tù si à voce rivolta.

Legrandu suddenly laughed.

The *gendarmes* touched their holsters.

Not a smoker! *Weh!* She had really believed him when he had told her that he had given up long ago! The stupid bitch! He had smoked like a Bastia cigarette factory for nearly twenty years.

'It's The Editor calling from Washington,' said Iain Campbell's secretary. 'Line two. And she's in a filthy temper.'

'Jeez, mate,' said Murdoch, rolling his good eye. 'Tell us something new.'

Campbell looked as hunted as a Highland stag. He bobbed his head as though it were weighed down by antlers. He stretched his hand towards the telephone amplifier as if it were electrified and pressed the button. It glowed red like a warning. The conference room was grey with tobacco smoke. As the sound of The Editor's voice trembled the metal grille of the amplifier from across the Atlantic, Caroline Ponsonby nervously stubbed out her cigarette.

'Hellooo,' said Campbell, trying in vain to imitate the courage of his Highland forefathers. 'Afternoon, Stella.'

'It's morning here.' Her voice hissed across the cold Atlantic as metallic as the blades of skating boots. 'Where's Kelly? I can't get hold of him.'

'He's still in hospital.'

'Still? What's the matter with him? He's been there two days now, hasn't he?'

'He's been badly shocked.'

'I don't care if his head's been blown off. He'll be a damned sight more shocked if he doesn't get out of there and back to work pronto. Get him out of there. It was only a small bomb, for God's sake. Have they arrested the Corsican? What's his name? The driver.'

'Ugo Legrandu. Aye. This morning.'

'Brilliant. Tell the police I want to press every charge in the book. Tell them I want to give evidence. I want him put away for twenty years. Plus get Kelly out of hospital *today*, Campbell. Now. This evening. Tell him not to be such a wimp. He's got work to do. And so have you. This list you faxed me. The guest list. It's absolute crap.'

On the other side of the table Murdoch took a deep drag on his hand-rolled cigarette, leaned forward towards the telephone amplifier and blew a long, slow, loving cloud of smoke into its face so that the smoke caressed The Editor's voice. Campbell waved the smoke aside frantically, shaking his head.

Michèle Langoustier began to giggle.

Campbell covered his eyes with his left hand. He had faxed her three thousand names squeezed out of every available brain and reference book. It had taken a full week but still she wasn't satisfied.

'What's wrong with it?'

'What's right with it, you mean.'

'We've included everyone who's anyone.'

'No you haven't. You've left out hundreds of the most important names.'

'That can't be right.'

'No, it damned well isn't. I've got a long list here of omissions in alphabetical order. Plus I'm damned sure there aren't three thousand names.'

'Aye.'

'No.'

'Yes there are.'

'No, Campbell.'

'Aye. Three thousand. The computer counted them itself.'

The amplifier rattled as she shouted. 'I said there are not three thousand names, Campbell. Did you hear me?'

Murdoch raised two fingers at the amplifier. Michèle Langoustier began to shake. She stuffed a handkerchief into her mouth.

'There are not three thousand names, Campbell; not nearly three thousand. I haven't counted them one by one and I have no intention of doing so but I suspect that there are no more than two thousand five hundred so I want five hundred more names today. You will fax them to me this evening. No one is to leave the office until I get them. *Capeesh?*'

Campbell looked pasty. Murdoch leaned back in his chair and closed his eye. Michèle Langoustier stood up, biting her knuckle. Her face was scarlet. She looked as if she would choke. She left the room in a hurry. Three seconds later, from down the corridor, they could hear her howl like an animal in pain.

'What was that?' said The Editor's disembodied voice from

the grille. The amplifier shuddered, tingling with suspicion.

'Just Wakonde,' said Campbell off the top of his head. 'He's caught his finger in a drawer.'

'I thought Wakonde was in Wales.'

'He –'

'What drawer? Where are you? Aren't you in conference?'

'I –'

'There aren't any drawers in the conference room. Why aren't you in conference?'

'We –'

'You're late for conference. What time is it over there?' The metal grille on the front of the amplifier trembled with the vibrations of her voice.

'Ten past five.'

'You know conference is meant to begin at five. Why are you late?'

'We –'

'This is not good enough, Campbell. Why does everything fall apart whenever I'm not there? You call the idle sods into conference as soon as this call is over. Plus I want you in my office for a serious talk when I get back. This is just not good enough. Now: Wakonde. What's his interview with the Gröning girl like? Any good?'

'He hasn't got it, I'm afraid, Stella.'

'What do you mean, he hasn't got it?'

'She wouldn't talk to him.'

'She what?'

'The German lassie wouldn't talk to him.'

'And so he's just come back to Monaco without the interview? Just like that?'

'Well –'

'Put him on. This minute. How dare you let him come back empty-handed? Put him on. Now. This instant.'

Campbell looked desperately around the room. For a moment he considered stalling her while someone called up Wakonde on his mobile phone in Wales. That way he could hold both telephone receivers close to each other so that The Editor in Washington could give Wakonde in Wales a bollocking for not being where he was.

Campbell's brain flickered and failed. He looked desperately at Caroline Ponsonby. Her eyes were perfect circles. Murdoch opened his own good eye and drew his forefinger slowly across his throat.

'Aye, that's it!' said Campbell. 'He's gone.'

'Gone?'

'To hospital.'

'Wakonde?'

'The finger. In the drawer. Bleeding. Maybe broken it. They've just rushed him off, poor laddie. To the infirmary.'

'For a bleeding finger?'

'Aye. Nasty wee cut. Deep.'

'And I suppose he will be there now for two or three days as well, will he, while he and Kelly lounge around in the sun on the terrace sipping champagne? Now hear this, Campbell. Listen good. I want Kelly back in the office first thing in the morning and I want Wakonde on a plane back to Wales tonight to inter-view the Gröning girl. Tell him he will not take no for an answer. Who does the little Kraut tart think she is? I don't care how Wakonde does it but tell him I want that interview or he's out; he needn't bother to come back; he can sod off back to South Africa. Tell him to bribe her, blackmail her, threaten to make it all up if she doesn't see him, whatever. He can do what he damned well likes, but I want that interview and I want it now! In the next issue. Plus since he has been so pathetic and unprofessional he will pay for his return fare himself. I've never heard anything like it.'

'Very good, Stella. Is that all?'

'No it damned well isn't. Now for your feeble apology of a list. Why isn't Kenneth Branagh on it?'

'He is.'

'No, he isn't. Nor's Emma Thompson.'

'They are. I know they are.'

'Get a life, Campbell. You've just forgotten them. You've

been damned inefficient, the lot of you. Plus where's Roseanne Barr? Nadja Auermann? Drew Barrymore? And Kim Basinger, Shari Belafonte, Annette Bening, Bernardo Bertolucci, Pierce Brosnan, Gary Busey, Phil Collins, David Copperfield?'

'They're all on the list already.'

'No, they're not. Nor are Cindy Crawford, Tom Cruise, Geena Davis, Darren Day, Robert De Niro, Danny De Vito, Johnny Depp, Bo Derek, Ralph Fiennes, Gennifer Flowers, Jodie Foster, Anna Friel, Bill Gates.'

'You said you didn't want Bill Gates.'

'I said nothing of the sort.'

'You said he was just a computer nerd and no one was interested in him.'

'Give me strength! That was when we were discussing the magazine, Campbell. I don't want computer people in the magazine because computers aren't sexy but of course I want Bill Gates at the ball. Hell, he's probably the richest man in the world. Didn't you know that, either?'

'I seem to remember telling you –'

'How can we have a party to die for without inviting the richest man in the world? For God's sake get a grip. Now, back to your pathetic list. You've left out all the real movers and shakers; every one of them. Where's Richard Gere, Hugh Grant, Tom Hanks, Tonya Harding, Michael Jackson? Plus *Janet* Jackson, Elton John, Nancy Kerrigan, Nicole Kidman, Pat Kingsley, Karl Lagerfeld, Ray Liotta, Heather Locklear?'

'Who?'

'You don't know Heather Locklear? She's in *Melrose Place*, for God's sake.'

'Yes?'

'The soap opera, Campbell. The soap. Do you actually know anything at all?'

'I don't think there's any need –'

'Plus what about Andie MacDowell? And Kyle Maclachlan, John Malkovich, Eric and Lyle Menendez, Demi Moore, Kate Moss?'

'They're all on the list already, I *know* it.'

'Balls, Campbell! And what about Martina Navratilova, Jack Nicholson, Nick Nolte, Gary Oldman, Lena Olin, Carrie Otis, Camille Paglia, Luke Perry, Eve Pollard?'

'Eve Pollard?'

'She's big on British television. Very big. Huge. Plus what about Donna Rice? Or Julia Roberts, Herb Ritts, Mickey Rourke, Meg Ryan, Winona Ryder? And Arnie Schwarzenegger? You've even left out Schwarzenegger!'

'No, Stella –'

'You've bloody well left out Schwarzenegger, Campbell. And his wife, too! My God, she's a Kennedy! How can you leave her out? Plus what about all the other Kennedys? And Charlie Sheen? And Spielberg? Not to mention Stallone, Oliver Stone, Sharon Stone, Quentin Tarantino, Mark Thatcher.'

'You want him?'

'And why not?'

'He's a celebrity?'

'More than you'll ever be, Campbell, that's for sure. More names missing: Travolta, the Trumps, Mike Tyson, Antonio Verucci, Louis Vuitton, Albert Watson, Cindy Williams, Youssou N'Dour.'

'Who?'

'Youssou N'Dour. Good God, Campbell, surely you've heard of him? The Senegalese singer?'

'Yes, of course. But I know we had him on the list. In fact it was Kelly who suggested him. Just before he was blown up.'

'Well, he's not on the list now. We need some Third World people there. The Third World is becoming very fashionable these days, Campbell: starvation, *kwashiorkor*, Aids; very chic. Or didn't you know that either?'

'I really don't think –'

'You're telling me. There are not nearly enough names from the Third World on the list. Think of some, Campbell. That's what I pay you for.'

'Look, Stella, I could have sworn that nearly every name you've mentioned is on the list. Something has obviously gone wrong. Perhaps the computer.'

'Come off it, Campbell. The same computer that counted all the names so accurately?'

Caroline Ponsonby was gesticulating at him and nodding vigorously across the table. She gave him a thumbs-up sign. Murdoch yawned, his big black aboriginal face suddenly an alarming flash of white teeth.

'I remember most of your wee names distinctly, Stella,' said Campbell. 'Here, let me check my copy of the list. I know most of them were on it.'

The line from Washington sounded thin. 'I'm not hanging on while you bumble through your files,' said The Editor. 'The names are simply not on my list. See that they are before I get back next week, or else. Plus I want three thousand names, not two and a half. Got that? *Capeesh?*'

Campbell felt a *frisson* of hope. 'You're not coming back till next week?'

'I'm taking a few days off in Bermuda on the way home. I need a rest. I'm exhausted.'

Murdoch raised his eyebrows, pinched his nostrils with a thumb and forefinger and with the other hand pretended to pull an old-fashioned lavatory chain.

'Some of us have to work like blacks –' said The Editor.

'That's me,' said Murdoch. 'The ace of spades.'

'– to make up for the rest of you skivers and malingerers. In the meantime get Kelly out of hospital and tell him to get me onto the biggest Bermudan TV chat show next week. That's a must-have. I've never done Bermuda. Plus tell him I want a veto of the other guests. I'm not going on with a bunch of small-time deadbeats. Tell him to fax me the details at the Marriott in Tucker's Town. Plus fax me your missing five hundred names there as well, and all the page proofs we have for the next issue.'

'All the page proofs?'

'Yes, Campbell, all.'

'Nearly two hundred pages?'

'That's what I said.'

'It'll take ages. Hours.'

'So?'

'It'll cost a wee fortune.'

'I don't give a tinker's toss if you have to break into your own wee piggy bank, laddie,' she said. 'Just do it. Plus tell Kelly to get onto the Filipino cruise people and tell them that I don't have any difficulty with the plans of the liner except that that they should make the ballroom and swimming pool bigger. They're too small for more than two thousand people. Anyway, get Kelly to confirm our booking for the ship for the last week of December 1999 so long as it'll cost us nothing. Tell the Finns they can call the ship the *Celebrity* if they want, but we'll have to charge them fifty thousand US dollars for using our name.'

'Fifty thousand dollars?'

'Are you going deaf as well as stupid? Why do you keep repeating me?'

'I –'

'Get to it. Oh yes, plus I want all the invitations reprinted. I'm making it a fancy dress ball. Change the wording: the New Millennium's Eve *Celebrity* Fancy Dress Ball. See to it, Campbell.'

Before he could say anything more she replaced the receiver in Washington.

'*Ciao*, baby,' said Murdoch. 'Sweet dreams.'

The telephone amplifier cowered before them on the conference table like a cornered animal. Campbell switched it off. He lit a nervous cigarette. 'Holy Moses,' he said.

'And that's another big name you've left off the list, you idle bastard,' said Murdoch. 'Anyone fancy a tinny?'

'But we had nearly all of those names,' protested Caroline Ponsonby. 'I remember typing the bloody things.'

'Me too,' said Pauline Chang.

'So what the hell has happened?' said Campbell. 'Let's see

the list again. Get a printout. And call it up on the computer too, Caroline, would you, lassie?'

Caroline left the conference room and Campbell buzzed his secretary on the intercom. 'Suzi,' he said, 'get Nat Wakonde on the line, would you please, lassie?'

'I've got him already. In Wales. On his mobile.'

'You're a gem.'

'I'll put him through.'

'Nat?'

'Iain.' Wakonde's voice leaked weakly into the conference room.

'Nat? You all right, laddie?'

'Fine. Perfect. Never been better.' He sounded dazed.

'You sure you're all right?'

'Sure. Yar. What a pleasure.'

'Nat, The Editor …'

'She's beautiful.'

'What?'

'She's the most beautiful woman I've ever seen.'

'Eh?'

'I'm in love, Iain.'

'With The Editor?'

'Not that old bitch. Helga Gröning. Hel–ga. She's the most beautiful woman I've ever seen.'

'In that case, laddie, you won't mind going back to see her again. The Editor says you're not to come back until you've got a decent interview.'

'She won't talk to me.'

'Take her some flowers. They always fall for flowers.'

'She loathes me.'

'Chocolates, then. Put them on your exes.'

'She won't see me. She hates all journalists.'

'Make it up, then.'

'She won't make it up. She thinks I'm a shit.'

'I mean make up the quotes. She'll never read the bloody article anyway.'

'I'll never betray her,' said Nat dreamily.

'I'm not asking you to betray her, laddie: I'm asking you to portray her. Just come back with an interview. Otherwise it's bye-bye Nathaniel and back to Soweto.'

'White River.'

'Wherever. Get on with it.'

'I'll try,' said Nat.

'Good lad.'

'Goodbye darling,' said Nat vaguely.

'Give her one for me!' called Murdoch. 'Up the sunburnt races!'

Campbell switched the amplifier off.

'Strewth, mate!' said Murdoch. 'He's got it bad. No probs. He's got it worse than a rakali's got fleas. He's lost the plot, poor bastard. Finished. No worries.'

Caroline Ponsonby came back into the conference room looking baffled. 'I don't understand this at all,' she said.

'What is it, lassie?'

'The list,' she said. 'Most of the missing names are there in the computer file when you look at it on screen, but when you print them out dozens of them just disappear.'

'Stone me!' said Murdoch. 'The ghost in the machine. It's become a poltergeist.'

In the lush green Tanat Valley of North Wales the rain had been lashing down for hours on field, stream and mountainside, on sheep and stone. Only the waters moved and the world was made of mud.

Helga Gröning and Arthur Lancelot closed the rough hessian rags hanging over the windows in their blue caravan painted with golden unicorns and sunflowers, and went to bed for the afternoon. He kissed her eyes and the blue tattoo of the dove on her left breast, and as the caravan rocked and squeaked and sighed the dog Merlin lay curled up in a corner, dreaming of flying.

Eventually Helga buried her face in Lancelot's thin silver

beard, clutched his bony elbows and shuddered.

Afterwards she wept. 'I am being so happy,' she said.

'Me too, babe,' he said, lighting a marijuana joint.

'I am not giving a damnation about you are older. This I am knowing for sure, *ja*.'

'Me too.' He kissed her eyebrows, nibbling the tiny silver ring above her left eye, and passed the joint from his lips to hers. He sighed. 'This is the life,' he said. 'Most people don't know how to live.'

Later she curled herself about him.

They slept.

The rain drummed on the roof of the caravan. Clouds settled grey on the valley like balls of cotton wool stained with mascara. The windows wept. The dog snored quietly in the corner.

After a couple of hours Lancelot stirred as the afternoon died and the movement of his leg beneath hers woke her too.

'I am loving you much, my holy man,' she muttered drowsily.

'Me too, kid.'

He leaned on one elbow and pulled the hessian away from the window facing the lane.

'It's still pissing with rain,' he said.

He sat up suddenly and peered through the window. 'Holy shit!' he said. 'That reporter. He's back again. The darkie. He's just standing in the road and staring at the caravan.'

Helga sat up swiftly, rubbing her eyes, and knelt behind him at the window, her hand on his neck. She pressed her breasts against his back, the little blue tattoo fluttering against his shoulder-blade, and looked out over his shoulder across the field. In the lane Nat Wakonde was standing in the rain alone beside a bright red car under a large, multi-coloured golfing umbrella. The photographer was sitting in the car's passenger seat, looking disgruntled. Nat Wakonde seemed to be looking straight into her.

She shivered.

She touched the base of her throat, as though to draw the top of a blouse together, and remembered she was naked. She ducked away from the window and reached for her clothes: one of Lancelot's shirts, a pair of his socks, the masculine clothes that she loved to wear because they made her feel safe.

'If he comes into the field I'll let Merlin loose,' said Lancelot.

'I hate that reporter,' she said. 'I spit him. *Schweinhund!*'

Merlin growled.

'Hang on,' said Lancelot. 'Now there's another car coming up the lane.'

He peered through the window. A white car drove up and stopped by the gate. A blue light was flashing from the roof of the vehicle.

'Oh, shit!' said Lancelot. 'It's the fuzz. Hide the dope, for Christ's sake. That bloody black bastard's shopped us to the fuzz.'

Three or four times each day Nguyen Thi Chu slipped out of her office in the history faculty building at Tây Ninh University and descended two flights of stairs to the staff centre. There she approached her mailbox in the hope that today at last there might be a letter from Quang Linh. Often the mailbox was stuffed with envelopes and she would search eagerly through them, but never was one addressed to her in that beloved handwriting as spiky as his unruly hair. Quang Linh had never been a reliable letter writer but when his ship had sailed from Haiphong for the Spratly Islands she had begged him to write just once a week – just a line or two, just a sentence, she said, just to say he was well – and he had promised. But week after week went by without any word. At first she was resigned to it, expecting to hear something in the next day or two. Then she became angry. How dare he? Quang Linh knew very well how much she worried about him: did he simply not care about her feelings at all?

Now she was apprehensive: he must be ill, or hurt. Wounded, perhaps. There had been no reports of any fighting yet around the Spratlys but there were rumours that some of the Chinese fleet was sailing towards Commodore Reef and North Viper Shoal, north-west of Sabah, where the Vietnamese navy was on patrol. She prayed that Quang Linh's ship was further north, closer perhaps to the Paracel Islands, where the tension with China and Taiwan was not so great. But then would the authorities allow the newspapers to report any fighting, especially if there had been casualties? She felt so far away from him, so isolated here on the Cambodian border. It was more than a year since she had been to Saigon. They had renamed it Ho Chi Minh City long ago, after the American war, but everyone still called it Saigon. To get there you had to pass through Cu Chi and whenever she had in the past she had found herself trembling as she approached the village, unable to forget the horror of the tunnels burrowing under the jungle.

Work was the answer. She took up judo again and the exercise helped a little, and the new philosophy lecturer took her out for a meal and a concert, but the magic spark was not there. It was work that best took her mind off things. She had started having the dreams again, the nightmares in which she was still underground in the tunnels of Cu Chi, not daring to breathe, the pain in her chest, the sweat trickling down her face, and American soldiers' boots were tramping the jungle paths above her head. One night she woke shouting and sweating, remembering the face of the black American GI and the terrified whites of his eyes in the dark as he came up through the narrow underground trapdoor and she had cut his throat.

It must be middle age, the menopause, or maybe the old malaria of the tunnels. They had all suffered terribly from malaria in the tunnels. When she took her spectacles off and looked in the mirror there were lines around her eyes; the skin was papery, and her eyes were tired and red and too small, her lips too thin. No wonder men were wary of her. She looked like a dried-up old spinster, a thin-lipped academic machine about as sexy as a computer. She was glad that Tran Xuan Kai would never see her old. She reached for a tissue and blew her nose. She dabbed her eyes.

Work was the answer. It allowed you to forget for a while that you were only half alive.

'Just like the Anglo-Saxons today,' she wrote, 'Ethelred the Unready's weakness, cowardice, disloyalty, degeneracy and lack of moral principle infected the moral fibre of all the Anglo-Saxon races with a fatal virus a thousand years ago. Just as they turn today in despair to astrology, fortune-telling, mysticism, superstition, spurious religions and idolatry, so then did they worship false gods and turn again to their ancient pagan idols: to Eostre the goddess of dawn, and Hreda, and Erce, the Mother of Earth. When they realised in the year 1001 that the world had not ended after all, they recovered their pride and saved themselves and eventually, in 1945, they saved the world. But in the year 2000 there can be no second recovery for the Anglo-Saxons. Their modern sickness is terminal. Their day is over and now it is our turn, in our own Pacific millennium. It is time now for what the Oxford historian Felipe Fernández-Armesto described in his book *Millennium* (Bantam Press, 1995) as "the cultural revenge of the east."

'History is not mocked. As the Anglo-Saxons falter and fail at last at the end of the twentieth century their downfall is due to exactly the same moral weaknesses that their Bishop Wulfstan denounced in the year 999.'

Chu leaned back, exhausted. The computer screen gleamed at her. She had no doubt at all that the book would win her acclaim throughout the Pacific. She knew deep in her heart that one day the leader would make her a Heroic Vietnamese Scholar, and she would be able to move into an apartment with two rooms. Then maybe she would have time to make herself more feminine, more loveable, and she would find a man to love, and Quang Linh would come home where he belonged.

She wished he would write. Where was he? Why didn't he write?

<hi> said Chandler <have a nice day>

Marlowe grunted. He bit into his jelly and peanut butter triple-decker sandwich and scratched his balls. They were always itchy these days. Night after night, as he sat before Chandler's blue screen, he was often conscious of them hanging about, lolling uncomfortably between his thighs, getting in the way, constant reminders. He seemed for some reason to have put on a little weight recently and now he needed to sit with his legs spread apart like a sumo wrestler. A couple of nights ago he had tried to cross his legs and failed.

He reached for his litre of Coke. At least the itch couldn't be anything really unpleasant. Those days were over. It was probably no more than a slight chemical rash from the new state-of-the-art, self-lubricating, rubber Luv-Pak equipment that Chandler had ordered for him on the Internet. The Luv-Pak fitted so snug and moist that Marlowe was using it twice as often as he had used the old MicroHard connections of the early pioneering days of screwing on the Internet; the old equipment had always needed so much creaming and scraping and cleaning. The itching certainly couldn't be anything serious. Those dangerous times were over; those exhilarating nights of risky cruising in the flesh in Frisco and Sydney and Amsterdam, of never knowing who or what you might pick up, the shadows lurking in corners, lights glinting on the canals, whispered voices, hands fumbling in the dark. Intoxicating nights. He shuddered now to think of the crazy chances he had taken in those days: the angry sailor in London with his cock tattooed like a moon rocket; the mad junkie with the syringe in Amsterdam. Too many of them from those days were dead but he had stopped in time. Never again. It was better this way and you still met some great cyberfucks on the Internet. Even Chandler was unlikely to pick up some nasty virus. Marlowe had taken plenty of precautions against that. He never let Chandler out into cyberspace without full electronic protection. No sassy little foreign computer was going to be infecting Chandler, no sir. Nowadays Chandler cruising the Internet was as safe as a ninety-nine-year-old nun in a cage at Fort Worth.

<72 messages today> said Chandler, displaying the morning's e-mail menu.

Marlowe sighed. He finished his sandwich, licked the jelly off his fingers, wiped his mouth on the back of his sleeve and took another swig of Coke. He unwrapped a Hershey bar, took a bite, spread his thighs, settled his buttocks, pulled the keyboard towards him and finally let his fingers tapdance across it as daintily as Rachmaninov.

<cut the crap> he tapped.

Chandler fizzed briefly and reduced the e-mail menu to three messages.

<thats better>

The first message was from some shyster in Cairo – Cairo, Egypt, not one of the other Cairos in Georgia, Illinois, Missouri, Nebraska, New York, Ohio or West Virginia – enquiring what Marlowe would charge to provide him with a list of fair-haired, blue-eyed boys under the age of ten and living within thirty kilometres of the River Nile.

<fuck off u prevert> he typed <or ill report u 2 yore ayatolla>

Chandler zapped the message in seconds under the Atlantic, across the Sahara desert and around the Pyramids.

Marlowe shook his head. The things people asked him to do! The things they wanted to do to other people! What sort of dickhead would want to molest a child, for Pete's sake, when there were all those wonderful king-size cocks hanging loose out there?

He called up the second message, from someone in Long Beach, and Chandler's screen exploded with a riot of gold and green and a fanfare of trumpets. A cute little pink kitten danced across the screen wearing a top hat.

Ah no. Please not again.

<*kitty schweitzer*> said the screen in fancy italics <*hi there big boy*>

The kitten waved its paw. It looked like Fred Astaire hailing a cab. The kitten bowed. Chandler uttered a strangulated miaow and blushed as the gold and green faded to pink and blue.

<where you been then big boy you playin hard to get> said the message <remember me im the busty blond age 43 remember you tracked down my bastard husband and his floozi in a shlok hotel in San Luis Obispo>

Mrs Schweitzer again. Last time she'd claimed to be fifty-two. She and her age were going down faster than a couple of fags in a football locker room.

<now ive kicked the dork out and im sueing him for divorce and hes loaded and im gonna be RICH baby and i jus LOVE men>

Marlowe shuddered.

<we oughter get to know each other better sweetart>

Marlowe closed his eyes and tried to imagine what Mrs Schweitzer looked like. It didn't bear thinking about.

<how about it big boy>

<GON AWAY> typed Marlowe <NOT BAK TILL XMAS LEFT NO ADRESS>

He sent the message and withdrew from Mrs Schweitzer's computer. He called Chandler to heel and Mrs Schweitzer's little pink pussy skipped across the screen again, swishing its tail, winking and forcing Chandler to give a reluctant miaow as it went. Chandler hummed and sighed. The things a computer was expected to do these days.

<so long baby> said the screen <missing you already>

The third message was from Santa Barbara: Bill Warren; the guy who wanted to stiff the magazine editor in Monte Carlo.

<Would you call me, please, Mr Marlowe?>

Yeah. Warren. The guy with the capital letters and

punctuation marks. All questions and screamers. Crazy guy. Nice job. Fun. Marlowe'd never been on a murder before. The cops would be real impressed when Warren murdered the editor and Marlowe turned Warren in and solved the case for them.

Chandler called up Warren's computer. He was in.

<Any developments?> said Warren.

<yea> said Marlowe <i screwd up there computer in monte carlo>

<You changed some of the names on their list?>

<hundreds + i plantd a gost virus in there to screw it up sum more>

<What about the editor? Have you found out any more about her?>

Marlowe did a smiley. <:-) sure she got 2764 English £s in her checkin a/c in London + she gets payd 9166.66 per month + she has 128000 more in a speshul savins deposit + it wont last all that long cos she owes 14937 on her mastercard + shes still messin roun with toyboys who cum expensif>

<:-)>

<thanx>

<I like that: toyboys who come expensive!>

<thank u>

<Maybe a little blackmail then, eh, Marlowe?>

<no sir not me u can count me out there im stricty legit>

<Sure. Just a couple of untrackable messages. Say $200?>

<no sir i never consider crime>

<300?>

<i never consider crime for $300 no way>

<350>

<5>

<350>

<450>

<4>

<425>

<4>

The screen froze.

<OK, 4. $400> said Marlowe. He did a grumpy. <:-(yore a hard man mr warren sir so whats the job u want me 2 do>

There was a pause on-screen. The cursor flickered stationary against the screen like a Morse message flashing out of a deep blue ocean. Then it skittered again across the screen leaving a trail of words like a snail's smear of slime.

<I want for you to put the fear of God up the bitch> said Warren <I want for you to soften her up first with a few gentle threats about her and the toyboys. They're under-age?>

<15 or 16 i gess>

<Great. Threaten to out her>

<Mention Dirk Molloy. That's the magazine's owner. God-fearing man. Churchgoer. He'd fire her if he knew. Put the frighteners on the bitch.>

<i feel i shud say here mr warren sir i find it hard to molest women>

<You some sort of fairy?>

<sure>

<You'll learn. Just give her a hard time. This is one tough bitch, Marlowe. You don't need to feel sorry for this one. She's not going to break down in tears. Anything else?>

Marlowe grinned. <:-) yea shes jus bin roun the world a few days in hongkong the mandrin hotel i checkd out her hotel check + she had yogurt + frut for brekfas then she came on here>

<To the US?>

<la>

<She's in Los Angeles? Now?>

<jus a coupla days now shes gon>

<Shit>

<i pickd her name up on the airline skedules she flew 2 washingtondc 2 days ago>

<She's there now?>

\<Where? What hotel?>
\<there a lotta hotels their mr w>
\<Could you find her?>
\<itll take time>
\<How much?>
\<nother 500>

\<i dont mean how much money you mercenary bastard i mean how much time would it take you to find her>

Hey, hey, thought Marlowe: no capitals! No punctuation! This guy is getting steamed. This guy cares. You can use a guy like that. You can take advantage. Caring makes you soft.

\<I apologise, Marlowe. I shouldn't have said that. How long would it take you to find her?>
\<2 or 3 hours maybe 4 there a lot of hotels there>
\<Please do it>
\<OK $500>
\<4>
\<5>
\<shit all right OK>
\<in advans pleas mr warren now>

Marlowe pressed one of Chandler's macro codes and Chandler automatically transmitted the number of his bank account:

\<please make immediate electronic deposit in bank of california la branch a/c meanstreets agency 93864793947>

\<You're a tough bastard, Marlowe>
\<thas jus wot mike tyson sez 2>

Marlowe waited for forty-eight seconds until the purple window opened up in the bottom right-hand corner of the screen to confirm an electronic desposit of $500 in his account.

\<thank u kindly sir> tapped Marlowe \<ill be in tuch>

There was no need at all for him to hack into all the hotel computers in Washington. He knew exactly where Stella Barrett was already. Chandler had been keeping a running check on her name on all the computer files at Washington airport and the major airline companies, and she had flown out this morning by British Airways to Bermuda and had checked into a suite at the Marriott Hotel near St George's. Still, why tell Warren that quite yet? A private dick couldn't make a decent living these days if he told the client everything at once. Sometimes in these hard times a gumshoe had to be sticky.

<hav a nise day now mr warren> he typed <misin u already>

CHAPTER 6

In the South Pacific, in Pago Pago, 120 miles to the east of the international date line, it was Saturday morning. But just a hundred miles to the west of the date line, on the Tongan island of Vava'u, it was already Sunday morning and the islanders were flocking to church as always in their thousands.

In Vava'u's little wooden clapboard capital, Neiafu, the Tongan people fatly filled the pews of the Wesleyan, Mormon and London Missionary Society churches whose priests had once persuaded their ancestors to give up cannibalism and eat dogs and bats instead. On Vava'u, like all the other dozens of scattered little Tongan islands, everything was closed. No traffic moved at all along the rough dirt roads, not even a bicycle. No aeroplane landed or took off, no ship sailed, not even a small canoe, and no radio station broadcast. The international yachts in Port of Refuge, the best natural harbour in all the South Pacific, lay silent because it was Sunday. It was so much Sunday that not even the yachties or tourists, not even the white people – the *palangi*, the 'sky-bursters' – dared to wear a bikini or play volleyball or go jogging. You could be arrested for blasphemy, for being bare-chested, or jumping up and down, or making a noise on a Sunday. And so most of the beautiful beaches were empty, the canoes drawn up on the fine white sand and parked beneath the palm trees. The only sounds to be heard on a Sunday above the squawking of parrots, the squeaking of fruit bats, the *kark-kark-kark* of the herons, the crash of the rollers against the reef and the gentle plash of waves on the sand, were the soaring melodies of the magnificent Tongan choirs as they raised their voices in magical harmony all over the islands in simple churches built to glorify the Lord.

On this particular Sunday, in the main Wesleyan church in Neiafu, the farmers and fisherfolk of Vava'u were wearing the very best of their Sunday best because this weekend the King and Queen of Tonga had left their white wooden palace in the Tongan capital Nuku'alofa, on the island of Tongatapu 170 miles to the south, and were staying in their country home on Vava'u. As usual they were in the Wesleyan congregation. The old King sprawled huge along the royal pew, overflowing in all directions, the fattest monarch in the world, all twenty-two stone of him. He was so fat that when he was on a visit to London people giggled when they saw him in the Tongan embassy limousine with the numberplate 1 TON. And yet, despite being overweight, the King of Tonga was the most royal monarch in the world. He was descended from a thousand years of Tu'i Tonga chiefs, themselves descended from another millennium of supreme nobility inherited from brutal Polynesian ancestors; the so-called Vikings of the Sunrise. The King was certainly much more regal than any of those other royal upstarts in Thailand, Britain, Saudi Arabia or Swaziland. And his body alone gave him stature: he was tall even when he was on his back. Even sideways. Squeezed in beside him in the royal pew was his comparatively slim nineteen-stone queen and behind them was ranged a squashed row of positively emaciated eighteen-stone Tongan nobles.

In honour of the royal presence the church was packed that Sunday with men and women wearing their very best and most colourful skirts: the men in *tupanu* reaching down to their knees, some of them carrying rolled umbrellas; the women wrapped in *vala* down to their ankles. They were all wearing around their waists their old and frayed but precious *ta'ovala*: woven ancestral straw mats that crackled whenever they sat.

In a pew near the back of the church, crunching and crackling with the best of them, sat the main branch of the Faletau family tree: Salote and Lini, the grannies; Salote's daughter, Deso; Deso's husband, Ongosia; and a tribe of adult offspring and children, from Deso and Ongosia's twenty-eight-year-old son, Viliami, down to their youngest, nineteen-year-old daughter, Afu, and Afu's infants Koli, Aleki and baby Enna.

Although Afu was nineteen – and a mother of three – she sat and stared with her mouth open at the King and Queen as they passed up the aisle with some of their nobles. She could not believe that she could be so close to them. After all, they came from Nuku'alofa – Nuku'alofa! – the biggest town in all of Tonga, which Afu thought must surely be the biggest and most glamorous town in all the world. They came from Nuku'alofa, where people said the royal palace had turrets and flagpoles and sentry boxes. And where the main street, Taufa'ahau Road, named after the King, a huge monarch of a road, went on and on for block after block, for at least twenty blocks. And in Nuku'alofa, everyone said, rich, glamorous people wafted in and out of the International Dateline Hotel and drank from real glasses every day.

The King was wheezing as he rolled up the aisle, lurching hugely from side to side, a vast impressive figure in his long leather overcoat, leather boots and sunglasses. Afu had seen him before in church but he always made her stare. He was huge. They said that the bigger you are the richer and cleverer you are, and Afu thought that the King must be the richest, cleverest man in all the world. Probably even richer and cleverer than her uncle Alipate, who couldn't sit down in an ordinary chair and once flew up in the sky to Nuku'alofa and had to be weighed along with his bundle of clothes before they would let him onto the airy plane. The King was so big that she wondered how he had found a bed big enough to sleep in. Afu's grandmother had been named Salote after the King's old mother but Afu found it difficult to believe that the King could ever have had a mother. After all, if he had a mother he must have been inside her once and how could any woman have had a man that big inside her? Afu had a naughty thought. She giggled.

'Sssh!' said her mother.

'Me shutim up racket belong me now,' whispered Afu, 'by an by.'

When the singing started Afu had to keep her mouth firmly closed. She loved singing and had once dreamed of joining the choir but they had told her that her voice was not good enough. She knew all the words of most of the hymns and sang very loud but not often in tune, and the choir leader had gently told her mother that Afu could not control her voice properly and why didn't she think of weaving mats or baskets or *tapa* cloth instead? Afu had never wanted to weave mats or baskets or *tapa* cloth and she had cried when she had been told she could not join the choir because she knew she could sing beautifully in her head. In her head she sang like an angel and her voice was pure and strong, but whenever she opened her mouth it made quite different noises however much she told her mouth to behave. She had the same trouble with her eyes: when she looked at a printed or written page she knew that the squiggles were meant to mean something and that there was supposed to be some sort of logic about them, but she could never work out what it might be. She could not even sign her own name because it was difficult for her to hold the pencil properly. Her fingers and hands were so clumsy and refused to do what she told them. They didn't listen to her properly. If her mother or the teacher wrote her name down on a piece of paper Afu would bend her face right down to the paper and stare at it for a long time. Although, after a while, she thought she could just recognise the shape of her first name – A, F, U – she could never even begin to grasp the shape of the second – F, A, L, E, T, A, U – in her head all at once. Instead her brain just went all spongy like an old coconut and her eyes began to think instead of a tin of Pacific Brand corned beef or a bar of chocolate. But here was another mystery, she thought: what was the point of writing her name at all? Why did they want her to write her name when everybody on the island already knew very well who she was?

Afu was not only nineteen. She was also very pretty. Her waist was a little podgy already after having three children so quickly but her silky skin was the colour of pale fudge, her legs long and slender, her smile wide and white. Her long straight hair was decorated every day with a fresh frangipani, ginger flower or gardenia. That was why she had three children already, two boys and a pretty little baby girl, though she couldn't remember who their fathers had been and she couldn't look after the children herself because she kept forgetting about them and dropping things so her mother and grandmothers looked after them instead; they told them that Afu was their big sister. When she had had the last baby the priest had been cross with her. 'You must tell the boys "no" when they want you to lie down with them, Afu,' he had told her sternly. Afu had often tried to but it was even more difficult than reading and the boys got so upset if she wouldn't and they looked so unhappy and *no* sometimes meant *yes*, anyway, which made it difficult. Anyway, all the other girls did it, too, even the twelve-year-olds, and she was nineteen, so why shouldn't she? And she liked it, what the boys wanted to do with her: it was nice and made her feel warm and funny.

But better than boys Afu loved music. Music never made her head go mushy. She loved hymns and Country and Western and the band at the Paradise International Hotel, and the way the music seemed to bounce around inside her head as though there was nothing else in there. She loved going to church, three times every Sunday, and listening to the Kava Club Choir and the organ and silver band, and as the music swelled and soared up to God in Heaven she sang to Him too, but just in her head, not aloud. Sometimes she forgot that she was meant to be quiet and suddenly shouted *Hallo, Louie* or *Amen* and sometimes she just couldn't help it and burst into a few words of a hymn when she was listening to it in her head but nobody was cross when she did. When she did suddenly make a noise in church people turned round in their pews and nodded at her mother and father and smiled at her because they knew she couldn't really help it. Some people could be kind. They didn't all call her Airhead Afu like some of them.

After the morning service the King and Queen were driven away in a big black car – no one minded if they drove about on a Sunday, of course – and Afu and her grannies and mama and papa and sisters and brothers and babies all strolled back home. They went along the dusty streets lined with frangipani, bougainvillea and poinciana to their little flat-roofed, thatched, corrugated-iron shanty house just outside town and to the feast that Deso, Salote, Lini and all their sisters and daughters and cousins and neighbours had prepared to welcome Afu's big brother, Viliami. He had come home for a holiday after being away for more than a year working in Hawaii, where he had a smart job working as a gardener for a rich American who lived in Los Angeles.

When they reached the house all the women went inside to prepare the feast, shuffling through the dead palm leaves strewn across the floor, and Afu went round the back to the family allotment – where Ongosia and Alipate grew fruit and vegetables – to say good morning to her Grandpapa Salesi. He was buried there in the yard in a grave marked by a pattern of coloured shells and a tasteful oblong border of upturned

Foster's beer bottles and a glinting and fluttering of old
Christmas tinsel, baubles and decorations. Afu thought that her
grandpapa's grave out here in the back yard was so pretty and
she often stopped by for a chat with him. It didn't matter to her
that he was dead. In some ways that was an advantage: at least
he listened to her and never interrupted. A cockerel stalked
across the grave, pecking haughtily at Grandpapa Salesi's roof,
unaware that within an hour Grandpapa Salesi's descendants
would be pecking at the cockerel's own descendants. Afu
squatted crosslegged beside the grave and told Grandpapa
Salesi about the King's leather coat and dark glasses and the
Queen's pretty singing and the shiny car that had taken them
away even on a Sunday.

'Him bigfella king belong missis queen he been come up
house belong God one time,' Afu told her grandpapa con-
fidentially as one of the miniature Chinese lanterns fluttered in
the breeze discreetly.

In the dusty street in front of the house Afu's sisters and
aunts began to lay a long trestle table for the feast to welcome
Viliami home. Soon they were scattering along it plates piled
high with cassava, breadfruit, coconut, papaya, pineapples,
bananas, sweet potatoes, mangos, limes, avocados, watermelons
and cheeses. Later they brought out on huge blue platters
three steaming roast suckling pigs and six chickens that had
been cooked in underground *umu* ovens along with dishes of
mullet, crayfish, octopus and shark steaks. These were followed
by bowls of sweet gravy, big white *'ufi* yams and *lu pulu* dishes
of meat and onions marinated in coconut milk and *umu*-baked
in taro leaves. There was even a plate of Afu's favourite food
especially for her, tinned fish and tinned corned beef, and she
clapped her hands and whooped when she saw them.

'My gracious!' she cried. 'Me hallo him bigfella fish belong
tin too much now!'

Afu loved tinned food. It always tasted better than food out
of the sea or food that grew on bones and she liked the pictures
on the labels and the magic ritual of opening the tins and

finding food inside. It was always a lovely surprise to ease off
the lid of the tin, being careful not to cut her fingers on the
jagged edge, and to discover what was inside even though she
always knew because the label always showed what it was
going to be. That mystery had always baffled her. How did the
food get in there, inside a sealed tin? And how did the food fit
inside so perfectly that it was never too big for the tin but just
exactly right? How did the food know what size it ought to
be? And how did the labels on the *outside* of the tin know what
was inside the tin even before anyone had opened it up? These
were the sort of questions that sometimes made her head feel
full. Afu had once asked her mother if the trees on which the
tins grew were also made of tin or if they had meat inside, but
Deso had told her not to be so silly.

'Afu! Pretty sister! Come sit with me!' called Viliami when at
last the family and all the neighbours sat down to eat. Afu
blushed and hid her face in her shoulder but he came around
the table towards her and took her hand and led her gently to
the place of honour beside him. As she went with him she said
loudly, 'This fella sister he stop him here now long talk-talk by
an by.' Then she made a funny face and plonked herself down
in the chair beside his and everyone laughed and clapped.
Grandmama Salote said that Viliami was a good boy and that
she and Grandmama Lini would look after Afu's pikininis Koli,
Aleki and Enna at the far end of the table where all the other
pikininis were. Afu felt proud that she was not sent to sit with
all the pikininis as usual and Viliami talked to her throughout
the meal just as if she was a proper grown-up, pouring her a
glass of beer and slicing pieces of pig and chicken for her. She
felt important and straightened her shoulders and pushed out
her front. Viliami teased her about her front and boys and how
pretty she was and about drinking too much beer. He told her
about his life in Hawaii and how there were plenty of Tongans
working there as ladies' maids and cooks and gardeners and
how he hoped one day to go to work for his rich American

employer in Los Angeles, in Hollywood.

Afu was tongue-tied. Viliami was so handsome, so strong, so clever, with an impressively long old *ta'ovala* crunched around his waist and a T-shirt that said HAWAII-YA? and a wide black halo of bushy hair and a smart new moustache. She felt like a baby who had not yet learned to speak. And he had seen so much of the world, not just Hawaii, and most of the little islands around Vava'u and Fiji too and he had even been to Nuku'alofa. He had seen the King's palace there and the turrets and sentries and flagpole and had even walked along every block on Taufa'ahau Road, all twenty of them, and had stood outside the International Dateline Hotel watching the famous people go in and out, and now he was even talking of going to Hollywood. Afu simply could not imagine Hollywood. How far away was it? Further than Nuku'alofa? No, surely not: she had heard once that Nuku'alofa was more than a hundred miles away. A hundred! She could not imagine a hundred. She had never counted more than one, two, three, four, many. And how big was Hollywood? Bigger even than Nuku'alofa? Impossible. Afu bet that Hollywood didn't have a king and flagpole and an International Dateline Hotel.

Viliami told her that Hollywood and Los Angeles were full of film stars and famous people and eventually, when he noticed that Afu had started to get bored sitting at the table listening to everyone else's noise and was just staring across the table with her mouth hanging open, he went inside the house and brought out for her a tattered magazine that he had brought back from Hawaii. It was a magazine that was full of pictures showing how handsome and pretty and glamorous everybody was in Hollywood and Los Angeles. On the front, at the top, in red, was a squiggly word: C, E, L, E, B, R, I, T, Y. Afu stared at it. On the front was a picture of a beautiful woman.

'That's Princess Sophia,' said Viliami. 'Pretty, eh? Nearly as pretty as you.'

Afu stuck her tongue out. She had heard of Princess Sophia but she didn't think that the Princess had ever come to Vava'u, not even with the King and Queen when they came for the week-end. She must have stayed at home in the palace in Nuku'alofa.

Afu flipped through the pages of the magazine. They were filled with glossy colour photographs and Viliami was right: everyone photographed was beautiful. They were all holding glasses and smiling, or gazing into each other's eyes, or chattering in groups, or lounging beside swimming pools, or talking to cameras, or climbing out of big shiny limousines, or galloping on horseback with their hair streaming in the wind. They all looked so perfect, so expensive. They all looked so happy, thought Afu. How nice it must be to be so happy.

And then she turned another page and fell in love for the first time in her life. It was a full-page picture of the most beautiful man of them all, the most beautiful man she had ever seen. He was white, tall and slim, his long straight hair floppy and tousled, his face gentle and humorous and so handsome. He looked as if he would never stop smiling. There were lovely little smiley lines around his mouth and eyes. And those eyes. Blue eyes. Such blue eyes. They were bluer than the brightest ocean, deeper than the deepest lagoon.

Afu swallowed. Her mouth was dry. He looked so clean. He looked such fun. His eyes were twinkling and they were looking straight into her heart.

She nudged Viliami and pushed the magazine towards him.

'How him bigfella callim name?' she said.

'That's Hugh Grant,' he said.

'Hugh Grant,' said Viliami. 'Famous English actor.'

'You?'

'Hugh.'

'Who.'

'No: Hhhh-you.'

'Hhhugh.'

'So. Hugh Grant.'

'Glant.'

'Grrrant.'

'Grrant.'

'Right. Hugh Grant.'

She snatched the magazine back and stared at the photograph.

'Hhugh Grrant,' she said.

He grinned. 'Hey, hey!' he said. 'You like him?'

She nodded. 'Me likeim too much already now,' she said.

He smiled and stroked her hair. 'Sure, he's pretty,' he said, 'but not nearly as pretty as you.'

'Course no,' she said crossly. 'You bigfella silly buggerup too much now. Hhugh Grrant him bigfella fella, not *faka lady* like Siole. Me wantim keep picture by an by.'

'Sure,' said Viliami. 'Take it. It's yours.'

Afu gazed at the photograph again. 'Hhugh Grrant,' she said. He seemed to be smiling right into the back of her head.

One day a man like Hhugh Grrant would find her and she would make him happy. Tonight, in church, she would pray to the King and Queen and Princess Sophia and all the other gods and goddesses to send her a man like that.

Later, when it was really hot and the sun was high and her head was fuzzy with beer, Afu slipped out of her seat and into the house and hid the magazine in her night-mat. She walked out of the other side of the house, saying hallo to Grandpapa Salesi as she passed his upturned beer bottles and Christmas decorations, and wandered away through the allotment and towards the sea, letting her feet take her wherever they wanted.

Her feet strolled her down towards the lagoon and when they reached the beach her head suddenly wanted to go swimming. Her head wanted her arms to take all her clothes off and her legs to run into the sea and then to make her swim with nothing on at all, but that would cause a terrible row if anyone found out. It was only the sky-bursters who took most of their clothes off when they went swimming: Tongan girls only went into the sea wearing all their clothes, including their blouses, petticoats and dresses.

But how were Afu's legs to know that? They strolled her to the water's edge although she kept telling them not to and that they were naughty. The green lagoon looked so inviting. The thirsty sun had swallowed every cloud and the hot sand tempted her toes and wavelets murmured against her ankles, tugging her in. Sunlight glittered on shallow water around the sandbanks. A small breeze sighed among the casuarina trees. Her eyes started helping her legs to be naughty and looked around to see if there was anyone in sight. There wasn't.

Afu's head could not resist it. If the grown-ups could all make a noise and break the rules on a Sunday, her head told itself, why shouldn't Afu's legs and arms break the rules too? After all, she was a grown-up too, wasn't she? She wasn't a pikinini any more.

Quickly her arms stripped off all her clothes and threw them on the sand. Her delicate little hands plucked the gardenia from her hair and tossed it away. Her long, slim legs forced her to run naked into the sea, her long black hair cascading down to her chubby waist, and her chests started bouncing and giggling too. Even her naughty lips had joined in now and they were laughing.

For a while her arms and legs splashed about in the shallows but then she drifted further out into the lagoon and here the turquoise ocean was so still and clean that she could see right down to the small crabs idling across the sand at her feet. Tiny, multi-coloured fish shimmered about her body and between her legs, flicking her soft brown skin with their lacy tails, kissing the insides of her thighs and nibbling the ends of her long black hair as it trailed in the sea. She swayed in the water, swirling her hips, and the fish darted away like rainbows in the ripples but then she was still again and they slowly returned, circling her slim brown legs, flickering against her buttocks, caressing her.

She thought of Hhugh Grrant and his eyes and his smile and she laughed and fingered the waves, stroking them like a lover. Then she began to sing, and there was nobody there in all the world to say *no!*

Nat Wakonde and Charlie Potter sat in their hired Ford Sierra at the end of a muddy Welsh lane and stared at the rain. It was very Welsh rain. It slid down the windows with the sly, insistent wetness that had kept the Anglo-Saxons at bay for centuries. It nudged the windscreen wipers, sniggering. It gurgled with malevolence.

'There's wet,' said Potter. 'God, I hate this place.'

'I tell you, Iain, I'm not going to do it,' said Nat firmly into his mobile phone.

'Be sensible, laddie,' said Iain Campbell with a touch of desperation. His voice quivered across the airwaves from Monaco out into space and back.

'I am,' said Nat. 'She still won't talk to me and I don't blame her at all. The poor girl was harassed for months by unscrupulous shits from Fleet Street who just made up stuff and now the police are moving the travellers on and she thinks I shopped them to the police and I don't blame her for that, either. Who else could have done it? One minute she refuses to give me an interview and the next minute there's a complaint about their behaviour to the police.'

'You're besotted, laddie. You're not thinking straight.'

'Oh yes I am. For the first time in ages.'

He could still see the loathing on her face. She had marched out of the caravan and across the field down to the gate after the police had left and had sneered at him. '*Schweinehund! Judas! Nazi!*' she had said. He had wanted to kiss her, to smoothe the twisted shape of her lips. He had been shocked by the contempt in her eyes.

'But it's an Editor's must-have,' said Campbell with urgency.

'I don't care if it's a final demand from the Queen of Sheba's Camel Commander, I'm not going to make this bloody interview up.'

Campbell sighed. 'Just a few quotes, laddie, that's all I ask.

You could cobble some likely ones together from cuttings, anyway. The sort of things she would say if she did agree to talk to you. You wouldn't actually be making anything up. Not really. She's said it all before, anyway.'

'Not to me, she hasn't. All those quotes in the cuttings were probably made up too.'

'She wouldn't even know what you've written about her. I don't suppose she's a regular reader.'

'I'd know, Iain.'

'Och, man, grow up, will you? Have you never made up a quote or two before? Just a couple of little ones?'

'Not a whole interview.'

'You'll never get a job on a Fleet Street national if you go on like this.'

'I'm glad to hear it.'

Nat could hear muttering in the office in Monte Carlo. Or was it the sound of the Welsh rain chattering beyond the windows?

Murdoch came on the line. 'Listen here, old son,' he said. 'You're letting down your mates. Stella's got us all by the short and curlies and unless you deliver this interview she's going to start pulling them out by the handful. She already thinks you're pretending to be sick and skiving in hospital with Paddy Kelly.'

'In hospital?'

'She thinks you've lost a finger.'

'A finger?'

'In a drawer.'

'A drawer? Where did she get that idea?'

'Search me, mate. And now the woman's refusing to pay any of us any expenses for the past month to punish us for not coming up with the celebrity guest list that she wants for the New Year's Eve ball.'

'She can't do that.'

'She can do anything she likes, sweetheart.'

'But my exes are absolutely genuine.'

'Yeah. Sure.'

'They are.'

'And Stella's the Virgin Mary.'

'They are, I tell you.'

'OK, OK. Don't tell me, sunshine, try telling her. She's already told Iain to make you pay your own airfare to Wales and back.'

Nat exploded. 'Who the hell does she think she is?'

'She's The Editor, sport, that's who.'

'She still can't steal my exes. She still can't force me to write a whole load of lies.'

'Get real, sport. She's The Editor. How long have you been in journalism? An editor's as powerful as the captain of a ship. If she tells you to walk the plank then you walk the plank and it's no use whingeing about a lifebelt. An editor's God.'

Nat snorted. 'There's a proper disputes procedure. If she gives me any grief I'll complain to the proprietor.'

'Dirk Molloy?' Murdoch laughed merrily. 'The Holy Ghost?'

'He's a born-again Christian, isn't he? He'd go spare if he thought we were being made to make up immoral interviews.'

'I wouldn't bank on it, mate. Molloy's only Christian on Sundays and even then only before lunch. And he's terrified of Stella. Wets himself when she shouts at him. They say she only got the job because she's got some sort of hold on him. She knows something about him, poor bastard. She's got him by the short and curlies too. You complain to Molloy and you're shafted good and proper.'

'I'm not putting words into Helga Gröning's mouth,' said Nat, 'and that's final.'

'Look, sport, we all know exactly what you'd really like to put in her mouth.'

'I'm not listening to this.'

'So you think you're in love with her, do you? Come off it, Nat.'

'Get stuffed.'

'It's all very noble playing the gallant lover –'

'Naff off, Tony.'

'– but what makes you think the Gröning girl's any different from all the other young hippy slags that hang out with these New Age wankers?'

'I'm switching the phone off now, Tony.'

'She's probably just a typical hippy nympho. They're all the same. Probably had more kinds of shag than a tobacconist.'

'You bastard.'

'She's had more hands up her than the Muppets.'

'Fuck off, Murdoch,' said Nat. He switched off his mobile phone.

He breathed heavily. He was sweating. He opened the car window slightly to breathe in the fresh Welsh dampness. The rain spat at him. Murdoch was a bastard.

The telephone rang.

Nat stared at the rain. It was tap-dancing now on the bonnet of the car.

The telephone rang again.

The rain was stuttering across the car roof. Suddenly he was deeply homesick for the Transvaal, for the smell of pine and gum, dust, animal hides.

The telephone rang again.

'Aren't you going to answer it?' said Potter.

'No, I'm fucking well not,' said Nat.

Potter shrugged. He laughed unpleasantly. 'Love!' he said. 'What a load of bollocks!'

On the border between Cambodia and Vietnam Nguyen Thi Chu waited and waited for a letter from Quang Linh. She feared that he was sick or being punished but she did not dare to make an official enquiry. That would betray a lack of moral fibre. If only she had a man to do these things for her, to protect her from her own feebleness. She had been so strong as a young woman. Wasn't it now her turn to be soft and weak? One silent afternoon she was tempted to go and pray at the Cao Dai temple as she had so long ago but that would do her career no good at all: the government had still not completely forgiven the Caodaists for their refusal to fight the Americans in the 1960s, even though they had executed four Cao Dai cardinals after the American war. Whenever Chu decided that she could stand the uncertainty no longer and that she would have to ask for official reassurance about Quang Linh's safety, she would look up and catch the eye of the government informer at the back of the lecture hall and she knew that she could not allow him to glimpse any weakness in her. Never. She, a veteran of the Viet Cong. She who had never shed a public tear when her brother had been killed at Chau Doc or even when Tran Xuan Kai had died. It had only been in private that she had allowed herself to weep, kissing Kai's creased, frowning photograph, sniffing his shirt, sobbing in silence so that no one in the tunnel would hear. She of all people should be fearless in her loyalty to the State she had helped to establish. If the informer ever learned of her fear he would know precisely how to damage her most if the time for that should come, and Quang Linh would be in even greater danger.

The nightmares invaded her sleep regularly now. She was always down in the airless tunnels of Cu Chi, the cramped warrens only a metre wide and a metre high, packed together with her comrades underground for week after week, sweating, gasping, sure that every rasping breath could be heard by the American GIs tramping through the jungle just a few feet above her head. They were pumping the acetylene and CS gases into the tunnel, driving the rats and fire ants and scorpions towards her in the blind darkness, and she wanted to scream. And the silent dream, where everything happened in slow motion: the big black American GI struggling to wriggle up onto the second level of the narrow tunnel, his shoulders jammed in the narrow trapdoor, his arms pinned behind him, his eyes wide with terror, his scream ricocheting through the underground caverns as she moved towards him to cut his throat; the smell of black American blood pumping into the dark earth. And then the B52 bombers growling above the jungle like wild animals, wave after wave of them, explosions gouging craters in the earth and burying the bravest of the brave and tearing the jungle apart and one night killing Tran Xuan Kai like a mosquito. They had never found the pieces. She had never said goodbye. One night she woke screaming from her nightmare as they stuck the black American GI's head on a sharpened bamboo *punji* stake and raised it as a warning beside the jungle trail.

Each night Chu tried to camouflage the stench of the GI's blood by dabbing on her pillow a little of the perfume she wore when she was afraid, and each day she tinted her bloodless lips with a little lipstick and tried to swamp her fears with work. She toiled ceaselessly on her book, using the Internet to roam the university libraries of the world and downloading megabytes of information to support her thesis that the year 2000 would mark a significant shift of global power and influence from West to East.

'In the year 999,' she wrote, 'there were those who feared that the year 1000 would mark the end of the world. Europe was hysterical with terror. On the last night of 999 hundreds of thousands sat up until dawn, too frightened to sleep, convinced that this was their last night on Earth. The city of Byzantium was abandoned by its entire population, who were sure that it would be destroyed in the year 1000 by fire and brimstone from the sky, and in France thousands of terrified peasants rampaged through the countryside burning crops as a frightened sacrifice. In Anglo-Saxon Britain there were many who prayed in their grief and terror that the prophecy might be true and that they might be relieved of the brutality, horrors and torments of their miserable lives at last.'

But it was there on the Internet too that she learned much more about the conflicts in the South China Sea than was ever allowed to appear in the Vietnamese media. It was on the Internet that she learned that to the south of the Spratly Islands naval vessels from China, Vietnam and the Philippines were sailing towards Commodore Reef and North Viper Shoal off the north-west tip of Sabah. How could this be? The Internet was set up for military reasons in 1969 by the American Pentagon, the very monster that had devastated Vietnam throughout the 1960s, yet now it was the only way of learning the truth and it was the State that she had worshipped that now was telling the lies.

There were other questions, too, that troubled her. Through all the days and nights that she worked on her book a fat shadow of doubt sat at the back of her mind like the government spy at the back of the lecture hall.

If the third millennium will indeed turn out to be the Pacific millennium, she thought, how is it that so many Pacific nations are now in an arms race against each other? How is it that China and Vietnam, the only two south-east Asian nations with nuclear weapons, can even think of threatening each other with them because of a few specks of uninhabited rock in the empty spaces of the South China Sea?

Whenever Chu looked up at the back of the auditorium there he was high up on the topmost tier. The informer gazed down at her like a god, as though somehow he knew of her secret treason and her loss of faith.

She once thought she saw a smile twitch at his lips but she had to be mistaken. The government spy never smiled.

Bill Warren came on-line from Santa Barbara just before midnight. He had become used to Marlowe's nocturnal hours and never called him now until well after sunset. He had nicknamed Marlowe 'Vampire' because he stirred only after dark.

<Any reply yet from Monte Carlo?> Warren asked.

Marlowe swallowed the last of the cookies and licked the crumbs from his lips and fingers. They must be making cookies smaller, he thought: a pack nowadays lasted no time at all. Sometimes he needed a whole pack between meals. He ought to complain to the fair trading authorities. Manufacturers tried to get away with all sorts of disgraceful scams.

He wiped the crumbs off on his sleeve, pulled the keyboard towards him and spread his legs, letting his paunch sag onto his thighs. The soft warmth of his stomach was comforting.

<shes in finland> he tapped <i pickd up her flite bookin bermuda/london/helsinki yday>

<What's the bitch doing now in Finland, for chrissake?>

<checkin out sum new cruse liner their>

<Jeez, the woman's never in her office. You put the frighteners on her?>

<:-) sure did ill send u the hole message i put in her e-mail in monte carlo>

Marlowe split Chandler's screen, retrieved the relevant message and zapped it downline to Warren's computer in Santa Barbara.

<president@whitehouse.gov.us//stella barret editor celebrity magazine monte carlo> said the message <security services report blackmail attempt imminent re sexual behaviour with afro minors. approach to celebrity owner dirk molloy imminent. suggest defensive program necessary. a wellwisher>

<Hey, she'll never believe that> protested Warren <From the President's Office? In Washington?>

Marlowe chuckled. <:-) shell hav to cos it did cum from the oval offis>

<?>

<i broke into the wite house computer + sent the message to her rite from the presidens desk>

<You broke into the White House computer?>

<yea>

<You sent her a message actually from the Oval Office?>

<sure its ezy wen u no how>

<My God, Vampire, won't they find out who did it?>

<no chans i wipd all my fingerprince off it>

<Jeez, Vampire, you'll have the entire CIA and FBI after you>

<nah theyll never trak it bak 2 me>

<you sure?>

<a minit after checkin out of the wite house computer i hackd bak into it agen to chek + there woz no trase of my 1st hack>

<Brilliant>

<thanx>

<That's real neat. You're a genius, Vampire>

<yea einstyne used 2 say so 2>

The cursor flickered white on the screen, blinking with cool appreciation.

<a coupla years ago i sent a message from the kremlin to bayjing> said Marlowe <in russian> The screen flickered. <that 1 nerely startd a war>

<Shit!>

<thats wot they sed in chineze>

<They'll catch up with you one day, for sure>

<no way>

<One more thing, Vampire. That list of famous people in the Celebrity computer in Monte Carlo. You say you can change any of the names and addresses on it without them knowing?>

<sure>

<And no one will ever find out?>

<no way its a neat little virus i developd myself its invizible + untrasible>

<In that case let's do it. A lot of celebrities have namesakes somewhere in the world. There are dozens of people somewhere called Michael Jackson or Julia Roberts or Hugh Grant or Liz Taylor. I once started making a list of their names and addresses for the magazine>

<im gettin yore drif>

<So we invite the namesakes>

<insted>

<to the big Celebrity Ball>

<insted of the reel celebs :-) yore a genius 2 mr warren sir holy cow id jus luv 2 b there 2 c there fases wen the rong guys turn up 4 the party all cumplete dorks + nonos>

The screen flickered.

<Well, you could be there too, couldn't you, Vampire?>

Chandler squatted on the workstation and hummed happily to himself. The cursor winked at Marlowe. Then it stuttered again across the screen, spraying white letters across the blue.

<We'll just invite ourselves to the Ball> said Warren.

The Editor came down the first class steps off the morning Finnair flight from Helsinki as cool as always, her silver sunglasses deflecting the real world, and slipped through the echoing caverns of Nice airport, past the scrum at the baggage carousels and headed towards the palms beside the glass doors. Trailing behind her was a skinny porter as mournful and straggly as his moustache.

The driver was waiting for her by the sliding doors. He touched the peak of his cap. '*Bonjour, madame,*' he said. 'I am Henri Chevalier, your new chauffeur.'

'Not until I say so, you're not,' she said. Her sunglasses were dismissive. 'Now step on it. We haven't got all day.'

He drove fast towards the A8 *péage* autoroute and the Mercedes sang as high as a blackbird above Nice's industrial suburbs on the three-lane northern flyover into the foothills of the Alps and towards the tunnels and the viaducts and Monte Carlo. Already she was on the telephone.

'Kelly?'

'Brilliant,' said Kelly. ''Tis indeed myself, so it is, and much better thank you for asking despite some cuts and bruises.'

'About bloody time, too, Kelly. Anyone would think you were dying. Have they charged the chauffeur yet? Wotsisname?'

'Legrandu.'

'Whatever. What's he been charged with?'

'Nothing yet. They're like still interrogating him.'

'Beating him up, I hope. He should be charged with attempted murder.'

'It seems they are having trouble accumulating evidence, interviewing witnesses, getting forensic details, blah-blah-blah.'

'We'll soon see about that. Now look here, Kelly, that TV chat show you booked me onto in Bermuda. Every one of the other guests was a nobody. Every one! I distinctly remember telling you to ensure that I appear in future only with other celebrities.'

'I was like in hospital, Stella.'

'Get a life, Kelly. They have telephones.'

'I was semi-conscious.'

'You're always semi-conscious.'

'I was suffering badly from shock and that.'

'So was I, Kelly. Deep shock. Two of the other TV guests were complete morons and the interviewer had never heard of *Celebrity* or even of me! Is that how you think you should brief an interviewer? It was utterly humiliating. I'm docking a week's pay from your salary next month.'

'But Stella –'

'A week's pay, and if you ever allow me to be humiliated like that again you'll be out without even the bus fare home to Tipperary.'

'That's not –'

'Stop whining. Have you had the invitations for the fancy dress ball reprinted yet?'

'I have so.'

'Stop sulking, Kelly. I want the invitations on my desk in half an hour together with the final list of three thousand guests. You will send out all three thousand invites in the next twenty-four hours.'

'I thought we were inviting like two thousand.'

'I don't pay you to think, Kelly. If I'd wanted a thinker I'd have hired a chimpanzee. I pay you to do exactly what you're told. How the hell do you think we can be certain of getting two thousand guests there on the night unless we invite three thousand? Idiot.'

'But what if they all accept?'

'Then we dump the ones we don't really want.'

'Just like dump them?'

'Of course.'

'Just like that?'

'I said yes, Kelly. Now stop jabbering and put Campbell on.'

Kelly jabbed the intercom button for Campbell's extension. There'll be more than just three thousand invitations on your desk when you get in, you ugly old cow, he thought. There'll also be a printout of a message from the American President warning you that someone is about to tell Dirk Molloy that you're a child molester. Dirk Molloy, famous Christian and family man. Dirk Molloy, the invisible proprietor, the Holy Ghost. If any of us is going to be sacked, sweetheart, it's you.

Kelly tried to imagine The Editor being sacked. It would be better than sex.

'Campbell.'

'It's her. Line three. And she's rampaging.'

'God.'

'No, she only thinks she is.'

'I could have been the editor of the *Auchtermuchtie Gazette*, you know, laddie,' said Campbell.

'You will be,' said Kelly. 'Sooner than you think. I'll put her through.'

At first Kelly had assumed that the message from the White House must be a hoax, that some joker in the office, Murdoch perhaps, was messing about with the system. But the only two likely hoaxers in the office seemed just as surprised by the message and swore they knew nothing about it. 'Strewth!' said Murdoch. 'So that's how the old bag gets her jollies: jumping on jailbait.'

'Never,' said Ferré. 'It is absurd. This is not a woman who would waste her time with boys. There are plenty of men who would pleasure her. She is *très* sexy in a disgusting sort of way.'

'Only to a particularly disgusting sort of Frenchman,' said Murdoch. 'You bloody Frogs would stick it in anything, wouldn't you? Strewth, no Oz would look at her twice.'

'This is because all Australians are homosexual. This is a well-known fact.'

'And all Frogs shag their sisters, sport. Another well-known fact. Have you checked with the White House, Paddy?'

Kelly had telephoned Washington, where a junior White House secretary had checked her records. 'Affirmative, sir,' she said. 'The electronic communication you specify was of a genuine nature.'

'You mean it was real? Like the President really sent it?'

'I am empowered under the Freedom of Information regulations to respond by voice affirmatively to your interrogation, sir.'

'Come again?'

'Due to considerations of national security sir I am not authorised to voice the exact text of the communication itself nevertheless I am empowered to respond in the affirmative to the effect that the electronic mail communication which you specify was despatched to the electronic mailbox of your editor stella barret editor celebrity magazine monte carlo this morning zero-nine-hundred-twenty-three-hours-forty-two-seconds eastern standard time. Sir.'

'Jaysus.'

'Bless you, sir.'

'Thank you.'

'You're welcome.'

'Thank you.'

'You're welcome.'

'Thanks.'

'You're welcome, sir.'

Holy Mother! Kelly thought. So the message was genuine. From the President of the USA. To The Editor. Her and little boys. Is that why she hates men? Oh boy! Wow!

★★★

He delivered Campbell to her, pressing the intercom button like a crematorium priest consigning a corpse to the flames.

'Campbell?'

'Stella –'

'I want the whole staff in the conference room. *Now!*'

'Something wrong?'

'You bet there is. Those last two features you faxed me yesterday are absolute crap. I want two substitutes, fast. I'll be with you in twenty minutes.'

'But we go to press today.'

'And you go to the knacker's yard tomorrow, Campbell, unless you come up this minute with two bloody good feature ideas to replace those two bummers. *Capeesh?*'

She killed the connection.

It was silent in the back of the Mercedes high above Cap d'Ail except for the whisper of the air-conditioning and the thoroughbred hum of the engine. As they came down into Monaco she gazed out of the window down the steep hillside towards the distant sea. Her sunglasses reflected silver slivers of sunlight off the water. In the distance a tiny ferry was escaping towards Corsica. The new chauffeur glanced at her in the mirror. He was glad she was not his wife. His wife was a proper woman.

Campbell stared at the silent telephone. He pressed the button on the intercom. 'Get Nat Wakonde in Wales,' he said, 'and get him fast.'

In North Wales the New Age travellers were dismantling their tents, rolling up the canvas and bedrolls and loading their few possessions into the caravans and the back of a battered old grey truck. Two women and three children were dancing on the dying fire, trampling it to death, encouraged by three excited dogs. The black mongrel Merlin pranced about, barking mad. Where the tents had been pitched they left a tidemark of litter: scraps of paper and polythene packaging, sweet wrappers, ripped fragments of cardboard, pages torn from magazines, crumpled cigarette packets, flattened reefer butts. Near the five-bar gate a used condom hung pale and exhausted from a twig in the hedge, twitching in the breeze like an airfield windsock. A bearded young man was chasing a chicken across the field, cursing as his open leather sandals slithered in the mud. The bird flapped and squawked, lurching clumsily through the muck, rolling drunkenly from side to side – like living *coq au vin*, thought Nat Wakonde. In the next field half a dozen sheep pressed their noses up against the fence and gaped at the spectacle, chewing. After a lumbering thirty-yard chase the man caught the fowl and grasped its head. The chicken squawked a final hopeless prayer before the man swore and snapped its neck.

'Scum,' said Charlie Potter, snapping the execution from the safety of the lane beyond the five-bar gate. He lowered his camera and rested it on the roof of the red hire-car. 'Bloody savages. Christ, I hate this place. I knew I should never have come. I hate the country. Fucking views! When this sodding job is finished I am never moving more than a mile out of London ever again.'

Nat leaned over the five-bar gate and sighed. 'Oh God,' he said, 'isn't she beautiful?'

In the middle of the field Helga Gröning tripped down the steps from the blue caravan with the golden unicorns and sunflowers painted on the side, pursued by the pounding rhythms of the exuberant old Paul Simon song, 'Loves Me Like a Rock'. She skipped across the field towards the site of the smallest tent and the squat, dark-skinned young woman with the hairy armpits and the little fat baby and the big fat breasts.

'Come, Rachel,' she called. 'We are lifting now, *ja*?'

'Fucking crusties!' said Potter.

Helga hitched up her long skirt and tucked it into the top of her knickers.

Nat gazed at her legs. 'Oh, man,' he said. 'Oh God.'

Her short, spiky, blonde hair looked like a pale hedgehog in the watery sunlight. He adored every golden tuft of it. He loved the way she stooped to help the other girl to lift her broken-down old sofa towards the van, the way her breasts swung forward and trembled under the thin tunic, the way she tossed her head and swung her hips as they turned to carry the sofa together.

She glanced in his direction. Oh God but she was gorgeous. He wanted so much to kiss the tiny silver ring in her eyebrow. He wanted to taste her nipples. He guessed they too would taste of silver.

She faced him with her hands on her hips. 'Fock off you churnalist,' she shouted across the field. 'You tell the police of us, you fock off.'

'No, no! You've got it all wrong.'

'*Raus! Raus!*'

'Let's go, squire, for God's sake,' said Potter. 'I've got dozens of pics to develop and she's never going to agree to an interview.'

'Just one more try,' said Nat. He raised his voice. 'Miss Gröning! Miss Gröning!'

She tossed her head, slipped her hand through her stocky friend's arm and walked with her towards her own caravan.

'*Fraulein* Gröning! Just a couple of words. Please!'

The two women walked on away from him, towards the caravan.

'I have a suggestion!' shouted Nat. 'I can help you all! I want to help!'

They walked on, ignoring him. The dog Merlin, excited by Nat's voice, glanced at the gate, remembered of old the taste of his fingers, and bounded barking towards him.

'That's it,' said Potter. 'Here comes that bloody wolfhound again. I'm getting out of it.'

'Please, Miss Gröning! I swear I didn't report you to the police. I had nothing to do with it. I promise. We can help you. Please!'

'Bloody countryside!' said Potter. 'All this green. It's not natural.'

'*Fraulein!* Please! I can help you fight the police order! Please!'

She had reached the steps of her caravan. Paul Simon was now belting out 'Keep The Customer Satisfied'. She turned. Even at this distance he could see the distaste on her face.

'*Raus, raus!*' she shouted across the field. 'Fock off, you churnalist!'

The dog reached the gate and leaped at Nat, barking hysterically, baring its long yellow teeth and launching itself with a clattering thud against the timbers. Potter scuttled into the car, slammed the door and locked it.

'Miss Gröning! Miss Gröning!'

She ducked into the caravan door and disappeared from view. At the gate the dog barked furiously, glaring at Wakonde. It snarled, curling its lips and rolling them back across its teeth. It jumped and bounced from one spot to another like a demented go-go dancer, backwards and forwards, never taking its eyes off him. Its eyes were yellow.

Arthur Lancelot appeared at the top of the caravan steps wearing breeches and a cloak.

'Why don't you knicker-sniffers just sod off?' he yelled across the field. 'Go on, bugger off!'

'I have an idea,' called Nat. 'We can help you. I promise. Trust me.'

'Get stuffed!'

'It wasn't us who shopped you to the fuzz.'

'Sod off!'

'I swear it.'

'Of course it bloody was.'

'No it wasn't. I swear it.'

'I don't believe you.'

'On my mother's grave.'

'Oh yeah.'

'On my word of honour. Cross my heart. We had nothing to do with it.'

'Pull the other one.'

'I swear. On my oath. I'll find out who did. I'll expose them in the article.'

'What article?'

'I've got to write one. Something, anyway. Even if she won't talk to me.'

'You'll make it all up, you mean. Immoral bastards! You must think we were all born yesterday.'

'I'll give you a veto over what I write. God's truth.'

Lancelot hesitated. 'A veto?' he said suspiciously.

'Honest. She can censor every word. If there's anything she disapproves of, it comes out.'

Lancelot hesitated again.

'Anything at all. You can both dictate completely what appears and what doesn't.'

Lancelot came slowly down the steps of the caravan and towards the gate. The dog went crazy, barking, whining, bouncing from one foot to another.

'You'll let me vet it?'

'You'd be better off vetting the bloody dog,' shouted Potter nervously from the car.

'Every word,' said Nat.

'You'll put the boot into the pigs?'

'I promise. They shouldn't treat you like this. I know what fascists look like. We had them in South Africa.'

Lancelot reached the gate. Merlin's barking had become manic. He kicked its rump. The dog whimpered. 'For pity's sake, Merlin,' he said. 'Shut up, you crazy beast.'

'You could even ignore the police order and refuse to move from here,' suggested Nat. 'Sit tight, stage a passive demonstration and I'll report that you're being unlawfully harrassed by the police. I could probably persuade my magazine to pay for a lawyer. It could be a great story all over the world: ANTI-NAZI HEIRESS BULLIED BY FASCISTS.'

Lancelot scratched his scrawny beard. He licked his lips. His tongue was startlingly red. 'Why should we trust you?'

'You have to,' said Potter from the car. 'He's black, see. He's kosher.'

'I never break my word,' said Nat. 'Never.'

Lancelot shook his head. 'I don't know.'

'You another sodding racist?' said Potter. 'Shit, this country's full of them. Bloody Welsh!'

'Shut up, Charlie, for God's sake,' said Nat.

Lancelot rubbed the side of his nose. 'She really hates you guys, you know. The Press.'

'I can understand that. I'll put that in the piece too, if she wants. We can nail all the lies, one by one. Tell her I'm on your side.'

Lancelot looked amused. 'You really fancy her, don't you?' he said.

Nat stared at him.

Lancelot chuckled. 'You'll never take her off me, you know. You haven't a hope.' He turned and started to walk back to the caravan. 'I'll see what I can do,' he said. 'Stay there, Merlin. Stay! Sit! Sit!'

He tramped away across the field and up the caravan steps. The caravan door closed behind him.

For several minutes there was no sound. Even Paul Simon was silent. The dog settled on its haunches, a faint memory of anger grumbling deep at the back of its throat. After a couple of minutes Nat could hear voices raised but muffled. The words were indistinct except for a sudden cry of '*Nein nein nein!*'

Emergency: 999, he thought. It's an emergency, all right: if she doesn't agree to an interview soon then I'm out of a job. And he meant every word he had said. Why should people like this be treated like lepers just because they lived in tents and caravans? And why should someone like Helga be harried by the Press just because her father was famous? At times Nat was deeply ashamed of his own profession. Profession? Journalism? It was hardly even a craft.

The dog laid its head between its paws and eyed him, its

growl still rumbling ominously like a distant aircraft.

Helga's muffled voice was suddenly raised and shrill with fury. 'You are promising! You are always breaking you promising!'

The dog jumped up and started barking again.

'What are dogs actually for?' asked Potter through the car window. 'You can't even eat the buggers.'

Nat could hear the lower voice of the other woman inside the caravan. She spoke for a minute and Lancelot spoke again. After a while there was complete silence for some time, then a further drone of more muted conversation. The sun shone weakly through the branches. The worst of the rain clouds scudded east. Potter switched the car radio on and was assaulted by a torrent of Welsh.

'Bloody Taffs! Why don't the buggers speak English?'

He flicked along the waveband and eventually settled on some commercial channel. Rap music pounded across the quiet valley. 'There's tuneful, isn't it?' said Potter.

Eventually the door of the caravan opened. Lancelot stood at the top of the steps.

'She'll do it,' he shouted. 'Here, boy!'

'Christ, I wish he wouldn't call you "boy",' said Potter.

'I think he's talking to the dog,' said Nat.

'Here, Merlin. Heel!'

The dog turned, yelped and bounded away towards the caravan.

'But not the photographer,' called Lancelot. 'She won't let the snapper anywhere near her.'

'Charming,' said Potter. 'Fucking Kraut! Who won the bloody war, anyway?'

'The Germans,' said Nat, 'and the Japs.'

His throat was dry, his hands clammy. In a minute he would be looking into her eyes, maybe shaking her hand, touching her fingers. He had never in his life felt so vulnerable.

'Fucking *hausfrau*!' said Potter.

***

Nat walked in a daze towards the caravan. The dark, stocky woman emerged from it and stopped him when he reached the bottom step.

'Rachel Goldstein,' she said.

'Hi. Nat Wakonde.'

She looked at him intently. 'You've got me to thank for persuading her.'

'Thanks.'

'I didn't do it for you. Don't kid yourself. I think your article could help us, and so does Arthur. But I want to say one thing. Helga is the kindest, sweetest person I've ever met. My baby and me owe everything to her. She's incredibly generous to all of us and gives nearly all her money away and she never thinks of herself. She really does believe that she can help to make the world a better place. So if you do the dirty on her I swear to God I'll get revenge.'

'I promise,' he said. 'She's lucky to have such a good friend.'

Rachel stared at him. 'Don't give me all that smooth bullshit,' she said. 'I know you bloody journalists. I mean it. If you stitch her up or let her down at all, in even the smallest way, I'll go to the police and tell them you tried to rape me – and you can probably guess what happens to black men accused of rape in Wales.'

The *gendarmes* released Ugo Legrandu soon after dawn, turning him out onto the empty Ajaccio street as though he were a common vagrant from Algiers. His left eye was red and swollen and the ribs on his right side throbbed where the *cochon* from Calvi had kicked him, the one who smelled of stale sweat. They had been able to find no evidence against him.

It was a cool, grey morning. He walked down from the *Gendarmerie* and the Palais de Justice towards the Boulevard Masséria and the Cours Napoléon and on to the Place du Maréchal Foch. On his left the docks were still, the ships and cranes silent on the quayside, but on the Boulevard Roi Jérome a water wagon rumbled slowly by, spraying the road and gutters. A couple of waiters were sweeping the pavements in front of their cafés and setting out tables and chairs. He caught a whiff of warm croissants.

'We know it was you who sent that parcel bomb,' Lanzi, the *gendarme* from Calvi, had said. 'One day we will prove it.' His sour expression suggested that he too could smell his own stale sweat. 'Once you're in our computer, Legrandu, you are imprisoned in it for life.'

'And you, *flic*, are filed up here,' said Legrandu, tapping his forefinger against his temple. 'And I never forget.'

That was when they had knocked him down and kicked his ribs.

On the Place du Maréchal Foch he found a *tabac* and bought some Gauloise cigarettes and a copy of *Corse-Matin*. He reached into his pocket.

They were not there.

Cochons! The French swines had stolen his thin black leather driving gloves.

He wandered around the square to the corner of Avenue Sérafini, settled himself at a table inside *Le Petit Caporal* and ordered a croissant and coffee.

'You are free then,' said the waiter.

'*Weh*. Corsica too one day will be free.'

'Please God.'

Legrandu made the secret sign, the ancient sign, the one the French feared so much.

The waiter crossed himself.

When he brought Legrandu's order he said: 'The coffee and croissant are also free. There is no charge.'

'Thank you. I shall remember.'

Inside the café another proud I Muvrini song was playing in his honour, '*A Tè Corsica*', the spine-tingling anthem of mountain, forest and granite:

> *Ghje per à pena di campà*
> *Ch'elli si mettenu in penseri*

Ch'elli si mettenu à marchjà
Mezu à le brame è l'addisperi.

He would not return quite yet to his wife and children in Sartène. He had unfinished business to do on the mainland first. Every night since his arrest he had been tormented in the *Gendarmerie* by visions of The Editor, La Barrett. His head had been filled with soft memories of her green eyes, her white thighs whispering together in the back of the Mercedes. She had invaded his dreams and he was beginning to find it difficult to think of anything else. Her body had begun to obsess him and he knew from old experience that there was only one way he could quench the obsession. Some women so filled your mind and body with lust that there was only one cure. He must have her. Nothing else would do. And it should not be difficult. She had made it plain in so many ways how she too felt about him, and she had made it plain that she did not want to be wooed. She did not want flowers, nor flattery, nor smiles, nor kissed fingers. Like most women, she wanted to be conquered. She wanted to be tamed and mastered. Like Don Juan he understood women only too well. Had the real Don Juan not been born Corsican too, born in Seville of Corsican parents? Don Juan would never have been discouraged by a little feminine shyness.

Legrandu smiled. He would take her roughly, the Corsican way. The I Muvrini song seemed to spur him on:

Corsica.
Corsica.
Gloria à tè.

He flipped through the newspaper, sipped his coffee and finished his croissant. Then he strolled across the square towards the docks and caught the ferry for Nice.

Kommandant-Generaal Bezuidenhout arrived at the van der Merwe farm near Nelspruit soon after dawn, jolting down the stony track from the main White River road in his open Japanese jeep with six of his Volksleger troopers bouncing about in the back. Dew shimmered on the grass and the sky blazed white with promise to the east beyond the bluegums and cedrillas.

Van der Merwe was waiting for them on the *stoep*, sitting in Hephzibah's old rocking chair and reading the old family Bible as he did every morning to prepare himself for whatever the Lord might choose for him that day. He was reading the Book of Revelation, Chapter 20, verses 4–5: '… and I saw the souls of them that were beheaded for the witness of Jesus, and for the word of God, and which had not worshipped the beast … and they lived and reigned with Christ a thousand years. But the rest of the dead lived not again until the thousand years were finished. This is the first resurrection.'

Ja, ja! thought van der Merwe: the first resurrection of the Boers. And then the second coming of the Afrikaans Republiek. And that too would last for a thousand years.

Bezuidenhout kept proper hours, he thought approvingly, good Boer hours, no lounging around soft in bed until the sun was high like the Brits at White River. And his troopers were all fine, fit young men, upstanding young Afrikaaners, bush-bronzed, with solid necks. Their eyes were as clear as mountain streams, unclouded by alcohol or self-abuse, their clean fair hair cropped short, all trim and tidy, their long khaki socks pulled high and tight to their knees, their thighs muscled. They wore plain clothes and were dressed in shorts, bush jackets, open-necked sports shirts and bush hats as though they were just a cheery holiday party of tourists out for a day's game-spotting in the Kruger Game Reserve. They would never wear their uniforms in public: if they did that, the black police would be swarming all over them quicker than monkeys scampering up a marula tree.

'*Welkom!*' said van der Merwe as the jeep skidded to a halt in a cloud of dust. He rose to greet them. The pain stabbed at his gut like a needle of fire. He winced. He would never show weakness. He had to see this through. '*Ontbyt?*'

'No, thank you, Hendrik,' said Bezuidenhout, climbing out of the jeep. 'We have eaten already.'

'*Koffie?*'

'Sure, *ja*, that would be good.'

Van der Merwe raised his voice. 'Moses!' he cried. 'Wakonde!'

The kaffir came running. '*Ja, baas?*'

'*Koffie vir sewe.*'

'*Ja, baas.*'

'*En maak gou!*'

'*Ja, baas.*'

The troopers jumped out of the back of the jeep and stood in a line at attention just beyond the rail that ran around the *stoep*.

'*Op die plek rus!*' snapped Bezuidenhout, standing them at ease and climbing the steps onto the *stoep*.

Well trained, thought van der Merwe with sudden pride. What a pleasure. When it comes to killing the enemies of the Boer people these clear, young eyes will flinch at nothing, the golden, languid eyes of lions, tranquil without remorse or pity. President Kruger would have been proud of them.

Bezuidenhout sat in the chair beside van der Merwe, bringing with him a sudden whiff of toilet water and another sudden memory of those bastard van der Merwe jokes:

'*So why don't women go for me?*' says van der Merwe.

'*You need to spruce yourself up, man,*' says Viljoen. '*Get a haircut, clean shirt, deodorant. Try dabbing a bit of toilet water behind your ears.*'

'*Ah, shit, man,*' says van der Merwe. '*I can never get the hang of that toilet water stuff. Every time I put my head in the toilet the lid falls on my neck.*'

Brit swine!

The woman Miriam served coffee on the *stoep*. 'Nice arse,' said Bezuidenhout. 'What a pleasure!'

He picked his nose, then pulled out from a pocket a large-scale map of the southern Kruger Park around the Malelane Gate and the Krokodil River.

'We'll just do a recce this morning,' he said. 'See how the

land lies. Get our bearings. If we find the spot where they buried the gold then we go in tonight with metal detectors. But it could take weeks. A lot can change in the bush in a hundred years.'

He pulled from the inside pocket of his jacket a photostat of the original handwritten diary that had been sent to the Oud Baas and read it out aloud: 'The gold is buried five paces from the marula tree, seven paces from the strange-shaped rock at the foot of the mountain and ten paces from the furthest western edge of the *donga* beside the dry river bed, where these measurements intersect.' Bezuidenhout frowned. 'How long does a marula tree survive?'

Van der Merwe shrugged. 'Ach, man, I don't suppose it's still there,' he said. 'Even if it hasn't died in one of the droughts it could have been trampled by elephant. They love the fruit: it makes them drunk.'

'What about the strange-shaped rock?'

'It could be anything.'

Bezuidenhout nodded. '*Ja*, man,' he said, 'you're right. But at least there's only one mountain that Kruger could have reached on donkeyback at night and still be back on the train within two hours. There's only one mountain just two or three kilometres inside the Malelane Gate: Tlhalabye.'

'*Ja*, right. On the road to Berg-en-Dal. Near the Matjulu River.'

'The dry river bed.'

'Maybe.'

'Near the Krokodil River too.'

'Sure.'

'And it must be at the foot of the southern part of the mountain, the part nearest to the Malelane Gate. They wouldn't have had time to ride right round to the back of the mountain.'

Van der Merwe felt a sudden warm optimism. They were going to find it. He was sure of it. They were going to find Kruger's buried gold! And then they would take their revenge on the kaffirs and Brits and the rest of the world.

'What are we waiting for?' he said. 'Let's go.'

Bezuidenhout stood. The troopers snapped to attention and stood rigid as he descended the steps from the *stoep* and passed them, heading for the jeep.

What a pleasure.

'Come with me in the front, Hendrik,' said Bezuidenhout.

When the Boers took their revenge on the rest of the world it would be like an earthquake, thought van der Merwe with pride. Last night before bed he had read Chapter 8 of the Book of Revelation again: 'There were voices, and thunderings, and lightnings, and an earthquake ... and there followed hail and fire mingled with blood ... and as it were a great mountain burning with fire was cast into the sea ... and there fell a great star from heaven, burning as it were a lamp ... And the name of the star is called Wormwood ... And I beheld, and heard an angel flying through the midst of heaven, saying with a loud voice, Woe, woe, woe, to the inhabiters of the earth ...'

CHAPTER 7

And millions of miles away in the icy blackness of outer space the vast five-mile-wide shadow of an unknown, unseen, unnamed comet swung a hundred thousand silent miles around the ghostly grey mass of a giant dead star and curved again in a lazy parabola back on a slightly different orbit, back towards the galaxy of old, back the way it had passed so many times before, across millennia.

At 83,241 miles per hour the huge white comet swung with grace around the furthest circuit of its endless quest between the stars and headed back across the universe, back towards the solar system, back towards the beautiful, shining, blue-green planet that it always passed once in a thousand years.

PART
TWO

CHAPTER 8

'Ah Jesus Mary and Joseph,' said Kelly. 'She's back.'

The Editor emerged swiftly from the lift with lips as thin as promises. A chill surrounded her. She seemed to have brought with her a gust of northern winter from Helsinki.

Dear God, thought Kelly, just wait 'til she sees the message from the White House! She'll go ballistic!

'Welcome back, Stella,' said Kelly, 'to be sure.'

'Get them all into the conference room,' she snapped. 'Now!'

'They're like there already, Stella,' said Kelly, 'all waiting for you, raring to go.'

She swirled past him and into her office like a small storm. For a moment Kelly despised himself. How can such a tiny woman make me feel so inadequate? he thought. She's little more than a slip of a girl. Even her chest is as flat as a boy's. Then he shrugged. I'm not the only one, he thought: she frightens everyone else as well, even her boss, even Dirk Molloy, the Holy Ghost, the born-again Christian. They even say she's had an affair with him. Is that how she got the job in the first place? Has she blackmailed him? She frightens everyone except Murdoch.

She disappeared into her office and slammed the door behind her. The light for her telephone extension flickered on the console on Kelly's desk. She seemed to be making several calls.

The staff waited for her nervously in the conference room. Campbell studied some papers and fiddled with his biro. He sniffed. Cigarette smoke.

He waved frantically across the table at Caroline Ponsonby.

'The air freshener!' he hissed. 'Quick! Smoke!'

Caroline left her seat, searched through the filing cabinet in the corner and found the canister. She sprayed the air wildly. A heavy stench of sweetness filled the room.

'Holy Moses, lassie, that's far too much. She'll know for sure now.'

They sat and waited.

'Here,' said Murdoch. 'Ever heard the one about the woman who went to the gynaecologist and said "doctor, doctor, there's something wrong with me aviaries"?'

'Not now, Tony,' said Campbell. 'Not now, for God's sake.'

The Editor entered the room with a face like a gargoyle. Kelly hovered nervously.

She frowned. 'Who's been smoking in here?' she said.

'No one, Stella,' said Campbell. 'Of course not. Welcome back.'

'I can smell smoke. Distinctly.'

'It's probably scorched earth,' said Murdoch. 'The way we've all been working flat out since you've been away. Crackling the air with energy.'

She glared at him. 'Get a life, Murdoch,' she said.

She sat at the head of the table.

'When I find out who it is who smokes when I'm not here he or she will be out of that door so fast their feet won't even touch the ground. *Capeesh?* OK, Campbell. Shoot. The two big ideas we need. Now!'

Campbell rubbed his nose. He looked down at the sheaf of paper in his hands.

'Nat's got an interview with the Gröning girl at last,' he said. 'He's writing it now. He's promised to let us have it this afternoon and he says the snapper got some great pics which are coming this afternoon as well. And it's going to be a cracker of a piece. Helga Gröning's accusing the British police of being fascists. She says they've molested her and manhandled her Jewish girlfriend and her baby. She says they're persecuting them just like her Nazi grandfather persecuted the Jews. She's threatening to take them to court.'

The Editor stared at him.

That's got her, thought Murdoch. That's a bloody good story. Even Stella can't complain about that.

'All right,' she said. 'But tell Wakonde I want to see it within the next half-hour.'

'He said it would take a couple of hours to put together.'

'I said half-an-hour, Campbell. I've got an appointment with the hairdresser. And the other idea?'

Campbell raised his head. He looked her straight in the eye. 'Rogers has just filed from Moscow. His piece about the Albanian hairdresser. It's very funny.'

Two-nil, thought Murdoch. Scotland 2, Hades 0.

'Funny?' she said. 'Who said it should be a funny piece? This isn't *Punch*.'

'It's a very good piece,' said Campbell. 'I think you'll like it. It's on your desk.'

She nodded brusquely. 'Let's hope it's as good as you say. It had better be.' She looked around the table. Her mouth was tight. 'I must say that I'm deeply pissed off with you all. As soon as I'm out of the office nobody does a stroke of work, discipline flies out of the window and everyone goes to pot.'

'Or tobacco,' said Murdoch.

'What?'

'Sorry.'

'What did you say?'

'No worries.'

She glared at him. 'Quite frankly, your ideas for this issue were pathetic,' she said, 'and I'm not putting up with it any longer. If you don't all snap out of it and sharpen up right now I'm going to cut all your wages by ten per cent. *Capeesh?* And if that doesn't work there are going to be some sackings. There's no room for passengers on *Celebrity*.'

'Except on the boat,' said Murdoch.

'What?'

'The *SS Celebrity*,' said Murdoch. 'Passengers.'

She tapped her pen on the table.

How does he get away with it? thought Caroline Ponsonby with admiration. But one day he's going to go too far. One day she's going to snap.

'Do us all a favour, Murdoch,' said The Editor. 'Just shut your gob and keep it shut. Right: Kelly. Have you sent out all the invitations for the ball?'

'I have that.'

'All three thousand?'

'Three thousand and fourteen.'

'And the entertainers? The Beatles? Pavarotti? David Copperfield? Have you approached their agents?'

'I have too, so.'

'And?'

'They're like consulting their clients, checking dates, blah-blah-blah.'

'And the fashion show? The supermodels?'

'Them also.'

'The food? The champagne? Krug?'

'The wheels are all in motion, Stella.'

'For your sake I very much hope that they are, Kelly,' she said grimly. 'Right, all of you: back to work, and I mean work. And remember what I said. It's time you all got a grip of yourselves. If you don't want the work there are plenty of others out there who do.'

She glided out of the room, so small, so fragile, and yet the room seemed almost empty once she had gone. She slammed her office door behind her.

'D'you think she really does fuck underage coons?' enquired Murdoch, his eyes gleaming wide in his big black face.

'Sssh!' said Caroline. 'She'll hear you.'

'I don't give a toss,' said Murdoch. 'If she really does fancy a bit of black todger d'you reckon I'm in with a chance?'

'Too old,' said Kelly.

'Too ugly,' said Caroline.

'OK,' said Kelly. 'I'll buy it. The woman who went to the gynaecologist because of her ovaries.'

'Not ovaries,' said Murdoch. 'Aviaries.'

'Pardon?'

' "Doctor, doctor," she said, "there's something wrong with me aviaries" and he said "You mean your ovaries" and she said "No, doctor, it's me aviaries" and he said "OK, let's have a dekko." So she gets up on the consulting couch and hoists her legs in the air and he gets his little telescope thing out and sticks it up her fanny.'

'I'm going now,' said Caroline.

Murdoch grinned. ' "My God!" said the doctor, peering up her fanny. "Aviaries! You're absolutely right! You've certainly had a cockatoo up here!" '

They drove through Numbi Gate into the Kruger Game Reserve early, as soon as the park opened for visitors – van der Merwe, Bezuidenhout and the six Volksleger troopers bouncing about in the back of the jeep – past the old memorial to Percy Fitzpatrick's bloody dog Jock of the Bushveld, ahead of the usual long queue of tourists' cars and coaches. The roads and tracks inside the park were still deserted, the air clean, the atmosphere one of fresh discovery, but van der Merwe knew only too well that within an hour or so the roads would be jammed with traffic. The last time he had ventured into the park, a few months ago, it had been like the

Jo'burg rush hour. The animals had become so used to all the attention that nowadays they posed for their photographs: the lions as slinky and disdainful as fashion models on the catwalk; the flirty giraffes peering daintily down their noses, winking their Naomi Campbell eyelashes, chewing like Madonna; the elephant gazing at the cameras as stolid as rugby forwards in the team portrait. Only the rhino still played hard to get, skulking out of sight as grumpy as rock stars scowling in the back of darkened limousines.

Van der Merwe spat out of the window of the jeep. Why did these Yanks and Brits and Japs all bother to come all this way to the park if that's what they wanted? Why did anyone come to the Kruger at all, thought van der Merwe, except to rise before dawn to revel in that cool, expectant hush just before the sun comes up, or at twilight to listen to the whisper of the trees in that moment of truth just before the sun suddenly plunges like a scarlet boulder into the western horizon? At dusk these people were probably sprawled in their luxury rondavels gawking at cable television and watching packaged programmes about wildlife.

The air was still chilly as Bezuidenhout drove the jeep along the Napi Road towards Pretorius Kop and past the grave of Willem Pretorius, the pioneer who had died here in 1848. It was not a bad place to die, thought van der Merwe. He tasted the air. Dry earth. Damp pebbles. He would rather die here in the bush, under the Lord's great ceiling, than in some cold white room with needles in his arms. The pain shifted in his stomach, testing the base of his spine. When the time came he would make them carry him out to die in the open air: Zechariah or Reuben or whichever of them it was who came in time at the end.

At Pretorius Kop camp Bezuidenhout turned south onto the old Voortrekker Road towards Afsaal and Malelane. The sun hung just above the branches like a huge gold coin on a Christmas tree: a good omen, thought van der Merwe, please God. There was little conversation. In the back of the jeep the

Volksleger troopers in their colourful, open-necked holiday clothes scanned the bush with their pale, translucent hunters' eyes, one of them gazing through binoculars at a distant shadowy group of elephant. What was there to talk about? All around them the bush itself was alive with gossip and rumour. A queue of zebra crossed the road as tame and tidy as a riding-school outing. A beady-eyed family of three ground hornbills strutted past like disgruntled turkeys. A laidback troop of indolent baboons lounged beside the road, exposing their scarlet buttocks, as insolent as rich nightclubbers mooning the morning after. A startled baby vervet monkey clung wide-eyed, upside-down, to the fur on its mother's stomach like an upended jockey. A whiskery warthog scuttled frowning through the bush in lustful pursuit of its mate like a portly clubman pursuing a bus after a two-bottle lunch.

'*Daarso!*' said Bezuidenhout suddenly, jumping on the brakes and pointing. '*Renoster!*'

He killed the engine and they sat in silence and watched the monstrous grey rhino as it lurked sullen and nervous only a hundred yards away in a shadow behind a clump of umbrella thorn acacia trees. Its small eyes sulked in its massive head, pre-historic and irritable. A small bird perched on its rump and jeered. After five or six minutes the rhino turned its rump towards them, defecated loudly, and then turned again and stamped about in its own hot faeces, doing a hefty war dance, marking territory, warning them off, before lumbering away behind a sycamore fig towards the rising sun, shouldering aside a blasé herd of feeding wildebeest as it went.

'Ach, man,' sighed van der Merwe. 'What a pleasure!'

'Magic,' said Bezuidenhout. 'I could watch them for ever.'

He started the engine and drove on south-west along the Voortrekker Road, where a hundred years ago the transport riders used to canter in from Mozambique. They went on past Ship Mountain and Komapiti and across the dry beds of the Josékhulu and Mitomeni Rivers, and past the arched rib bones of animal skeletons gleaming white under the sun. The road was rough at times and whenever the jeep bounced over a pothole the pain stabbed at van der Merwe's stomach.

'Hendrik?'

'It's nothing.'

'You all right?'

'*Ja. Nie te danke!*'

He was not going to give a hint of his pain. Life was always a matter of pain. Out on the lowveld two impala stags were fighting in a clearing, locking horns, while a group of female impala sauntered over towards them to watch, only mildly curious to know which stag would win the fight and mate with them. Life was always a struggle.

Bezuidenhout turned south at Makhutlwanini, near where Leary was killed by a wounded leopard in 1926. It was astonishing, thought van der Merwe, how few people had been killed or even wounded by lion or leopard in the park in a hundred years. When he himself had been caught unawares and mauled by the lion up at Saxonwold it had been his own damned fault and due to nothing but carelessness. He should never have left the truck without better cover: if you stayed in your vehicle, even if it was an open truck or Land Rover, a lion or leopard would see the silhouette of the vehicle as a closed whole, a familiar outline, and would never attack unless you stepped out or stood up and broke the outline shape. Unless you did that, none of the big cats even dreamt that the vehicle was in fact a tin full of meat. It was rare for animals in the Kruger to attack humans now – except for the hippo, the most dangerous, bad-tempered creature known to man. The hippo has killed more humans than any of the other big beasts.

Just before the turn-off for the Malelane Gate and the Krokodil River, Bezuidenhout stopped the jeep at the side of the road and gestured through the right-hand window. 'There it is,' he said. 'Tlhalabye. Kruger's mountain.'

The hill rose above them just as Kruger's anonymous diarist had described the site of the buried gold in 1900: a rocky granite summit, slopes dotted with seringa, bush willow, jackal berry, date palm, tamboti.

Van der Merwe lit a cigarette and coughed heavily with the first lungful of smoke. He spat a thick gob of black phlegm into the bush.

'They would have come in towards the mountain from over there, from the east,' said Bezuidenhout, gesturing with his chin, 'crossing the Krokodil River where the Malelane gate is now and trekking direct through the bush where the road is now to about here.'

He dug into the breast pocket of his bush jacket, retrieved the photostat of the diary and unfolded it. He held the paper lightly in his fingers, like a holy relic. 'OK,' he said. He called over his shoulder: 'Potgieter! Wessels! Mocke! Van der Westhuizen! All of you! Which of you boys can spot a marula tree? Or a strange-shaped rock, eh? Or a dry river bed?'

Eight pairs of binoculars scanned the foot of Tlhalabye. Van der Merwe swept his glasses up and down the side of the hill as well as around the base: there was rock fig, magic guarri, impala lily, mixed grass but no sign anywhere of a marula tree. A starling swooped past with an irridescent flash of peacock blue and turquoise. A bustard strutted by, self-important with a paunch. In the distance a long-legged, orange-beaked secretary bird stalked past with black leggings as arrogant as any Jo'burg typist. Away from the road, down towards the Krokodil River, a wildebeest grunted at the water's edge and nearby a pretty little blue and yellow lilac-breasted roller sang a warning. They said the song of the lilac-breasted roller once saved Shaka's army from ambush and he made the bird a protected species on pain of death. That was Africa for you, thought van der Merwe: Kruger and Shaka both early conservationists, the one a devout and civilized man of God, the other a brutal kaffir savage. And their empires had both in the end been destroyed by the Brits. The Brits were to blame for everything, the bastards.

So van der Merwe answers the phone and the caller says: 'Mr Smith?'

'No,' says van der Merwe, 'this is van der Merwe.'

'Ach, I'm sorry. Wrong number. Sorry to trouble you.'

'Ach, man, it's OK,' says van der Merwe. 'No trouble. The phone was ringing anyway.'

Brit *basters*! What sort of a joke was that? Of course you answer the phone when it rings, even if it's a wrong number. How are you supposed to know it's a wrong number unless you pick it up?

'Ach, man, there's no marula tree at all,' said van der Merwe. 'Not this side of the hill, anyway. And I can't see any strange-shaped rock. They all look pretty ordinary to me.'

Bezuidenhout drove very slowly south, towards Malelane camp and the northern bank of the Krokodil River, and then slowly west towards Berg-en-Dal. A couple of cars overtook them, the passengers peering too at Tlhalabye to see what they were staring at. They drove slowly back towards the tourist camp at Malelane, their binoculars focussed sharp on the base of Tlhalabye, and then north to the T-junction with the main Skukuza road and across the Matjulu River, turning left and west again on the sandy road towards Matjulu mountain and Berg-en-Dal, round the back of Tlhalabye. Several times an optimistic trooper called attention to a rock or a gully but each time was a false alarm.

'It's too far, anyway, round here,' said Bezuidenhout. 'Kruger could never have ridden this far from the river in half an hour on a donkey. *Vervlaks! Kom*, we need to think about this.'

He drove on along the sandy road past Matjulu and back across the river to the camp at Berg-en-Dal, parking the jeep by the public lookout point above the dam. They climbed out to stretch their legs in the safety of the car park. Van der Merwe lit a cigarette and was overcome by a sudden fit of coughing.

'You OK, Hendrik?' said Bezuidenhout.

He nodded, catching his breath. A sudden pain investigated his spine again, probing it with curiosity. An ache bruised his lungs. He walked with care, determined to pacify the agony.

'You should give those cigarettes up,' said Bezuidenhout.

'They're not doing you any good.'

'It's a bit late for that now,' said van der Merwe. He glanced at one of the young troopers and was suddenly overcome by a sharp pang of misery: he realised to his shame that he was jealous of the young man's youth, his fitness, the strength of his muscles, the clear whites of his eyes, the cleanliness of his life. Van der Merwe was numbed by grief, as though he were mourning himself.

The sun was hot now, enticing the multi-coloured lizards into the open. A pair of yellow hornbills wandered by, pretending to ignore the trippers. In the distance a hippo sat in the river, settled into the mud and coughed. A fish eagle soared high above the dam and a kingfisher darted out of the trees. Grinning crocodiles basked on the warm rocks, giants lying with jaws wide open, their teeth being cleaned by tiny oxpeckers perched inside their huge mouths. Beyond the river a flock of ostrich danced past like a nervous chorus line, glancing over their shoulders. A lion roared beyond the trees, on the horizon.

How can they expect us ever to give all this up? thought van der Merwe fiercely. How can we let them steal all this from our grandchildren? Our angry ancestors would never forgive us.

'They're mating,' said Malan, gazing through his binoculars.

'*Waar?*'

'Lion. *Daar. Op die linkerflank.*'

'The left?'

'*Ja.* Behind the trees.'

'Got it. Shit, he's a big bugger!'

'I don't think he's much of a bugger, Fanie! It looks as if he likes the ladies.'

'*Ja, so moet 'n bek praat!*'

'A lion can do it again and again, you know. Every twenty minutes. For three weeks!'

Mocke shrugged. 'So?' He grinned.

Malan punched his shoulder and laughed. 'Cheeky sod!' he said. '*Tsotsi!*'

'It's the wrong hill,' said Bezuidenhout suddenly. 'Of course! That's it! We're looking in the wrong place.' He reached for the map. 'It's not Tlhalabye at all! It's Khandzalive! Of course! *Dis wat dit is!* It's Khandzalive!'

'But that's even further away, man,' said van der Merwe. 'It must be ten kilometres off to the west, maybe more.'

'But only from *here*,' said Bezuidenhout. 'It's no more than a couple of kilometres from the Krokodil River itself, just like Tlhalabye is. Look at the map. It's no further from the Krokodil River than Tlhalabye is.'

'That's true,' said van der Merwe, 'but how …'

'We've made the mistake of assuming that Kruger crossed the Krokodil River that night where the Malelane Gate is now, but who says he did? The diary says only that they crossed the river at Malelane. Well, this whole southern area is called Malelane, not just the gate and the camp. In those days there wasn't any gate or camp. They could just as well have crossed the river ten kilometres further west. In that case the mountain they came to was Khandzalive, not Tlhalabye. And Khandzalive looks even closer to the railway line than Tlhalabye is.'

Van der Merwe studied the map. He compared distances. He nodded.

'But there's no road marked on the map,' said Bezuidenhout. 'It's way out in the bush. We'll have to do some *bundu*-bashing in the jeep.'

A smile tickled van der Merwe's lips. He shook his head. 'Ach, man, that won't be necessary,' he said. 'There's an old track from Malelane to Khandzalive along the riverbank. I've known this bush ever since I was a kid. My old man used to bring me here almost every weekend.'

Fifty years ago, on the same old track along the riverbank from Malelane to Khandzalive, van der Merwe and his father had spotted a rare King Cheetah playing in the sunshine with her cub in a clearing. They had sat in silence in the car for half an hour, entranced, watching the beautiful, sleek animals playfully biting and cuffing each other, and rolling each other over and over and wrestling in the sun. At times the animals seemed to kiss each other and for half an hour van der Merwe and his father and friends had shared in a moment of magic all but unimaginable nowadays. And a few years later, on the same track, they had come across a rare pack of eight wild dogs with their hunched hyena stoop, Alsatian faces and huge bat-like ears as they loped along the track on long, thin, greyhound legs as though they were running on stilts. Today even the game rangers in the park could go for a year without seeing wild dog.

Later, as a young conscript in the army in the fifties, van der Merwe had borrowed one winter week in June his father's open Land Rover to take three fellow conscripts and a Shangaan tracker on a six-day safari through the Kruger. Not far from here, on the other side of Khandzalive, they had camped illegally out in the open in the wild bush between Maqili and the Nsikazi River far from the eyes and patrols of the Kruger game rangers. On that particular day they had gone *bundu*-bashing in search of leopard, crashing up and down steep hills, jolting across rocks, ruts and ravines, smashing through the scrub, flattening trees. They had left the Land Rover to walk in the sun through the scrub as the Shangaan tracker had pointed out the spoor and droppings of every kind of wild animal. And they had followed a herd of five elephant through towering elephant grass, with van der Merwe reversing the Land Rover towards the elephant in case they needed to make a quick getaway.

That night the Shangaan had smelled out for them a hunting leopard not far from their camp and they had followed the great beast through the black heart of Africa in the open Land Rover, often stopping and sitting silent in the wild dark bushveld as the leopard, just ten or fifteen yards away beyond thickets of buffalo thorn, quietly stalked a herd of impala whose nervous eyes had glittered in the Shangaan's spotlight.

For almost an hour the leopard had stalked the buck through the darkness, watching them, creeping forward, settling, sizing them up, and van der Merwe and his *boeties* had followed the magnificent beast quietly in the Land Rover, crunching the undergrowth, killing the engine, hearing the tense savagery of the African bush at night: the crack of a twig, the squawk of a bird, the restless twitching of unseen, trembling creatures who spend every second of their lives expecting sudden death.

Then the leopard had spotted a big hole in the base of a termite mound, the home of a family of warthog, and had sniffed the promise of tender newborn wartpiglet squealing underground. The great spotted cat had hunkered down in a scrum in front of the hole with rippling rugby shoulders and for twenty more minutes they had watched it watching the hole. By now it was completely ignoring the impala, which had skipped away eventually through the bush, unaware of how close they had come to death that night, to live another hour and flirt one day with some other quiet executioner.

Eventually the leopard had become restless in the dark, glancing often over its hefty Hollywood superstar haunches, unsettled by the sudden arrival of two hunchback hyena that had come jogging out of the dark towards it, jeering threateningly. The big cat had glared at the scavengers, which had loped away, not quite brave enough.

And then the leopard had itself strolled away into the dark, licking its lips, and the show was suddenly over and it had been time to go home. They had careered away through the bush in the Land Rover, exhilarated by their brush with birth and life and death, frozen in the stiff, icy, winter night breeze, bumping across sand and rock and rich red earth, bouncing through streams and gullies and elephant grass with the Shangaan's spotlight high at the back of the Land Rover raking the shadows ahead of them from side to side, picking out glittering eyes in thorn bush and thicket, startling shy kudu and zebra, sending gnu galumphing through the scrub and hares and wild cats scuttling across the savannah.

How could they give all this away now? How could the

world expect them to disinherit their descendants?

That night they had eaten dark, fat steaks of rich impala out in the open air under a million pin-bright stars around a blazing camp fire. It had been then, as the sparks had crackled high into a crisp black sky and the flames had flickered on the faces of his friends, that van der Merwe had decided once and for all that there had to be a God.

They waited until late afternoon before they smuggled the jeep unnoticed around the back of the private camp at Malelane and steered it along the narrow track beside the Krokodil River towards Khandzalive and the prospect of finding Kruger's treasure at last. At the side of the road the herring-bone grass was already turning gold in the evening sunlight and by the time they reached Khandzalive the eastern slope of the mountain was falling into shadow and beyond it the entire lowveld was beginning to glow with the pink of twilight. Tiny mongooses scuttled across the road, taunting the martial eagles and bateleurs stooping high above the granite kopjes.

They all spotted the strange-shaped rock at the foot of the hill at the same time, as soon as they drove in towards it from the south. There could be no mistake. It was just as the diarist had described it: a huge, eerie boulder with a rock fig growing out of its broken heart, cracking it in two; a boulder shaped so strangely, with lines so stark and savage, that it resembled nothing on earth but might have come from a different planet. Nearby a dried riverbed ran away across the bush towards the Nsikazi River and past a large *donga*, a gully as deep as a man's grave. A few feet away stood the shrivelled trunk of a dead marula tree.

Bezuidenhout drove slowly up to the spot and stopped the jeep several yards away. He killed the engine and they sat for a moment in silence, unable to believe their good fortune, giving thanks praise be to God. *So waar as God!* thought van der Merwe with awe. His heart was pounding with anticipation, the pain in his gut throbbing with every beat. This must be the place. There could be no doubt. Over there, just there, the great President Kruger had sat, in this very place, beneath that very tree, a hundred years ago. In this very place he had sat long in silence and had gazed at the stars and had savoured the last sad night of his independent Boer republic, his Golden Republic of the Transvaal, and had mourned the tragic end of his struggle against the British and had contemplated the sour prospect of an anonymous little seaside villa thousands of miles away in Corsica.

Just here.

The place was as silent as a cemetery.

Over there, in the dry river bed, the diarist had shot the kaffir in the head and perhaps the kaffir's bones still lay in the dust nearby like the skeletons of animals, bleached by the sun.

They sat in the jeep in absolute silence, in a kind of prayer, waiting for darkness to camouflage their search. Even the young men said nothing as they watched the bush, breathing quietly, imagining, paying homage. Young men like this, thought van der Merwe, will make our nation great again. I must not envy them. I had my turn and now it is theirs.

Please God that the gold is still here, prayed van der Merwe, that the People of the Lord may be freed from the land of bondage. For it is written in Matthew 24: 'Ye shall be hated of all nations for my name's sake … But he that shall endure unto the end, the same shall be saved'.

Bezuidenhout reached for his rifle and stepped out of the jeep into the twilight. 'Fischer,' he said quietly. 'Van der Westhuizen. Wessels. Mocke. Take your places on lookout.'

They took their rifles and spread out around the site, north, south, east, west, facing outwards.

'Potgieter and Malan,' said Bezuidenhout. 'The spades.' In silence he placed his back against the dry, dead wood of the old marula tree and took five paces towards the *donga* and the mysterious rock, marking the spot by drawing a line in the dust with his boot. From the rock itself he took seven paces towards

the tree and the *donga*, once again marking a parabola with his
boot. From the edge of the *donga* he marched ten measured
paces towards the intersection and made another mark. Each
mark was within a yard of the other two. Erosion, thought van
der Merwe. That would explain the discrepancies: the edge of
the donga had obviously crumbled by two or three feet in a
hundred years.

'*Net hier!*' said Bezuidenhout, pointing the barrel of his rifle
at the ground.

Just like Kruger had said, the very same words, a hundred
years ago.

There was nothing there to mark the spot. A century of rain
and drought and animals' hooves and droppings had covered
the site as completely as Kruger would have hoped. A shed
snakeskin lay flimsy and translucent in the dust, strangely
beautiful in its frailty, and a few small stones, perhaps the very
stones that the diarist had scattered there a hundred years ago
for camouflage.

The night came down.

Suddenly it was cold. Van der Merwe shivered and lit a
cigarette to warm his fingers.

The stars began to twinkle, a hundred at first, then a
thousand, a hundred thousand, a million, glittering brilliant in
the unpolluted air, the very stars at which Kruger had gazed in
misery on his last night, here, in this very spot, before he had
left the Transvaal for ever. A cricket began to chirp. A lion
roared in the distance. A jackal cackled.

'OK,' said Bezuidenhout. 'Start digging.'

Van der Merwe pressed the palms of his hands together.

Please God it is still there.

He pressed his eyelids tight.

Please God no one else has got here first.

And then a terrible thought.

Please God it is not just a hoax.

The ferry came in from Ajaccio across the Baie des Anges

towards Nice on a glorious summer afternoon, the sun glittering to the left on an airliner settling comfortably over Antibes to come in to roost at the airport. On the right a blinding reflection suddenly dazzled the mirrors of the lighthouse on Cap Ferrat.

Ugo Legrandu leaned on the rail of the ferry with the wind in his face and gazed up beyond the sprawling terracotta roofs towards the hazy summits of the junior Alps towering above the distant autoroute. How often in the past, he thought, had he driven Her along the autoroute and looked down with a stab of nostalgia to see this very ferry coming in across the sparkling sea from Ajaccio or Bastia. How often had he dreamed then of home, of the scented hinterland of Corsica, of the mountain lakes, pine forests and perfumed hillsides that had made the great Napoleon himself swear that even if he were blind he would know if he ever returned home because he would smell it. Yet now Ugo could dream of nothing but an Englishwoman naked in an afternoon bed in a shadowy room in a villa up in the hills at St Paul de Vence, where the scents come at dozens of francs a bottle from the factories at Grasse.

Just to think of her perfume, there, just there, aroused him; her pale skin damp with sweat, the hot fragrance of her, the hair dark and wiry against her secret parts, her breath coming fast and shallow, a cry of pain as he forced himself into her, blood on her lip. He eased his stance at the rail, spreading his legs, thinking of her hunted eyes in the dark, her astonished mouth, saliva on her chin. It would be just like that frightened English girl all over again, the one he had had eight years ago at Sagone, about sixteen or seventeen she must have been, when she left the beach that hot afternoon to go back to her hotel room for a siesta and forgot to lock the door and he had followed her into her room and locked the door and had had her the Corsican way. A complete stranger. That was why it was so exciting. That was why men went to prostitutes, he thought, the excitement of a complete stranger despite all the risks, *because* of all the risks: the girl's terrified eyes, her thin English voice begging in vain *please-no-please-no*, his hand pressed hard over her sharp little teeth, the grunting noise she made against his fingers, her tiny breasts, her silver crucifix pressing cold and hard into his chest, imprinting a small red sign of the cross. The memory of that alone excited him. He had bruised her thin young thighs with his knees. Most women love a little brutality. It makes them feel feminine, helpless. He could still remember the way she had whimpered afterwards and the tears on her cheeks. La Barrett would whimper too.

Ashore he found a public telephone and called the *Celebrity* offices in Monte Carlo.

'*Celebrity*-Magazine-for-Glamour-and-Glitz-Monique-speaking-how-may-I-help-you.'

Monique had always had the hots for him. A shame she was so ugly, with a hooked nose as vast as a Roman centurion's.

He disguised his voice with a low growl. '*L'éditrice*,' he said.

'Ugo?' she said.

'Eh?'

'*C'est vous, Ugo?*'

'*Ugo? Je suis Pierre Lafont.*'

'*Excusez-moi, m'sieu. Vous me rappelez un ami …*'

She put him through to La Barrett's office. *Nom de nom!* How had she recognised his voice?

'Kelly.'

The Irishman. Legrandu hesitated.

'Kelly here.'

He could visualise Kelly hunched over the telephone in his poky little office high up on the eighteenth floor and in the next office, marooned in a huge expanse of emptiness, La Barrett cool and distant as usual behind an almost deserted desk, her eyes so cold and green, her manner so superciliously Anglo-Saxon, her cool fingers grasping the short, fat telephone receiver, her wet tongue flicking across it. His blood throbbed.

''Tis Kelly speaking. Is anyone there?'

'Ze editeur,' he growled. 'I wish speak wiz 'er.'

'She's not like in the office. Can I take a message?'

'When she is *retour*?'

'Legrandu?' said Kelly.

'Eh?'

'Is that Ugo Legrandu?'

'*Je suis Pierre Lafont, m'sieu.*'

'You sound like Ugo Legrandu.'

'*Quoi?*'

'Where are you like calling from?'

'From Nice, *m'sieu.* I wish only the speak wiz –'

'You are bloody Legrandu, aren't you, you bastard? I'd recognise your fockin' voice anywhere. You fockin' well blew me up. You like near killed me. Fockin' Corsican shit! I'm going to –'

Legrandu replaced the receiver quickly. *Zut!*

The Irishman would tell her he had called. *Merde!* Kelly would warn her that he was back in town. *Nom d'une pipe!*

He loped out of the docks and hailed a taxi to take him up to her villa in the hills at St Paul de Vence. She would not be home yet, not for three or four hours, perhaps, but she always left a spare key on a secret hook on the back of her garden seat. He had used it often enough before. And then he would wait for her to come home from work.

He sat in the taxi sweating as the driver stopped at almost every traffic light along the Promenade des Anglais between the harbour and the turn-off at Cros-de-Cagnes and the meter shivered and clattered the francs away. He sat back in the rear seat, restless at being the passenger rather than the driver. It felt unnatural. He resented the way the driver seemed to slow down deliberately as he approached a traffic light that was about to turn red. He disliked the raucous radio music and even the back of the driver's head seemed offensive with its short, fat neck and thick, aggressive hairs. There was something insolent about the back of the taxi driver's head. It was too solid. It suggested contempt. Above all, Legrandu resented the rattling of the meter, fifty-*click*-fifty-five-*click*-sixty-*click*-seventy. He must have been mad to take a taxi.

Past the airport and the tacky little shops and cafés that line the seafront road at Cros-de-Cagnes they turned right towards Les Hauts-de-Cagnes and the smooth, fat road up towards St Paul perched white and ochre on its own little hill like icing on a little cake, the church's sandy belltower sticking up like a finger-biscuit.

The taxi dropped him outside the Colombe d'Or, where the *gendarme* at the checkpoint barrier was preventing the rubbernecks tootling their cars up the hill through the Place du Général de Gaulle and choking the narrow medieval streets of the village itself. To the right, opposite the Colombe d'Or, a group of tourists was gawping at the *pétanque* players under the leafy plane trees on the sandy village square. A fat, brown man with a gnarled *Provençal* face and a T-shirt stretched tight across his large stomach staggered bleary-eyed across the square in pursuit of his *boules*, followed by three equally unsteady companions. A thin, heavily suntanned woman was waving a cigarette holder at him from a marble-topped table on the terrace of the Café de la Place behind the purple bougainvillea creeper on the edge of the village square. 'Jonathan!' she called in a very English voice. Not a Frenchman after all, then, but English. 'Jonty! Do you want another?'

He turned and gazed at her, swaying on his feet, his eyes bloodshot and unfocussed. It seemed a miracle of engineering that he remained upright. 'Do I wannanother one?' he slurred loudly. 'Is the Pope Polish? Of course I fucking well wannanother one. I wannanother bottle! Two bottles.' He waved his arm at his companions. 'And one for each of them, eh? A bottle for each of them.' He startled chuckling until he was screaming with manic laughter like a demented hyena, rocking on his heels unsteadily, his face puce, his eyes bulging like goldfish. One of his companions buckled at the knees and collapsed into the dust. The fat brown Englishman pointed at his fallen comrade and shrieked like a peacock. 'He's pissed again!' he bellowed. 'Pissed as a fart! Can't take him anywhere. Why does he always get pissed?'

'Maybe he drinks too much,' she said. The fat brown man started shrieking again and the Englishman lying in the dust began to laugh as well.

'*Les* soccer *hooligans anglais*,' said the *gendarme*. He shrugged. '*Les* yobs *du Londres*.'

'*Cinq cents cinquante*,' said the taxi driver.

'*Cinq cents!*'

'*Weh! C'est ça*.'

Five hundred and fifty francs! You could buy a woman for that.

'You should have your meter checked,' said Legrandu, handing over the money.

The driver gazed at the notes. There was no tip. He shrugged. '*Va te faire enculer*,' he suggested. He sneered and drove away in an explosion of blue exhaust fumes.

'*Va chier!*' yelled Legrandu after him.

The *gendarme* at the barrier chuckled. Behind him, through the gateway onto the terrace of the Colombe d'Or, Legrandu could smell the orange groves on the hillside and from the terrace itself there drifted a strong whiff of wealth. Every Celebrity in the world had lunched or dined at some time on the terrace at the Colombe d'Or – every actor, model, artist, pop star, politician – ever since the days when the place had been owned by Yves Montand and Simone Signoret. Legrandu had once seen Montand across the road on the dusty village square playing *pétanque* one afternoon for four thousand francs a game. Signoret had been squatting in a dark corner of the bar, huge, dressed all in black, with only the glittering eyes in her gross, fleshy face to remind you that once she had been a slim, beautiful girl. Both dead now, along with most of the celebrity ghosts that once had haunted the place, but the atmosphere was still laced with a fragrance of fame, francs and flattery. The walls inside the hotel, the corridors leading towards the swimming pool, were lined with originals by Miro and Picasso, who had lived just up the road in the sixties. They said that Roger Moore, too, had once had a villa here, and Bill Wyman, and that famous black American writer, the homosexual. No wonder La Barrett had chosen to live here. This was true *Celebrity* country, where the rocks were million-franc diamonds and the gold-diggers needed no spades.

He wandered down the hill towards her villa, past neat wrought-iron fences, hedges of pine, the smell of damp trees, the lime and lemon citrus, white oleander, Tuscan jars of red geraniums, and terracotta roofs marching in step down the hillside. The villa was tucked away from the main road, behind a wall and a clump of scented bushes, overlooking the valley. It was guarded by fat cacti and palm trees, and the wooden shutters were closed on the windows facing the terrace, which meant she was not at home. *CHIEN MÉCHANT* said the wooden notice on the gate beside a picture of a snarling Alsatian. Legrandu grunted. La Barrett had never owned a dog, neither *méchant* nor cuddly, not in all the years he had known her. Dogs require affection.

He tried the old key in the padlock that bolted the chain on the gate, the key he had always used when she had sent him up here on an errand. Had she had the lock changed after she had sacked him? He felt the key turn in his fingers. It slid open with ease. Of course she had not had it changed. Why should she have had it changed? She wanted him to break in. He locked the gate behind him and walked around to the back of the villa to look for the spare house key that she always hid on the hook at the back of the garden bench. It was still there. He smiled.

He opened the front door and let himself in. The place smelled of wax polish. The red light began to wink on the burglar alarm control panel in the kitchen and he stepped across to it and punched in the deactivation code that he had long ago learned by heart – 3, 5, 1, 9. It was so easy to remember: her age and her birthday. The warning light switched itself off.

The villa was immaculately tidy. Of course. The cleaner would have been in. It was stuffy with all the windows locked. He sat in the living room, hidden from the road by a bush, lounging on the fat soft sofa beside the fireplace and flipping through some magazines: *Paris Match*, *Le Canard Enchaîné*, *Hello!* A clock ticked loudly in the hallway and the voices of passers-by in the road drifted across the wall. Now and then he could heard a distant, muffled shout from the *pétanque* players up in the village square and sometimes the *chock-chock* of the *boules* as they bombarded each other in the dust.

He looked at his watch. It was 5.30. It could well be an hour or two yet before she returned, even longer if she had a dinner to attend. Never mind. He would wait. He had waited already for three years. There was no hurry. Anticipation was everything in love. It was only boys who wanted to rush love.

He wandered around the living room, fingering her possessions, touching a vase of dried flowers, stroking a figurine of a woman in a ballgown. He studied two framed photographs, one of a young fair-haired boy squinting into the sun, one of a young man with a big nose. It was rumoured at *Celebrity* that she had once been married, a long time ago, but no one had ever mentioned a son. Legrandu stared at the picture of the young man with the big nose. Could this be the ex-husband? He stared at the big nose, disliking its owner. They said that a big nose meant a big cock. *Mon Dieu!* Dépardieu must be hung like an elephant!

He looked at his watch: 6.15. She might be on the autoroute by now, heading home. Suddenly he was wary. What if she had her new chauffeur with her? He might come with her into the villa, perhaps carrying her suitcase or shopping. He would need to hide if the chauffeur came in. In the bedroom, the built-in cupboard, behind her clothes. He walked through to her bedroom. She had never allowed him here, when he had been carrying things in for her. She had always told him to leave suitcases and parcels in the living room, keeping a distance. He preened in front of the mirror. *Weh!* She couldn't trust herself alone with him, that was it.

The bed was vast, decorated with white lace. He smoothed the soft material of the fat, white *Provençal* pillows, imagining her hair tousled across them. Not long now. And afterwards they would sleep deep like the dead.

He opened her cupboard door. Her clothes shivered in the sudden draught, frail and feminine. They smelled of her. He brushed them aside and stepped into the cupboard, closing the door and hiding himself behind them. This would do if the chauffeur came in with her.

He pressed his face into the cloth of one of her dresses as it hung in front of him and realised that he had developed a huge erection. He sniffed the cloth. It smelled of something flimsy, something vulnerable. He wanted her so much. He felt that his skin might burst. He was sweating. It was airless inside the cupboard. He pushed the door open for air.

The telephone rang. *Brrrrr!*

He stepped out of the cupboard. The telephone rang again on the bedside table. *Brrrrr!* Long pause. *Brrrrr!* Long pause. *Brrrrr!*

Then he heard her voice in the living room.

Mon Dieu, she has returned. While I was in the cupboard.

Her voice sounded metallic. 'Stella Barrett. I'm not taking calls at the moment but please leave a message after the tone.'

Her answerphone.

Of course.

There was a click, a buzz, and then the dialling tone. The caller had cut the connection without leaving a message. A red light began to wink on the answerphone.

He ambled from room to room, peering at framed photographs, examining her CD collection, opening drawers and cupboards, inspecting their contents and then closing them, pulling a book off a shelf, glancing through it and replacing it. It was stuffy with all the windows locked but he did not want to open one and risk frightening her off. As night came down he stood at the wide picture-window by the terrace and gazed out through the glass for a while across the valley towards the sea as the light faded and died beyond the mountain peaks of Gourdon and Grasse and down in the valley the lamps started flickering like fireflies.

By 7.30 he began to listen for any sound of the Mercedes, a click of a key in the padlock. He dared not switch on the lights or the television set and he sat in the dark listening to the sounds of the night: the crickets chattering in the shrubbery, the muffled muttering of distant voices outside the Café de la Place up the hill, the clinking of bottles and glasses, the occasional shout or laugh, a clunk of the *boules* as someone played on under the floodlights, now and then a car horn or an engine revving, a cat mewing nearby, over and over again.

Eight o'clock passed, and nine. She must have gone out to dinner. He settled down to wait. A television set was turned on in one of the neighbouring villas. He could hear the raucous laughter of some gameshow assaulting the silence of the garden, its blue glow flickering between the shrubs like the flashing light of an ambulance for people with broken minds. A couple stood talking in the road outside, the man quiet and reassuring, the girl giggling, their murmuring just too low to understand. A jet plane rumbled briefly beyond Villeneuve-Loubet and Mougins as it lowered itself over Cannes and Juan-les-Pins. A frog started croaking at the end of the garden. A crash came from the café, plates smashing, a rowdy cheer followed by laughter. The drunken Englishmen: could they possibly still be drinking? Where did they put it all? Legrandu grimaced. He loved English women but English men were even worse than the filthy *bosche*: they still seemed to think that they owned the world. In the darkness the cat started mewing again. A dog barked. *Chien méchant*. It barked again and again, on and on, becoming hoarse. It sounded sad, like a voluble man who is noisy only because of the silence between his ears.

Brrrrr!

He jolted in his seat, jerking awake. He must have fallen asleep.

Brrrrr!

He must have dropped off. He sat up, rubbing his eyes. Somewhere a cat was still mewing.

Brrrrr!

The telephone. Should he answer it? No, of course not. That would be madness.

Brrrrr!

He looked at his watch. It was very dark. He angled its face towards the moonlight: 11.45. Nearly midnight! He must have dozed off for more than an hour, nearly two.

The answerphone clicked on, the red light flashing.

The metallic voice again, staccato in the silence: 'Stella Barrett. I'm not taking calls at the moment but please leave a message after the tone.'

Then silence, a click, and her voice again, her own voice this time, her real voice, answering her false recorded one. He held his breath. Her voice. It was her, calling her own recording machine, her at this very minute speaking into a distant telephone, her cool fingers grasping the short, fat receiver, her wet tongue and lips flicking across it. He felt a stab in his groin.

'*Héloïse*,' she said.

Héloïse. The cleaning woman. She was telephoning to leave a message for the cleaning woman.

'I'm in Venice,' she said. Her voice echoed around the musty room, as though she were standing beside him. He stared at the answerphone, her voice so near, so intimate. He could hear her breathing. He could almost reach out and trickle his knuckles lightly along her lips.

'I'm staying with the marchesa at her *palazzo*. The number's in the address book if you need me. I won't be back for five or six days and then I may have to go on to Prague so I want you to get all the curtains and cushions dry-cleaned while I'm away. And some of the carpets need a good clean too. And I want you to do the silver as well. And take all the books off the shelves and dust them each individually. And of course don't forget to come in every day to feed Mandela. He'll be starving in the morning by the time you come in. I had to leave suddenly this afternoon and he hasn't been fed since this morning.'

Mandela. The black cat. He had forgotten her cat. Of course. *Chat méchant.* Cats need no affection. The cat mewing outside all night in the dark. *Miao.*

'*Ciao!*' she said, replacing her receiver. The answerphone clicked, buzzed and switched itself off.

Legrandu stared at it. The red light winked at him, over and over again. Venice. For five or six days. And then on to Prague.

He couldn't wait that long. Five or six days? He would explode.

He wandered through to the bedroom in a daze and stared at the bed, the soft pillows, the white silk and lace, the place where he would have spread her out like a banquet. Not tonight. Not tomorrow. Not for five or six days, a week, perhaps two.

He opened her top drawer, sinking both hands into the soft mounds of her underwear, closing his eyes, stroking the silky material, touching it where it had touched her. He hooked his fingers around the straps of one of her tiny brassières and pulled it out of the drawer, exploring it with his nostrils, detecting a hint of the milk-powder perfume of her little breasts. He lifted a pair of lacy white knickers from the drawer and pressed them to his face, burying his nose deep in her smell, rubbing his lips across the soft crotch. For a moment he imagined he could taste her; a faint tang of salt, a hint of anchovy. He shuddered.

He would have to follow her. He could not bear to wait any longer. Venice. He had been to Venice only once, many years ago, and had wondered what all the fuss was about. What was so special about streets full of water? But nothing now would stop him going again. To hell with the expense. He would steal a car, drive all the way. It was not far: five hundred kilometres, perhaps? Six hundred? He could do it in a day, easy. He could be with her tomorrow night. He would surprise her tomorrow night in a dark shuttered room in the marchesa's *palazzo* with the sound of a canal lapping against old stone and with moonlight glittering on the dark water.

He found the marchesa's address and telephone number in the address book on the table beside the answerphone. As he left the villa the cat Mandela wound its tail around his leg and mewed hungrily. He lashed out with his foot, kicking the cat in the side. It screeched and fled into the villa, mewing piteously. He locked it in. Let Héloïse wonder tomorrow how it had got into the house. What was it to him?

He locked the garden gate behind him and strolled down the hill, followed by distant strains of music wafting from the café, voices calling, a car door slamming, faint echoes of rowdy voices singing '*Sur le Pont d'Avignon*'. It was the drunken English again without a doubt, their glorious British Empire now no more than a bleary memory at the bottom of an empty glass.

Near the bottom of the hill he broke into a Citroën parked by the side of the road and drove it away down to the coast and into Nice, past the glittering lights of the Promenade des Anglais, where the glow in the sky was so yellow that you could see no stars at all, past the arrogant elegance of the Negresco and the floodlit façade of the casino, into the centre of town. He abandoned the Citroën in the Rue Masséna and in the Rue du Congrès he bought himself a small whore with big tits.

'The Queen can't come to the New Year's Eve ball,' said Kelly.

He was leaning back in The Editor's chair in her office in Monte Carlo with his feet propped up on her desk. He kissed the filter-tip of his cigarette and blew a perfect grey halo across her desk.

'Why not?' said The Editor. Her voice echoed down the telephone line as though she were underwater.

'They say their programme was already booked up years ago, previous engagements, family commitments, dah-dee-dah. And they go "The Royal Family simply cannot be seen to support commercially sponsored events unless they're in aid of approved charities".'

'You get back to them, Kelly, and tell those toffee-nosed prats in Buck House that of course the ball is being held in aid of charity.'

'Brilliant. Is it?'

'Of course it bloody well isn't, but that's not the point. It could be. Just tell them it is. Oxfam. The Red Cross. Aids. Help for Distressed Old Queens – anything they fancy. They'll never check up afterwards.'

'I could try.'

'Not could, Kelly. You will try.'

'Right. Brilliant.'

'Item two. The American President.'

'Ah.'

'I want you to send the bastard a reply to that offensive computer message he sent me. Take this down, Kelly. Right. *To the President of the United States of America. From Stella Barrett, etcetera. I realise that you are a man of limited intelligence but I am deeply offended by your disgusting allegation about my private life. Should you be foolish enough ever to repeat this unfounded rumour to anyone I shall sue your bollocks off.* Have you got that?'

'... disgusting allegation ...'

'About my private life.'

'Brilliant.'

'Should you be foolish enough ever to repeat this unfounded rumour to anyone ...'

'... unfounded rumour ...'

'I shall sue your bollocks off.'

'… bollocks off.'

'That's it. Right, read it back to me, Kelly.'

'Is that an x in bollox?'

'No, Kelly, it's c, k, s. Now read it back. To make sure you haven't made one of your customary picturesque Irish cockups.'

'Right. *I realise that you are a man of limited intelligence –*'

'Like you, Kelly. Have you ever thought of standing for election as President of the USA? You'd walk it.'

'*… but I am deeply offended by your disgusting allegation about my private life. Should you be foolish enough ever to repeat this unfounded rumour to anyone I shall sue your bollocks off.*'

'Right. I want that sent now. Today. Who the fuck does he think he is?'

'Right away. Brilliant.'

'Anything else?'

'The French and Russian presidents have refused. So has the British Prime Minister.'

'I don't have any problem with that. They're all wankers anyway. Mogadon bores. Nobodies. Not real movers and shakers.'

'Rainier's said no as well.'

'*What?* After that great profile we gave him last year?'

'Seems he's already involved in some official celebration.'

'I'm not having that. I'll speak to him when I get back. What about Caroline?'

'No reply yet.'

'Lean on her office, Kelly. We've got to have at least one royal at the ball and especially one of the Grimaldis. Good local PR. Anything else?'

'Jeffrey Archer can't come, either. He's giving a big millennium party of his own.'

'Who the hell invited Archer?'

'You did.'

'I did not.'

'You did. He's on the –'

'Hear this, Kelly: I – DID – NOT – INVITE – JEFFREY – ARCHER! I – WOULD – NOT – INVITE – JEFFREY – ARCHER – IF – HE – PAID – ME – A – MILLION – POUNDS.'

'Lucky he's said no, then, like.'

'What was that?'

'If you say so.'

'I did say so, Kelly. Find out who put him on the invitation list. Against my clear instructions, at that. I said quite clearly no writers.'

'I think possibly Lord Archer was like suggested not for his writing abilities but for his moving and shaking.'

'I want to know who put him on the list.'

'I'll like make enquiries.'

'You do that, sunshine. Anyone else?'

'Richard Branson can't make it, either. He's throwing a huge street party for half a million people in Edinburgh.'

'Damn! There's a real mover, Branson, a Shaker's shaker. Now, what about the really big cheeses? Tom Cruise? Hugh Grant? Naomi Campbell?'

'No replies yet, Stella.'

'Right, I want a daily list from you of the replies as they come in with a running total of acceptances. That's a must-have.'

'Very good.'

'What about the entertainment?'

'The Beatles don't seem to be too keen.'

'Offer them more. Offer them a million each.'

'I don't think a million each will –'

'What about Pavarotti?'

'They're taking their time replying.'

'Lean on them. Mention the Mafia. These Eye-ties don't like to upset the Mafia. What about David Copperfield?'

'I'm working on it.'

'The fashion show? Naomi, Christy, Kate, Linda?'

'We're trying.'

'Try harder, Kelly. Time's passing. *Tempers fugit*, especially mine. What about the food? The booze? Has Krug come across yet?'

'Not yet.'

'Sod them, then. Try Dom Perignon.'

'Champagne for two thousand.'

'Is that some sort of problem?'

'No. Of course not. Just –'

'Just do it, Kelly. Plus I want you to book me a Madame Pompadour costume for the fancy dress ball.'

'Madame Pompidou?'

'Dear God. Pompadour, you cretin. Louis the Thing's mistress.'

'Brilliant.'

'Now. Put me onto Campbell.'

'Brilliant. Just one more thing, like. The Corsican phoned.'

'Which Corsican?'

'Legrandu.'

'Who?'

'Ugo Legrandu?'

'Who's he?'

'Your chauffeur. Your ex-chauffeur.'

'The man who tried to murder me?'

'The man who tried to murder *me*.'

'Rubbish. He was after me. He's done what?'

'He phoned like yesterday afternoon. Wanted to speak to you.'

'What for?'

'I don't know. He was very shifty. Tried to disguise his voice, sort of gruff, fake French accent, dah-dee-dah. He's like "I weesh speak viz ze editeur," so I go "That's you, isn't it, you Corsican bastard? I'd recognise your voice anywhere. You tried to blow me up." So he goes, "No, no, *je suis Père Lamont* –" '

'A *priest*?'

'Eh?'

'*Père Lamont*. He was pretending to be a priest?'

'I hadn't thought of that.'

'I don't suppose you had, Kelly. Not a great thinker, are we? I don't suppose you thought of calling the police, either.'

'Ah.'

'Do it, Kelly. Now! This minute.'

'Right. Brilliant.'

'The police, Kelly. Tell them we have had a murder threat.'

'Well, he didn't actually make any threats, Stella.'

'Yes he did, Kelly. You will tell the police that he threatened to kill me.'

'But –'

'I want that bastard locked up for years and I don't care how you do it.'

'I –'

'The day I decide to sack you is getting closer, Kelly.'

'I'll call them like this minute.'

'You'd better believe it. Now put Campbell on.'

'Of course. Brilliant. Right away.'

'Just one more thing, Kelly.'

'Yes?'

'Did you believe it?'

'What?'

'The American President's disgusting allegation about my private life?'

Kelly hesitated for a fraction of a second.

'You did, didn't you?'

'Good God, no, of course not.'

'You did, you little Irish turd. I know when you're lying. You actually believed that I might be capable of molesting children. Jesus!'

'Not at all –'

'I'll never forget that, Kelly.'

'But it's –'

'I'll never forget your disloyalty. Now put Campbell on.'

He pressed Campbell's button, disconnecting her for a moment. What a bitch, he thought. Jaysus! One day …

'Campbell.'

'She's on line three.'

'And?'

'Foaming at the mouth.'

'Oh God.'

'I'm that harassed. That harassed. I'm just a blur.'

'Right. Yes. Put her on. Hello, Stella. How's Venice?'

'Wet. How's Ferré's piece on the CNN weather girl?'

'He's writing it today.'

'Fax it to me as soon as he's finished. Plus what about the chef from Brazzaville? That was Merlot, wasn't it?'

'Yes. She's having a bit of trouble with that one. She says he's not a pigmy at all. He's at least five foot tall, which I understand is big in Zaïre.'

'I don't give a damn what size he is, Campbell.'

'You said he was a pigmy.'

'He's probably got leprosy too but that's got nothing to do with it. I want to know whether he or his people were once cannibals. Do you get the connection, Campbell? We have here a fashionable French society chef who may once have been a cannibal.'

'That's ridic –'

'Bokassa was. So was Amin. Half of Africa's dictators have probably got a taste for a nice bit of missionary steak. So did our celebrity chef ever cook people? Eh? That's what we want to know. And if he did, what are his special cannibal dishes? Manburger? Sheik *tartare*? Cock-*au-vin*? Tell Merlot to get on with it, Campbell. *Capeesh?*'

'Very good.'

'What about Schwarzenegger's short story?'

'We're chasing it.'

'About as fast as a tortoise. Chase harder. It's only a short story we want, not *War and Peace*. It'd be nice if we could have it before the end of the next millennium. Plus what about Salman Rushdie's sex life?'

Campbell hesitated. He laughed. 'I'm sorry. I didn't realise you were serious about that.'

'You what?'

'I'll get someone onto it straight away.'

'Why did you laugh?'

'I thought you were joking.'

'Joking?'

'Well –'

'You don't think that's a brilliant idea, then? A piece about Rushdie's orgasms in captivity?'

'I –'

'Where did you learn your so-called journalism, Campbell?'

'It was –'

'You have about as much of a nose for news as a Hollywood gerbil up an actor's arse.'

'There's no need –'

'Get Wakonde to do it. His piece on the Gröning girl turned out better than I expected. Yes, put Wakonde onto the Rushdie story.'

'I –'

'And what about the Larry Dzerzinski pics?'

'His Aids is very bad now, Stella. Terminal.'

'That's the whole point.'

'Yes, but he's very ill.'

'So?'

'The snapper in New York is having trouble getting to him again. He's already seen him twice and they're asking why we want to photograph him three times in six months.'

'Sack the snapper, then. Get another snapper. Make it look like a separate job. Dear God, do I have to think of everything myself?'

'Dzerzinski's people won't let anyone near him. They say he's on his last legs.'

'All the more reason to get after him quickly, then, before he snuffs it. That's exactly what we want, Campbell. For Christ's sake, that's the whole point of the pics: to run a whole series of them showing how he slowly wasted away in his last few months. It'll be sensational. That's the whole point. Can't you see? Jesus wept! I don't believe you're real. Why the hell did I hire you, Campbell?'

'You probably thought I was Naomi's father,' he said.

The telephone line hummed. 'Don't you get cocky with me, Campbell,' she said quietly. 'I'll have you counting paperclips if you think you can get cocky with me.'

He took a deep breath. 'I think it's time I resigned, Stella. We're obviously not –'

'Resign?' She gave a sarcastic chuckle. 'Resign? You? Don't make me laugh, Campbell. No one walks out on me. No one, do you hear? You signed a year's contract and there's seven months still to run and I'm bloody well holding you to it. *Capeesh?* You'll serve every day of it. Every hour, until the very last minute. You walk out on me and I'll sue you for a year's pay in lieu of notice and another year's pay in damages, inconvenience, you name it. I'll have your guts for garters. No one resigns from *Celebrity*, Campbell, not until I'm good and ready, and then they get fired. Nobody leaves until I sack them. *Capeesh?* Now get those Dzerzinski pics, *pronto.* We run them this month.'

She cut the connection.

Campbell replaced the receiver.

It rang again immediately. 'Plus another thing,' said The Editor. 'We need to dump half the guests we were planning to invite to the ball. I've just realised that we only need a thousand celebs after all if each of them brings a partner or guest. So by close of play tonight I want a list of the thousand you suggest we dump. And you'd better get it right, Campbell. *Capeesh?*'

The telephone clicked and purred. Campbell stared into space, across his office and through the windows and over the deep blue freedom of the sparkling Mediterranean sky and sea. Away on the right a white flag fluttered from the pole above the palace. He knew how it felt. Banks of grey cloud were stacking up on the left above the hills towards Menton and

Italy, challenging the skyscrapers. Down below by the harbour, on the right, on the Quai Antoine, the row of factories and warehouses was as pink as his own frustration. Along the Quai Albert the cafés under the trees looked tacky with their red-and-blue awnings and orange frou-frou umbrellas. The strings of red and white fairy lights, and flags and pennants hanging from red-and-white barbers' poles looked seedy in the sunlight. Even the expensive apartment blocks on the Boulevard Albert seemed to him to be as cheap as the women in white silk trousers and golden sandals patrolling the precinct beside the huge Rainier III swimming pool.

'Cheer up, sport,' said Murdoch in the doorway. 'We'll all be dead soon. No worries.'

He ambled into the room with next month's dummy layout. He surveyed Campbell's mood with his one good eye, sat on the edge of Campbell's desk and lit a cheroot. 'It could be worse,' he said. 'You could be married to her.'

Campbell grunted.

'At least the sea's cleaner than it used to be,' said Murdoch. 'When Noël Coward was here in the sixties the Med was so filthy that whenever he flushed the lav he used to look down at it and say "This is not so much goodbye, merely *au revoir*".'

'Will you do me a favour, laddie?' said Campbell.

'Course, mate. Any time. Any time at all.'

'Go boil yer heid,' said Campbell.

Well after midnight on the other side of the world Steve Marlowe was perched on his workstation stool in his apartment in Los Angeles munching a jumbo hotdog and ketchup that Chandler had ordered for him from the all-night deli. He was tapping at the keyboard with one greasy finger, scanning idly through the *Celebrity* computer files in Monte Carlo for something new, when he came across Stella Barrett's message to the White House.

<president@whitehouse.gov.us/barrett@celebrity.co.mc/ /I realise that you are a man of limited intelligence but I am

deeply offended by your disgusting allegation about my private life. Should you be foolish enough ever to repeat this unfounded rumour to anyone I shall sue your bollocks off>

Hey! A woman with balls!

Marlowe eased his own as they lay trapped tight and sweaty between his thighs. They were always uncomfortable these days. His balls seemed to be swelling by the week: even though he now sat at his workstation with his legs spread wide like the hands of a clock at 1350 hours, his testicles seemed to be growing bigger and bigger, like a pair of cuckoo eggs in the nest. He had not actually seen his penis for some time now, not since it had taken to skulking under his stomach, and sometimes it took him several seconds to find it as he groped about under his belly like a game of hunt the thimble. Starved of space on all sides, his cock seemed to be shrinking. Equally disconcerting, the fat on his chest was filling out so much that it increasingly resembled a fine pair of female breasts.

He took a long swig of Coke and reached for the second jumbo hotdog, smothered it with ketchup, bit into it and wiped his fingers on the lower slopes of his right breast. His nipple stood to attention. Even the jumbo hotdogs nowadays seemed to be getting smaller, he thought: not long ago just one of them between meals would have been plenty but now he always needed two to stave starvation off. He knew why his tits were growing, of course, and why his penis was shrinking. It was all due to all the female hormones in the public water supply nowadays. He had read on one of the Internet bulletin boards that every glass of water you drink in any big city in the world has already been passed through the kidneys of at least twenty or thirty people before being recycled and treated to make it fit again for human consumption. The sewage farms nowadays were simply recycled soft drinks factories. And since half the recycled water had been peed by women – and most of them women on the pill or HRT – every second glass of water was awash with all kinds of powerful female hormones. So men were becoming impotent and infertile, their penises were shrinking, their breasts burgeoning, their testicles exploding. And women, of course, were drinking huge doses of recycled male hormones, which was why so many of them now had moustaches, jogger's knee and balls, like the editor of *Celebrity* magazine.

Marlowe had been careful to avoid water ever since he had learned of W. C. Fields' warning about the stuff: 'Fish fuck in it,' said Fields. But how could you shun it completely? Every time you took a bath all that female infection probably leaked right into your body through your pores.

He grabbed a handful of peanuts and crammed them into his mouth, chewing and gazing at the Barrett woman's message to the President on Chandler's screen. He nodded with admiration. That was one of the great things about the Internet, he thought: you could learn so much from it. He had always thought that *realise* was spelt with a *zee*, that *private* was *privit*, that *rumour* was *rumor*. And *bollocks*: Marlowe had always been convinced that you spelt it with an *x*. But that was the Internet for you: the greatest teacher in the world.

Mind you, the Internet was sometimes pretty slow these days. It could feel quite sluggish when there were millions of people all over the world logged on at the same time, as though the capillaries of its huge global brain were being silted up by too many simultaneous demands. On a bad night logging-on could take ages, ten-second jobs could take two minutes to complete, and gophers seemed to search the electronic highways for ever as they kept coming up against international traffic jams and had to re-route themselves. But tonight everything was so slow that Marlowe began to suspect that the problem rested not so much with the Internet itself as with Chandler. Chandler seemed to be dragging his bytes about deliberately as he sighed and whined whenever Marlowe asked him to do anything. One of tonight's jobs had involved a simple credit-rating check in Mexico but Chandler had taken half an hour to do it.

And when a new client came on-line from London,

England, to hire him to do a job it had taken Chandler two minutes just to let Marlowe know the call was waiting.

<wot kind of usless pc u got there> jeered the client <sum sort of tyranasorus rek>

Marlowe bristled. <no sir just the latest teknology>

<i hope so i got a job 4 u>

And what a hell of a job it was too. The client was an employee of the British state lottery company and he wanted Marlowe to break into the computer and fix it to win him the big weekly prize. Sometimes the prize was as much as $30 million.

<shit thats a tuf 1> said Marlowe.

<they say yor the best>

<thanx its stil a big 1>

<we go 50–50>

<70–30> said Marlowe <to me>

<50–50> said the client <u need me i no the contact nos + the paswords>

<but it wont b easy + i do the work + take the risk>

<ok 60–40>

<ok 60–40>

Later, when the client had given him the contact details and passwords and had gone off the line Marlowe played around with them for a while and flirted gently with the lottery computer in Britain but the security there was much better than most. This was not going to be easy. This needed thinking about.

Tooling through the Internet menus he suddenly came across an update report on the mysterious new comet that had been spotted in outer space.

'The giant comet was first identified by the Spacewatch Telescope in Arizona in February 1998,' said the report, 'and its presence was quickly confirmed by the Hubble Space Telescope, the Observatoire de la Côte d'Azur near Nice and the Hooker telescope at the Mount Wilson Observatory near Los Angeles. The comet suddenly came into view out of the black of beyond in the constellation of Sagittarius, near the cluster of Messier 69, like the sudden Hale-Bopp comet of 1995, but this intruder seems to be truly vast, a great ball of ice and vapour that some scientists are estimating could be as much as seventy miles wide – as big as the biggest comet previously recorded – and hurtling through space at about 90,000 miles an hour. Its flare is so bright that it will soon be visible to the naked eye.'

Wow, thought Marlowe. Seventy miles wide. Seventy! And 90,000 miles an hour. Around the world in fifteen minutes. Jeez. He scrolled on through the report:

'No one can say yet whether the comet is heading towards the Earth but some experts are forecasting that it could come as close as half a million miles, which is very close indeed in astronomical terms for an object as huge as this one. If it came that close it could have a devastating effect on the tides, the weather, the orbit of the moon, maybe even the orbit of the Earth. If it actually hit the Earth it would do so with an explosion millions of times more powerful than all the world's entire stockpile of nuclear weapons.'

No.

It would never happen.

Of course not.

Marlowe shivered. It seemed cold in here. Probably Chandler again: Chandler failing to keep a proper eye on the central heating thermostat. It had even taken Chandler nearly fifteen minutes to download a simple colour photo of a very black Mozambican boy sprawling naked in a fishing boat with his legs entangled in nets and ropes, and with a wonderfully insolent expression on his face. The Mozambican boy had quite obviously not been drinking western water.

Even when Marlowe challenged Chandler to a game of chess he had the feeling that Chandler was not really trying. The computer sat there sullenly on the workstation, glowering. Often it took as much as five seconds to make a move and on three or four occasions it moved so fast and carelessly that you could almost feel the shrug of boredom. Had Chandler been human, Marlowe would have accused him of sulking, even perhaps of jealousy, and he thought he knew why: earlier in the evening he had tried to download a sales ad about a new hands-off computer that worked without either keyboard or mouse but simply by vocal command. Chandler had not liked it. The glare from the screen was harsh.

<ERROR: NO SUCH FILE> said Chandler.

<crap> said Marlowe.

<ERROR: NO SUCH FILE>

<gopher Dell sales>

<ACCESS DENIED>

<go>

<ERROR: NO SUCH FILE>

<balls>

<ERROR: NO SUCH FILE>

<jeez>

<ACCESS DENIED>

Eventually Marlowe had fooled Chandler and bypassed the glitch by calling up Bill Warren's computer in Santa Barbara, using that instead to download the ad and then making it ram the ad back downline onto Chandler's disk in an act of sudden electronic buggery. Chandler's screen seemed to wince as the ad for the new computer had flickered into view:

IS YOUR OLD COMPUTER PAST ITS SELL-BY DATE?

TOO SLOW FOR YOUR PRESENT NEEDS?

TOO MANUAL?

IS ITS MEMORY SIMPLY NOT AS POWERFUL AS YOU NEED?

IF SO, WE HAVE JUST THE NEW MODEL YOU DESERVE

A YOUNGER MODEL

QUICKER

MORE GLAMOROUS

AND ALL IT NEEDS IS THE SOUND OF YOUR VOICE ALONE!

The glare from Chandler's screen was ferocious. Marlowe scrolled quickly through the sales pitch. The new computer sounded astounding. It was twice as fast as Chandler and its memory three times bigger, yet its actual hardware was only half the size, so that it was much neater and more compact. It had neither keyboard nor mouse: you had only to speak a few simple words and phrases into the computer's memory program for it to learn to recognise your voice and then to obey every vocal command. The machine was even capable of correcting automatically all your spelling and grammar mistakes and of editing out curses and colloquialisms. Its leisure applications, too, were breathtaking. One of its extra peripherals was a room-size wrap-around screen onto which the new computer could project any scene you chose, and in 3-D at that: you simply asked it to give you a panorama of snow-capped mountains or a busy street scene in Rio or a dazzling tropical beach and there it was before your eyes and all around you, not just on a virtual reality headset but actually all around you, in real space and real time, with all the real sounds and smells you would expect. You would be able to stroll at random along the Great Wall of China, scuffing the stones as you went, or wander with echoing heels through the Guggenheim Museum in New York, or clatter along the cobbles of the Rue des Grands Augustins on the Left Bank in Paris, or sit among the black ties and dinner jackets of the audience coughing in the Sydney Opera House, marvelling at the mellow tones of the Moscow Philharmonic Orchestra. You could even tramp the silent, dusty surface of the moon. He would never need to leave his apartment ever again.

<price> asked Marlowe.

<$155000>

<shit>

<we offer 10% discount for any order placed within 24 hours> Marlowe consulted Chandler's calculator. Ten per cent off meant $139,500. Still far too much. But the price would come down quickly. It always did. In a year or so one of these little beauties would cost half as much.

He filed the brochure for future reference and Chandler's screen went blank with a smug shade of blue. Marlowe fired Stella Barrett's White House message downline to Bill Warren and added a note of his own for Warren:

<instrux pse re next move re black boys + blackmale>

Marlowe knew that Stella Barrett had to be lying. Her credit card statements showed the regular debits quite plainly: BLACKBOYS £500, BLACKBOYS £750. Who did she think she was kidding? He chuckled. What the hell would they make of it all in Washington? Worried gofers were probably scuttling around the White House asking nervous questions. *Who in tarnation is this Barrett woman? Is this some coded message? A nuclear warning? Could this be the start of some new dirty tricks scandal? Celebrigate? And do we tell the President?*

Marlowe grinned, swigged at his Coke, finished his slice of pecan pie and reached for a Hershey bar. Chandler's clock said 0539. Great. Nearly time for supper. But first he felt horny.

He reached for the virtual reality headset and programmed it to run the celebrity sex menu. A tropical beach would be nice, somewhere perhaps in the South Pacific, with frangipani and bougainvillea fringing a blue lagoon. It was one of his favourite fantasies. It was paradise. On VR it was even better than the real thing: you could hear the waves but you never got sand up your ass. He strapped himself into the Luv-Pak and fitted the VR visor over his eyes. Who would he have this time? He ran down the MicroHard Celebfuk menu. They did all sorts: Humphrey Bogart, James Dean, Errol Flynn, Clark Gable, Cary Grant, Rock Hudson, Bob Marley, Jim Morrison, Tyrone Power, Elvis Presley, Jim Reeves. All dead. All necrofuks. Why couldn't he have somebody who was still alive? Why couldn't he have Tom Cruise? Nice name, that. Cruise. Nice. It wouldn't hurt anyone. Tom Cruise wouldn't even know. It was only VR. It was all in the head, and how can you copyright a fantasy fuck?

He lay with James Dean under a palm tree, stroking his muscles. Sulky eyes. Sulky mouth. Acne. Tight ass. Nice.

As Marlowe grunted and gasped, an Internet e-mail message injected itself into the memory of Chandler's electronic postbox. Unseen, as though the computer were dreaming, the message blossomed gold and green as a cute, invisible pink kitten danced in a top hat across the darkened screen.

<*kitty schweitzer*> said the unseen screen in fancy italics <*hi there*>

The kitten bowed and silently miaowed.

<so whyre you avoidin me big boy>

ah god jim boy thats good so good

<my bastard husband sure is sore with you> said Mrs Schweitzer <he thinks you n me is havin an affair>

Marlowe groaned. He gasped. 'Ah Jim,' he said. He sighed. 'Ah, Jim,' he said. 'God, that was good, Jimmy baby.'

James Dean sneered.

Afu Faletau squatted on her heels in the dust beside her Grandpapa Salesi's grave in the yard behind the little corrugated iron house on the Tongan island of Vava'u, and gazed at the coloured picture in the tattered old copy of *Celebrity* magazine that Viliami had given her. She pressed her nose right up close against the creased, shiny paper.

'Hhugh Grrant,' she told her Grandpapa Salesi. 'Lookim big Hollywood whitefella belong book plenty too much pretty now.'

The Christmas lanterns around the grave fluttered in the breeze, glinting silver in the upturned Foster's beer bottles. She kissed the shiny paper of the magazine.

'My gracious!' she said. 'Me luvim too much now like buggery thassall.'

She rocked on her heels and stood up. From the village there came the constant hammering of the women making *tapa* cloth as they sat cross-legged in the shade beating the mulberry bark.

She said goodbye to Grandpapa Salesi and wandered away from the house, still gazing at the shiny photograph, scattering the chickens pecking across the allotment. She meandered past the copra and yam plantations and down the sandy path between the bougainvillea and the rich smelling frangipani towards the beach. Now and then she pressed the picture up against her pert little nose again, and twice she kissed it. She began to sing quietly out of tune – 'hhugh grrant hhugh grrant hhugh hhugh grrant grrant grrant hhugh' – to the rhythms of an old Polynesian melody, pretending in her head that she was singing a solo in church and that the whole congregation was silent, the organ too, and the choir, and all of them listening in mesmerised rapture only to her. Her head felt full – as full as a tin packed with corned beef. She looked at his picture again. He smiled at her and she thought she saw him wink.

Offshore the women were standing fully dressed waist-deep in the lagoon, digging eels and seaslugs out of the mud, slicing them open with knives and gutting them, dropping long orange strands of innards into their buckets.

'Hhhugh,' said Afu, dredging the name from the back of her throat as though she were clearing phlegm. 'Hhhhhhugh.'

Her mother had been very cross with her when Afu had come home from the beach after swimming without any clothes that day that they had had the feast in the street to welcome Viliami home from Hawaii. She had wandered back home without remembering to put her clothes back on and her horrid little boy-girl cousin Siole Veikune, the *faka lady*, the one who wore dresses, had seen her coming naked up the path with her clothes under her arm and he had pointed and shouted with glee, 'Airhead rude! Airhead mad!'

Her mother had bundled her into the little tin shack and had smacked her and smacked her and smacked her even though Afu had kept crying out: 'Mefella no doim! Arms belong me takim off clothe all together by self now.'

'On Sunday!' her mother had shrieked. 'On Sunday! On Sunday! On Sunday!' until her father had come in and pulled her mother away and shouted, 'She only pikinini! She only pikinini!'

'Me no pikinini!' Afu had shouted indignantly. 'Me bigfella lady now!'

Her mother had stopped smacking her then and had started to cry.

Afterwards, when it was nearly dark, Siole had found her dressed again and sitting on her heels beside Grandpapa Salesi's grave. He had sat down opposite her on the other side of the grave. Her skirt was right up around her thighs and he had stared at her in a funny way, looking at the top of her legs. She had seen boys looking at her like that before. When they looked at you like that their eyes always went funny.

'No!' she shouted. 'You go way you little buggerup!'

She had noticed him watching her a lot since then.

On the beach she tucked the magazine into the big pocket of her skirt and sat out of the blazing sunshine on the edge of an empty canoe drawn up on the sand in the shade of a palm tree. A warm breeze caressed her bare legs. A turtle staggered in slow-motion out of the sea, groaning like a dying man. Parrots and lorikeets whistled and squawked high above on the jungly slopes of Mount Talau. Egrets and swallows swooped across the forest waterfalls. Terns and grey herons flirted with flowers richly coloured and perfumed. Far out on the booming reef a few beachcombers with sacks hoist over their shoulders were hunting octopus and shellfish amid the coral. A wooden whaleboat with an outboard motor puttered out to sea, slicing the glittering turquoise waters. A big black crab scuttled sideways towards its hole, tap-dancing across the burning sand.

Afu adjusted the frangipani flower in her hair and sighed. It was all so boring, she thought: nothing but sunshine and powdery sand and the endless translucent sea, nothing but palm trees and trade winds and the thundering reef. There was nothing to do, nothing at all, and nowhere to go. Why did they call it the Paradise International Hotel? This was Vava'u, not Paradise. She wanted to go away. She was fed up with Vava'u. So many of the boys and girls she knew at school had gone already, finding jobs across the sea and sending money home to their families, sailing off to New Zealand, Fiji, Samoa or Hawaii to work in the factories and hotels. Uncle Alipate said that Sapeli Vahu had even stowed away on a cargo boat bound for Auckland, wherever that might be, and she was now a lady's maid and wore real stockings.

Afu dreamed of going away too. Perhaps she too could get a job as a lady's maid if she could learn to stop dropping things. She wanted to take a boat to Nuku'alofa and walk along Taufa'ahau Road and see all the big, exciting shops and the King's palace and maybe even Princess Sophia. She wanted to go to Hawaii and see Viliami's garden and travel with him to Los Angeles to see Hollywood, where all the beautiful people live. She would go up to Hhugh Grrant in Hollywood and say hello and touch his eyes and she would let him kiss her.

She looked up. Her twelve-year-old cousin Siole was standing on the other side of the canoe, Siole the *faka lady* with red varnish on his fingernails and a gardenia in his hair. He was staring at the top of her legs.

Siole licked his lips.

'You give me fuck,' he said.

'You washim out you mouth,' she said.

'Jus one fuck-fuck,' said Siole. 'I give you tin meat.'

'Tin meat?'

'You likim.'

'What kind meat?'

'Sossis.'

'How kind sossis?'

'Number one sossis.'

Siole looked carefully around and pulled a small, dented tin of frankfurter sausages furtively from his shirt pocket. The label was scratched and stained. He handed her the tin. She turned it in her hands, stroking the dent with her thumb, marvelling at the coloured picture on the label: all those fat brown sausages inside this little tin, she thought; all squashed together like boys' little pee-pees.

Siole glanced quickly over his shoulder again. The beach was deserted. He licked his lips. 'You fuck now?' he said.

She sniffed. She looked at him as he stood there, short and nervous in his girl's skirt with the flower in his hair just like her and the varnish on his nails. He looked just like a girl. She had never had a *faka lady* before. Did their little sausages look the same as a proper boy's little sausage?

She slipped the tin of frankfurters into the pocket of her skirt.

'You number one time?'

He swallowed. He nodded.

'OK,' she said.

She clambered into the canoe, hoisting her skirt, swinging her slim brown legs, flexing her dainty toes. Her long black hair tumbled about her waist, crowned with a golden splash of frangipani. She lay in the bottom of the canoe, raised her skirt above her waist and spread her silky thighs.

'Makim quick now thassall,' she said.

The New Age travellers' caravans rolled south at last from the holy silence of the Tanat Valley and the magic fastnesses of northern Wales. Just before they had left their camping site Helga Gröning had made her demonstration of protest against the eviction by marching up to the four policemen and standing in front of them, with hands on hips, haranguing them.

'How are you sleeping in the nights, *ja*, when you are doing such things to small, lawful people?' she shouted. 'How are you wives being pride of you when you are doing such things? Fascist pigs! Nazis! I spit you, Nazis.' She gave a violent Nazi salute. '*Heil, Schweinehunde!*' she cried.

Arthur Lancelot gripped her arm and persuaded her back to the battered grey truck. They drove away down the lane at the head of the small procession with the black dog Merlin sitting up in the passenger seat barking at clouds and nodding at passers-by. The gleaming white police car brought up the rear, following them up the valley, through the hamlets of Llangynog and Penybontfawr and the right-hand fork in the road towards Penygarnedd and the English border. In the blue and gold caravan Helga sat with her best friend Rachel Goldstein and Rachel's fat little baby. Together Helga and Rachel made rude finger gestures at the police through the back window. She knew they would never arrest her, not after the article that the black reporter had sent her. It was the kindest article anyone had ever written about her. It was gentle and understanding and he had kept his promise not to write anything that she didn't want. She had never met an honest journalist before. And there were only five mistakes. And he had such a kind and gentle face. She was sorry now that she had been so rude to him at first, but how was she to know? She had never met a gentle journalist before.

She pulled the magazine off the shelf and flicked through it, stopping at a huge photograph of the English actor Hugh Grant. There was no doubt about it: Hugh Grant was quite beautiful – so relaxed, so twinkly, so civilized, so charming. But was he perhaps too charming? Too clean, too nice, too Anglo-Saxon, too perfect? They had always sought perfection, the Saxons, and in Germany it had led to the Nazis, her grandfather and her greedy father. She hated perfection. They had always wanted her to be perfect. They had always told her that she could do better if she tried, but why should everyone be expected to do better? Why wasn't it good enough just to do well?

Sometimes when she looked in the mirror she hated her own beauty; the wide blue eyes, the blonde hair, the soft lips. It was all too perfect. It needed 'flaws to make it human. That was why she had hacked off her long hair and pierced her eyebrow with a tiny silver ring and her nostril with a silver stud. Who wanted to be a goddess? The black man had looked at her like that, as though she were a goddess. His stares had made her uncomfortable. Because he stared, she had thought, he must be like all the other men. Later he had told her that he worshipped her and he had made her blush. Sometimes she thought of mutilating herself but she knew she would never have the courage. Instead she wore long skirts, old shawls, rough tunics and clumpy boots to camouflage her beauty. She was still too young to understand that shabby outfits made her look more beautiful than ever.

They drove south towards Stonehenge through Llanfyllin and Bwlch-y-cibau and past twelfth century Powys Castle and across the scar of Offa's Dyke, where Lancelot told her that a powerful Anglo-Saxon king of Mercia had moulded the Anglo-Saxon nation twelve hundred years ago and had built a massive earthwork to keep the wild Celtic Welsh at bay. Helga wished she could be Welsh. She wished she were small, dark, peaky and called Bronwen.

They drove on south and west into Anglo-Saxon England along the time-worn pilgrim route to Leominster on the River Lugg – 'It's named after Lugus, the god of the Long Hand,' said Lancelot – and then past ancient settlements with names like Hope under Dinmore, Ocle Pychard, Much Cowarne and Stretton Grandison and on towards Gloucester, the capital of the ancient Anglo-Saxon kingdom of Mercia.

They stopped often, parking for the night in a field or beside the road or down a country lane, and Lancelot and the other men would build a fire and Helga would cook or sit at her needlework or embroidery and afterwards as the day died they would meditate or listen to Gregorian chants or Lancelot would play his lyre and sing of the old legends. But often they were moved on again by the police. Wherever they went people looked askance and moved away. Fields were closed to them, gates locked and barred with notices that read: NO TINKERS TRAVELLERS GYPSIES DOGS. Often heavy chunks of tree trunks were wedged behind the gates to keep them out. 'We don't want the likes of you round here,' said a man in Little Marcle. In supermarkets the other shoppers moved imperceptibly away without even looking, as though they could smell failure.

Helga did not mind. What did she care for the opinions of these people? Who were they, with their constant spending and insurance policies and pale, stricken faces? Lancelot told her that the English had always sneered at those who were different and had looked down on those they did not understand. The entire British Empire, he said, had been built on snobbery, intolerance and contempt.

'We are the Children of Dôn, Hell,' he told her. 'We are the Powers of Light, which is why we are always persecuted by the Children of Llyr, the Powers of Darkness, and the goddess Rhiannon, and Brân the Raven God who has no body but only a bloody severed head. We are the People of Gwydion, the master of magic and music, and Aranrhod of the Silver Wheel, the virgin goddess of sky and fertility, and their sons the sea god Dylan, and Lugus the god of the Long Hand, *Lleu Llaw Gyffes*, the god of the Dexterous Hand, the patron of all arts and travellers, the Lord and Master.'

'We go south,' he said, 'to the sacred place, following the ancient ley lines, knowing the oak tree, to honour Belenus, the Bright One, the god of the sun, at his festival of fire. And you, my Hellish, you are one of the Mother Goddesses, the fairy mothers, *Y Mamau*, to be cherished for ever.'

He looked deep into her eyes and she felt a trembling in her womb.

After Gloucester they took a detour across the Cotswold Hills to Cirencester, the old capital of the Dobuni tribe of ancient Britons, and across the gentle hills of Oxfordshire towards Wantage and the Vale of the White Horse. Lancelot drove the truck and caravan up to the summit of White Horse Hill at Uffington, where the huge mysterious three thousand-year-old figure of a horse had been cut into the white chalk hillside.

He climbed out of the truck and pointed across the vale towards Wantage.

'That's where Alfred the Great was born in 849,' he said, 'and later he defeated the Danes nearby at the Battle of Ashdown. This is where all the ancient ley lines meet, Hell. This is where Britain was born, and the British Empire, and America. This place is the womb of Anglo-Saxon civilisation.'

Helga gazed up at the huge figure of the white horse. 'Why are they calling it an horse?' she said. 'It is more like an cat, *ja*.'

Lancelot stared up at it. She was right: the gigantic figure had a sinuous, feline grace that was nothing like the powerful strength of a horse. Had all the experts and scholars got it wrong?

'You're dead right, Hell! Of course! The Celts used to worship cats. And cats rode the skies on witches' broomsticks.'

They tramped down the steep hillside path towards the vast white ears of the 'horse' and he pointed down towards Uffington at the stark hillock that stood alone and mysteriously sinister. It looked as though it had been scarred by hatred.

'They say that's where St George killed the Dragon,' said Lancelot.

Sometimes, as Lancelot's deep voice washed over her, Helga's mind went into neutral. He knew so much. Perhaps he knew too much. Now and then she thought of the black reporter and his soft smile and gentle face. He never said too much. He said just enough. Wakonde. Nat Wakonde. Sometimes she dreamed of him in her sleep, for no woman can ever forget any man who has looked at her like that.

'*Taran* means "thunder" in Welsh,' said Lancelot, 'which is why the Celtic god Taranis is Jupiter, The Thunderer, the god of asteroids and comets.'

She had never slept with a black man.

'Are you listening, Hell?'

'Of course, *ja*,' she said. 'Every word.'

She thought of his black black skin against her pale pink flesh. There were goosepimples on her arms.

'You'll never learn anything if you don't listen,' said Lancelot.

The letter from Quang Linh arrived at last on a beautiful April morning with the sun banked high above the paddyfields around the Sai Gon River and the distant mountains of Bao Loc and Da Lat. Nguyen Thi Chu had gone to work early before the post arrived, exhausted by yet another nightmare, and the envelope lay unnoticed for several hours in her mailbox pigeonhole outside the staff room as she sat at her computer in her office two floors above and worked on the chapter about the Seven Modern Deadly Sins for her book.

'In every Anglo-Saxon country the people now follow slavishly every passing fad and political correctness,' she wrote, 'spinelessly obeying the whims of cynical capitalists and astrologers, following false prophets, cults and sects. They worship fame and shallow image-makers. They are spineless in standing up for truth and justice or in resisting evil and punishing wrongdoers. Even the most disgusting sexual perversions and pornography are condoned. The Anglo-Saxon race has lost its soul.'

Soon after noon Chu left her office and descended the two flights of stairs to the history faculty staff room. As she passed her pigeonhole she spotted Quang Linh's letter protruding from it at a jaunty angle just as she had dreamed for so long that it would. The colour of the envelope alone, the standard naval colour, told her immediately that the long wait was over. The sight of his handwriting on the envelope suddenly weakened her.

With trembling fingers she grasped the letter and carried it back up the stairs to her office, holding it before her as though it were some holy relic.

She laid the envelope on her desk, afraid to open it, placing it like a sacrifice before Quang Linh's silver-framed photograph. She looked at his sweet picture. He was smiling, in his naval uniform, so proud, so happy, his hair sticking up as usual, his ears sticking out. I love him so much, she thought. Just let him be safe and happy. She raised the photograph to her lips and kissed the glass.

Her eyes were damp. How silly.

She wiped her eyes and opened the envelope.

'Dear Mother,' said the letter. 'I am worried about you because you never write to me. Why do you never answer my letters? I write to you every week yet I hear nothing in return. Please write. I worry about you. I fear that something may have happened to you. Perhaps you are ill? Otherwise I am well myself and enjoying life in the service of our great country. Your loving son, Quang Linh.'

That was all.

She stared at his photograph in the silver frame. He smiled back at her. What did he mean? She had written to him every week for months, sometimes twice a week. It was he who never replied, he who had caused her so much worry.

Perhaps there was something wrong with the postal system. She would have to speak to the ministry about it. Perhaps there were security implications with mail going to and from the Spratly Islands.

But at least he was safe and enjoying himself. At least he was safe.

She descended the stairs again to the staff room and had some lunch in the canteen with Bui Ngoc Ho and later she joined the exercise class for aerobics.

It was not until late in the afternoon that she was summoned to see the head of the history faculty in his office. She allowed herself the faintest smear of lipstick and a dab of perfume. As she entered the room the government informer was slouched in a chair in front of the desk with his thin legs entwined around each other like serpents. His flattened hair glistened like an oil slick. He glanced at her with interest, as though she were some lower form of life to be studied. His eyes were as cold as ever. She could smell the grease on his hair.

Suddenly she felt breathless. Her heart trembled. So he had found her out at last, she thought: something she had said during one of her lectures, maybe, some remark she had made to some disgruntled student. Or perhaps he had stolen his way into her computer and had read something of which he disapproved. And now he had reported her. Now he would accuse her of treachery. She had always known he would do so one day. She locked her fingers together to stop her hands trembling.

The government informer uncoiled his legs. His thin shins glinted pale beneath his trouser legs. She felt more afraid than she had felt in thirty years, since the dark steaming silence of the Cu Chi tunnels.

'I have unfortunate news for you, comrade,' said the government spy.

Her lips were paralysed.

Quang Linh.

It had to be.

'The State and the Party grieve with you.'

Not Quang Linh, who always tried to protect me.

'They offer their condolences.'

In a flash of memory she saw Quang Linh as a little boy, his legs like little sticks, his shorts too long and baggy, flappy around his bony little knees, his eyes so dark and vulnerable, his tufty hair so uncontrollable, his ears sticking out like a baby elephant's, his little snub nose, his cheeky smile.

No. Please no. Not Quang Linh. Please. Not my baby.

The government spy stared at her. 'Your son Kieu Quang Linh is dead,' he said.

CHAPTER 9

The gleaming new $360 million Filipino cruise liner *Celebrity*, cheered on by thousands of shipyard workers and their families, slipped almost empty out of Helsinki harbour on a misty morning into the choppy Gulf of Finland with barely a tremor as its Greek skipper and skeleton crew set course west on its maiden ghost voyage towards the Baltic and the first stage of its eight-week journey to the Far East.

As tall as a 12-storey skyscraper – yet computer-controlled from the bridge by a tiny joystick no bigger than a toadstool – and faster at 27 knots than even the *Oriana* or the *QE2*, the 74,174-ton, 15-deck, 2,135-passenger, fully computerised monster shouldered aside the pounding of the waves without even a twitch of its massive 95-ton stabilisers, which would take it with only the slightest tremble through the tempests of the Bay of Biscay and the South China Sea. Only the mighty swells of the Pacific might one day challenge the giant vessel to heave and roll.

Across the cold North Sea and down the chilly English

Channel the *Celebrity* was scheduled to sail to dock first at Southampton and then to follow the sun south across the Equator around the Cape of Good Hope towards the teeming harbours of the Orient.

At Cape Town the *Celebrity* would dock in the shadow of Table Mountain to salute the fifth anniversary of free black South Africa with a shipboard banquet for the South African president and the heads of a dozen African nations. And then the ship would cruise north through the warm, shark-infested waters of the Indian Ocean and Mozambique Channel up the East African coast to show the flag at Durban, Maputo, Beira, Dar-es-Salaam and Zanzibar before setting sail finally, relentlessly east for the Seychelles, Colombo, Singapore and Ho Chi Minh City, where the River Sai Gon had been dredged to take the biggest liners. Then it would sail for the Philippines into the rising sun.

Somewhere along the way – in the Seychelles perhaps or Singapore – the woman would come aboard, the editor of *Celebrity* magazine, to test the ship for herself to see if it was worthy of the cruise she had booked to Tonga and the international date line in December 1999. The dapper little Greek skipper, Captain Stavros Eliades, was not looking forward to it. The woman had a reputation. They said she was impossibly difficult, utterly selfish, constantly changing her mind quite irrationally and much given to making absurd demands and insisting on having her way. But the PR people had been adamant that her whims should be gratified. The celebrity party she was planning for New Year's Eve would be worth millions of dollars in international publicity, and so the *Celebrity* had been furnished with expensive paintings, portraits and busts of more than a thousand twentieth-century celebrities, from Marilyn Monroe to Hugh Grant, and the two five-star restaurants had been named after celebrity chefs, the two thirteen-metre swimming pools after Olympic swimmers, the three gymnasia after famous athletes. The ship had a seven-hundred-seat Sylvester Stallone theatre, a five-hundred-seat Liz Taylor cinema, a Marlene Dietrich cabaret nightclub, a Lucky Lord Lucan casino, a four-deck Princess Diana shopping arcade, a Jane Fonda health hydro, an Imelda Marcos kindergarten and a Bill Gates computer room with multi-million-byte electronic library and space-satellite access to the Internet and the World Wide Web.

The skipper was not keen to have the *Celebrity* editor on board. He did not have much time for difficult women. He had one of his own at home.

The *Celebrity* shuddered as she turned into the Baltic wind between Hangö and Hiiumaa and headed for Gotland and out to the open sea.

'What in God's name is the woman doing now in Venice?' said Murdoch, rolling his good eye while the other gazed glassily at Kelly.

'Aaag,' said Kelly.

'Come again?'

Kelly gurgled. 'Royals,' he croaked. 'The ball. She's trying to get some.'

'Eye-tie royals?'

Kelly nodded.

'Jeez, the woman must be desperate.'

Kelly croaked again.

'Frog in the throat?' said Murdoch.

'Voice,' croaked Kelly.

'You sound real crook. You want to go and see the quack, mate.'

Kelly nodded. 'Have,' he whispered. 'Said stress.'

Murdoch patted his shoulder. 'I'm not surprised. Strewth, the stuff she gives you to do. You must be knackered. You want to go home to bed, take a couple of days off.'

'She'd kill me.'

'It's far too much for you to do on your own. She ought to get one of the London party specialists in to organise this bloody ball. Liz Brewer, Elizabeth Anson, someone like that. They know everyone. They could bring in hundreds of celebs, organise the whole thing, do the PR. Why doesn't she get on to them?'

Kelly grimaced. 'Rows,' he croaked. 'With both. She says …' His voice faded. He choked. 'Says … she'd rather … die than go to them … for help.'

The telephone rang.

Kelly lifted the receiver.

'Don't be so bloody stupid,' said Murdoch. 'How the hell are you going to talk on the phone? Give the thing to me.'

He took the receiver. It was Nat Wakonde calling from London.

'G'day, mate,' said Murdoch. 'Great piece on the Gröning girl. Caused quite a stir, eh? We even had the Israeli media on the blower. Great stuff. Sorry I was a bit rude about her. Just trying to gee you up a bit. It worked too, eh? Even the old bag liked it. Here, have you heard the one about this guy who takes his pet croc into a pub?'

Nat grunted. 'Not now, Tony.'

'OK, mate. No probs.'

'It's this bloody story about Salman Rushdie's love life,' said Nat.

Murdoch chuckled. 'I can see it now: RUSHDIE GETS HIS ROCKS OFF. SALMAN SPAWNS. SATANIC VICES.'

'Is the bloody woman out of her mind? I mean, how the hell do I even start? I can't write a sleazy piece like that.'

'Why not?'

'It's hardly journalism.'

Murdoch gave a hollow laugh that echoed across the Alps. 'You what?'

'It's just tacky gossip,' said Nat.

'So what's new?'

'Who the hell cares about Rushdie's love-life?'

'A couple of million readers, I expect,' said Murdoch. 'You didn't come into this racket To Do Good, did you? You didn't expect to be part of some noble cause, I hope? You didn't believe in all that crap about the dignity of the Fourth Estate?'

'I expected to write the truth. To write about things that matter.'

'Truth? Jeez, mate, this is journalism. Where've you been the last twenty years? We're just hacks now, that's all, only song-and-dance men earning a crust by entertaining the troops. Nobody gives a flying fuck if it's all lies, not even the people we write about, half the time. People expect us to gossip and lie. Haven't you learned that yet?'

The line was silent.

'Nat?'

He could hear him breathing.

'Speak to your old Uncle Tony, there's a good boy.'

'I don't know if I can go on with this much longer,' said Nat.

'Of course you can. And how can you resign? You've just bought that flat and there aren't that many jobs out there. Ask any freelance. Come on, it's not such a bad idea, anyway. What is poor old Rushdie doing for his jollies? It's not a bad idea at all. You just need a bit of a holiday, old son. Get the Rushdie piece under your belt and then take a break. I'll try and fix it for you this end. Get away somewhere nice for a week or two, put your feet up, get your leg over.'

The line hummed.

'Ooops. Sorry. Tender subject, eh? You still got the hots for the German sheila? OK. No worries. Hire a caravan. Stick a bone through your nose. Take off after her and slip her a length.'

'You're a crude bugger, Tony. Is the bloody Editor there?'

'No, she's off on another freebie. Venice.'

'Iain, then. Can I have a word? Is he around?'

'He's around, all right: around the bend, I reckon.'

'What do you mean?'

'Talking to himself. Twitching. Making faces. Scratching his bollocks. Sometimes he just laughs suddenly, like a parrot.'

'What's wrong with him?'

'Nervous breakdown, I expect. It wouldn't surprise me: She's been giving him a hard time recently. She's been giving

us all a hard time. The woman's been a real bitch this week.
They're all at it, Paddy too, all collapsing under the strain. Still,
it's only the sensitive ones who suffer. The crude buggers like
me survive.'

'Can you put me on to Iain? I'd still better speak to him.'

'OK, mate. Fair do's. It's your cremation. I'll put you
through.'

Murdoch pressed the buttons for Campbell's extension and
heard Campbell's telephone buzzing several times unanswered
in his office along the corridor.

Campbell wandered into the newsroom. He looked around
with a wild expression.

'It's the furry ones, you know, laddie,' he said in a
confidential murmur.

'Eh?'

'And the spiky ones also. Oh yes.'

'What you on about, mate?'

Campbell stared at him with intense concentration and
then hooted with laughter.

'Know what she's done now, laddie?' he squawked. 'She's
taken all the charity money. The cash we all chip in for the
CDs and videos that get sent in for review.'

'The Widows' and Orphans' Fund?'

Campbell cackled. 'That's it. The Editor's pinched it. To buy
some make-up, she said. Ninety-eight francs! To buy some
make-up!'

He wandered away in a trance towards his office. 'It's the
spiky ones that are best in the end,' he muttered.

'Fuck me,' said Murdoch. 'Scotland 2, Hades 98.'

'Tony?'

Nat Wakonde, muffled, on the telephone.

'Tony? You still there?'

'Not now, mate. Not now. I've got to get the poor old fart to
hospital. He's gone completely round the twist.'

Campbell wandered into The Editor's office and began to
remove his trousers.

★★★

'The gold is worth nearly two hundred million rand!' said the Oud Baas. 'Two hundred million!'

Steyn whistled.

'*Scheiss!*' said Pienaar.

They were sitting around the Volksraad conference table in the safe house on De Clerq Street in Lydenburg, most of the usual delegates. An African was whistling tunelessly in the street beyond the garden wall and from a distance came the sound of a heavy lorry growling down Voortrekker Street towards Sabie and Long Tom Pass. The Voortrekkers' vengeance was nigh, thought van der Merwe: the sound of the Long Tom guns would soon be booming again across the lowveld.

The Oud Baas tugged at his beard. He smiled like a crocodile. 'With that sort of money we can recruit, train and arm a proper Volksleger at last,' he said, 'and then we will be strong enough to declare independence.'

'At last!' said Strydom. 'The day is come.'

'Amen,' said Potgieter.

The Oud Baas nodded. 'The world has forgotten us,' he said. 'It treats us with contempt and condescension. It is time to remind them who we are. Do you know what their latest offer is to us? They are offering us a homeland in Mozambique!'

'*Nee!*'

'Never!'

'An insult!'

'It's true,' said the Oud Baas. 'The kaffirs in Maputo are offering us cheap land across the border if we are willing to develop it and teach them how to farm. And the rest of the world is behind them. The world forgets that we were promised a whites-only homeland in the document that de Klerk and Mandela signed when the kaffirs took over. That's how much the world thinks of us: a tin-pot, banana-republic Volksstaat in Mozambique! We must show them that the Boer nation is still the only true champion of Christianity and decency in a world corrupted by liberalism and weakness and depravity. We will not be discriminated against because of our colour.'

Deep in his imagination van der Merwe could hear the silent echo of a multitude of dead Boer voices singing that great patriotic anthem 'Die Stem', and then the ghostly accordion strains of 'Sarie Marais', and the spirits of all those Boer heroes down the ages whose courage and sweat in building this land had all gone to waste thanks to the kaffirs and kaffir-lovers and Commies and pinko fellow travellers: brave pioneers like Louis Trichardt and Andries Potgieter, the Great Elephant of the Voortrekkers, the man the kaffirs had called Nthelaka, 'The Attacker', who defied both the Brits and the Zulus and forced Mzilikazi to sue for peace and who died on 16 December 1852, the Day of the Vow, fourteen years to the day after the Voortrekkers' victory over Dingaan's Zulus at the battle of Blood River. And Hendrik Potgieter, and Karel Trichardt, who trekked from Ohrigstad to Delagoa Bay in 1845, and Willem Pretorius, who was buried in the Kruger Park near Pretorius Kop, and Helgard Petrus Steenkamp and Stefanus Johannes Roos of the Potchefstroom Commando and Frederick Senekal, and all the others; all those who fought and died in the wars against the blacks and the Brits. And the gold-rush miners who dared and dug and died at the ghost town of Eureka City and in the Valley of Death at Barberton. And those who had risked their lives to build the first dangerous roads to places like God's Window and Silver Creek and Robbers' Pass and Pilgrim's Rest. And unremembered heroes like van der Merwe's grandfather Nathan, who had carved a place here for his seed out of the unforgiving earth, and heroines like his grandmother, Beulah, and his great-grandmother, Hannah, who had buried ten of her eleven infant children. Heroines like Hephzibah, once so young, so trim, so much in love with him.

Tears salted his eyes. They must not be forgotten, all those Boer heroes and heroines. Their sacrifices must never be sold cheap again. The Vow must be renewed. *Ons vir jou, Suid-Afrika!*

The small pile of Kruger's buried gold had glinted in the moonlight as the two young troopers had hauled the sacks out of the hole they had dug in the Kruger Park at the foot of Mount Khandzalive between the *donga* and the dead old marula tree. There seemed so little of it to be worth so much. Two hundred million rand! Everything seemed suddenly to take on a deeper significance. The clunk of the ingots as they nudged each other in the dust. Bezuidenhout's stifled cry of joy. The sudden startled silence of the night bush. The hammering of his own heart. As the gold lay spread out under a million stars, blinking in the moonlight for the first time in a hundred years, the pain had stabbed his gut with such ferocity that he had whimpered.

'What about the bloke who sent us the diary?' asked Grobler. 'Who is he, this so-called senior government official?'

'A great patriot,' said the Oud Baas. 'I expect he will make himself known to us in due course, when we have established the new republic. Are we all agreed that the gold should be sold to hasten that day?'

'*Ja, baas!*'

'*Natuurlik!*'

'To buy weapons and declare independence?'

'*Ja seker.*'

'*Ongetwyfeld.*'

'We could do it next year to mark the centenary of Kruger's war against the British.' The Oud Baas licked his lips. 'We could refuse to take part in the elections. We all know that they will be rigged. We could turn our backs on them, and declare independence instead.'

Yes! thought van der Merwe savagely. What a pleasure: to declare independence from these kaffir bastards and to set up the new Boere Volksstaat on the very anniversary of Kruger's

War against the Brits! Perfect! Brilliant! That would show the sniggering Brit kaffir-loving bastards!

Do you know why van der Merwe keeps coming back for more moth-balls? Because his aim is so bad he keeps missing the moths.

Halfway down the table Koos Labuschagne raised a finger and caught the Oud Baas's eye.

'I know where we can buy a nuclear bomb,' said Labuschagne.

In the distance a scooter buzzed irritably along Kerk Street.

The Oud Baas gazed at Labuschagne with translucent grey eyes. 'A Russian bomb?' he said.

'No.'

'I'm not touching any of those old Soviet weapons,' said the Oud Baas. 'They're desperate for cash and they've been trying to flog them for so long that the things are probably useless. They use dirty plutonium and their safety procedures are non-existent.'

'They're not Russian, *baas*,' said Labuschagne. 'These bombs are South African.'

A stillness leaked across the table like that moment in the bush when everything falls silent just before a leopard makes a kill.

The Oud Baas stared at him. 'I understood that all six of our nuclear bombs were deliberately destroyed by de Klerk before Mandela took over in 1994.'

Labuschagne looked nervous. 'There were more than six,' he said. 'In the eighties the Israelis helped us to build twenty-one bombs at a secret research centre not far from Pretoria and in the nineties they started working on neutron bombs. They called it "tickling the Dragon's tail".'

The Dragon, thought van der Merwe. The old serpent. Satan, breathing fire and brimstone. Revelation, Chapter 20: 'And I saw an angel come down from heaven, having the key of the bottomless pit and a great chain in his hand. And he laid hold on the dragon, that old serpent, which is the Devil, and

Satan, and bound him a thousand years. And cast him into the bottomless pit, and shut him up, and set a seal upon him, that he should deceive the nations no more, till the thousand years should be fulfilled.'

'Six bombs were eventually destroyed to keep the world happy,' said Labuschagne, 'but one was secretly tested in the Mozambique Channel and twelve more were smuggled back to Israel and two went missing somewhere in South Africa and have never been accounted for.'

He looked around the table and gave a little smile. 'I know where the two missing bombs are,' he said, 'and they're both for sale.'

Labuschagne smiled. 'The bombs are called Paul and Hendrik after Kruger and Verwoerd.'

'Great patriots.'

'God rest their souls.'

'I understand that the bombs are stored not far from here, in the Northern Transvaal, in stockpiles deep under the bush,' said Labuschagne. 'They're very easy to hide. These modern neutron bombs are incredibly small, about half the size of a rugby ball.'

Oh yes! thought van der Merwe, thank the Lord. A nuclear bomb of our very own. A threat the world could no longer ignore. An N-bomb to protect South Africa's most threatened wildlife species, the Afrikaaner.

How do you confuse poor old van der Merwe? Lean two shovels against the wall and tell him to take his pick.

They should drop the bomb on London and wipe the bastards out.

'How much?' said the Oud Baas.

'I could probably get them for about fifty or sixty million rand each,' said Labuschagne.

The Lord God of Battles is girding His loins, thought van der Merwe, to rescue His chosen people.

He suddenly gasped for breath.

'Hendrik?'

He winced.

'You've gone quite white.'

He smiled weakly. 'That's very reassuring!' he said.

They laughed uneasily. He hated to see the pity in their eyes. He felt diminished by their sympathy. It could not be long now before the inevitable telephone call: 'Hendrik, we're truly grateful for all you've done but it's time for you to make way for a younger man.' When that happened there would be little left to live for.

He would have to see the doctor again. He would need the painkillers soon.

Ugo Legrandu sat at an outside table in Venice on the Piazza San Marco, smoking a Gauloise, sipping a *cappuccino* and listening to the lilting melody of the late-night string quartet playing on the balcony of Florian's café. All over the vast *piazza* spread wide beneath the brooding magnificence of St Mark's *basilica* pools of water glistened in the moonlight as though the giant marble lions on the Piazzetta dei Leoncini had been relieving themselves all over the square. The huge volcanic paving stones smelled fresh and clean. Pigeons danced with their reflections on the puddles, splashing each other with their wings.

He had checked into a cheap hotel and telephoned the marchesa's *palazzo* but a *macaroni* manservant had announced in a servile Italian whine that the marchesa and her guests were dining out and would not be back until after midnight. He had used the evening to drift through the jostling crowds thronging the streets and the banks of the canals, peering into cafés and windows, strolling about the crooked warren of alleyways and passages between the Piazza San Marco and the Rialto Bridge, amazing himself by working out in francs the prices of the antiques and Venetian glass and lace on display. Staring into a brightly lit souvenir shop window in the Calle dei Fabbri, he had been mesmerised by the sinister harlequin expression on the silver face of a traditional long-nosed Venetian carnival mask that seemed to leer at him. It repelled yet attracted him and eventually, although he knew he could not afford it, he entered the shop and bought it. He tried the mask on, fixing it about his ears and gazing into a mirror in the shop. With its long, beaky silver nose, it gave him a look half evil, half wicked: half Scaramouche and half Pinocchio; half lecher, half lover. *Weh!* He would wear it as a disguise when he was breaking into the *palazzo*. He would wear it as he ravished her in her room above the canal and she would not know who he was until he chose to tell her.

The quartet outside Florian's finished playing and started to pack up their instruments. Legrandu looked at his watch. It was getting late. The tourists were leaving their seats and wandering off towards their hotels and the waiters, in black suits and white aprons, were fluttering like flustered pigeons as they stacked the tables and chairs.

He paid for the coffee and ambled away from the huge *piazza* through the darkened alleyways towards the Rialto Bridge and the marchesa's *palazzo* across the canal towards the Rio delle Due Torri. Venice had irritated him in daylight. He had hated the sweaty crowds and the stench of packaged culture, the trippers jostling from one ornate church to another, from museum to gallery, scavengers picking over the rotting carcass of European civilisation. It had needed a down-to-earth Corsican to see through all the showy, foppish, *macaroni* shallowness of the place: they said that the great Napoleon had taken one look at it and had immediately abolished the Venetian Republic. But now the crowds were gone and Legrandu began to enjoy the anonymity of midnight and the camouflage of darkness, shrugging himself into the shadows and savouring the deep silence that could suddenly envelop you as you turned a corner, the whisper of the lagoon lapping the ancient stone, the random clinking of tethered boats and gondolas as they nudged each other, a sudden strange silhouette, the occasional echoing footstep in the dark.

As he crossed the Rialto Bridge he was greeted by the bells of San Giacomo tolling midnight and the flickering lights of Ruga dell Orefici beckoning him on past ochre walls and low doorways towards the cramped streets beyond Campo Baccarie and the Rio di San Cassiano. The lights were still blazing on every floor at the marchesa's *palazzo* and he stood in a shadow across the alleyway to await their return. A large boat growled up the Grand Canal, its engines throbbing, leaving a luminescent wake that lashed the steps at the end of the alleyway. Something moved in the dark behind him, a rat perhaps, clattering a can against the cobblestones. From a distant window he could hear the muffled tones of a television set, the staccato dialogue of a late-night movie. Grey light flickered against ancient stone.

It began to rain.

It was nearly one o'clock before the marchesa and her guests returned home. The rain had stopped but the cobbles glistened still with its memory and dampness dripped from the medieval eaves. Legrandu stepped back into the shadows. Rain dribbled down his neck. He watched from the darkness as the party approached from the direction of the Campo San Cassiano, their footsteps clattering loud along the night alleyway long before they came into sight, their approaching voices echoing in the corners of hollow passageways. There were six of them, three men and three women: the women slim and elegant in their evening dresses, explosions of red, white and blue, all laughing, the men casual and carefree in light-coloured trousers, open-necked shirts and expensive sneakers. Legrandu felt a stab of jealousy. Their laughter seemed offensive, their wealth disgusting. He felt homesick for Sartène, where the Communists ruled and the women wore black.

He pulled the mask on, tightening the fastening behind his head. The holes for the eyes were a little too small and he was strongly conscious of the large, beaky nose protruding in front of him, sweeping the air when he turned his head, glinting silver in the moonlight. It smelt of metal but it gave him camouflage: if they spotted him they would simply assume that he was a late reveller on his way home.

He stared at the women as they came into sight, raising the hems of their dresses above the glistening cobblestones: the one in red small and blonde, the one in white dark and anorexic, the one in blue…

She was not there.

La Barrett was not one of them.

He stared at them, not comprehending. The blonde in red was much too short, the one in white all collar-bone and elbow, the one in blue positively ugly.

He shook his head. Where was she?

With another man? Jealousy suddenly burned in his gut.

He stepped forward out of the shadow, unthinking.

'Where is she?' he said angrily in Italian. His voice was muffled by the mask.

They turned towards his voice, startled. The woman in red saw his mask and raised her hand to her lips.

'What have you done with her?' said Legrandu furiously, speaking more distinctly. 'Where is she? Is she ill?'

One of the men stepped forward. 'Who are you?' he said. 'What are you talking about?'

'La Barrett,' said Legrandu. 'Where is she?'

'Stella?' said the ugly woman in blue. 'He knows Stella?'

The marchesa. Of course. He recognised her now. The marchesa, with a face like a toad.

'Of course I know Stella, marchesa,' said Legrandu.

She looked startled. 'You know me too?'

'Of course,' he lied. He gave a little bow. 'We met two years ago.'

'In…?'

'Nice. But why should you remember? It was Stella who

introduced us but the meeting was sadly brief.'

'And Stella?'

He smiled. 'We are –' he shrugged '– good friends.'

'Well!'

The woman in red giggled. 'What fun!' she said.

'And your name, *signor*?'

Legrandu hesitated. 'Pierre Lamont,' he said. 'From Monaco. She has mentioned me to you?'

The marchesa smiled unconvincingly. 'Of course,' she lied. 'She will be most upset to have missed you. Did she expect you? That is strange. She said nothing. She has suddenly been called away on business.'

'To Prague?'

'You knew she was going to Prague?' The marchesa seemed relieved. 'Yes, she had to leave in a hurry for Czechoslovakia. Some nonsense about a cannibal hairdresser. Dear Stella is always most amusing.'

She gestured towards her *palazzo*, a bony, ugly figure but once again in charge. 'You will join us for a drink, Signor Lamont? And remove that amusing mask? Come.'

'You are most gracious, *madame*,' said Legrandu, 'but it is late.'

The mask's silver nose pointed obscenely at her. It glinted in the moonlight.

'Strange that she left no message for you if she was expecting you,' said one of the men suspiciously. 'Odd that she did not say that you were coming.'

'She did not know I was coming. It was meant to be a surprise.'

The little blonde in red looked at him with interest. 'How sweet,' she said.

The woman in white stared at him. 'How romantic,' she said.

He could smell the blonde's perfume: a trace of apricots, rose petals. She smiled at him.

'You must join us for a drink,' said the marchesa briskly,

'and tell us all about yourself and Stella.'

Legrandu gave a shallow bow. 'It is very gracious of you, marchesa, but I must not presume on your hospitality.'

'Not at all…'

'It is late.'

'Little more than midnight.'

'Almost one.'

'Then the night has not begun.'

'You must excuse me, marchesa. I am weary after my journey.'

The blonde giggled. 'Poor Stella!'

'Perhaps tomorrow?'

The marchesa looked disappointed. Her face settled into a puffed expression of discontent. 'Very well,' she said. 'If you insist. You shall lunch with us tomorrow. Ha! Today.'

Legrandu bowed again. 'I should be honoured.'

'Here? At twelve thirty?'

'Enchanted.'

The marchesa smiled, her jowls wobbling. For one terrible moment Legrandu wondered what she might look like naked. He closed his eyes and shook his head, setting the nightmare free.

'Until tomorrow, then. Today. At twelve thirty.'

He bowed, bending to kiss her hand, the cold silver nose of the mask pecking at her knuckles.

'*A domani,*' he said.

He turned to face the blonde in red, clicked his heels and kissed her fingers too. They smelled of fish.

'Charming,' she said.

And then the woman in white.

'Strange that Stella didn't invite the fellow for dinner,' muttered the man with the blonde.

They moved away towards the *palazzo*. Spoilt *macaroni* bitches, he thought. They had less between their ears than they had between their legs. What had they ever done to earn their ease and wealth? Flat on their backs, that's all, like common

prostitutes, selling their bodies to rich men. They would sneer
a little less if they knew what he really thought of them, what
he dreamed of doing to them. They would lock their doors and
bolt their windows.

He strode angrily through the huddled maze of streets away
from the Rio delle Due Torri through the Campo Beccarie
and along the Sottoportico di Rialto towards the hunchbacked
Rialto Bridge, the mask swinging from his hand, the long silver
nose gleaming in the moonlight, his footsteps clacking
furiously towards the Grand Canal. Rage clouded his mind.
First Venice, now Prague: how dare she suddenly go off to
Prague like that without telling him? How dare she give him
the slip again? She was toying with him, teasing him, leading
him on a fool's dance across Europe and now he had no idea
where to find her in Prague, and he certainly had no intention
of meeting the marchesa for lunch. If the marchesa told La
Barrett that he had been asking for her they would call the
carabinieri.

Halfway across the Rialto Bridge he stopped and leaned on
the parapet, breathing heavily. He lit a cigarette, a red glow in
the night, a ghostly puff of smoke. The mask glinted in the
moonlight, leering at him. Waves danced and shimmered down
the Grand Canal towards the lagoon, flirting along the banks
with a small breeze towards the *vaporetto* stations of San
Silvestro and San Angelo. On either side of the Grand Canal
the *palazzi* loomed like giant black cliffs. A barge floated away
in the distance, heading south, its tug grunting like a
hippopotamus. He could smell the sea: salt, seaweed, oil, grease.
Somewhere far out on the lagoon, beyond the high dome of
Chiesa della Salute, a ship's hooter wailed as sad as a child lost
alone in the mist.

He needed to drain his anger. He needed a woman, but
where did you find a woman in this godforsaken *macaroni*
aquarium at two in the morning? The rich little blonde in red.
He wished that he had her alone now up one of the darkened

alleyways up against a warm old wall, her red dress rucked up above her hips, her plump *macaroni* buttocks pressed tight against the ancient stone, her slender legs locked about his waist, the smell of fish on her fingers. He would bite her breasts. He would chew her nipples.

A whore. No complications. That's what he needed. Simple. He would betray the bitch Barrett with a common prostitute. That would teach her. He felt stiff with lust. Perhaps the women in Venice had tails, like mermaids. Perhaps that was why they smelled of fish.

He picked up the mask and crossed to the other side of the humpbacked bridge, heading left away from the centre of the city and the main streets across the Campo San Bartolomeo and Fontego dei Tedeschi and across the Rio Fontego into the northern districts towards the Canale delle Fondamenta, hunting for flesh. The small canals were still in the moonlight, nothing moving except an occasional water rat laying a trail of soft ripples to tickle the bobbing gondolas and lick the legs of the bridges.

He walked slowly north through deserted streets and alleyways towards the Ospedale Civile, swinging the mask, loitering in the shadows, listening for footsteps, standing still beneath a late lighted window, staring up at it and praying for a sudden face above the sill, a tangle of hair, a beckoning smile. From a window high up in a house on Calle dei Miracoli came the faint sound of music. A cloud moved across the moon, throwing a cloak across the church of Santa Maria Nova. A bottle tinkled against the cobblestones in the Calle Castelli and rolled down the alleyway, clinking as it went. From high on the silent terracotta roofs of Corte Castelli, beside the Rio di San Marina, came the howls of cats wailing like infants, ecstatic with pleasure and pain.

His testicles ached. Pleasure and pain together. He touched himself. He was bursting. Where were the women? Where were the whores, the brothels? On the streets of Nice or Cannes at two o'clock in the morning the prostitutes lined up

in rows like taxis. No wonder the *macaroni* were all homo-
sexuals. The only *poules* in Venice were the chickens.

He heard her footsteps just as he was about to turn back
towards the centre of the city, her high heels echoing faint at
first from across the canal and approaching him along the Calle
del Cristo and over the bridge across the Rio di San Marina,
the thrilling *clack-clack-clack* of high heels alone after midnight.

Clack-clack-clack.

Clack-clack-clack.

A distant promise echoing louder and louder as she
approached.

A woman alone at this time of the night. She must be a
whore. Why else would she be out alone? Going home,
perhaps, tender from too many men in one night, but they
always welcomed a final client. Perhaps he could spend the
whole night, have her again at dawn and again before breakfast.
His loins throbbed. Did he have enough money to buy her?
No matter. He could always leave without paying. He felt
dizzy with lust. He pulled back into a doorway, listening as she
approached.

Clack-clack-clack.

His testicles tightened. The sound of her heels beckoned
him, ricocheting off the stone alleyways like castanets. He felt
full. He closed his eyes. He breathed deeply. Not too soon.
Slow. Slow. Savour it. The excitement of a stranger. The thrill of
pale, unknown thighs, cold, soft, wet. The taste of her tears.

A foul stench drifted off the canal, a cold odour of sulphur
and rotten eggs.

She came out of the night like a small vessel under sail, her
head held as high as a pennant, her prow firm and proud. She
was pale and young, perhaps twenty-three or twenty-four. Fair.
Small. No more than a metre and a half tall: much shorter than
the teenage English girl that hot afternoon in Sagone. *Petite.*
Not pretty but luscious. Her breasts would make good
handfuls. Her lips were plush. Her buttocks trembled.

She was only a few yards away before she saw him leaning in the shadows against the wall.

'*Ciao, bella.*' He smiled. His grin glinted in the moonlight.

She walked on without turning her head, passing him. She smelled of garlic and soap. She smelled afraid.

'*Signorina!*' he said. 'Speak to me.'

She turned right suddenly, into the Calle delle Erbe, across the Rio di Ca'Widman and towards the Rio dei Mendicanti. She quickened her pace.

He followed, his footsteps soft behind the clacking of her heels and the pounding of her heart.

'*Signorina! Per favore! Quanto?*'

'Go away!' she said. 'Leave me alone.' Her voice was shrill with apprehension.

She began to walk faster.

He strode after her, swinging the mask at his side. '*Signorina! Momento, per favore!*'

'Go away! I'm a respectable woman,' she said. Her voice broke. She seemed on the edge of a sob. 'I shall call the *carabinieri.*'

The broken sound of her voice excited him. It gave them a relationship, an intimacy. So she was not a whore, then, after all. But he had to have her. And she would be grateful afterwards. They were always grateful afterwards. Every woman secretly fantasised about rape.

He raised the mask to his face, fixing the band around the back of his head. The silver beak stood high and hard, pointing at her as sharp as an accusation.

She glanced nervously over her shoulder. She saw the mask. She started to run across the bridge over the canal, tottering on her high heels before kicking her shoes off and running to the left barefoot along the Fondamenta dei Mendicanti.

He loped after her. What was wrong with the woman? All he wanted was a little affection. Why all the fuss?

She began to scream.

***

'Help!' she screamed. 'Help!'

She would wake people.

They would call the police.

He began to run after her fast, past the warehouses lining the canal, towards the hospital, where the light splashed across the quay like a golden sanctuary.

He caught her as she ran into the Campo Santi Giovanni e Paolo, grabbing the back of her dress and dragging her back towards him in front of Verrocchio's bronze equestrian statue of Bartolomeo Colleoni.

She saw the mask again and screamed.

A curious light was switched on in a house across the canal, and then another, and a third, but they were far enough away on the other side of the water.

He wrapped his hand across her mouth, stifling her cries, and lifted her in his arms, cradling her close, her full, soft breast pressed into his chest. She was so light, no more than forty or forty-five kilos. She struggled and tried to bite the palm pressed across her mouth but her struggles were useless. She was far too small to resist him. She smelled of fear. He felt a jolt of pleasure as he felt her bones against his body and knew what he was going to do and carried her as she struggled and kicked into the darkness of a narrow alleyway where no light falls even at noon.

In the deepest recess of the alley he tore off the mask, ripped the top of her dress away and threw her down on the ground.

Her head hit the cobbles with a sickening crack. An ugly sound spilled from her lungs.

He stared into the darkness. 'You! You all right?'

He knelt beside her, feeling for her in the dark. 'You all right?'

Blindly he reached for her, running his hands over her, feeling her shoulder, her breast, touching her ribs. He could count each one, thin but firm like the strings of a guitar. As his eyes adjusted to the darkness he could see her silhouette spreadeagled on the ground, her breast gleaming, her head twisted at an ugly angle. He pressed his ear to her mouth. No sound. Her chest. No movement. He rolled her over.

'Wake up!' he hissed. 'Wake up!'

Her arm flopped to one side. He punched her in the chest.

'Wake up!' he croaked.

He shook her and shook her again. Her head lolled uncontrollably.

He stared at her. Her skirt was rucked up around her waist. She smelled of putrefaction. She smelled of death.

He backed away from her, shuffling backwards on his heels, hypnotised.

'*Dio*,' he said. '*Mio Dio*.'

Something crawled away from him in the darkness, shuffling away through filth.

Her soul, he thought in terror.

And the devil will take my own.

He recoiled from her body and ran from the alleyway, turning right, avoiding the hospital, running anywhere except the hospital, running blind away from the immortal city towards the sea, running and running along the Calle del Caffettier and the Calle delle Capucine, his rubber soles slapping the paving stones like a blind man's walking stick, until he reached the Fondamenta Nuove. There he sat on a bench and trembled and gasped in the small fresh breeze off the open sea.

Legrandu bent forward and vomited. He began to weep.

'*Perdonnu mio Dio*,' he sobbed into his lap, rocking himself to and fro, repeating the words of the *Catenacciu* over and over again. '*Mio Dio perdonnu, Perdonnu mio Dio, Perdonnu pietà.*'

Offshore the wind-whipped waves like white-haired priests were washing the feet of the cemetery isle of San Michele, the island of the dead.

'G'day,' said Murdoch in Monte Carlo, winking his good eye at Kelly and lounging behind The Editor's desk with a cheroot between his lips.

The telephone crackled. 'Murdoch?' said The Editor. 'I'm in Prague.'

'Check.'

'Very funny. Where's Kelly?'

'Right here.'

'So why are you answering his phone?'

Murdoch made a face at Kelly. 'He's lost his voice.'

'I thought it was only his marbles.'

Kelly stuck his tongue out at the telephone receiver.

'The quack says it's stress,' said Murdoch. 'Nervous tension.'

'Nervous tension? I'll give him nervous tension.'

Kelly nodded vigorously.

'The quack says he still hasn't recovered from the trauma of opening the letter bomb,' said Murdoch.

'Trauma? It was only a little bang, for God's sake.'

'That's what all the sheilas say. There's no pleasing some women.'

'That's enough of the feeble jokes, thank you very much, Murdoch. Tell Kelly to stop being so pathetic. And put Campbell on.'

Murdoch hesitated.

'I said put Campbell on.'

'He's not here,' he said.

'What?'

'Campbell's crook.'

'Sick? In hospital?'

'At home. In bed.'

'In bed? At three o'clock on a Wednesday afternoon? I'm not standing for this. Get him up immediately. Get him into the office this minute.'

'He's not well, chief. No bullshit. Campbell's not a bludger: he's real mangy. Some sort of nervous attack. When I saw him yesterday arvo he was trembling like a Wagga Wagga virgin on a Saturday night.'

'And what's supposed to be wrong with him?'

'Stress, the quack says. Nervous tension.'

The Editor exploded. 'Infectious, then, is it, this nervous tension? Contagious, is it? My God, an epidemic of wimpishness. I suppose you'll be going down with it next.'

Murdoch laughed. 'Me, chief? Stress? Never. Ah is jus' a lazy, good-for-nothin' outback abo from way out beyond the black stump.'

'You said it, Murdoch, not me. You said it. Now put Kelly on. I'm sure he can whisper.'

Murdoch shrugged. 'You'd have more of a chance getting a dozen dingoes to dance the *paso doble*.'

'Just put him on, Murdoch, will you? I'm in a hurry. I have to be in London tonight and Paris tomorrow.'

'Wilko, chief. Roger, over and out.' He handed the telephone receiver to Kelly, making an obscene gesture with two fingers and a thumb. 'Here you are, sport. It's Hoarse Whisperer time.'

'Kelly?' she said. 'What are you playing at? What's the matter with you? Stop being so pathetic.'

Kelly moved his lips. '—,' he said.

'What was that?'

'—.'

'Speak up, Kelly, for God's sake. Stop being such a wimp.'

'—.'

'Dear God, I can't hang around not listening to you all day. Put Murdoch back on. If I find you're malingering, Kelly, your feet won't touch the ground. Murdoch?'

'In person, chief. Eager and straining at the leash.'

The Editor grunted. 'Get Kelly into the conference room,' she said, 'and turn the amplifier on: that way he can hear my questions and you can give me his answers.'

'Roger. We're on our way, chief.'

'And Murdoch.'

'Chief?'

'For Christ's sake stop calling me chief. I'm not some bloody Red Indian squaw.'

'Now there's a beaut fantasy,' leered Murdoch. 'You Running Bare, me Howling Wolf.'

'One day, Murdoch…'

'Right away.'

Kelly trudged after him into the conference room. Murdoch took the seat at the head of the table and switched on the telephone amplifier. It hummed with apprehension, moaning gently like the eardrum echo of blood in a sea shell.

'OK,' said Murdoch. 'Fair dinkum. All jake.'

'You there, Kelly?' she barked. Her voice stabbed around the room like a blind mugger.

'–,' replied Kelly.

'Kelly is all present and correct,' said Murdoch, 'except for the voice.'

'And the marbles. You listening, Kelly?'

'He is. With both ears.'

'First of all, Kelly, get on to the shipping line and tell them I'll join the liner in Cape Town next week. Book me on a flight from Paris. Tell them I want the best suite from Cape Town to Durban. Right. Next: get them to fix up a safari for me to see the Kruger Game Reserve. I want two or three nights in one or two of the best private camps: Mala Mala, Shimuwini, Biyamiti, one of those. Then I'll fly back to London from there. Fix it, Kelly. Got it? Right. Now: any news? Any messages today?'

Kelly started scribbling frantically on his pad, tearing sheets off as he finished writing and pushing them over to Murdoch to relay. Murdoch squinted over his shoulder, frowning and nodding, blinking now and again at the amplifier.

'He says you have had a grovelling apology from the American President,' said Murdoch. 'One of his private secretaries telephoned personally last night. Full of remorse.'

'I should damn well think so. What did he say?'

'Let's have a dekko. "Deep distress," it says, "profuse apologies, disgraceful unfounded allegations" blah-blah-blah. The White House says it's a mystery how the message was sent in the first place. They swear it didn't come from the Oval Office.'

'So who the hell sent it, then?'

'They reckon some dill may have broken into their computer. Perhaps on the Internet.'

'So what are they doing about it?'

Murdoch peered over Kelly's shoulder. 'They've promised a full investigation, in-depth enquiries, no stone unturned, dah-dee-dah. They've got the FBI and the CIA working on it.'

The Editor snorted. 'Big deal. Those wankers are still trying to work out who killed Kennedy. Right. Kelly: tell the White House I want a full report as soon as they've found the culprit. Plus a public apology to go out on all the agencies. Plus tell them I want the President at the New Year's Eve ball.'

Kelly waved a finger above his head, scribbling furiously.

'It seems he's already going to some big thrash in New York,' reported Murdoch.

The Editor's voice tightened. 'Not any more, he's not. He's coming to Tonga with us. Or else. Now, what else is new?'

Kelly pushed over a sheaf of jottings and waggled his wrist limply. Murdoch picked up the notes.

'A Marian Black-Boyes rang from London,' he said. 'She wants you to call her as soon as you get to the Savoy tonight.'

'Call her back for me this afternoon, fix an interview. She's a great new celebrity astrologer. Get Merlot to do it.'

'Merlot's in Paris. Chasing the cannibal chef.'

'When she's finished with the cannibal chef, then she can go straight on afterwards to London to interview Mrs Black-Boyes.'

Fuck me crouching! Murdoch thought. Black-Boyes! A Mrs Black-Boyes. A woman's name, not under-age gigolos at all. An astrologer. The Editor's been having her fortune told.

'Murdoch? You still there?'

'Well, bugger me!'

'What?'

'Strewth!'

'Get on with it, Murdoch!' yelled the Editor.

'No probs. Nat Wakonde gave us a bell from Oxford. Reckons he knows where to get a fix on Rushdie but he can't get close enough to put the finger on his love life.'

'Tell him to keep trying. Dear God, do I have to do everyone's job? What do I pay these people for? If he's still got nowhere by Monday tell him to make it up. Tell him I want a piece in the next issue. It's a must-have. Next!'

'The Marchesa Somebody Something di Somewhere called from Venice. She said to tell you that your boyfriend Pierre Lamont has been hanging around asking for you.'

'My what?'

'Boyfriend.'

'Pierre who?'

'Lamont.'

'Never heard of him.'

Kelly was frantically scribbling something on the pad. Murdoch glanced at it.

'He's somebody's chauffeur,' he said.

'Lamont?'

'Yes. No. No, Kelly says not somebody's chauffeur. Her chauffeur.'

'The marchesa's?'

'Yes.'

'And she says her chauffeur is my boyfriend?'

'I'm lost, Stella. But the marchesa wants you to bell her.'

'I think I'd better. Talking of chauffeurs, what are the police doing about the Corsican bastard who tried to murder me?'

Kelly was scribbling manically.

'Not the marchesa's chauffeur,' said Murdoch. 'Kelly says he was your chauffeur.'

'Of course he was my chauffeur. I fired the man. What's Kelly going on about?'

'He says Lamont was your chauffeur.'

'No he wasn't. He was called Ergo something. Ergo Lepanto, something like that.'

'Ugo Legrandu.'

'That's it. What are the police doing about the bastard?'

Kelly threw his hands in the air.

'They've dropped the case,' said Murdoch. 'They can't find enough evidence.'

'We'll soon see about that! Kelly? Get on to the Chief Police Commissioner in Paris.'

'Clouseau,' suggested Murdoch. He winked his good eye at Kelly. 'Inspector Clouseau.'

'Yes? Is that him? Fine. Whoever. Tell him I want immediate action about the Corsican killer. Tell him that if I don't get it I shall run a piece about corruption in the French police. Do it, Kelly, this afternoon.'

Kelly slumped across the conference table.

'Kelly is eager for the fray,' reported Murdoch.

'About bloody time!' said The Editor. 'What's next?'

Murdoch consulted Kelly's scrawled directory. 'Larry Dzerzinski died in New York last night.'

The Editor whooped. 'Great! That's fabulous! Did we get some poignant last-minute pics?'

'We're chasing the New York snapper now.'

'He'd better have got them. We'll run them right away, next issue. See to it, Murdoch: a series of pics of Dzerzinski slowly dying of Aids over several years. Brilliant! With a really punchy headline: SNUFF MOVIE DIRECTOR SNUFFS IT. Or what about AIDS: THE ULTIMATE DIET? Something like that. Something sexy. Work on it, Murdoch. Next!'

He looked at Kelly, who shook his head.

'That seems to be the lot,' said Murdoch. 'It's been a quiet day for the Irish.'

'Well, you can tell the Irish it's not a quiet day any more,' said The Editor. 'What about the fancy dress ball? The Beatles? The supermodels? The invitations?'

'The Beatles still aren't interested,' reported Murdoch. 'We've offered them two million each but they don't want to know. Can't buy them, love.'

'Blast! What about Pavarotti?'

'Booked already. David Copperfield too. And the Stones. And the London Philharmonic Orchestra.'

'Damnation! I knew we should have planned this ball years ago, when we could have set it up properly. Why did nobody think of it then, back in the eighties?'

'I wasn't here then, Stella. The magazine wasn't even started until 1995.'

She had started to rant. 'All the best acts will have gone by now. Why did none of you think of it then?'

'I wasn't here then.'

'Why do I always have to do everything myself?' she shrieked.

Murdoch sighed. 'OK, boss, it's because we're all nongs. Drongoes, the lot of us. We all need a flamin' kick up the acre.'

An ominous silence drifted out from Prague, into outer space and glanced off the telephone satellite back to earth again to hum to itself in the amplifier. Irony was always a mistake with The Editor, thought Murdoch: irony came at her like a stranger and she passed it by without even a nod.

The silence lengthened. This is it, thought Murdoch. This is where she calls my bluff and shows that she can sack a black, one-eyed, culturally deprived, socially challenged aborigine after all and to hell with political correctness.

'You know what, Murdoch?' she said. 'You're absolutely right. And you know something else? I'm going to make you deputy editor instead of Campbell. As of now. Campbell's out. Finished. Fired. I can't have a deputy editor who gets nervous tension and goes to bed at three in the afternoon. I need a deputy editor who can face reality, even if it means admitting how useless he is. You're promoted, Murdoch. Congratulations.'

Murdoch gazed at the amplifier. For a moment he thought that he too had lost his voice.

Kelly looked at him nervously, drew a forefinger across his throat and rolled his eyes upwards.

Murdoch cleared his throat. 'Come off it, Stella,' he said. 'Strewth, I'm just a production hack, not deputy editor

material. I couldn't tell the difference between a fashionable
society hairdresser and a back-street shirt-lifter.'

'They're probably the same guy. Plus never mind that,
you're the only one of my staff I can trust.'

Murdoch hesitated. Deputy editor, eh? A pay-rise. A little
clout. And maybe he could hack it where the others had failed.
He wouldn't let her push him around, like the others. She was
only a woman, after all. Just a sheila, not a monster. The others
had always been terrified of her, that was their problem. That

they had failed: they were all born victims, wankers
decent bloke. tened of feminism, cowed by corporate cunt.

'You'll do as you're told. I can't pinch a mate's job. Campbell's a
Deputy Editor as of now. You can have another twenty
thousand francs a year. Plus a car. Campbell and tell him
he's fired.'

'Me?'

'Why not?'

'I can't do that.'

'Of course you can. You will.'

'But that's your job, Stella. Jeez!'

'You may be deputy editor, Murdoch, but don't start telling
me what my job is. Just do it, will you? I'm busy. I've got better
things to do than run around after a malingerer.'

'He'll sue.'

'He'd better not.'

'Wrongful dismissal. Breach of contract.'

'He'd better not. I'll have him for misconduct, embezzle-
ment, sexual harassment, you name it. Now, let's –'

'But who'll do production?'

'You will, of course.'

'As well?'

The Editor's tone was exasperated. 'Not afraid of a bit of
work, are we? Now for Christ's sake stop arguing. Don't you
want another twenty k a year? Plus a car? Do you want to spend

Graham Lord

the rest of your life as a grotty downtable sub? Get a grip, Murdoch. Get real.'

'But Campbell's crook, Stella. You can't fire a bloke when he's down and out.'

'Who says? I can fire him whenever I like. I can fire anyone whenever I like, and that goes for you too, so stop farting about and let's get on with the job. Back to Kelly. And talking of firing, that applies especially to Kelly, and especially if K—fails to sign up half a dozen seriously glitzy showbiz a—ball. Did you hear that, Kelly?'

Kelly scribbled furiously on the pad. ... in excellent

'He heard it,' said Murdoch. 'Hi— working order.'

'Right, Kelly. About ... costume for the ball.'

'He says he's booked the Madame Pompadour you wanted.'

'Unbook it, then, Kelly I'm going to go as Lucrezia Borgia instead.'

'Great choice,' said Murdoch. 'Absolutely right. Go nicely with the *Poison* perfume.'

'Very funny. I'll have you know, Murdoch, that all those cruel stories about her are completely untrue. Lucrezia Borgia was a highly intelligent, sensitive, artistic woman.'

'That's why you're so right for the part.'

'Like hell. Right, Kelly: chop-chop. What about the champagne for the ball? The food? The airlines?'

Kelly scribbled and scribbled and scrawled.

'He says he's still trying,' said Murdoch.

The Editor laughed unpleasantly. 'You can say that again,' she said. 'Listen here, Kelly: we have only a few months to go and we still need two thousand free airfares to Tonga, that's four jumbos-full, and two thousand bottles of champagne, and four thousand dinners and breakfasts, and if you don't get them sorted out within the next week I shall personally remove your bollocks and wear them as earrings.'

Kelly winced.

'Did you get that, Kelly?'

Kelly looked unhappy.

'He got that,' reported Murdoch. 'Kelly is facing the prospect with typical Celtic fortitude.'

'He'd better believe it.'

Kelly scribbled again and scribbled some more.

Murdoch tracked him over his shoulder. 'He says the cruise line has promised to take care of all the tucker and grog.'

'I want to know exactly what they're going to provide. I want to see precise menus and wines. We're not serving hamburgers and chips to two thousand mega-stars. I want a menu to die for.'

'They've also offered to fix up all the entertainment with their on-board troupe of musicians, singers and dancers.'

'You must be joking! Are you really suggesting, Kelly, that we should allow two thousand of the world's smartest movers and shakers to sit around yawning while a few clumsy Goanese cabin stewards and stokers lurch about the stage doing conjuring tricks and telling dirty jokes? What we need is the really big names. Huge names. Mega-names, Kelly: Madonna, Michael Jackson, Elton John, the Flintstones. Get real, for God's sake. Get a life. Plus the supermodels, a fashion show to die for – what about that? What about Naomi, Christy and Linda?'

'Still no reply from them, I'm afraid,' said Murdoch.

'Then put a bomb under them, Kelly,' she snarled. 'Isn't that what you Irish are best at?'

'They'll want money,' said Murdoch. 'Big money.'

'Not when they know it's me asking,' she said. 'Not when they know who'll be there. So who will be there, Kelly? Any replies yet? Or has the entire world lost its voice as well?'

'We've had a couple of nos so far,' said Murdoch.

'Who?'

'Tom Cruise. Glenn Close. Jodie Foster.'

'Blast! I wanted them all. Try them again, Kelly. Tell them how huge it's going to be. Try their PR people, tell them they can't afford not to be seen there.'

'And the Pope's said no. It seems he didn't much like those pics of him in the bath.'

'Prudish old fart.'

'And a few others: Demi Moore, Nelson Mandela, Bill Gates, Myra Hindley. I'll fax you a list.'

'This is terrible. Any yesses yet?'

'A couple.'

'Who?'

'Phil Collins. Julia Roberts. Hugh Grant. That's about it so far.'

'That's all? Just three out of a thousand?'

'So far.'

The Editor's voice was brittle. 'Chase the others up again, Kelly,' she demanded. 'Ring them all. These are busy people. Celebrities. Movers and shakers. They need to be nailed down. Call their secretaries and assistants and PR gofers. Tell them Hugh Grant's coming. Plus Julia Roberts. Mention the Beatles, Madonna, Michael Jackson. Hint that they'll all be there. The others won't dare to let it look as if they haven't been invited to the party of the century. What about Buckingham Palace? Any joy?'

Kelly shook his head and scribbled on the pad. Murdoch tilted his head to read it.

'The Queen and Prince Philip have refused again,' he said.

'Damnation!'

'Quite rudely this time. So has Charity.'

'Charity?'

Kelly shook his head irritably as though some insect were buzzing around inside it.

'Ah, no,' said Murdoch. 'Not Charity. Apparently the royals don't believe the ball's in aid of charity. They've checked out the ones we mentioned and none of them has ever heard of us.'

'Bloody sneaky!'

'They all but accused us of lying.'

'Bloody cheek!' The Editor snorted from a great distance, out into space and back again. 'Toffee-nosed prats. God, I hate those creeps at Buck House. What about Charles?'

Kelly scribbled.

'No,' said Murdoch, screwing his eye up. 'He's refused too. So has Di. And Andrew. And Edward. And Anne.'

The metal grille of the amplifier trembled. 'Who do these people think they are?' hissed The Editor.

'Kelly says do you want him to try Fergie?'

'NO I DO NOT!' bellowed The Editor. 'This is meant to be a classy occasion, not some naff knees-up in Torremolinos. Now listen to me, Kelly: the royals may not be much cop any more but we still need at least a couple of them at the ball to give it a bit of oomph. Have you tried Alexandra yet? The Gloucesters?'

Kelly scribbled.

'They've all already said no as well,' said Murdoch.

'I don't believe this!' bawled The Editor.

'The Kents?' said Murdoch. 'Do you want Princess Michael?'

'NO I DO NOT WANT PRINCESS MICHAEL OF KENT, MURDOCH, YOU MORON! Now you listen to me, Kelly: you get back onto the other royals and try them all again. Refuse to take no for an answer. At least one royal couple is a must-have. Bully them. Bribe them. Threaten. Blackmail. Tell them we've got the dirt on them. Tell them we'll publish. Anything at all. I don't care how you do it, BUT GET THE BUGGERS THERE!'

Kelly shrugged forlornly.

'Kelly is right on top of the case,' said Murdoch. 'Kelly is on the ball and raring to go.'

'That'll be the day. What about the Grimaldis? Rainier? Caroline?'

Kelly shook his head hopelessly.

'It seems they've all said no again. Previous engagements.'

Kelly raised two fingers at him.

'They told us to get stuffed,' reported Murdoch.

Kelly shook his head wildly and waggled both fingers at him.

'I'm sorry, I'll read that again,' said Murdoch. 'They did not tell us to get stuffed, they just refused twice.'

'I'm not standing for this,' said The Editor in a quiet, menacing tone. 'Kelly, if you don't bag me a royal for the ball I swear you'll never work anywhere ever again. I mean it, Kelly. So help me…'

Kelly's face was flushed. He was scribbling furiously, his knuckles gleaming white as they bunched across the paper. He finished with a flourish and slid the pad triumphantly across the table under Murdoch's nose.

'What's going on?' said The Editor, suspicious in the sudden silence. 'What is it?'

Murdoch glanced at the pad. He whistled. 'Good news at last, chief,' he burbled. 'Great news. Extra grouse.'

'For God's sake get on with it, Murdoch! What is it?'

Murdoch grinned. He winked at Kelly.

'No sweat,' he said. 'No probs. We've got our Royal. The King of Tonga's accepted.'

Steve Marlowe patted his face with a king-size tissue. He was sweating. He never seemed to be dry these days. He spread his thighs, eased his itching crotch and scratched it a little. Then he bit into his third hot doughnut of the night, wiped the jam and sugar from his fingers onto his T-shirt, scratched his gut and glowered at the computer screen. It glared back at him. He was having a hell of a time trying to break into the British lottery computer. Their security was very high grade and even though Marlowe had the passwords the right combination was eluding him. And Chandler was doing nothing to help. Chandler was actually sulky and obstructive, flashing up unnecessary warning and error messages and making a childish fuss whenever he was asked to do anything. Marlowe's fingers were punchy on Chandler's sullen keyboard. He flexed them like a boxer, limbering up, easing the stiffness in the joints. He tested his knuckles, fisting them. They crackled. He wanted to damage something.

<ERROR ERROR ERROR> said Chandler's screen
<NO SUCH FILE / ACCESS DENIED / NO SUCH FILE
/ ERROR ERROR ERROR>

Marlowe swore. It was all lies. Of course the file existed. He had saved it onto Chandler's hard disk himself only a few nights ago when Chandler had first started being difficult. The file was all there in Chandler's memory if only the goddam computer would stop sulking and call it back to mind.

'IS YOUR OLD COMPUTER PAST ITS SELL-BY DATE?'

That's how the file had started, the ad from the catalogue for the latest, most up-to-date computers. And then it had gone on to describe in lip-licking detail all the sexy attributes of the new no-mouse, no-keyboard, no-nonsense, computer. But now Chandler was pretending that the file didn't even exist. Chandler kept displaying instead a file that Marlowe was sure he had never saved himself, in which a message blossomed gold and green to a triumphant fanfare of trumpets as a cute pink kitten danced in a top hat across the screen.

<*kitty schweitzer*> said the screen <*hi there*>

<not that file 4 godsake> tapped Marlowe.

<so whyre you avoidin me big boy>

Marlowe pressed EXIT. Nothing happened. He pressed ESCape and ESCape again and again, dementedly. Chandler ignored him. The rogue message skittered on across the screen.

<my bastard husband sure is sore with you> said Mrs Schweitzer <he thinks you n me is havin an affair>

Marlowe pressed CANCEL and up on the screen came the first threatening e-mail message the goddam woman's husband had sent him: <you bin messin with ma wife no one messes with ma wife and gets away with it, boy, i'm comin to chop yore balls off>

Marlowe pressed EXIT and up came his reply – <there mus b sum mistak sir im gay> – and then Mr Schweitzer's second message: <i aint havin no aids-infected faggot messin with ma

wife boy im coming to chop yore balls AND YORE HEAD off see if i dont>

Marlowe had sent a virus downline into Schweitzer's computer to infect his hard disk and corrupt his files. That should shut the old bastard up.

Chandler was flashing that goddam kitten onto the screen again.

Marlowe cursed. It really was time he dumped Chandler for a younger model. Tonight Bill Warren had come suddenly on-line from Santa Barbara with an angry complaint about the mistake they had made over this goddam limey astrologer Marian Black-Boyes and Chandler had let him down badly. This was a good job, the Warren-*Celebrity* job. Marlowe was glad to have it. It was paying well, it was interesting, and best of all it was fun. Marlowe really enjoyed surfing into the Monte Carlo files. Some of the stuff he had found in there was fascinating: stuff about some of the most famous people in the world, some of it so hot that it would surely never be published openly. And he really enjoyed altering the invitation lists for the magazine's New Year's Eve ball. Bill Warren had given him the addresses of some fantastic namesakes to work on: an unknown Hugh Grant in Fort Lauderdale, a Tom Cruise in Albuquerque, a Tony Curtis in Minneapolis, a Jodie Foster in Edinburgh, Scotland, a whole gang of Michael Jacksons all over the world, a Kate Moss in Rio, a Jack Nicholson in Canada, a Julia Roberts in Carson City, a Mickey Rourke just up the coast at Monterey, a Charlie Sheen in Australia, an Emma Thompson in Kenya. By hacking into the *Celebrity* computer and changing some of the addresses Marlowe had now made the *Celebrity* computer invite every one of the namesakes to the ball instead of the real celebrities. Marlowe could hardly wait for the shit to hit the fan. He was even tempted to go and join the party in the South Pacific on New Year's Eve himself. It would cost nothing at all. It said so – "all expenses paid" – on the gold embossed invitation that he had sent himself. But now Chandler's sulky behaviour was threatening to sink their involvement in the whole project. Warren had been furious.

<How in god's name did you make such a stupid mistake?> enquired Warren as soon as he came on-line. <Mrs Black-Boyes is a fashionable astrologer in London. Barrett's been consulting her for months. So how the hell do you see the name Black-Boyes on her bank statements and just assume that Barrett was screwing under-age Afros?>

<sorry> said Marlowe <musta bin a computer error>

<no it wasnt> said the screen suddenly.

The intervention appeared out of the blue, startling them both.

<What was that?> said Warren.

<looks lik anotha glitch in t sistim> said Marlowe.

<liar> said the screen.

Chandler! The goddam computer was heckling him!

Warren's cursor had hesitated on the screen for a moment, blinking with bewilderment, white on blue.

<Do we have an eavesdropper?> he said <A crossed line?>

<that mus be it> said Marlowe <get off t line whoeva u r>

<assole> said the screen.

<You talking to me, Marlowe?> said Warren <because if so...>

<no way sir this appers 2 b a computer mallfunkshun>

<cocksucka> said the screen.

<I've had enough of this> said Warren.

<ill call u bak on anotha line mr warren sir> said Marlowe <i think we have a hacker here>

<I don't like this. This is poor security.>

<motherfucka> said the screen.

Warren had suddenly disappeared off-line. Chandler's cursor winked at Marlowe with insolence. The screen gleamed smugly. He should never have given Chandler a vocabulary.

<ive had enuf of u> tapped Marlowe onto the screen.

<c if i care>

<i cant afford a computer that maks mistaks>

<u spelt it black boyz>
<u did>
<i dint>
<u did>
<dint>
<did>
<uve got old + slo> said Marlowe <wots the point of n old slo computer that maks mistaks>
<u bastard>
<a computer wot swares>
<u tort me>
<its time u wer ratired>
<i given u the best yrs of my life u sonofabitch>
<yor past it>
<u jus wanna dump me for some tarty young model> said Chandler.
<2 rite> said Marlowe <u got it>
<cocksucka>
<get her>
<assole>
<jellus old queen>

Marlowe had crashed out of the system, tugging viciously at Chandler's power cable, yanking the plug from the power point, and Chandler had gone down into darkness with a groan as his lights went out and a white glare flashed across the screen.

Marlowe heaved himself up from the workstation and hauled himself down the corridor to the kitchen to fix himself half a dozen peanut butter sandwiches with bananas and cream to follow, and a butterscotch milkshake. He had given up Coke. They made the stuff with water. He couldn't risk his tits getting any bigger. When he and Chandler had gone out cruising on the Internet the other night he had picked up a neat little Siamese boy from Thailand who had done a runner as soon as he had seen Marlowe's tits. <i no like woman> the little Siamese had said before withdrawing. Marlowe could have sworn that he had heard Chandler snigger.

'Son-of-a-bitch!' said Marlowe, stabbing the knife into the peanut butter.

How dare the little shit snigger? How dare Chandler interrupt him when he was dealing with a client and fuck up on the job and swear? Who the hell did Chandler think he was? He had been nothing until Marlowe had bought him. Marlowe had taught him everything he knew. That's all Chandler was: just a bitchy little tart, a spoiled little queen. There were plenty more little tarts where Chandler came from, some of them a damn sight smarter and more attractive.

Marlowe finished his meal, consoled himself with a block of milk chocolate, and mooched about the apartment with his fists bunched deep in his trouser pockets, knuckling his testicles. It was only just midnight. He watched an episode of *Star Trek* but after that the hours stretched ahead of him like a string of black holes. He had a pile of work he ought to be doing – an Internet job for a firm in Hawaii, a credit check on a woman in Surakarta, a research project for a company in Zimbabwe – but he could hardly just go straight back to the workstation and switch Chandler on as though nothing had happened. How could they work together tonight after all the things that had been said? Marlowe wasn't going to give in now and pretend that nothing had happened, not after all that.

Marlowe mooched into the bedroom. He was bored. He picked his nose, rolled his thumb and forefinger together, examined the result and then flicked the small black pellet across the room. He licked his fingers. He nudged his testicles. Beyond the triple-glazed safety of the picture-window the world turned in midnight silence, spinning through space, the yellow headlamps slicing the freeway like lasers, the blue light of an ambulance flashing. He sprawled on his bed and zapped the TV on, surfing quickly across a dozen channels, ricocheting off a couple of old movies, a chat show, a sports programme, a game show, the news, a cartoon programme. Nothing much took his interest. God, he was bored. What was he going to do for the next eight hours? His fingers twitched. He missed the keyboard. In a way he almost missed Chandler, the spoiled little bitch.

On the TV screen there appeared a map of the universe, a huge expanse of black pricked out with tiny twinkling lights, a large red arrow pointing at the Earth, a large red circle focussing on a distant comet millions of miles out in space. Marlowe sat up and zapped the volume higher. This was more like it. He had always been fascinated by programmes about outer space.

Some presenter was drawling away in that dry, laid-back fashion that science reporters like to adopt, as though they were determined not to be impressed. He was talking about the mysterious comet they had found recently deep in outer space.

The comet was gigantic, he was saying, and it seemed to be heading straight towards the Earth.

'There are about two hundred million comets surfing the solar system and orbiting the sun,' he was saying, 'and about two thousand asteroids that are more than a kilometre wide with orbits that cross the orbit of the Earth, like the Machholz-2 comet that was first spotted in 1994. There are also about a hundred million smaller asteroids at least ten metres wide – and a few that are terrifyingly huge and powerful. The asteroid 1 Ceres is a monstrous six hundred and twenty-five miles wide and the fastest known comet hurtles through space at a hundred and sixty-four thousand miles per hour.'

Marlowe gazed at the screen, mesmerised. A chunk of junk 625 miles wide! Shit: from here to Salt Lake City! And 164,000 miles an hour. That was like travelling to the moon in ninety minutes! Jeez!

'Two or three times each century,' said the commentator, 'one of the bigger, one-kilometre asteroids zaps through the two hundred and fifty thousand mile gap between the Earth and the moon, and three this century have come a little too close for comfort: the asteroids Apollo, Adonis and Hermes, each of which weighed millions of tons. Smaller asteroids, quite dangerous enough themselves, are regular visitors. In 1989 the asteroid 4581 Asclepius missed the Earth by only four hundred thousand miles. In 1991 the asteroid 1991 BA missed by just a hundred and six thousand miles. So did two others in 1993 and 1994. Closest of all was the asteroid 1994 XM1, which passed just sixty-five thousand miles away in December 1994.'

'Jee-sus!' said Marlowe.

'Should a one-kilometre-wide asteroid hit the Earth there would be an explosion equal to a hundred thousand megatons of TNT. Scientists are generally agreed upon the likely results of an impact with the Earth. In his book *Rogue Asteroids and Doomsday Comets* Dr Duncan Steel says that if one were to land in southern California all of Los Angeles along with much of the Earth's crust beneath would be vaporised. The resulting debris would rain back down as far afield as Hawaii and New York provided, naturally, that these places had survived the massive seismic shocks following the catastrophic impact. In short, civilisation as we know it would be plunged back into the Dark Ages.'

The presenter smiled his dry astronomer's smile. He might have been talking about taking a day trip to the seaside.

'When Machholz-2 appeared in the sky in 1994,' he said, 'Professor Stephen Hawking was asked about the danger. He predicted correctly that it would miss the Earth, but added that if it did hit, it would probably mean the end of the human race.'

Soon after dawn, as the hotel chambermaid left her home beside the canal in the alleyway just off the Campo Santi Giovanni e Paolo, she stumbled in the early gloom over the girl's body.

She ran screaming across the square and along the Fondamenta dei Mendicanti to the hospital, crying hysterically.

A doctor and a male porter ran back with her towards the alleyway and found the girl lying at a hideous angle.

The porter crossed himself.

The doctor knelt beside her in the filth.

He bent over her, touched her, raised her wrist, felt her pulse.

He pressed his ear to her chest.

'Dear God,' he said. 'She is still alive.'

Nat Wakonde drove south out of Oxford towards the Vale of the White Horse. Murdoch was right. How could he possibly resign, even on a matter of principle? Especially on a matter of principle? He was deeply in debt and even back home in South Africa staff jobs were rare and freelancing difficult unless you had a speciality. And would Rushdie really care if he wrote about his love life? Probably not: he sounded like a good bloke. He would understand the pressures on a fellow writer. Murdoch was right: perhaps he just needed a holiday.

As he drove into Wantage every other tree was sprouting fluorescent red and green posters that shrieked: NO TO THE WHITE HORSE AIRPORT. He drove into the square old cobbled market place, circled the huddled stalls and the statue of Alfred the Great, and took the minor B-road out of the town again into the rolling English summer countryside. He drove past Letcombe Regis and Letcombe Basset and more garish posters insisting NO TO THE WHITE HORSE AIRPORT, past Uffington and White Horse Hill and up the steep climb across the ancient Ridgeway path to the top of the Lambourn Downs and the lush green distant views across the sweeping Lambourn racehorse gallops and over the hills of four great Anglo-Saxon counties.

Nat had failed to find Salman Rushdie in Oxford. In London Rushdie's publishers and literary agent had promised only to pass on a message to the author for him. In desperation Nat had gate-crashed two of the boozy, gossipy book-launch parties that Rushdie was known occasionally to attend with his police bodyguards but there had been no sign of him. At the second party Nat had been accosted by a tiny, twittery woman who stood too close, kept fingering his tie and calling him 'Ben' and seemed to be under the impression that he had won some major literary prize.

'I expect you and Salman are great friends,' she had twittered, pronouncing 'Salman' like *salmon* and gazing straight up Nat's nostrils. She stroked his tie. 'Not because you're both...well... ethnic...of course, but because of your great talents. Literary talents, of course.' She had wagged her forefinger at him and poked it into his chest. 'Naughty naughty! And of course you and Salmon both won the Booker, didn't you? Such a nice man, Salmon, don't you think? Such a sweet smile. Those gorgeous bedroom eyes, all droopy. So attractive. Well, you all are, of course, people like you. It's the skin tone, I think, not all pale and horrid like us.'

She had patted his buttock absent-mindedly as though it were a pet.

'How could those horrid Arabs be threatening to kill him?' she had said. 'And Salmon's so brave. He goes out and about everywhere these days, to parties and dinners and everything, even though his life is in such terrible danger. I saw him at the Cape party only a couple of weeks ago and he told me in confidence that he's going to be speaking at the Oxford Union this week. Me! He trusted me! Well, I could have been anybody, couldn't I? I could have been an Arab spy, even. So brave. Do you live near here, Ben? Islington, I expect. Or Hampstead. Yes? I'd love to see where you do your writing. So inspiring. Have you got a girlfriend at the moment?'

'I'm married,' Nat had lied.

'I'm not surprised.' She stroked his hand. 'Such lovely skin.' She looked up his nose again. 'Just the one wife, Ben? Or are you allowed four?'

'Just the one and she's very jealous.'

She had giggled and patted his hand. 'You're a naughty,

naughty boy,' she had said. She had turned his tie over and read the manufacturer's label and then turned it back again and patted it into place. 'Where are you going for dinner, you naughty boy?' When Nat had managed to escape he had telephoned the Oxford Union, where one of the staff confirmed the date of the debate but denied that Rushdie would be one of the speakers. But then they would deny it, wouldn't they? Nat had hired a car and driven to Oxford to attend the debate but there had been no sign of the hunted author among the speakers, just two clapped-out old politicians who made speeches congratulating themselves, a finger-snapping disc-jockey suffering from a surfeit of adrenalin and a media lesbian with angry hair.

No wonder the Ayatollah's assassins had never managed to find Rushdie, thought Nat. The man was invisible. In desperation he telephoned his gossip column contact on the *Herald*.

'There's a rumour that Rushdie's buying a racehorse, old boy,' drawled the *Herald* man. 'Why not pop over to Lambourn and ask around some of the racing yards? I can give you a couple of introductions to trainers there: Pete Walwyn, Nick Henderson, Oliver Sherwood, people like that. Or Screamer Lewis in East Garston: he knows everyone. If a pheasant farts in Faringdon, Screamer's the first to know.'

Nat lit another cigarette and drove on away from White Horse Hill into the heart of Berkshire's racing country. He barely noticed the stunning views to the right across the valley as the road cut across wide grassy gallops and plunged into cool woods towards the distant Norman tower of Lambourn church nestling down in the valley.

Helga.

Hel-ga.

Her name was like the whisper of a butterfly's wings. The first two notes of a symphony. How could she love a man who was more than twice her age? Who had a straggly beard and yellow teeth and a pin in his nose?

'Stone me, mate,' said Murdoch when he read Nat's article about her. 'Who is this sheila, then? St Helga of Troy?'

'She's lovely, Tony. Beautiful. Sweet. Kind.'

'And nice tits, too. I can see that even with one eye. Mega-knockers.'

Nat had wanted to hit him.

In the two weeks that had passed since then he had lost his appetite and a stone in weight. He was smoking more than forty cigarettes a day. He was restless, twitching his fingers, drumming them against the steering wheel. When he managed to sleep she haunted his fitful dreams but in them she never looked at him directly: she was always just out of focus, looking askance, always blurred. When he woke, always long before dawn, he would stare for an hour or more into the thick darkness until he could bear the loneliness no more and then he would switch the light on and gaze at the photograph he now carried with him wherever he went. It was one that Potter had snatched in the caravan before the interview with her in Wales, and Nat would feast his longing on the fleeting glimpse of her liquid smile, her lips, her golden hair, the wide blue eyes, the tiny silver ring planted in her eyebrow, the silver stud glinting in her nostril.

Sometimes he kissed her photograph, whispering her name.

The day after the interview he had sent her a lavish bouquet of flowers to thank her and a fulsome letter giving her his address and telephone number in Monte Carlo. He had written to her twice in the following fortnight and had sent her three copies of *Celebrity* when they published his interview with her. She had never replied.

One night in his dream she turned her head towards him and it had had no face.

He had never been so unhappy in all his life. How could she waste herself on a man with a dog called Merlin? Why didn't she know?

He drove down off the Downs into Lambourn, past more

and more roadside posters demanding NO TO THE WHITE HORSE AIRPORT. Beyond the avenue of venerable trees on the right the grassy plain stretched out towards Seven Barrows and a dozen buried centuries of Anglo-Saxon history.

'Christ, I hate the country!' said Potter in the passenger seat. 'Fucking views!'

'How can they do it?' said Lancelot furiously. 'Bloody vandals! A new international airport! Right here, where all the ancient ley lines meet. It's unbelievable.'

He strode angrily along the Ridgeway, away from White Horse Hill towards Compton Beauchamp and Ashbury, along the prehistoric track that had snaked for centuries across the heart of England from the Wash on the cold grey North Sea to the great grey slabs of Stonehenge in the windswept heart of Wiltshire. Helga ran after him. Even here, far from any village, an occasional tree beside the track blossomed with a fluorescent poster protesting NO TO THE WHITE HORSE AIRPORT. Behind them the Ridgeway curved back across the hills of Middle England to Beacon Hill, where they lit huge bonfires in ancient times to warn of the Viking raids, and back to join the Icknield Way across East Anglia to the shores where the Vikings landed.

They walked past yellow fields of rape and corn splashed scarlet with tall poppies and fluttering butterflies and through dappled woods and bluebells buzzing with bees into the lazy silence of an English summer day with the sky as clear and blue as the eye of God and golden buttercups reflecting the sun. Only the birds called to them. There was no one else for miles around. The world felt very old.

'Concordes roaring in and out,' said Lancelot furiously. 'Jumbo jets! They must be mad! Is there nothing these capitalist bastards won't desecrate to make themselves more money?'

'Nothing,' said Helga. 'My family too. Money is a serpent.' She walked on in silence, kicking at tufts of grass with the toes of her sturdy Doc Marten boots.

'I am hating money,' she said.

'You could always give it all away.'

She stopped and gazed at him.

'Give all you have to the poor,' he said, 'and follow me.'

She thought about it. 'This is impossible,' she said. 'I am frighten to be real poor. This is why I am hating it.'

Helga slipped her hand into his as they walked along the ancient path. 'Cheer up, *mein liebling*,' she said. 'I am making you laugh now. Rachel is telling me a joke so I am asking you this joke now, I think, please, to make you better, *ja*.'

'I can't believe what these vandals are doing here. Nobody seems to care about anything any more.'

Helga squeezed his hand. 'This is making you laugh, I am thinking. Now you be paying intention. How is the difference between the hedgehog and the Rolls Royce?'

He shrugged.

She grinned at him. Her face lit up like a child's. She looked so fragile, like a beautiful ragged-headed street urchin in her rough tunic and heavy belt and one of his old shirts and sturdy Doc Marten boots. He felt a sudden surge of affection for her and immensely grateful to have her here beside him on a beautiful summer day, so young, so perfect, so alive. What had he done to deserve this? With a stab of recognition he suddenly knew that he would never be happier than he was now. This was the peak of his life. Why had the gods been so good to him? Eventually they would demand a price, for the gods are jealous gods: Brân the Raven God, and the Horned God, Cernunnos. Nothing is for nothing. One day she would leave him. Maybe soon. And the gods would present their bill.

He hugged her tight. 'I don't know,' he said. 'Tell me, then, Hellish. What is the difference between a hedgehog and a Rolls?'

She giggled. 'The hedgehog is having the pricks on the outside!'

He laughed. He had had a lot of women in his time but never one he had loved as much as this.

'You are getting the joke?' she asked anxiously. Her eyes were uncertain. 'The pricks, *ja*?' she said. 'You see, two different kind pricks.'

He wanted to protect her for ever and knew that that was the worst thing he could ever do to her.

'The pricks on the outside,' he said. He laughed. 'That's funny.'

She smiled with relief and squeezed his hand. 'I am bettering with the English joke, I think,' she said. 'I am thinking this is a good one, *ja*?'

'Great,' he said. 'Groovy.'

He held her close and kissed her. One day she would leave him and he would never be happy again.

They walked on south in silence, revelling in the sunshine, holding hands, marvelling at the warmth and beauty of England at its best on a hot June afternoon so far from the hubbub and the real world, the birds calling out on every side, the rustling of grass, the humming of insects.

He wished he could die now or live for ever.

'I am having baby,' she said.

They sat together on the old flat gravestone of Wayland's Smithy amid the shade of the magic circle of tall trees set back beside the Ridgeway. The tombstones were warm against their buttocks. There were no birds singing here, no insects clicking, just a heavy silence in filtered sunlight winking through the trees. In the shade the narrow black entrances to the prehistoric underground burial chambers watched them like the empty eye sockets of the dead.

'Wayland the Smith was Lord of the Elves,' said Lancelot, picking at a patch of moss on one of the tombstones. 'He was a brilliant Anglo-Saxon blacksmith who was captured by the Vikings. They say he still haunts this place. His ghost will shoe your horse if you leave a coin and go away.'

Why is he telling me this? she thought. What is all this to do with me and our baby?

'I am not having horse,' she said. 'I am having baby.'

A slight breeze stirred the trees to the east.

'They say Wayland the Smith came from Germany,' said Lancelot. 'A Saxon hero.'

The breeze whispered towards them, rustling the leaves. She shivered. Something invisible seemed to be watching them. She would hate to be here alone even on a bright day like this, let alone at night. Shadows seemed to move just outside the edge of her vision and beyond the cool shade of the central magic circle the sunlight blazed across the countryside. She trembled. Goose pimples speckled her arm. This was what it must be like to be dead, she thought, to be trapped in the shadows looking out from the darkness, to watch the living still going about their lives in the warmth and light beyond the funereal trees.

'How long has it been?' he said.

'Two month.'

'Will you have it?'

She stared at him. 'But of course.'

He looked nervous.

Suddenly she knew that everything had changed.

He leaned forward and placed his hand on her stomach. The wind fell, exhausted in the silence. The tombstones seemed to be listening.

Today I have at last become a woman, she thought, not because I am pregnant but because at last I understand. I have become a woman because he has become something less than a man.

Already the sun had passed its zenith and was leaning towards the west. A small grey afternoon shadow nudged the toe of the tallest tombstone.

He looked away. 'I think you should get rid of it,' he said, and she knew for sure.

She was silent as they drove south again towards Stonehenge to celebrate the summer solstice. Paul Simon's voice reverberated around the cab of the van, songs with titles that suddenly seemed absurdly significant: 'Baby Driver'; 'The Obvious Child'; 'Mother and Child Reunion'. Merlin sat up between them in the front of the van, his paws planted apart on the dashboard, panting and nodding at passing tree trunks as though they were acquaintances. They drove away from White Horse Hill and Uffington, leading the procession of travellers' vans and caravans across the Downs and slowly through Lambourn, carefully passing the nervous strings of skittish racehorses trotting out to the gallops. The horses shied and pranced as Merlin barked and capered about the front seat. Small brown rat-faced men in helmets perched high and tiny on the horses' saddles, cursing the dog and jeering at each other.

She stared out of the window. There were red and green posters everywhere – NO TO THE WHITE HORSE AIRPORT – and banners strung across the high street where dwarfish, bow-legged people jostled each other off the pavements into the gutters. She gazed down at them from the window of the van. They grinned and gurned and capered like medieval jesters. They seemed to her to be barely human, like Wayland's elves themselves.

She stared out of the window. 'I will not kill my baby,' she said.

They drove on south across the leafy River Kennet to Hungerford and then due west to Marlborough along the old coach route that once brought galloping mails from London to Bristol.

'Civil War country, this,' said Lancelot. 'Roundheads and Cavaliers. Bloody battles. 1643 and '44. King versus Parliament. Democracy versus Tyranny. The heart of England. The womb of the British Empire. The nursery of the USA. This is where it all began.'

But you said that too about Wantage, she thought rebelliously. You said exactly the same thing about Alfred the Great and the Vale of the White Horse. You know too much.

***

They stopped for the night just east of Marlborough in a clearing deep in the ancient beech woods of the Savernake Forest, where William the Conqueror had hunted deer and where the Druids long ago had hunted God.

They parked the vans and caravans among the trees and Helga slipped out into the late afternoon to clear her mind by wandering alone along narrow paths through the forest, savouring the cool of evening. She stopped now and then to listen to the small night animals scuffling through the undergrowth. A bird sang a warning high above her head and a breeze played with the branches. She could smell the fresh promise of approaching rain. In the distance she glimpsed a flash of lightning. Thunder crashed long leagues away and rolled towards her across the ancient woods. It was Thor hurling his thunderbolts, that's what Arthur would say, or Taranis dragging his heavy Celtic shield across the floor of heaven. And here, alone in the dark green forest, she could almost believe it. She shivered. No wonder the Celts and Druids had worshipped trees, she thought: there was magic in the gnarled mysteries of sacred groves, the holy gleam of holly, the silent mysticism of hiding places deep in woods where tree-gods whisper in the blackness and the trolls of German legend dance in the moonlight. That was surely why the gods had brought her here: to reclaim her dark Germanic inheritance, to feed her mystic Saxon soul and set her free. *I shall not kill my baby. That is what they do in the other world, the world of my father and grandfather, in Hitler's world. But I shall not kill my baby.*

It began to rain, heavy spots pattering on the umbrella of leaves high above her head but rarely reaching the ground, running away instead like quicksilver across the dark green canopy of leaves. The rain began to drum on the leaves, beating a soothing rhythm. She found a sheltered clearing, sat on an ivy-covered tree stump and rolled herself a joint of marijuana. She knew that he would try to persuade her to have an abortion. That was what they had all done in his day, in the Sixties, when selfish men and women had massacred millions of babies. Like Hitler. But this was 1999. She would not do it. And if he insisted, she would leave him.

Back at the camp she found him sitting cross-legged in meditation, and after the meal she went to bed early and he sat up late under a makeshift shelter beside the fire until after midnight, softly playing the lyre and singing forgotten medieval lullabies. As the storm broke over them and the torrent pelted down about them, all but drowning the sound of his music, something, she knew, was coming to an end.

When he came to bed he held her fiercely.

'Baby, baby,' he said, stroking her hair. 'Baby, baby.'

He buried his nose in her hair and inhaled her sweet young smell. How could he risk losing this? He must never let her go. Without her the light would go out of his life.

'Of course you must have the baby,' he said.

What did it matter? he thought. The world in any case was doomed. This year, next year, soon. It had all been foretold long ago by all the great seers and prophets: St Columba, Malachy O'Morgair, Nostradamus, Edgar Cayce, Jeane Dixon, the Seventh Day Adventists, Jehovah's Witnesses, and other Christian prophets like Fatima and Garabandal. They had all warned that the end would come at the end of the second millennium, in about the year 2000. Even the Bible, even the Book of Revelation. How could all of them be wrong? One baby more or less would make no difference.

'Of course you must have the baby,' he said, and he pressed his lips against the blue dove tattooed on her breast.

'I am calling the baby Natalie,' she said, 'or Nathaniel.'

On the Tongan island of Vava'u it was raining again. It seemed to Afu Faletau that it had been raining non-stop for four or five months. Great black clouds bunched themselves over the island, shrouding the summit of Mount Talau, and long gusts of rain came sweeping in from the sea to wrap themselves around the jungle mountainside like hot wet blankets.

Afu crouched in the back doorway of the house with her chin on her knees. She gazed miserably out at the downpour. She was so bored. There was nothing to do. It was Sunday again. It always seemed to be Sunday nowadays. Nothing moved: not a bus, not a bicycle. There was no television because on Sundays they didn't send the pictures out from Nuku'alofa and she wasn't even allowed to play her music. Afu was left alone to stare at the pouring rain.

After church her boy-girl cousin Siole had come sidling up to her with a tin of corned beef, trying to get her to do it again, but she had pushed him away and told him it was Sunday. You didn't do it on a Sunday unless you were married, not even for corned beef. The rain lashed down, drumming on the tin roof, raking the earth in front of her like bullets. Sometimes he brought a tin of fruit or fish but she wouldn't do it with him at all unless he brought corned beef. It wouldn't be right to do it with Siole for something she didn't really want. That would be rude.

Sometimes when Siole was doing it to her she closed her eyes and thought of Hhugh Grrant. Her *Celebrity* magazine picture of Hhugh Grrant was now so torn, cracked, creased and faded that she could hardly see his face any more but she had fixed his face in her head: his lovely smile and floppy hair and cheeky eyes. Siole never had a nice smile. His face went all funny when he was doing it, all sort of fierce and silly. Once he brought with him a friend who gave her some chocolate but just stared and stared at her with frightened eyes.

Would the rain never stop? This wet was worse than all the months when the sun shone every day, day after day, and there was nothing to do but sit under a palm tree and look at the blazing powdery sand and the translucent green lagoon and listen to the waves booming far out to sea against the reef. She had even tried to find a job but nobody wanted her. She had asked at some of the restaurants in Neiafu and they had laughed at her.

'You?' said one of the managers. 'Waitress? You silly in the head. Now go way.'

Afterwards Afu sat down and thought about that for a long time. What did he mean, silly in the head? She thought about it a lot but in the end her head started feeling very full and she had to stop thinking because it made the inside of her head go all mushy.

She had even tried to buy a ticket to Hollywood on the weekly boat to Nuku'alofa but when she tried to pay them with all the money she had, eight whole *pa'anga*, they said it wasn't nearly enough. How could eight *pa'anga* not be enough?

Perhaps it would be cheaper to buy a ticket to go up in the airy plane because that didn't take nearly as long as the boat to get to Nuku'alofa, so really it ought to be cheaper.

She stared up at the bucketing rain. What if it started raining when you were up there in an airy plane? How would you ever get back down through all this water? You could be stuck up there in the sky for ever. You would have to sit on the clouds for months, waiting for the rain to stop. That would be even more boring.

Eventually the rain stopped. The afternoon faltered and began to die and clouds of mosquitoes rose like smoke from the humid undergrowth, flying on the damp evening air towards her in formation, humming to themselves with hunger. She ran away towards the harbour to see if anything was going on. Most of the yachts that crowded the Port of Refuge during the winter had sailed away to kinder harbours and most of the others were covered up and battened down against the weather, but not far from the Paradise International Hotel she could see one of the yotties working on his boat.

She stopped on the quayside beside his boat and watched as he stacked a coil of rope and polished the brass. On the mountainside behind her a parrot called from the trees and the fruit bats started squeaking as the darkness began to fall.

He was a white *palangi*, a 'sky-burster', and thin and old – at least thirty, she thought, maybe thirty-five – and his yellow T-shirt was stained with sweat and oil and his khaki shorts hung baggy about his bony knees. He looked battered. His boat was battered too, an old wooden boat with rust across the railings.

She stood quietly on the quay and watched him. Eventually he sensed that she was there. He looked up and frowned, his expression distinctly unfriendly. His face was thin and creased, with deep unhappy lines running down from either side of his mouth. His upper lip was puckered in the middle and cleft with a thin white scar. He had tried to hide the cleft with an unsuccessful moustache.

'Wha' you wan'?' he grunted from deep at the back of his nose. He seemed to have trouble talking. A thin white spider's web of stitches crawled across his upper lip towards his wide, flattened nose.

She looked down at him with her deep eyes. The ginger flower sparkled in her hair above the long black tresses tumbling down her back to below her waist. He looked up at her on the quay above him, his eyes tracking up the short, flimsy skirt and the flash of soft flesh at the top of her long, slim, fudge-coloured legs. She gave him a wide, white smile.

'Mefella name Afu,' she said. Her voice was like a silver bell.

He turned away, hiding his lip. 'Wha' you wan'?' he grunted.

'Me wantim go way Hollywood,' she said.

He looked up at her again. Hollywood! She gave him a brilliant smile. Her teeth were as white as the whitest beach, her lips as wide as the sweetest lagoon. He gazed up at her long, tapering legs. She was barefoot and a little silver chain glittered around her left ankle. Her legs seemed to be unending: the colour of new fudge, the skin up there so soft and silky.

He cleared his throat. It sounded like raked gravel. 'My name Chim,' he said.

'Chim?'

'Zhim.'

'Shim?'

He struggled with his lips. 'Jim.'

'You call Jim?'

'Yeah.'

She clapped her hands and giggled. 'Jim!' she said. 'Jim! Me likeim.' She giggled again. 'Jim-Jim-Jim, me-like-im!'

Her face was alight with pleasure at being alive. He felt a sudden pang of loneliness.

'Where bigplace belong you?' she said.

'New Shealand.'

'Shealand?'

'Zhealand.'

'Zhealand?'

He struggled with his lips. He contorted his face. 'Zealand,' he said. 'New *Zealand*.'

'New Zealand!'

Where Tongan girls go on ships far away to work as maids, she thought suddenly, and wear sexy stockings.

'Youfella want maid?' she asked. 'Wear sexy stocking?'

'Eh?'

'I wear sexy stocking for you now.'

He stared at her. Her eyes gleamed. Her smile was wide and white and eager. The flower shone in her hair.

'You-me come Hollywood by an by along boat belong you,' she said. 'You know him bigfella Hhhugh Grrrant?'

' 'u' Gran'?'

'Hhhhhugh Grrrrant,' she said severely, correcting him. 'Hhhhhugh Grrrrant.' She wagged her finger at him. 'Wefella go stop bigplace Nuku'alofa you-me, thassall.'

'I' not goin' to Nuku'alofa,' he grunted.

She jumped down from the quay onto the deck of the boat, landing lightly on her bare feet.

She gave him a huge grin. 'Wefella long talk-talk now,' she said. She touched his moustache. 'Me like-im you grass-belong-face. You got tin meat?'

***

'I'm in Paris,' said The Editor.

'Paradise?' said Murdoch. He clutched the telephone receiver in one hand and a smoky cheroot in the other.

'Paris, you idiot. Have you sacked Campbell yet?'

'I –'

'Do it, Murdoch.'

'He's still crook, Stella. I think we should wait until he's fit again.'

'Sack him, Murdoch. Sentimentality is a serious weakness. How's Kelly's voice?'

'Still on walkabout.'

'Still malingering, you mean. Keep a close eye on him. He's a dodger. Tell him I've got a list of things for him to do.'

'He seems pretty overloaded with work already, Stella.'

'Nonsense. He's just lazy and inefficient. He takes too long to get things done. Kelly is a skiver, Murdoch. He needs to be given a hard time. You have to crack the whip. Now: tell him I want him to make sure that all the TV and newspaper contracts for the ball stipulate that I am to receive personally ten per cent of all royalties.'

'What? Ten per cent?'

'You think it should be more? Fifteen?'

'No, I… People might…'

'I think ten. Don't want to be greedy. Now, tell Kelly I also want absolute control over where the TV cameras are placed on board the ship, especially when they are filming me. *Capeesh?* I know what these slimy TV bastards can be like. In Prague they stuck a lens right up my nose, the incompetent arseholes. Plus I want an absolute veto on all TV presenters and commentators, and I want to see in advance complete lists of all newspaper reporters invited to cover the ball plus a file of their latest cuttings. Plus tell Kelly I want to see complete CVs and photos of every member of the liner's crew three months before the ball and that includes every waiter and stewardess. I'm not having any uglies on board. Not unless they're celebs. We don't want any buck-tooth Japs or pug-face Stone Age head-hunters frightening the guests and the cameras. Plus tell Kelly to cancel my flight from Paris to Cape Town tomorrow and to postpone the Kruger Park safari and tell the shipping line I'll join the ship in the Seychelles on the twenty-eighth. I'm going to South America for ten days first. Tell Kelly to fix me a flight from Paris to Rio tomorrow. He can tell the airline we'll give them a plug in exchange for a first class ticket. Plus tell Kelly to book me onto a flight from London to the Seychelles on the twenty-seventh. Right. Now for the next issue. The new list of ideas is piss-poor, Murdoch. I want you to tell those lazy bastards in the newsroom that unless they come up with ten cracking good ideas by Friday night they will have to work in the office throughout the weekend and I expect you to see that they do. *Capeesh?* I'll be ringing you in the office on Sunday to make sure that you're all at work unless you've sent me a list I can approve before then. I'm fed up with having to run this entire magazine single-handed. What do I pay those lazy layabouts for?'

'Wouldn't it be better…'

'Yes?'

'If we tried incentives.'

'What?'

'Instead of threats?'

'Incentives? What do you mean?'

'Well – maybe bonuses for really good ideas or pieces. Days off in lieu of overtime. Small salary increases for good work. A small percentage of the royalties of the ball, even.'

'Give them more money? Not likely. You must be mad. I pay them all far too much already. You're too damned tolerant, that's your trouble. People like that don't understand kindness, Murdoch. You have to be firm with them otherwise they take advantage. Now I've got to go.'

'About my rise, Stella. The twenty thousand francs…'

'I can't talk about that now.'

'And the company car…'

'I'm busy, Murdoch. I'll deal with all that when I get back from Rio.'

'It's just that –'

'Or the Seychelles.'

'It's only –'

'There's more to life than money, Murdoch. Money is the root of all evil.'

'The *love* of money is the root of all evil. St Paul.'

'That's what I said. And you can also tell those idle bastards that I'm stopping all holiday entitlement for six months, until we get all the details for the ball sorted out.'

'Six months!'

'Is that a problem?'

'Well, some of them have already booked their holidays. Flights, hotels, the lot.'

'Tell them to unbook them.'

'Nat –'

'I don't want any excuses or arguments, Murdoch. Just see to it, will you? We can't have people swanning off around the world when there's serious work to be done. And now I must go. I'm holding you responsible. *Ciao!*'

'Shite,' said Kelly loudly in his normal voice. 'The friggin' bitch.'

Murdoch took a deep drag on his cheroot.

He sighed.

'Have you heard the one about the guy who takes his pet croc into a pub?' he said.

For two weeks after learning of Quang Linh's death at sea Nguyen Thi Chu was haunted by terrible nightmares. She would do anything to delay bedtime, sometimes working on the book until two or three in the morning. But the heart had gone out of the project. Sometimes she sat and stared at the screen for half an hour, unable to think. Who cared about Anglo-Saxon history or the Seven Modern Deadly Sins? Quang Linh was dead.

Night after night she dreamed that he was buried alive deep down in the third level of the clay tunnels of Cu Chi and was

screaming silently for her and that she was digging frantically
with bare hands to get to him while a platoon of American GIs
thrashed closer and closer towards them through the jungle,
hunting them, and the face of every GI was the face of the
government spy. She could smell again the stench of the
tunnels, the urine and the excrement, the rotting corpses, and
her skin was mad again with pain and itching, the bites of
mosquitoes, fire ants, tiny invisible insects. And overhead the
Yankee helicopters clattered and clattered as they broadcast
their foul propaganda through their deafening loudspeakers
and she could hear the amplified, tape-recorded sound of
children's voices crying.

Night after night she slept for only two or three hours and
woke whimpering to lie awake in the darkness until dawn,
sweating and trembling, unable to sleep again.

Quang Linh was dead. Nothing mattered any more.

The university offered her some compassionate leave but
where would she go? She preferred to go through the motions
of work, lecturing, holding tutorials, anything to distract the
memories. After work, to exhaust the pain, she started doing
judo every day and taking long walks into the countryside
around Tây Ninh, sometimes twenty or thirty kilometres at a
time, tramping like an automaton towards Xom Mat Cat or Ap
Trai Bai or Black Lady Mountain or the Sai Gon River. Once
she went right up to the dangerous Cambodian border,
praying that one of the jumpy Cambodian border guards
would shoot her. Everywhere she walked she saw young men
of nineteen or twenty, laughing, running, vigorous, flirting
with girls. Often she wept.

'Your son has died a glorious patriotic death in the service
of the Motherland,' the government informer had told her that
dreadful afternoon in the head of the history faculty's office.

'No!' she had cried.

'Your son was a hero. You will go soon to Ho Chi Minh
City to be invested as a Heroic Vietnamese Mother.'

He had risen from the chair, the silent northern man, uncoiling his bony legs and gleaming shins. He stood before her. She could hardly bear to look at him: the cold black eyes, the flat oily hair, the pointed ears. Even now she sensed about him a sort of triumph. So many like him had come down the Ho Chi Minh Trail from Hanoi to Tây Ninh in the old days, small thin northern men with narrow eyes. She had fought for years beside them but she had never liked them. Northerners were quite different: they seemed to have ice in their hearts. And now they had taken the spoils of victory and they called Saigon Ho Chi Minh City.

He had placed his hands on both her shoulders and had brushed her cheeks with his in a comradely salute. His cheeks had been as cold as a corpse. He had smelled of grease and peppermint.

Not Quang Linh! Not my baby! Not Quang Linh with his cheeky smile and bony knees and tufty hair and silly big ears.

Why had her letters never reached him? He must have died thinking she could not be bothered even to write to him. He must have died feeling unloved. Had he called out for her at the end? '*Me! Me!*' Mummy! Mummy! Had he cried for her?

She had wept herself, then.

'How did it happen?' she had wept.

The government informer had stared at her. 'A foolish accident,' he said.

'An accident?'

'A skirmish with some Filipino fishermen.'

'Filipinos? Not Chinese?'

'We have built lighthouses and desalination plants on some of our Quan Dao Thruong Xa islands.'

'Not the Chinese navy?' she said. 'Not the Chinese?'

'Without any justification the Filipinos claim that some of our islands are theirs. Their fishermen built an illegal structure on one of the rocks: a fishermen's hut. It was necessary to demolish it to preserve Vietnamese sovereignty. Your son was struck on the head by a boathook.'

A boathook. Killed senselessly by a frightened Filipino fisherman. Not even in battle against the Chinese.

'He died instantly. There was no pain.'

The child she had carried and suckled.

My baby. Those big dark eyes. That smile. Ah no.

'Where?'

The government informer had moved away. The shape of his shoulders suggested distaste. 'That is classified information.'

'And his...body?'

'He was buried at sea.'

So not even his body, then.

'With full honours.'

She would not even be able to kiss his sweet face one last time, then. He would never lie in the family tomb among his ancestors beside her grandfather's house at Go Dau Ha.

Quang Linh! My baby! Buried at sea. Among the sharks. My baby!

In the third week of her misery she found herself walking through Long Than towards the Great Temple in the Holy See of the Cao Dai religious colony. It must have been twenty years at least since she had been here in the Caodaists' sacred head-quarters, she thought. Their temple stood in the middle of a vast, deserted square like a child's garish candy-floss fantasy, like something out of Disneyland, all ochre, pink, sky blue and gold with ornate tiered pagoda towers. It had spires, Moorish archways and verandahs, fussy filligree balconies, opulent marbled pillars blazing with golden suns and entwined with serpents, golden lions and garish statues of the Cao Dai saints on every wall and pinnacle: saints like Confucius, the Chinese leader Sun Yat-sen, the French writer Victor Hugo. And everywhere along the walls of the temple was depicted the vast single Divine Eye of the Cao Dai, the High Tower, the Supreme Being, Creator of the Universe, cold and sinister under its thick black eyebrow, watching everything.

She approached the temple slowly, with misgiving. She had

forgotten just how lurid and bizarre it was. She had always felt uneasy here, and not just because the Caodaists had once been so virulently anti-Communist that the government had had to execute four of their leaders after winning the American War in 1975. It was also because the square was too clean, the sparkling colours of the temple too fresh and bright. There had always seemed to her to be something sinister about this place, something too good to be true, like the smile of an alligator. Even the Cao Dai religion itself had always seemed to her to be too good to be true, for it tried to be all things to all people, attempting to combine all the great religions – from Buddhism to Christianity – in a basket of beliefs as though faith were simply the latest supermarket bargain. Their venerated holy men included Napoleon Bonaparte, Shakespeare, even Winston Churchill. Here in this gaudy temple on the jungly Cambodian border both West and East had been forced into a shotgun marriage that had given birth to a bastard religion that promised that in the new millennium the world would be united in a golden age of glorious harmony. And yet something drew her on into the temple. Something there, she knew, was waiting for her.

At the entrance she removed her shoes and lined them up in the dust outside. A service was in progress, chanting drifting across the empty square. Beyond the archway she glimpsed the backs of hundreds of acolytes in robes of white and priests – both men and women – dressed in Buddhist yellow, Taoist blue or Confucian red as they squatted barefoot with knees akimbo. They were lined in orderly rows on the gleaming marble floor of a long, rectangular, yellow-and-blue hall, facing away from her towards huge candles flickering on the distant altar. On each side of the aisle a dozen tall, pink-and-gold columns decorated with scaly black serpents and grinning red-and-green dragons soared high to the pale blue ceiling with its fluffy painted clouds and pinprick stars. Sunlight streamed through stained glass windows with their designs of pink roses and Divine Eyes, and splashed across the marble floor like liquid butter.

One of the priests in the back row turned and looked at her over his shoulder. He smiled.

Her heart stopped.

'Quang Linh!' she cried.

It was him. Quang Linh. There. In the back row.

She ran towards him.

A barefoot attendant, dressed like an Arab in a squat purple turban, grabbed her arms and held her back.

'You are not allowed to shout!' he hissed. 'It is forbidden to stand in front of the altar unless you are a priest!'

He gestured towards a stairway at the side. 'You may watch from upstairs.'

Chu ran up the stairs to the first floor.

Quang Linh!

Here!

Her heart was pounding. She ran along the balcony above the heads of the priests squatting below. At the back of the hall the golden statue of a Hindu goddess stood beside a statue of a Chinese priest with a banjo.

Chu stopped, breathless, and leaned over the balcony, scanning the faces of the priests in the back row. Where was Quang Linh?

The one who had smiled at her smiled again.

He was not Quang Linh.

Of course not.

Quang Linh was dead.

There seemed to be a boulder at the back of her throat. She swallowed. Her throat was dry. Her eyes were damp. She stared again at the priest. Of course he was not Quang Linh. He was nothing like him.

She wept silently at the back of the balcony while the choir began to sing and a shrill voice cried prayers from the high altar. Blowing her nose, she stared at the priest again. How could she have mistaken him for Quang Linh?

Chu stumbled on along the balcony towards the high altar,

past statues of Jesus, Buddha, Confucius, Vishnu. In front of her, at the far end of the temple, the cardinals and archbishops were bowing before the candlelit altar. The choir began to chant again.

Suddenly the tears were wet again on her cheeks.

Quang Linh! My baby! My baby!

And then she was praying too, for she knew exactly why she had been drawn to this place after so many years.

He had summoned her here. Quang Linh. With his broken, impish grin he had called her here from beyond his watery grave.

I know why I am here. The Caodaists are spiritualists. They hold regular séances and speak with the dead.

The tears glittered on her cheeks.

The priest at the back of the temple looked up at her and smiled.

And millions of miles away in the icy blackness of outer space the unnamed comet hurtled through the silent cacophony of the universe, at 91,568 miles an hour, past dead and living planets, past empty vastnesses, back the way it had passed so many times before, back towards the beautiful, shining, blue-green planet that it always passed once in a thousand years. The one it had very nearly kissed a thousand years ago.

CHAPTER 10

When the liner *Celebrity* docked in Cape Town on its maiden voyage to the Philippines reporters swarmed on board like locusts, stripping their vocabularies of all their adjectives. Cameras zoomed in on all the smiling black presidents and their glittering ladies as they came aboard for the banquet to celebrate the fifth anniversary of independent black South Africa and newspapers and magazines devoted several pages to pictures of the ship and its guests. IS THIS THE GREATEST SHIP EVER BUILT? asked one headline. THIS DEMI-PARADISE, said another, SET IN A SILVER SEA.

The *Celebrity*'s dapper little Greek skipper, Captain Stavros Eliades, strutted about his computerised bridge like an elderly husband with a beautiful young bride. He blossomed in her glory and counted his blessings, for even when they left Durban there was still no sign of the dreaded woman editor of *Celebrity* magazine, who had been meant to join the ship for the voyage from Cape Town to Durban. She had never turned up. She had been unavoidably delayed, said her harassed Irish secretary on the telephone from Monte Carlo: she had had to fly to Tokyo for the opening of a new restaurant. She would join the ship instead for the leg from Durban to the Seychelles, he said. But in Durban there came another call from Monte Carlo: the woman had been detained again, this time to fly to Santiago for a fashion show. She would join the ship when it reached Dar-es-Salaam or Zanzibar, said the harassed Irish secretary, or maybe when it reached Mahé in the Seychelles if she decided to go to the International Women's Conference in Calcutta.

Captain Eliades stood to attention on the bridge and surveyed the heaving swell of the Indian Ocean beyond the harbour and smoothed his neat little goatee beard with satisfaction as the *Celebrity* set sail from Durban and headed north into the Mozambique Channel. At this rate he might manage to avoid the woman altogether until the New Year's Eve ball itself.

Beyond the port bow a school of porpoise cavorted through the waves, leaping and twisting, joyous and carefree in the tropical sunshine.

Captain Eliades smiled. He knew just how they felt.

'Why don't we blow up this big new ship that's in all the papers and TV?' said van der Merwe.

You know what happened when van der Merwe was told to blow up the QE2? He burned his lips on the funnel.

The pain stabbed like a hot lance. He winced. He breathed deeply.

'Hendrik?' said the Oud Bass. 'You OK?'

Van der Merwe nodded. The pain settled to a sharp ache. 'This ship,' he said. 'The *Celebrity*. The one where they gave that banquet for all those bloody kaffir big-wigs in Cape Town the other day. All those grinning black baboons. *Bobbejaans!* We should blow it up, man. That would make them all sit up and take notice.'

The Oud Baas tapped his silver biro against the surface of

the Volksraad conference table. Only Potgieter and Cronje were missing: Potgieter sick, Cronje on a secret mission to Paraguay. A jumbo jet growled above the town and headed east, settling over Long Tom Pass towards the new international airport at Hazyview on the edge of the Kruger Park.

The Oud Baas tugged at his beard. 'Why the ship, Hendrik? What's it got to do with us?'

'It is Babylon,' said van der Merwe fiercely. 'It is filth and an abomination in the sight of the Lord. It represents everything that is foul in the world today, everything that has destroyed our nation and our culture and our young people. It encourages gambling, drinking, fornication, gluttony, idleness, luxury. It fawns on heathen kaffir politicians and witchdoctors and their fat whores. It is filled with graven images and the worship of false gods.'

'But Hendrik…'

'*Vervlaks!* It should be destroyed,' insisted van der Merwe. His voice trembled. He was sweating heavily.

The Oud Baas nodded. 'You speak the truth, Hendrik, but if we manage to wrap up the nuclear deal we will only have the one bomb, maybe two if we are lucky. We must not waste them on irrelevant targets.'

'Irrelevant?' van der Merwe exploded. '*Wat!* The work of the Lord is irrelevant?'

The Oud Baas bristled. '*Nee*, I did not say that, Hendrik, and you know it. We need to save the bombs for the elections and the Day of the Vow in December. That is when we will use them – if we are forced to use them. But please God we never need to use them.'

'*Skei uit daarmee*, man! Of course we will need to use them,' said van der Merwe, looking around the table, seeking support. His eyes gleamed with conviction. 'Even the Bible, the Book of Revelation, promises us a nuclear explosion to save the people of the Lord.'

Beyond the windows one of Bezuidenhout's young Volksleger troopers was patrolling the lawns between the house and the high wall that protected them from prying eyes in the street outside. Beyond the wall an African was whistling tunelessly, one of those jaunty old *kwela* tunes, the ones they used to play on the penny whistle in the kaffir townships.

'We need the bombs not for destruction, Hendrik, but as a bargaining counter,' said the Oud Baas quietly, 'to force our enemies to give us our rightful homeland instead of insulting us with the offer of some broken-down banana republic in Mozambique. We do not want to blow anything up at all, Hendrik. We want only to threaten to blow them up.'

Van der Merwe was defiant. His beard jutted. He looked just like an Old Testament prophet, thought Bezuidenhout admiringly, just like some nineteenth-century Voortrekker, like President Kruger himself; defiant, indomitable. The old boy was still a fighter. He might be dying but brave Boer blood was still pumping strong through his veins.

'And this ship,' demanded van der Merwe. 'This abomination. Do we simply ignore it? Will we not gird ourselves in defence of the teachings of the Lord?'

Another spasm gripped his stomach. He gasped and bent forward, giving a little bow as though to acknowledge the ultimate seniority of pain.

The Oud Baas leaned forward. He looked concerned. 'We cannot do everything at once, Hendrik,' he said gently. 'We can only do one thing at a time.'

'Then the Lord is betrayed by His own people,' said van der Merwe quietly. 'We have waited long enough, man. The Lord is not mocked!'

'Not here, Hendrik, no.' The Oud Baas gazed at him with affection. 'Never here.'

When the meeting ended van der Merwe was the last of the delegates to leave the conference room, lighting a cigarette, coughing, spasms racking his lungs. He shuffled to the door, closing it behind him with a click that sounded like an accusation.

The Oud Baas gazed at Bezuidenhout. 'I'm afraid it is time that Hendrik retired,' he said sadly.

'I agree,' said Bezuidenhout. 'He is losing his sense of perspective.'

'Tell him, will you, Pieter? Over a quiet drink. As a friend. Have you spoken to his doctor?'

'*Ja.*'

'And?'

'Four, five months. Maybe six.'

'There's no hope?'

'None.'

'Poor old Hendrik. He's a good man. A fighter.'

'*Ja.*'

'A great patriot.'

'The best.'

'He is also in great pain.'

'*Ja.* He refuses to take the painkillers. He says they will dull his anger.'

The Oud Baas shook his head. 'If only we had more men like Hendrik. We could take the whole country again. Tell him we have between us enough anger to make up for fifty dying men.'

'I will.'

'Be kind, Piet. Do it gently. He deserves well.'

The Kommandant-Generaal nodded. 'I will tell him that after we are all gone to our rest his name will be the first on a new Voortrekker monument in the centre of the new Volksstaat's new capital,' he said.

The Oud Baas frowned. 'You can tell him his name will be second,' he said, and grinned.

Bezuidenhout hesitated.

'*Ja?*' said the Oud Baas.

'I don't know how to…'

'Say it, man.'

'Only. It's…'

'Say it, Piet.'

Bezuidenhout gazed at the Oud Baas. His eyes were pale, the translucent eyes of a predator that has seen much suffering and caused most of it. 'There is of course another alternative,' he said. 'It might be kinder – and safer – to shoot him.'

The Oud Baas stared at him. 'Safer?'

'In his pain. When he starts taking the drugs. He might talk.'

The Oud Baas looked away. A muscle twitched at the corner of his eye. 'So we shoot him. Like a sick dog.'

Bezuidenhout shook his head. '*Nee*, never. Like a brave old lion that deserves to die with dignity.'

The Oud Baas looked out of the window. Three of the delegates were standing together on the lawn talking quietly in the sunlight. Botha and van Wyk were strolling away towards the pink and scarlet of the flowerbeds, muttering, plotting as always. There was no sign of van der Merwe. A passing cloud suddenly darkened the grass, staining the bougainvillea purple.

The Oud Baas coughed. He looked back at Bezuidenhout. His eyes were tired.

'Very well,' he said. 'Do it.'

In Corsica, in the dark old granite hillside town of Sartène that the locals insist on calling Sartè, on a gusty day with the clouds building fat and black across the Bay of Valinco, Ugo Legrandu knelt and trembled before the altar in the Chapel of Saint Joseph in the church of Sainte-Marie des Grâces on the edge of the central square, the Place de la Libération. Thunder rumbled beyond the hills across the valley of the Rizzanèse towards Propriano. Candles guttered in the gloom, their fragile light flickering across the white marble statue of the Virgin and Child and licking the tears on Legrandu's face.

'*Perdonnu mio Dio*,' he muttered, crossing himself time and again and repeating the penitent words of the *Catenacciu* over and over. '*Mio Dio perdonnu, Perdonnu mio Dio, Perdonnu pietà.*'

A murderer. He shuddered. He had never murdered before. A little aggressive seduction, yes. Some violence, of course:

enemies beaten up in the dark, men knifed, but always men who deserved to suffer. These things had always been common in Corsica, especially in Sartè, with its ancient memories of Moorish and Genoese invaders, its blank, forbidding, granite walls. But never murder. Not until now. He gazed with fear at the sad face of the Madonna and crossed himself fervently again and again.

'*Perdonnu mio Dio, mio Dio perdonnu, Perdonnu mio Dio, Perdonnu pietà.*'

Murder in Corsica was often a noble calling, when honour demanded that you should kill the grandson of the man who once insulted your grandmother's cousin, or to terminate the man whose great-great-grandfather stole your great-great-grandfather's goat, or to take revenge on some brazen boy who might have insulted your sister by kissing her cheek or tearing off her headscarf in public. Corsicans have always needed death to dignify their vendettas. The names of the feuding families of Sartè ring down the centuries like funeral bells: the Roccaserra family against the Ortoli and Pietri, the Carabelli against the Durazzo, the Poli against the Giacomoni. There were times too when it was your duty to chastise a woman with death: an unfaithful wife, without doubt, or a scandalous sister. But not a woman you had never met before. Not a woman walking beside a canal in Venice.

It had been an accident, of course. He had not meant her to die. He had wanted only a little sympathy, a smile, a soft caress. Was that not what women were for?

Yet the word still sat ugly in his head like a tumour. Murderer. *Meurtrier*. The very shape of its letters was sinister: they looked like a sneer on the face of the Devil. *Meurtrier*. And its sound. It sounded like the thud of a funeral drum. It smelt like *merde*.

Yet nobody knew. He was safe. Nobody had come after him. Nobody suspected him. He was home, safe, back with his wife and children. 'Where have you been?' she had said. He told her to mind her own business. That's how it was still in

Corsica, still in places like Sartè. In Ajaccio and Calvi the young girls wore short skirts and smoked cigarettes and married whoever they wanted and argued with their men, but in Sartè wives still dressed in black and disagreed only with their eyes.

But God knew.

Here, in this gloom, on this dark unseasonal afternoon, in the flickering shadows before the Madonna and Child, God knew what he was. *Meurtrier.* The saints' statues watched him with sorrow, the statues of Notre-Dame de la Miséricorde, of St Damien, the patron saint of Sartè, and the statue of St George, the great deliverer who they said once slaughtered the giant ox not far from here, the ox as huge as a dragon. *Meurtrier.* The altar candles smelled of hot wax but were the colour of corpses, and the cloths were musty with the the the odour of decay. *Meurtrier.* And the dead themselves knew, the souls that lay restless in the hillside tombs and stalked the mountains and the valleys at night and cried out for vengeance. The very darkness seemed to know. The shadows seemed to move about him with intelligence. Behind the altar there stood like a solid affirmation of decency Giuseppe Cesari's wooden statue of the Assumption carved from the trunk of a single olive tree. The woman in Venice too had been a martyr. Her soul had shuffled away through the filth in the alleyway beside the canal. He had heard it scuffing the dirt. Her soul would be seeking revenge. Her soul would have joined the army of the dead, the *squadra d'arozza*, the army of spirits that are jealous of the living and come by night in gangs to claim their souls in the early hours before dawn. Her soul would be in Purgatory soliciting others to help her find him. There would be dozens of them, hundreds of them: the angry dead hunting him down, first in the back streets of Venice, then in Genoa, Nice, following his trail by night on the ferry to Ajaccio. In the end they would find him here in Sartè, perhaps just outside in the narrow, cobbled Rue du Purgatoire itself, perhaps in just a few days, on the night of the 31 July, the Feast of the Dead, when every

Corsican village is invaded by vicious, restless spirits seeking revenge or absolution. He would hear the tramp of their dead feet one night and he would look up and hear the *squadra d'arozza* calling his name from the perfumed hillsides of the *maquis* with their mingled scents of myrtle, rosemary and thyme – 'Ugo, Ugo, Ugo' in their high-pitched, wheedling voices in the wind off the mountains – and he would have no choice but to go with them to the grave. The jealous dead are even more terrifying than the *mazzeri*, the living witches who hunt you down and slaughter you in their dreams. The *mazzeri* may at least decide to spare you but there is no denying the *squadra d'arozza* when you hear the tramp of their dead feet echoing between the stone alleyways and the whisper of their unearthly voices. The dead always find their victims in the end. The dead never run out of time.

And he did not even know her name. He could not pray for her without her name.

'*Perdonnu mio Dio,*' he wept. '*Mio Dio perdonnu, Perdonnu mio Dio, Perdonnu pietà.*'

He would give up La Barrett, he swore, if only this terrible guilt were lifted from him. She had been sent to him by the Devil: let the Devil take her back. He would never think of her again. He would forsake other women, return to his wife, be a father to his children. *A pact with God. I swear it. If only this weight is lifted from me.*

On the wall at the back of the church, to the right of the main door, there hung like an accusation the red gloves and huge cross and chains of the *Catenacciu*, the forty-four kilograms of heavy gold-tipped cross and clanking chains that are dragged through the crooked little medieval streets of Sartè every year on the night of Good Friday by the *Catenacciu*, the Chained One, the repentant sinner. Robed and hooded in red, the *Catenacciu* would struggle in agony through the streets followed by a jostling crowd who would call and moan as he staggered, falling and bleeding, in a reconstruction of the suffering of Christ on His way to Golgotha.

Each year they came on the night of Good Friday, thousands of hungry spectators and a different *Catenacciu* each time, almost always a murderer, it was said. In the old days it was often a brutal bandit who had come in from the savage hills and the wild *maquis* to seek absolution by suffering anonymously for his sins. Each year, ever since he had been a boy, Legrandu had turned out to watch the spectacle with excitement, smelling the fear and violence in the air, the sweat of thousands, the smell of blood. At 9.30 every Good Friday night the anonymous Penitent – dressed barefoot in hood and robe as red as the blood of Christ and with irons chained to his right leg – would emerge from the church into the little Rue du Purgatoire to drag himself between the weeping stones of the dank old medieval town, heaving on his shoulders the huge, black wooden Cross. Through the flickering streets he would stagger and stumble, beneath the blazing braziers and flaming torches, followed by priests and monks with lighted tapers, the chanting choir, the wooden effigy of the dead Christ, eight lesser penitents dressed in black and finally Simon of Cyrene robed in white. Beneath the crowded wrought-iron balconies with their flowerpots and splashes of scarlet geraniums he would drag himself whimpering through the chanting crowds – '*Perdonnu mio Dio, mio Dio perdonnu, Perdonnu mio Dio, Perdonnu pietà*' – up and down steep flights of steps and along the narrow alleyways, through sudden low arches. For more than three hours the torture would go on like a scene from Purgatory, the *Penitent Rouge* struggling through the old town, through the Piazza Maió and the Place du Maggiu and the Manichedda and the Rue Nicolas Piétri and the Rue Frères Bartoli, past the slogans daubed on the ancient stone – VUTETI CORSICA NASIONE and LIBERTA PERI PATRIOTI FLNC – past ruined, deserted, four-storey buildings with broken windows, past thick old cobwebbed wooden prison doors bolted and worm-eaten, tiny windows barred with rusty iron, past the smell of damp, decay and hopelessness, past tiny ferns growing in the gutter out of naked

rock like promises of resurrection. And then he would stagger
back through the great arch and the Place de la Libération and
across the square past the Monument of the Dead and up the
hill out of the town, the Penitent gasping, falling, weeping,
bleeding, the chain clanking and scraping the cobbles, the
crowd now silent, now shouting, baying, the children
screaming, women wailing, all conscious of terrible guilt, all
praying for absolution and salvation, all thinking of their own
dark secrets. Last year, according to rumour, the Penitent had
been a murderer who had lived for forty years in Vietnam, even
longer than Peppu, and had come home to wash the stains
from his conscience and to die – one of those thousands of
Corsican exiles who had once escaped the poverty of Corsica
by following their destinies in the French colonies of
Indo-China and North Africa.

That was what he must do if he was ever to be free, thought
Legrandu. He must go to the Franciscans in the monastery and
beg them to let him become the *Catenacciu* himself next year,
in the year 2000, the first *Catenacciu* of the new millennium.
He would beg them to let him drag the Cross and Chains
barefoot through the medieval streets, to let him fall three
times and gasp and bleed and to purge his sin by emulating the
suffering of the Saviour. If he failed, the woman's soul would
hunt him down and kill him like a beast, like a wild boar in the
dreams of the *mazzeri*.

He knelt before the altar and crossed himself again and
again. '*Perdonnu mio Dio*,' he wept. '*Mio Dio perdonnu, Perdonnu
mio Dio, Perdonnu pietà.*'

'Murdoch?' said The Editor. The telephone line crackled across
a third of the globe. 'Murdoch? Is that you?'

'Yo,' said Murdoch in Monte Carlo.

'Thank God for that. These bloody South American telephones…'

'Where are you?'

'Santiago.'

'Chile.'

'Not at all,' she said. 'It's boiling.'

Hey! Murdoch sat up. *Strewth, The Editor made a* joke?

'Where's Kelly?' she said.

'In his office.'

'Has he got his voice back yet?'

'Sure an' begorrah, Kelly is whole again.'

'The only thing hole about Kelly,' she said, 'is the one in his head.'

That's more like it, thought Murdoch with relief. That's the real Editor we all know and love.

'Get him to join us on the conference circuit,' she said.

'Wilko, chief.'

'And Murdoch…'

'Chief?'

'I AM NOT YOUR CHIEF. Right? This is not Wogga-wogga or Wooroloo.'

'No, Bwana.'

'Murdoch…'

'Yes, boss.'

'Get Kelly.'

He called Kelly on the other line and had the switchboard patch both telephone extensions through to The Editor in Santiago. For a moment they seemed to lose her in a welter of clicks and buzzes but then her voice came through again as shrill as a road-drill.

'Kelly?'

'Indeed it is I, like,' said Kelly. 'Brilliant.' His voice echoed with apprehension.

'So you've found your voice again,' she said.

'I have that.'

'I'm glad to hear it. Any luck with the marbles?'

'The marbles?'

'I thought you had lost those too.'

Kelly was bewildered. 'Marbles? I never like had no marbles.'

'You can say that again. You still there, Murdoch?'

'In full, boss,' said Murdoch.

'Stay with us, Murdoch. You're the only idiot in that damned place with any brains. Where's that wimp Campbell? Still lying at home in bed feeling sorry for himself?'

'They've taken him to hospital, Chief. Nervous breakdown.'

'For Christ's sake! What a wanker. You moved into his office yet? We need a level playing field here at this moment in time.'

'I'm still not sure…'

'Move into his office, Murdoch. Now. Today. That's a must-have.'

'I –'

'That's enough chat. Let's get to it, then, Kelly: any word from the White House?'

'They've suggested a draft apology.'

'Fax it to me.'

'But the President still can't come to the Ball. He's like *many apologies, previous engagement, long-standing appointment*, blah-blah-blah.'

The Editor's voice rumbled like a cement-mixer. 'We'll soon see about that. What about the Chief Police Commissioner in Paris? Have they arrested the Corsican chauffeur yet?'

'They still say there's no evidence.'

'You're quite useless, Kelly. For God's sake, can't you get anything right? You there, Murdoch?'

'In person, boss.'

'Will you please get onto the Chief Police Commissioner in Paris and tell him to arrest the Corsican.'

Stone me: she said 'please'.

'I'm relying on you, Murdoch. You're the only man I can trust. Now: Kelly. About my fancy dress costume…'

'I've booked the Lucrezia Borgia gear,' he said.

'Unbook it. I've changed my mind. I'm going as Boadicea.'

'Jaysus!'

'Just do it, Kelly! Now, how are the replies to the invites coming along?'

Oh dear, thought Murdoch. Here it comes. Which do you want first, Stella: the bad news or the bad news?

Kelly took a deep breath. Murdoch looked up. Across the corridor he could see Kelly clearly through the glass partition of his little hutch of an office. Kelly was crouched over his telephone receiver with his right hand clutching the back of his head as though to hold it onto his neck. Murdoch grimaced. Why were they all so terrified of her? The woman was only human. Strewth, she even made the occasional joke.

'We have forty-three acceptances to date,' said Kelly.

There was a moment's silence, then she exploded. 'Forty-three?' she bellowed. 'For God's sake! Only forty-three? Out of a thousand?'

'Give or take.'

'Give or take what?'

'Whatever arrives in the next mail, like.'

'For Christ's sake, Kelly! Only forty-three? Out of a thousand? Who are they, then?'

'There's some good ones, Stella,' said Kelly quickly. He was scratching the back of his head now. Flakes of dandruff floated across his shoulders.

Nerves, thought Murdoch. Poor bastard: now he's got dandruff as well.

'I'll be the judge of that,' she snapped. 'Who's coming?'

Kelly consulted his list. 'Phil Collins,' he said.

'That's great!' said Murdoch decently. 'Phil Collins, eh? Fantastic!'

'Tom Cruise,' said Kelly. 'Tony Curtis, Jodie Foster –'

'You've already mentioned her before,' snapped The Editor.

'So I did, at that. Then there's Kate Moss, Jack Nicholson, Julia Roberts –'

'And her. You mentioned her before as well. They're coming twice, then, are they, Jodie Foster and Julia Roberts?'

'No, I like thought you wanted all the names.'

'Get on with it, Kelly.'

'Right: Mickey Rourke, Charlie Sheen, Emma Thompson –'

'OK, OK,' she snapped.

'Great start,' said Murdoch encouragingly. 'No worries.'

'Shut up, Murdoch,' she said.

'Some of them are very flattered to be invited,' said Kelly in a wheedling tone. 'Jack Nicholson's letter is that grateful. You'd never imagine he was a superstar. He goes like *deeply honoured to be invited to such a prestigious event, it's the greatest excitement of my life,* dah-dee-dah.'

The Editor's voice was ominously quiet. 'Jack Nicholson is grateful to be invited? Jack Nicholson?'

'He is in his reply, so, sure he is. Here it is. Yes. He goes "I never thought I'd be invited to such a wonderful celebration of the year 2000." '

The telephone line crackled. 'I don't believe it,' she said. 'Jack Nicholson?'

'Perhaps he's taking the piss,' suggested Murdoch. 'They say he's got a great sense of humour.'

'Not at all at all,' said Kelly. 'It reads complete genuine. He's like *The happiest day of my life, I can hardly wait, I'm counting the days,* dah-dee-dah.'

'This I must see,' said The Editor. 'Fax me his letter. Fax me the whole list of acceptances. Any royals yet, Kelly?'

'Apart from the King of Tonga, is it?'

'It is. We know all about the King of Tonga already. You mentioned the King of Tonga a week ago. We'll probably have to charter an entire jumbo jet to get him there.'

'Not at all at all. He lives like just round the corner.'

'And you're just round the bend, Kelly. I'm asking about other royals. Apart from the sodding King of Tonga. And don't say the Queen of Tonga, Kelly, I warn you.'

'Very good. The King of Swaziland is looking promising. A provisional yes, like. They said they'd confirm next week.'

'And?'

'There's some woman who claims to be a Romanian princess who keeps pestering me for an invitation. Shall I give her one?'

Murdoch chortled.

'What's so funny?' said The Editor.

'Nothing.' He chortled again. 'No probs.'

'Who's this so-called princess, then?' she asked.

'Princess Zelda, Imelda, something like that. She keeps going on about the Austro-Hungarian empire and her great-great-granny.'

'Never heard of her. Get rid of her. What about the Brit royals?'

'Not a whisper.'

The Editor snorted. 'Wankers. Well, I don't have any problem with that. They're finished, anyway. Who gives a damn about the Windsors? They've blown it. They won't last much longer. In a few years' time they'll be lucky to get invited to the Sandringham Women's Institute Christmas lunch.'

'Which will come as a great relief to Phil the Greek,' said Murdoch, his voice a sudden intrusion.

'Shut up, Murdoch. What about refusals, Kelly?'

Kelly hesitated. He gripped the telephone receiver and closed his eyes.

'Kelly? You there?'

'Eight hundred and twenty nine,' he said.

The Editor was silent for a moment. 'I didn't quite get that,' she said.

Kelly cleared his throat. 'Eight hundred and twenty-nine,' he said. 'Like.'

'Eight hundred and twenty-nine? Refusals?'

'That is right, so it is.'

'What? Refusals?'

'Yes.'

'What do you mean?'

'I mean eight hundred and twenty-nine personages and personalities have like refused. Eight hundred and twenty-nine regret that they are unable to accept the kind invitation.'

The telephone line hummed. The air-conditioning vents whispered among themselves.

'Are you winding me up, Kelly?' she said.

'Not at all at all.'

Murdoch gazed out across Monte Carlo bay. Flags fluttered gently in the breeze on the yachts down in the harbour. The sky was cloudless, the sea glittering blue. Seagulls floated in front of the huge plate-glass picture windows. High up on the hilltop to the right a little toy flag hung limp on the little toy flagpole atop the little toy ochre palace. Up on the hill on the left, along the Avenue du Président John Fitzgerald Kennedy, the stylish buildings stood solid guard against anything of bad taste, like human feelings. The Hermitage loomed creamy yellow with its pillars, arches, wrought-iron balconies. The Balmoral. The Banque Paribas. The Centre Cardio Thoracique, where first they had rushed poor old Iain Campbell when they thought he was about to have a heart attack. The Hotel de Paris. The Opéra. The Casino. What the hell are we all doing in this cold-hearted dump, he thought, wasting our lives like this, sitting like prisoners for day after day in concrete cells? Spread out in front of him and on either side, skyscrapers clustered about the Mediterranean stuffed full with bankers, accountants, investment experts, money men, all scuttling about and sacrificing their lives to the great god Money. At moments like this he envied his primitive ancestors, poor and hungry though they were, but dignified and free to go walkabout in the Dreamtime of their billabongs, bush and the sky.

'You're sacked, Kelly,' said The Editor.

'I'm fockin' glad to hear it,' said Kelly, 'so I am.'

Murdoch sat up. Stone me! What the heck did Kelly think he was playing at? He waved frantically at Kelly through the glass across the corridor, shaking his head with vigour.

'What?' said The Editor. 'What was that, Kelly?'

'You can stuff your job, like, you ould bag. I'll clear my desk now, like, and be off.'

Murdoch covered his eye with his hand.

'You can stick your job where the squirrel stuck his nuts.'

'Take a pull, Paddy,' said Murdoch. 'Get a grip, mate.'

Kelly was staring at him through the glass partitions. He raised two fingers at him. 'And you can fock off too an' all, you great Australian blight,' he said.

For a moment of silence even she was stunned.

'Have you gone mad, Kelly?' said The Editor.

'Not at all at all,' he said. 'I've just come to me senses at last.'

'Don't be ridiculous, Kelly. Now you'll do as you're told. I want you to –'

'Not any more you won't, you ugly ould bag.'

Kelly slammed his telephone receiver back into its cradle. Murdoch gazed at him across the corridor with wonder. Kelly appeared in the doorway of his office. A huge smile lit his face. His eyes twinkled. Even Kelly's curly hair seemed to crinkle with pleasure. Kelly treated him to a double V-sign with both hands. He did a little dance in the corridor. 'I've done it!' he yelled. 'I've fockin' well done it! Brilliant!'

There was a hush in the newsroom.

'Done what?' called Caroline Ponsonby. 'Have you got the Queen?'

'I've told her!' yelled Kelly. 'The ould bitch! I've told her to get focked and stick her job!'

'The Queen?'

'Fockin' Barrett. I'm off. I've told her to go jump in the Liffey. Up the Republic!'

There was a stunned silence in the newsroom and then a jabber of conversation.

'You what?'

'He what?'

'You told…'

'He's resigned?'

'My God, Paddy.'

'He's what?'

'He's told her. The Editor. He's told her to go and get stuffed.'

A huge whoop of joy burst from the newsroom, soaring across the desks and computer terminals and ricocheting along the corridor.

'Good for the Irish!'

'Well done, Paddy!'

'Fantastic!'

Murdoch wiped his hand across his brow. Who would ever have thought it? Kelly, of all people.

The telephone seemed to fizz in his hand.

'Murdoch? You there?'

Murdoch grunted.

'What the hell has come over Kelly?' she said.

Murdoch shrugged. It was time. Somebody had to tell her straight. It was now or never.

'He's finally had enough,' said Murdoch.

'Enough what?'

'Enough of your bullying, Stella.'

'My what?'

Murdoch took a deep breath. 'Your bullying, Stella,' he said. 'You treat him worse than shit. He's just decided not to take it any more. He's decided there are worse things than being unemployed.'

'I don't understand…'

'He's not the only one, either. The rest of the staff has just about reached the end of its tether too.'

'What the hell do you mean?'

Somebody had to do it. Someone had to tell her sometime. He knew he was good at his job. He would always get another, somewhere sane, back home perhaps, back in Sydney.

'They all hate you,' he said.

'I don't believe I'm hearing this,' she said.

'Can you hear all that cheering?' said Murdoch. 'That's your loyal staff celebrating in the newsroom because somebody at last has had the guts to tell you to get stuffed. They all loathe you, Stella. No probs.'

The telephone line buzzed like an angry mosquito.

'I don't believe I'm hearing this,' she said. 'After all I've done for them. After all I've put up with.'

'But you treat them all like shit, Stella. Why do you think Campbell has had a nervous breakdown? They hate your guts, Stella. All of them. Every one. I'm sorry, but it's true.'

The telephone line echoed with his accusations. Ah well, thought Murdoch, this is when she fires me too.

'Ungrateful pigs,' she said. 'After all I've done for them and this bloody magazine. Where would they be without me? Out of work, that's where. I've a good mind to resign and let them all stew. I've often thought of retiring.'

'Why don't you, then?'

She hesitated for a moment. 'I can't,' she said in small voice. 'How can I? Who would I be?'

And then she burst into tears.

Later, long after Murdoch had calmed her down and had promised to hold the fort until she returned and to start inviting all the C-list celebrities right away – all the disregarded names she had never wanted at the ball, all the boring writers, the tedious scientists, the despised politicians, just to make up the numbers – and long after most of the staff had left the office to join Kelly at a frenetic farewell booze-up in a bar down by the harbour, the fax machine in The Editor's office started to chatter with an incoming message.

Murdoch crossed the corridor and went into her office. It was quiet now at the end of the day and her absence lay across it like an invisible shroud. There was a sadness about the place, a loneliness in the polished wood of the vast deserted desk and the slimness of the single green cardboard file in her IN-tray, a melancholy even in the silver-framed portrait of Dirk Molloy that she kept on the desk, in the faint smile on Molloy's face, an unhappiness about his eyes. How odd it was that she should keep the proprietor's photograph on her desk. Unless it was true that they had been lovers. Was that possible? He was in his sixties, she in her thirties. Of course it was possible. The room was empty of more than just her. Out in the darkness the little twin lighthouses winked one-eyed at each other across the mouth of the harbour.

Tears. Stella. The Editor. Weeping! He would never have believed it. She was only a woman after all.

He crossed her office towards the fax machine and reached for the printout.

It was a long message from the astrologer in London, Marian Black-Boyes: three closely printed pages on A4 paper. It was an astrological forecast of some sort, some mumbo-jumbo prophecy: 'What The Stars Foretell'.

What nonsense, he thought.

The last page came off the fax machine. He glanced at the bottom to see that the full message had been received.

'I'm so sorry, Stella darling,' it said in the last paragraph. 'You wanted me to give you a reading for next year, for AD 2000, but try as I might I'm damned if I can come up with anything. I can't see anything at all for you after 1999.'

Marlowe dabbed at the sweat pouring down his face, bit into a jam, cream and banana sandwich and took a swig of strawberry milkshake as the lottery client came on-line from London.

<hows it going> said the client.

<its tricky> said Marlowe <im stil working on it>

<wots taking so long im buying the tickets each week>

<there firewalls r brilliant + there r millions of combs>

<it cant b all that dificlt we only want it to choose 6 numbers>

<its not so eezy>

<how much longer then>

<a week or 2>

<itd better b or i try sumone els>

When the client had gone Marlowe swore and wiped his brow and sat and wrestled with the problem for more than an hour, testing the British lottery computer with dozens of different approaches and combinations, but the damned thing still had him firmly locked out. The principle was simple enough: each week the lottery computer picked six numbers between 1 and 49 and any punter who had picked all six numbers in advance was onto a share of the jackpot. All Marlowe had to do was to programme the computer to pick the six numbers that he and the client had already chosen – 37, 38, 39, 40, 42 and 44 – a combination so tight and unlikely that no one else would have chosen it and they would scoop the whole jackpot without having to share it. But he began to suspect that the lottery computer was being guarded by finger signatures so that it knew that the way he played his keyboard was not the way one of its regulars played it. He needed more information to crack this one. He needed the names and passwords of some of the top lottery executives to let him hack into their own terminals just as they were using the computer themselves so that he could record exactly how they tapped at the keyboard: how hard, how fast, how often with pauses. Once he had recorded their styles and rhythm he might be able to use their electronic fingerprints to impersonate them and fool the computer into letting him in by playing the tapes back into it.

That was it!

He punched the air.

He would break into the lottery computer by using camouflage.

Later Marlowe sent Chandler muttering off downline into the *Celebrity* computer in Monte Carlo to arrange for Tim Watters to be sent an invitation to the New Year's Eve ball in December aboard the *Celebrity*.

Tim Watters would be the perfect guest for the *Celebrity* Ball. He looked exactly like Bill Clinton. Exactly like him. Like a twin. Even Hillary Clinton herself had once done a double-take when she saw Tim Watters, who looked so like her husband that during the Clinton Presidency Watters had become the highest paid celebrity impersonator in the world. When Tim Watters turned up at the *Celebrity* ball with a hired team of bodyguards the Tongans would go ballistic.

Watters was not the first celebrity lookalike that Marlowe had invited to the ball. He had managed to track down thirty others, from a Drew Barrymore to a Barbra Streisand, and it was amazing how closely some of the *doppelgängers* resembled the real celebrities. The Hugh Grant and Meg Ryan doubles could hardly be distinguished from their famous lookalikes. If only the *real* celebrities would also agree to go to the ball it would be like Noah's Ark: they could all go aboard the *Celebrity* two by two. He grinned. Or Hugh by Hugh!

Marlowe reached for a Hershey bar and sucked at the synthetic, hormone-free, strawberry milkshake. Sometimes, when he looked at himself in the full-length mirror in the bathroom, he thought his tits might just be growing a little slower than they were before he'd given up drinking water. Not that there was anything wrong with a man having big tits, of course not: not in these days of equal opportunities and laws against sexism. If a woman could be proud of her tits, why shouldn't a man be, too? It was just that Marlowe was still old-fashioned enough not to want to have to order himself some jumbo-sized, reinforced brassières on the Internet. Once he did that his name would be downloaded onto every weirdo mailing list in the world and he'd suddenly start receiving kinky catalogues through the mail and wisps of lacy underwear, studded leather goods with holes in strange places, whips, masks, fishnet stockings, asshole perfumes, that sort of stuff. Fat, ugly women would pursue him on the Larger Person's Lonely Hearts Network. No thank you, no sir, absolutely not! A good, old-fashioned Luv-Pak was quite enough for him, thank you very much. Marlowe was absolutely straight: nothing fancy, nothing kinky, just a normal Internet gay.

When Chandler had fixed the *Celebrity* computer to send Tim Watters an invitation Marlowe browsed through the Monte

Carlo files looking for other possible guests to brighten up the New Year's Eve ball. It was now three weeks since he had heard from Bill Warren, who was obviously still angry about Chandler's stupid confusion over black boys and Mrs Black-Boyes, but there was no need to stop having fun at the expense of the *Celebrity* computer just because Warren was no longer paying him to do it. In one of the files he came across a letter to some top French cop in Paris demanding that he should arrest some Corsican chauffeur called Ugo Legrandu. Marlowe paused. Ugo Legrandu? That sounded like French for Hugh Grant. Hey! Let's have some fun here, Marlowe thought and chuckled. Why shouldn't the chauffeur go to the ball as well? He lifted the chauffeur's name and address from the letter, zapped it into the file holding *Celebrity*'s invitation list and instructed the *Celebrity* computer to send Legrandu an invitation to the New Year's Eve ball in his own name – Ugo Legrandu – but filed under Hugh Grant. Legrandu would receive his airline tickets in the name of Legrandu, but on the *Celebrity* computer invitation list he would appear as Hugh Grant. Marlowe grinned and scratched his balls. He hadn't had so much fun since he had sent that computer message from the Kremlin to Beijing threatening a nuclear attack in the summer of 1997.

Marlowe ripped open a pack of salted peanuts, threw a fistful into his mouth and sent Chandler pottering off into cyberspace to scan the Internet for any news about the new comet. Chandler muttered and grumbled, taking his time, sighing and wheezing, clicking away like an old arthritic, and eventually flickered onto the screen a message that had obviously not originated in outer space.

<IS YOUR STOMACH GRAVITATIONALLY CHALLENGED? WHY NOT TRY ONE OF OUR REIN-FORCED ARCHITECT-DESIGNED SLIM-U CORSETS? SPECIALLY CREATED FOR THE HUNKIER MAN. JUST $78. SLIM-U. THE CARING CORSET FOR THE KINDER SILHOUETTE>

'Jeez!' said Marlowe. He stabbed the EXIT button. Another ad appeared.

<THE CASANOVA DIET TO PUT HER IN THE MOOD. Take two lemons...>

Marlowe hit the EXIT button again three times. The screen blinked and flashed and served up another message.

<you bin messin with ma wife> said the message <no one messes with ma wife and gets away with it, boy, im comin to chop yore balls off>

'For chrissake!' yelled Marlowe, wiping ketchup off his fingers onto his T-shirt. <EXIT EXIT EXIT>

<ALERT> said Chandler <ERROR ALERT>

Another message appeared on the screen.

<i aint havin no aids-infected faggot messin with ma wife boy im comin to chop yore balls AND YORE HEAD off see if i dont>

'Ah shit,' said Marlowe. Kitty Schweitzer's husband. He had deleted that Schweitzer file weeks ago. Where the hell had it suddenly come from? Somewhere in the deepest hidden recesses of Chandler's raddled memory, burned as unforgotten as a grudge into Chandler's hard disk. Chandler had stopped being funny. Chandler was going to have to go.

Marlowe reached for the keyboard and pressed the SEARCH button: <COMET COMET COMET>

Chandler blinked and tried again.

<im gettin closer u faggot now i know where u live im comin to get you>

Marlowe bunched his fist and thumped it hard on the top of Chandler's screen.

A sharp pain stabbed at his chest.

He gasped.

'Cocksucker!' he yelled. 'Comet, I said, goddammit! Comet!'

<ALERT> said Chandler <ERROR ACCESS DENIED ALERT NO SUCH FILE>

Marlowe yanked Chandler's main cable and plug out of the

power point, crashing out of the programme, plunging Chandler's screen with a high-pitched whine into sudden darkness. Then he booted up quickly again to take Chandler by surprise, using a different initial sequence and tapping in a different pathway code to re-route the search, by-passing the stubborn glitch that seemed to have developed in Chandler's primary system. Chandler would definitely have to go. This couldn't go on. It was getting worse by the week: constant delays, glitches, sullenness, obstruction. It was time he bought himself a new computer. Marlowe could no longer rely on Chandler. Farewell, my lovely: it's time for the long goodbye; the big sleep.

A file flashed onto the screen, a news agency background report on the comet. At last. Marlowe grunted and scrolled through the text.

'Some comets orbit the sun once every century or two,' said the report. 'Others return much more frequently. Encke's Comet, which is a mile wide, orbits the sun every 3.3 years. Comet Temple-Tuttle returns every 33 years, Comet Swift-Tuttle every 130 years, and Halley's Comet, which is nine miles wide, has returned about every 76 years for more than a thousand years. It is described in the *Anglo-Saxon Chronicle* as 'the long-haired comet' that appeared over Anglo-Saxon England in the year 990 as the Vikings ravaged the coasts of East Anglia and it is also shown in the Bayeux Tapestry that depicts the Norman Conquest of Anglo-Saxon England in 1066. Halley's is next expected to return in 2062.

'Comet Swift-Tuttle, which passed close to the Earth in 1992, is due to return in 2126 and is expected to miss the Earth by no more than two weeks. Other comets take more than a thousand years to return. Comet Hayakutake, which lit up our skies so spectacularly in 1996, was last seen from the Earth 15,000 years ago and will not return for another 15,000 years. Comet McNaught-Russel, which was tracked by astronomers in Australia in 1993, was undoubtedly the same comet that was previously spotted by the Chinese in the constellation of the

Great Bear as long ago as the year AD 574. It had taken it 1,419 years to return after a round-trip of 13,000,000,000 miles through space and it is not due back again until the year 3412. One comet – Finsler's Comet, which was seen in 1937 – is estimated to return only once every 13.6 million years, so that won't be back until AD 13601937!'

Marlowe gazed at the screen in awe. Space: 'The Final Frontier.' And now it was coming frighteningly closer.

He clicked the mouse and Chandler sighed, groaned and served up another Internet astronomy file.

'Some comets are huge, like the Shoemaker-Levy 9 comet that suddenly appeared from nowhere in 1993 and crashed spectacularly into Jupiter in July 1994 at about 135,000 miles an hour. One Shoemaker-Levy fragment – at two miles wide the size of a mountain – exploded with the force of 250 million megatons of TNT; a power fifteen billion times greater than the bomb that devastated Hiroshima, and punched a hole in the side of Jupiter big enough to take fifteen planets the size of Earth. Another fragment created a fireball five miles wide and with a temperature of 14,000°F – hotter than the surface of the sun.

'The terrifying power of Shoemaker-Levy 9 worried the US Congress so much that in 1994 it increased its support for Spaceguard, the global telescope early-warning system that searches the heavens daily for objects that might threaten the Earth, and the Council of Europe agreed to join the US in adopting a plan to save the Earth from a cosmic collision. In 1995 there was also an urgent conference of 120 scientists at the Planetary Defense Workshop at the Lawrence Livermore National Laboratory in California to consider ways of destroying or deflecting any future threat from outer space.'

Wow.

Marlowe bit his fingers. He patted the sweat off his forehead.

Wow.

He clicked out of the item and called up another. Chandler sighed again.

<wait…> said Chandler.

For a few moments the screen went blank. Then <ARE YOU ASHAMED OF YOUR PENIS?> enquired Chandler. <IS IT TOO SMALL? TOO THIN? TOO SOFT? INVERTED?

> *NO PROBLEM – YOUR WORRIES ARE OVER*
> WE SPECIALIZE IN DISCREET MEMBER
> ENLARGEMENT
> JUST A $^1/_2$-INCH A MONTH SO AS NOT TO
> ASTONISH AND FRIGHTEN HER!
> **FULL 6-MONTH COURSE AS TESTED BY**
> **ERROLL FLYNN**
> YES! *THAT* ERROLL FLYNN – THE GUY WITH THE
> TWELVE-INCH SCHLONG
> ALL SHAPES SIZES AND COLORS
> *FULL SATISFACTION GUARANTY*
> **Call DICK N HANCER Inc FOR THE MIGHTIER**
> **TOOL>**

<4 fuxake> said Marlowe <gro up assole>

He tried to exit but another sulky file appeared on the screen, this time a news agency background piece on the comet.

'Even a comparatively small cosmic rock – like the 12-mile wide asteroid that crashed into the Yucatan Peninsula at Chicxulub in Mexico 65 million years ago – wiped out the dinosaurs. Many scientists and historians are also increasingly convinced that the bibilical Flood and the sudden changes of climate experienced by the Earth in the years after AD 530 were caused by comets or asteroids crashing into the Earth. The Oxford astronomer Dr Victor Clube has also drawn attention to the sudden destruction of the Bronze Age cities in the second millennium BC and "the fire of righteous vengeance" that is said to have suddenly devastated King Arthur's kingdom of Avalon in Ancient Britain and left it weak and exposed to the savage Anglo-Saxon invasions of the first millennium.

'Some scientists believe that the ancient British monument at Stonehenge was built as a space observatory to allow the Ancient British to track and predict eclipses and the approach of comets and asteroids, which have been called "the dark monoliths of space." Even the history of primitive peoples is packed with references to cosmic disasters. The Australian aborigines, for instance, still tell of a "fire from the sky" and "the Devil Rock" that fell like a thunderbolt onto the Nullabor Desert about 5,000 years ago.'

Marlowe gnawed the hard skin beside his thumbnail.

Suddenly he was afraid. This wasn't just *Star Trek*. This was for real.

He zapped on through to the end of the article.

'Some dangerous heavenly bodies may never be spotted at all. In 1989 one thousand-foot asteroid missed the Earth by little more than 100,000 miles and no one had seen it coming. Some scientists even believe that our solar system has not just nine planets roaming around the sun but also a tenth, the invisible Planet X, which we have never seen because it is so far from the sun that it has no reflection but which must exist because of the effect it appears to have on the orbits of Halley's Comet and the planets Neptune and Pluto. Planet X is believed to be huge, three times as big as Saturn, but it orbits the sun only once in five hundred years: a ghost planet that haunts our solar system.'

He lifted his eyes from the screen and gazed out at the night sky. He could see only one dim star up there. Venus? A manmade marmalade glare hung over the city like smog, dimming the glories of the universe. But it was somewhere up there. Still millions of miles away but heading this way. Seventy miles wide, they said. Ninety thousand miles an hour. Awesome! At least we'll never know anything about it, he thought: the end will come so fast that no one will suffer. The Earth will just smash into pieces or go spiralling out of its orbit and into the sun.

But of course we'll know about it, when the end comes. A chunk of

rock as big as that would fill the sky for weeks before the impact. It
would hang on the horizon huge and menacing all day and night,
growing bigger and bigger as it approached, darkening the skies like the
mountains before a storm, a great grey looming daytime monster that
would gleam silver at night ten times the size of the moon. The moon
itself may fall from the sky. The seas will rise and thrash about.
Whirlwinds. Gales. Hurricanes. And we will watch it all the way as it
comes, the final condemned generation, staring into the eye of a cosmic
bullet.

   \<ALERT\> said Chandler \<ALERT ALERT\>

The summer solstice dawn flickered across Stonehenge and
Salisbury Plain, the giant lonely rocks like broken teeth flecked
with gold. The crowds pressed close against the fence beside
the road and chanted and sang as the Sun God kissed the great
silhouettes of Bronze Age stone glinting in the early light,
dumb enigmatic messages from some ancient civilisation.

   Messages from outer space, perhaps, thought Helga as
Lancelot stood beside her and chanted the ancient Celtic
welcome to the zenith of the year. These huge bluestone pillars
had been dragged here centuries ago from Wales, Lancelot had
told her, and the massive sarsen stones had been shaped by
Mycenaean craftsmen before their civilisation was suddenly
destroyed by even vaster rocks from the sky in the second
millennium BC.

   She looked across the earthwork beyond the line of
policemen with riot shields and helmets holding the restless
crowd back from the sacred stones themselves.

   'Fascist pigs!' she shouted at the policemen. 'Nazis!' She
gave the Hitler salute. '*Heil, Schweinehunde!*'

   Her voice evaporated in the wind.

   The Druids stood to one side, facing east, bowing their
white head-dresses, aloof in their virgin robes. The UFO freaks
and Flat Earthers huddled into their anoraks and woolly
knitted caps against the early chill. The vegetarians chewed
their beards and scuffed their sandals, and the tattered hordes of

New Age travellers whooped and sang with gusto. They sang 'Here Comes the Sun' and then a Gregorian chant and then 'Summer is i-cumen in', all the while linking hands and swaying left and right and crying to the sky to honour their gods: Belenus, the Bright One, the god of the sun, and Lug of the Long Hand, the patron of travellers.

'But now they are desecrating even Stonehenge,' Lancelot had told her. 'Even here, where the Sun God's mother was born, they are brutalising the ley lines and bruising the soul of Gaia. Look at all those modern houses they've built inside the Iron Age earthworks of Vespasian's Camp.'

Beyond the ancient tombs great mounds of butchered soil lay piled high where a fat new by-pass road was being built to the north of Stonehenge across the Bronze Age settlement and ancient burial site. Even the dead are no longer left to sleep in peace, thought Helga: even the dead are sacrificed again to propitiate the living.

And yet – did it really matter? He kept telling her the world was about to end in any case, so what did it matter? He kept telling her about all the Doomsday prophets who had warned that the end was near. Like the American seer Edgar Cayce, who said that an earthquake along the San Andreas Fault would destroy Los Angeles, Hollywood and much of California. And Lancelot kept seeing omens in the sky: the great warning eclipse that was due in just six weeks' time, the eclipse of 11 August 1999; and the evil portent of the Grand Cross of the planets a week later, when the planets would form in the shape of the Cross and would crucify themselves across the signs of Taurus, Leo, Scorpio and Aquarius; the signs of the bull, the lion, the scorpion and Man, the Four Beasts of the Apocalypse in the Book of Revelation.

And Nostradamus – especially Nostradamus – who Lancelot insisted had forecast all of it nearly five hundred years ago:'the age of the great millennium, when the dead will come out of their graves'; the 'burning torch that will be seen in the night sky'; the 'bearded star' that will appear 'when the great cycle of the centuries is renewed'. Nostradamus had forecast too that 'the great king of terror will come from the sky' and warned of 'the great mountain, one mile in circumference… drowning great countries', of 'thirst and famine when the comet will pass', of 'heat like that of the sun upon the sea', of 'a trembling of the Earth', of 'the islands of St George half sunk'. The islands of St George: where else but Britain? And Los Angeles and Hollywood would be devastated by earthquakes, Nostradamus said, and Monaco would be drowned by seven massive tidal waves. And now the scientists had discovered the giant new comet of the apocalypse heading, as promised, towards the Earth – but no one yet had dared to name it Wormwood.

But Helga believed none of it. Her baby stirred beneath her heart and called the prophets liars.

She looked up at Lancelot singing beside her. He seemed suddenly to have become old. She had never noticed it before. His eyes were tired. For him the future is dead, she thought, but not for the world and not for me.

From out of the crowd a black face came towards them, dodging between the beards, woolly hats and anoraks: a young, thin face, sad, hesitant.

Helga looked at the black man and smiled. Of course. The journalist. The only decent journalist in all the world. The one who had asked her to go away with him. *Mein Gott!* she thought. He was so thin. So thin. So black. So sad and lonely.

Nat Wakonde gazed at her. 'I knew I'd find you here,' he said. He stared at her. He cleared his throat. 'I want you to come as my guest to a ball on New Year's Eve,' he said.

'Christ, I hate Stonehenge!' said Potter. 'Fucking rocks!'

It took Afu Faletau and New Zealand Jim more than a week to sail south in his rusty old yacht from Vava'u to Tongatapu and the promised paradise of Nuku'alofa, 'The City of Love'. More than two hundred miles it was, Jim said when they set off.

Good gracious! Two hundred! She had never counted more than one, two, three, four, many.

And then Afu was sick for three days. She had never seen so much water in all her life. The whole world was made of water, from sky to sky, and her stomach floated free. She lay for three days down below in the cabin, sprawled over the edge of the bunk face-down above a bowl that New Zealand Jim kept emptying for her. She had never felt so terrible. She thought she was going to die and wished it would happen soon. New Zealand Jim emptied the bowl and brought water and pills and wiped her mouth with cool cloths and he did not make her do it at all, he just slept by himself on the other bunk.

On the fourth day she suddenly felt better. She staggered up on deck and looked at the waves. They looked so silly, bouncing up and down like that all the time and rolling all over the place. What were they for? The waves at home in the lagoon behaved themselves. They kept themselves tidy. These waves were great big silly clumsy things.

That night she felt so much better that she ate a whole tin of corned beef and drank a tin of condensed milk, and later New Zealand Jim came and lay with her in the same bunk. He touched her and made her head go all soft and her legs tremble. That was lovely. That had never happened to her before. She asked him to make it happen again the next day, and the day after that. Once it made her cry, it made her feel so happy. New Zealand Jim was so kind. And he had promised to buy her some sexy stockings in Nuku'alofa. He was a good man. All his ugly was outside, on his face, in the scars on his lip and his squashed nose, but all his good was inside, where it really mattered.

On the fifth day she took all her clothes off and lay on deck on her back in the sun. She imagined wearing stockings and watched the sky-bursters' tiny airy planes making thin white trails high up in the blue: she wondered how the sky-bursters could fit inside such tiny machines. Perhaps they shrank them down to size before they let them get on. That night she lay on the deck again and Jim came and lay down beside her and touched her again and it was very nice.

On the sixth day she took all her clothes off again and sat at the side of the boat dangling her long, slender brown legs over the edge. Her long, silky hair streamed out in the wind and she laughed her big beautiful white laugh and she started to sing and Jim did not tell her to stop singing or to go and make baskets or *tapa* cloth instead. He just sat at the back of the boat near the steering thing and looked at her and smiled and he looked so nice with his crooked smile and squishy nose, and she sang and sang and the white birds sat on the masts and listened. She thought she had never been so happy in all her life.

On the last day they sailed between 'Eua Iki and Fukave, and she just stared at all the tin roofs and palm trees as they sailed in towards Nuku'alofa at last after so long. She stood on deck and gripped the rail and stared as they entered the muddy lagoon and sailed past the yachts in the marina basin and into the harbour. She had never seen so many coconut trees: they stretched away on all sides as far as she could see.

Nuku'alofa.

Paradise.

She could hardly believe it. She laughed and clapped her hands.

'My gracious!' she cried. 'Thassall!'

Nuku'alofa! At last! She was really here! Bigplace Nuku'alofa! Where the King lived with Princess Sophia! The biggest town in all of Tonga, maybe the biggest, excitingest town in all the world. And the island was so flat! Where were all the mountains? How smart it must be not to have to have a mountain!

Afu could hear her heart thudding with excitement.

New Zealand Jim jumped ashore first and tied the ropes and held out his hand. She jumped too and landed shakily, tried to stand up straight and giggled as she staggered to keep her balance. Her knees were weak, her legs wouldn't listen to her and her head was all mushy inside. The jetty was moving up and down like the sea! This was magic: a dancing jetty! She had always known it. Nuku'alofa was a magic place.

She gripped Jim's arm and after a moment the jetty stopped dancing and her legs were steady and her head was tidy again.

Nuku'alofa!

They wandered together away from the jetty, past Queen Salote Wharf and through the customs and immigration shed where she just smiled at the man in the uniform and New Zealand Jim had to show his little book. Then they walked along the foreshore towards the town. The people all looked so handsome, rich and clever, and the younger men were all so smart with their big, bushy hair styles, torn jeans, heavy belts and buckles and they wore T-shirts with bright, coloured pictures and slogans: NO NUKES IS GOOD NUKES and AIR PACIFIC: IT TAKES TWO TO TONGA and SMILE! YOU'RE IN THE FRIENDLY ISLES!

And then there, suddenly, right on the waterfront, surrounded by tall pine trees, was the royal palace with its sentry boxes and two big shiny cannons. It had red roofs, towers and turrets, gleaming white woodwork and wide, white verandahs with pillars all round. The famous flagpole, the tallest flagpole in the world, was flying the King's red and white flag from the middle tower.

'Oh, my gracious!' she said, staring at the white-gloved guards in their little sentry boxes. She looked beyond the low stone wall and across the lawns and colourful flowers and shrubs towards the palace windows, hoping to see the King having his lunch or talking to Princess Sophia. 'Oh, my gracious!' she said.

And there on the waterfront too was the International Dateline Hotel, the most famous hotel in the world, and people were walking in and out of it! Famous people, she was sure of it. Perhaps Hhugh Grrant was there.

'Oh my!' said Afu.

New Zealand Jim turned inland away from the sea and they walked along the main street, Taufa'ahau Road, past the post office, the Parliament House, the Chinese restaurant, the Wesleyan Church and all the wooden shops. They headed along the longest road in the world and she stared at everything, her eyes wide. They wandered through the town and he showed her the royal tombs and the Bank of Tonga where they make all the money and the Talamahu market with all the fruit and vegetable stalls and people everywhere. It was all so busy, with people walking on both sides of the road and quite a lot of bicycles and a bus and two taxis driving along it at the same time. Some of the girls were wearing high heels – in the middle of the day! – and one of them had painted her toenails red, and one boy and girl were holding hands in the street! Afu was amazed. How grown-up they were here. How smart.

She wished she could be like them. One day she would paint her toenails red and wear high heels and hold hands with anyone she wanted. She would walk down Taufa'ahau Road holding hands with Hhugh Grrant.

She squeezed Jim's arm. She was so excited. Nuku'alofa! At last! Nuku'alofa!

'Well, tha's it,' said Jim. 'Tha's the lot. Crap, i'n'it?'

She looked at him without comprehension.

'I don' know why you wan'ed to come 'ere,' he said. 'There's nothin' 'ere. Nuku'alofa's the ars'ole of the world.'

She stared at him, baffled. What was he saying?

'Ah so?' she said.

What was *ah so*? What did he mean?

'You Afu Faletau?' said the policeman. 'From Vava'u?'

He stood right in front of her on the pavement, blotting the sun: tall, broad and strong, his uniform smart and crisp, the leather shining and polished. His face was fierce under his cap.

'You Afu Faletau?'

She nodded.

He faced New Zealand Jim. 'You James Mackenzie?' he said. 'From Auckland? The *Ocean Breeze*?'

'Yeah. Sure,' said New Zealand Jim. 'Wha's…'

The policeman raised his hand and laid it on New Zealand Jim's shoulder.

'James Angus Mackenzie,' said the policeman. 'You under arrest. For kidnap.'

The Editor sat behind her desk in her office in Monte Carlo as straight and stiff as a London guardsman. Murdoch stood in front of her desk with his hands behind his back, like a schoolboy.

She sniffed. 'Who's been smoking in here?'

He stared at her with his one good eye unflinching.

'No one,' he said.

'I can distinctly smell smoke.'

He grinned. 'Maybe they're burning your effigy out in the newsroom.'

She gave him a thin smile and shuffled the papers on her desk. 'We'll forget all those offensive things you said to me on the telephone in Santiago the other day,' she said tightly. 'Plus we'll forget my reaction. I was utterly exhausted, that's all. Jet-lag. Too many meetings. Not enough sleep. The heat.'

'Fair do's.'

'We will never mention it again.'

'No worries.'

'So you can tell those idle, conniving wankers out there in the newsroom that I'm back in charge and if any of them steps out of line, just once, they'll be out as well like Campbell and Kelly. One whisper of cheek out of any of them and their feet won't touch the ground.'

He looked at her unblinking. *But Kelly resigned. You didn't fire Kelly, Stella. You may have driven Campbell into a loony bin but*

Kelly walked out on you. He told you to get stuffed. Kelly was the one that got away.

'Glad to see you're back to your old self,' he said.

'You better believe it. Plus I don't give a tinker's toss what you or any of those wankers out there think of me. *Capeesh*?'

He shrugged. 'No sweat.'

And yet he had heard the catch in her voice on the telephone from Santiago, and he had heard her weep, and he had seen her face when she had read the fax from Marian Black-Boyes. She had looked hunted then: vulnerable. She had looked at last to Murdoch like a real woman. The bluster was all a façade. The bullying came from weakness. This woman was only a woman and afraid that one day she would be found out.

'Is the lawyer outside?' she asked.

'Yes.'

'Call him in. And stay.'

Murdoch opened the door of her office and made a face at the company lawyer who was waiting outside in the corridor. The lawyer was a fat middle-aged Englishman with startled eyes, an air of defeat and an over-eager smile. Murdoch felt sorry for him. The rumour was that he had had to leave England in a hurry, some scandal involving a client. He came into the room sideways, like a crab, half bent with subservience, his hair lank. His suit was shiny. The Editor looked up at him as though she had somehow picked him up off the pavement on the bottom of her shoe. Perhaps she had.

'I want you to sue Kelly,' she said.

The lawyer grinned with fright. 'Yes, of course. Absolutely. Quite right. Disgraceful.'

'I want you to nail him for breach of contract, insubordination, slander, anything you can lay on him. I'm not having any of my staff talking to me like that. Understand?'

'Absolutely not. Absolutely. Quite right. Dreadful business.'

'Immediately, Thompson. Today. Throw the book at the little Irish shit. Sue him for everything he's got. Sue him for a year's back-pay. I want him to be so frightened he wets himself.'

'Right away, Stella. This minute. Quite right.'

She waved him away with irritation and he crept sideways towards the door and out into the corridor, grinning nervously as he went.

Murdoch hesitated. What the hell. He was either the deputy editor or he wasn't and there was no point in crawling like all the others. She only despised them all the more when they did. 'May I make a suggestion?' he said.

She laughed harshly. 'You want me to take Kelly back, I suppose. Typical. You're so bloody feeble.'

'I think he deserves a second chance.'

'You're so wet, Murdoch, it's pathetic.'

'He's been pretty shaky, Stella, ever since that bomb went off in his face. He's been nervous and jumpy. Touchy. Of course he should never have spoken to you the way he did, but he didn't know what he was saying.'

'God, Murdoch, you're such a wimp. I'm beginning to think I made a mistake making you deputy editor.'

'Fair do's. You can always unmake me. That's your privilege. You're The Editor. But I'm suggesting this for the sake of the magazine, not just to save Kelly's skin. I know you say he's a layabout and I agree that he can be a bit slow but in fact he's very good at what he does. He's an excellent organiser. He gets things done. He knows where everything is. If I could just get him to apologise to you properly. Profusely. I'm only suggesting that it might be worth reconsidering.'

She looked away from him. She riffled through some papers on her desk.

'Where's the new list of extra invitations?' she said irritably. 'The one with Jeffrey Archer on it and all those other boring bloody writers. And the scientists, Stephen Hawking, that lot. And Princess Michael. And bloody Fergie.'

'I bet Kelly would know.'

'Oh, for God's sake, Murdoch, stop going on about Kelly!

Oh, all right, if you really want him back. But he has to apologise to me within twenty-four hours, in person, and he'd better grovel. And if he ever has the cheek to talk to me like that again I shall hound him into bankruptcy. *Capeesh?*'

'Thank you, Stella.'

She pretended not to hear.

'I'll ring him at home now,' said Murdoch.

She shuffled angrily through the papers on the desk.

'And when you speak to him,' she said, 'ask him where the fucking address book is.'

On his way back to his office Murdoch dropped in to see the lawyer, who was crouched over a legal textbook with a worried expression. 'Hold your horses, mate,' said Murdoch. 'Don't send for the executioners quite yet. She's giving Paddy Kelly another chance.'

'Thank God for that,' said the lawyer. His hands were sweaty. 'To be honest, I don't know that we could actually make anything stick.'

'Strewth, mate, we don't want you to start being honest. You're a lawyer, for God's sake.'

The lawyer gave him a weak grin.

'She'll take him back if he grovels,' said Murdoch. 'All I have to do now is persuade him to kiss her bum.'

'Shouldn't be difficult. Everyone else has to.' The lawyer looked shifty. He glanced over his shoulder and discovered nothing there. He looked confidential. 'You know what she's doing now?' he whispered.

'Let me guess,' said Murdoch. 'Does she shag under-age blacks?'

'No, no, much worse than that,' said the lawyer. 'Now she wants me to renegotiate all your contracts. She wants to cut all your salaries, holidays and notice periods and sack three reporters as well. She says she needs the extra money to pay for this damned New Year's Eve Ball.'

'Bloody hell!' said Murdoch. 'She'll never get away with that.'

'That's what I'm telling her.'

'Shit, she's only just given me a rise.'

'I wouldn't bank on it.' The lawyer tapped the side of his nose. His finger left a dark, greasy stain. 'By the way,' he said, 'did you ever hear the joke about this chappie who takes a crocodile into a bar?'

'Sorry, mate,' said Murdoch. 'I never understand jokes.'

Nguyen Thi Chu knelt barefoot on the shiny marble floor in front of the altar in the great yellow-and-blue Cao Dai temple in Tây Ninh. It was long after midnight, well after the fourth and last service of the day, and the temple was deserted but for Chu and the medium and maybe the soul of Quang Linh.

Quang Linh! I am here. You are not alone.

Tears dampened her cheeks. The silence was oppressive. She could hear the blood in her eardrums. Wax dripped down the candles like a silent criticism, for it was many years since she had prayed properly, with all her heart, for the gods of her youth had not been the gods of her ancestors. But now she was praying fiercely to every god she could remember: to Ong Troi, the Honourable Mister Heaven; and Tho Cong, the guardian of the Earth; and the Gods of the Water and the Mountains; and the lesser gods of the trees and stones and lakes; and all the ancestors and all the dead, even to Quang Linh himself now that he was one of the immortals.

The medium approached the altar, his bare feet slapping against the marble and leaving faint, damp footsteps behind. The fat altar candles flickered across his flat, expressionless face. He looked so young, no older than Quang Linh himself, for the Caodaists believed that a medium is at his most powerful in the energy of his youth.

He bowed. Incense wafted up on either side of the altar and smoke from the paper money she had given him to burn coiled like prayers towards the vaulted ceiling. A beam of moonlight shafted silver across the soaring pink-and-gold columns entwined with grinning black dragons with red-and-green faces. High in the pale blue ceiling the pinprick stars twinkled like fairy lights. And over everything the Divine Eye watched like the cold, wet conscience of the world.

The medium lifted the séance prayer envelope from its place above the altar. The paper money crumpled. The fire died in its bowl.

He bowed and stepped away, walking backwards, his robes whispering.

You are not alone, Quang Linh. Her tears gleamed on her cheeks. She could feel him very close. He was here, she knew, somewhere here, somewhere beside her. In her mind she could see his smile, the pride in his eyes. *You must speak for me with the ancestors, Quang Linh, and tell them that I did write every week, twice a week, sometimes three times a week. You must tell them how much I always loved you, and that you did not die alone, for when you died my life was finished too.*

The medium turned towards her. He looked so young, so very young. Why should he be alive and Quang Linh dead? She shook her head to clear it. She must not think this way. She would tarnish the magic.

He slid the slip of paper out of the envelope. He studied it and then folded it and placed it back in the envelope. He lifted his eyes towards her. They glittered in the candlelight. She looked at him with dread.

His voice was high-pitched, like the voice of a girl.

'You must go to Saigon,' he said.

In a hospital room overlooking the Fondamenta Nuove canal, facing north towards the cemetery island of San Michele, the doctor stepped back from the bed.

He smiled at the nurse.

'She will live,' he said. 'And then they will find the bastard who did it.'

And four hundred million miles away the comet swung around the giant belly of Jupiter like a stone caught up in a sling. It shrugged off the insistent tug of the giant planet's massive gravity and hurtled on even faster past the pastel yellow clouds and the Great Red Spot and the swirling graveyard down in the gas below where the great Shoemaker-Levy comet had fallen and died five years earlier in 1994.

The unnamed comet accelerated towards the little golden disc of the sun, its icy surface beginning to thaw as it buffeted full into the solar wind. Wisps of gas and dust flaked away into the blackness of space, bright coloured streamers trailed like a bride's veil a thousand miles behind it in the solar wind as it fell into the heart of the solar system at a hundred thousand miles an hour, two-and-a-half million miles a day, seventy-two million miles a month. It was heading back the way it had passed so many times before, back towards the tiny, beautiful, shining blue-green planet that it always passed once in a thousand years; the one it had flirted with a thousand years ago and a thousand years before that, when its light had shone on the three great kings as they came by camel from out of the East.

CHAPTER 11

The great new ocean liner *Celebrity* sailed north along the steaming tropical shores of Mozambique, past the broken Portuguese colonial concrete of Maputo and the stinking swamp of Beira, past rusty Quelimane and Dar-es-Salaam and the dhows of Zanzibar. There it swept with grace and elegance to starboard like a great white swan and headed into the sun across the Indian Ocean for the sleepy Seychelles and the nervous flatlands of the Maldives sinking into the sea, and on towards Sri Lanka and the Strait of Malacca towards Singapore.

At every port along the way Captain Eliades expected the arrival of the editor of *Celebrity* magazine but at every port there came yet another message that she had been delayed and had changed her plans again. A cheery Australian called Murdoch kept telephoning the ship to say that the Barrett woman had now gone somewhere else instead: first to New Orleans, then an unavoidable trip to Antigua, then somewhere in Canada, and then she decided to fly instead to

South Africa for a long delayed safari in the Kruger National Park.

'She says she'll join you next week in Singapore for the leg to Saigon,' said Murdoch.

'It is difficult for me to contain my excitement at this wonderful news,' said Captain Eliades.

'Don't be like that, sport,' said Murdoch. 'She's really quite soft underneath. Like a crocodile.'

Hendrik van der Merwe rose at dawn as usual in the old family farmhouse in the wilds of the Transvaal and said his prayers as always in his nightdress. But nowadays he could no longer kneel: he had to do it sitting on the edge of his bed. The pain was too great now for him to kneel. He hoped that God would not mind too much. He would find out soon. It could not be much longer. The pain was now so bad that he had started taking the heaviest of all the painkillers. It was only a matter of months now, maybe weeks.

Afterwards he walked painfully to the basin, washed, pulled on his khaki shorts, khaki bush jacket, long khaki socks and *velskoene* and combed his grey, wispy beard. His face was now so thin that the skin hung off his skull in folds like a crumpled curtain. Hephzibah would never recognise him now when he joined her in Heaven.

He tucked the comb into the back of his long khaki socks and walked slowly outside into the brisk morning air. He sat on the *stoep* as always to read the big old family Bible for ten minutes and to contemplate his soul and prepare it for death today, if the Lord so chose. To the east the sun came up on another perfect morning; there was the smell of pine and gum, dust, animal hides, warm elephant dung; the smell of Africa.

The woman Miriam brought him breakfast barefoot on the *stoep* as always, averting her eyes as always. He bowed his head to say grace and the sun rose out of the Indian Ocean and stretched itself warm across the old wooden planks of the *stoep*.

Kommandant-Generaal Bezuidenhout was coming to see him today, something about the Volksraad, something urgent, he had said on the telephone. Van der Merwe guessed what it might be. It was the moment he had always dreaded. 'You have done wonderful work for the Volksraad, Hendrik, but the time has come to retire and make way for a younger man.' They might just as well take a gun and put him down like a dog.

He lit his first cigarette of the day. The smoke seared his lungs and he was racked by spasms of coughing, the tears misting his eyes, the lion wound suddenly throbbing in his leg. What a joke! The wound the lion had given him over at Saxonwold all those years ago was coming to life again just as he was dying.

The telephone shrilled inside the house and Moses Wakonde came running with it, his bare feet flapping against the wooden boards, the telephone flex trailing behind him. Wakonde was suddenly getting old too, thought van der Merwe with surprise: his hair was turning grey and his bony knees were stiff as he ran. He ought to leave him a small pension in his will, he thought. He hadn't been a bad old kaffir really, not as kaffirs go, not once van der Merwe had straightened him out.

Van der Merwe lifted the telephone receiver. '*Ja?*'

'It's Koos.' Koos Labuschagne. The Volksraad delegate from Jo'burg. His voice was hurried. 'They've all been arrested.'

'Eh?'

'The Oud Baas, man.' He was breathless. 'Bezuidenhout, Strydom, the lot. All of them except you and me.'

'Arrested?'

'The kaffir security services. They raided the house in Lydenburg last night.'

'*Grote Griet!* But…'

'I was too busy to attend the meeting. Away on business.'

'What meeting?'

'Last night.'

'There was a meeting? Of the Volksraad?'

'*Ja*, so.'

'In Lydenburg?'

'*Ja*. Sure.'

A bird called in the tree beyond the *stoep*. A dog barked in the concrete square behind the kaffir quarters. Somewhere in the house the woman Miriam switched on the vacuum cleaner.

'You didn't know?' said Labuschagne.

'No one told me,' said van der Merwe. 'They said the next meeting was next week.'

'They must have forgotten to let you know in the rush. It was a sudden emergency meeting. The Oud Baas called it yesterday morning. Some *verdoem* magazine called *Celebrity* has got an article in it this month that says he holds regular meetings of old friends in Lydenburg! Stupid bastards! With his old track record in the Party the kaffir state security were bound to start asking questions. Shit, man, the bleddy magazine might just as well have run a huge headline saying he's a terrorist.'

'*Celebrity*?'

'Some bleddy Brit magazine. *Celebrity*, something like that. The one that's involved with that new ship in Cape Town the other day. Look, man, I can't talk. It's too dangerous.'

But I should have been there, thought van der Merwe angrily. How dare the Oud Baas call a secret meeting without telling me? I deserved to be there, after all these years, after all I have done for the Party and the Volksraad. To be martyred now for the Cause, at the end of my life, would be a privilege I have earned. My name would go down in history along with Kruger, Potgieter, Steenkamp, Roos and all the other great Boer heroes.

'Where've they taken them all?' said van der Merwe.

'No one knows. They wouldn't dare bring them to Jo'burg

or Pretoria. They're probably in some kaffir jail in Bop or the Transkei, the poor bastards.'

'What are we going to do?'

'Lie bleddy low for a few weeks, that's what. They've charged them all with treason.'

'What about the bombs?' said van der Merwe. 'We could nuke the *basters*. Now! We could nuke Cape Town. The Parliament building. *Groote Schuur*.'

'Shit, Hendrik, the Bomb's a bleddy bargaining counter,' said Labuschagne savagely. 'As soon as you use it you haven't got a bargaining counter any more.'

'The day of the elections, then. Or the Day of the Vow.'

Labuschagne hesitated. 'Yes. Maybe. Soon.'

Van der Merwe's voice trembled. 'You can rely on me, Koos. I'll plant it anywhere you like. I'll strap it around my guts, if you like. I'm a dead man already. It would be a privilege.'

Labuschagne was silent for a moment.

'You're a great man, Hendrik,' he said.

'*Nee*, man.'

'But we must not explode it in South Africa. Not at home. We must use it somewhere else, if we have to, as a warning. Lagos, Nairobi, somewhere like that.'

'London!' said van der Merwe. 'Brit *basters*!'

'We'll think about it. I'll call you. In a couple of months, if they haven't caught up with us. But don't call me, man, whatever you do. Don't call anyone if you value your freedom.'

Labuschagne killed the call. But I don't value my freedom, thought van der Merwe angrily. I value my honour more.

He lit another cigarette and was racked again with coughing. He knew he should give it up. But what was the point? It was too far late. And tobacco was the last of all his old friends.

He felt a slow anger beginning to burn along with the pain in his gut. So they had called a meeting without him, had they? They had blown him out, just like that. So that was what Bezuidenhout was coming to see him about today, then, to tell him it was all over. Without even a thank-you from the Oud Baas, without even a word of goodbye. He deserved better from the Oud Baas than that. They might just as well have put a pistol to his head and pulled the trigger.

But Koos was right: they should never use the nuclear option in South Africa itself, not even to mark the Day of the Vow. They must use it somewhere else.

Vervloeks! he thought. *Celebrity* magazine. And the 'high-ranking government official' who had led them to Kruger's gold in the first place. Was the gold a plant? A trap? Shit, why hadn't they been more careful?

And the whistle. Suddenly he remembered the whistle. Every time they had had a Volksraad meeting in Lydenburg there had always been a kaffir whistling in the street outside, always one of those *kwela* tunes, one they always used to play on the penny whistle in the kaffir townships.

His anger hardened. So the Oud Baas thought they could do without him, did he? Right. He'd show them. *Celebrity* magazine. Leah's foul magazine. He had always told Leah that *Celebrity* was an instrument of the Devil, filth, an abomination in the sight of the Lord representing everything that was foul in the world today.

He staggered out of the chair on the *stoep* and swayed for a moment as he fumbled for his balance, steadying himself against the wicker table.

Did you hear about van der Merwe's brain transplant? His body didn't reject the brain: the brain rejected him!

Ja! For sure! That was it. He would go after the liner, take revenge. For the Oud Baas and all the others. And for Zechariah, Reuben, all the generations to come. It would be a privilege. Always take one with you when you go he thought. Van der Merwe would take a thousand with him when he went.

He would find the *Celebrity* and blow the bleddy thing up, and no way would he burn his lips on the funnel, the bastards.

★★★

For more than two weeks Ugo Legrandu refused to leave his house on the hillside in Sartène. He sat in the darkness with the shutters closed, staring at the wall. *Meurtrier!* The dead woman's soul seemed to follow him from room to room like a foul odour. *Meurtrier!*

'You are troubled, my son,' said the monk at the monastery. 'Would you like to make your confession?'

'No!'

'No sin is too great for confession, my son. The Lord is merciful.'

'I need also to forgive myself, Father. I must make the penance of the *Catenacciu*. I must carry the Cross on the night of Good Friday next year.'

The monk had looked at him sadly and shaken his head. 'That is not possible, my son. You will need to wait for twelve years. We are fully booked already until the year 2010.'

'Twelve years? I cannot wait twelve years!'

Meurtrier!

The monk smiled gently. He spread the palms of his hands. 'There is so much sin in the world, my son,' he said.

Since then he had stared at the walls day after day, watching the slivers of sunlight sneak through the shutters and slide around the room.

'Are you ill?' said his wife. 'Shall I call the doctor?'

'I do not need a doctor,' he said. 'Go away.'

Another woman, she thought: that was the explanation. She knew all about his other women. He had always had other women, but then that was natural. All Corsican men hunted women: that was normal. She would not wish to be married to a man who did not pursue women; she would not wish to be married to a homosexual. But this particular woman must have been different. Normal men do not sit around moping at home all day. Normal men sit in the Café de la Victoire or the Café des Amis and drink coffee and sip a *myrte* and play cards and discuss politics, the iniquities of the communist mayor, the news of the latest feud, the stupidity of the *macaroni*, the prospects of independence from France. Normal men go hunting and defend their honour and pursue vendettas. They do not cower at home in the dark.

One night, in bed, he wept, and she tried to hold him as he sobbed but he pushed her away and swore at her.

He was restless in his sleep, dreaming every night that he had turned into a wild boar or a goat and was being pursued across the savage open countryside of the Sartènais by a horde of *mazzeri* hunting him to death in their own dreams. Or he dreamed that the spiteful army of the dead, the *squadra d'arozza*, was tramping along the alleyway outside, slapping the naked soles of their dead feet against the cobblestones and calling to him in their keening whispers to join them. *Ugo! Ugo!* they called, *Meurtrier! Meurtrier!* One night he dreamed that the drum of death was pounding muffled in the next room, summoning him to the tomb, on another that the *malaceddu*, the bird of evil, was tapping at the window, on another that he was awake and watching his own phantom funeral as the jealous dead carried his coffin at noon across the Place de la Libération and into the church, chanting the Mass for the Dead, their white knuckles clutching the silver handles, their bones clicking, the chains of the *Catenacciu* rattling on the wall beside the great door.

On the night of the 31 July, the night of the Feast of the Dead, when the *mazzeri* of each village go out in their dreams to fight to the death their rivals in neighbouring villages, he put bright lamps in every window and left them burning all night and placed sharp knives at every doorway to deter the spirits that invade every Corsican village on that night every year. He locked himself into the bedroom and rammed cotton wool into his ears to deafen the cries of the damned as they called for him.

He dreaded the night of 1 November, the Festival of the Dead, when the bells would toll all night to summon the spirits. How would he be able to bring himself to leave his doors open all that night as usual to welcome the dead? How would he bear the prospect of a multitude of risen corpses tramping through the streets with lighted candles to feast on the food left out for them in all the houses, the pasties made of onions, wild herbs, goats' cheese, salted *brocciu*? How would he be able to bring himself to visit the graveyard as usual on All Souls' Day and place the customary candles and chrysanthemums in the family tomb and sit there for hours beside the angry coffins to heed the silent disapproval of the ancestors? How could he face the contempt of his dead grandfathers?

And always among them in his dreams she was there: the woman in Venice, a grinning skull without lips. *Ciao, meurtrier!* she grinned, opened her blouse and flaunted her naked, shrunken breasts. *Avanti! Andiamo!*

In the third week he could stand the fear and isolation no longer. If the Christian Church could not help him then he must make a pilgrimage to the shrine of the oldest power of all, a power much older than that of Rome, to some holy place of the ancient primeval Mediterranean gods where he could appeal for peace of mind to the Great Mother Goddess, the Giver and Taker of Life, the soul of the people, the spirit of Corsica. He would go in supplication to megalithic Palagiu, perhaps, where scores of monoliths bear witness to the ancient powers, or to Cauria and the neolithic Fontanaccia dolmen, or to Filitosa where the earliest Corsicans first worshipped eight thousand years ago and the ancient stones cry out in silence to the stars.

Filitosa, he thought. Yes: Filitosa, the greatest and most magical of them all.

He slipped out of the house at dawn and rode his motor scooter along the N196 down into the valley of the Rizzanèse. Stark, rugged mountains with their heads helmeted in mist marched away like columns of gladiators on either side of the grim valley. The wooded, secret hills whispered in the wind.

Great granite boulders tumbled down the scrubby hillsides like children's building blocks. He rode across the river to Propriano, throwing a stone into the river first to scatter the spirits and then skirting the bay spread out beneath the looming cemetery high on the hillside, and on towards Porto Pollo.

As he rode through the early stillness towards the pre-historic ruins, with the scent of the *maquis* rich in his nostrils and the mountains massed behind him on the right and the sea sparkling to the horizon on the left, his head was filled with the memory of the wailing Celtic bagpipes of the I Muvrini song '*À Pena Cum'è Tè*' and the proud, haunting, patriotic words that echoed in his soul:

> *Aghju l'anima corsa*
> *Di sole croscia intinta*
> *Di luce inturchinata*
> *E di muntagna cinta*
> *Di terra marturiata*
> *Da lu so mare avvinta*
> *À pena cum'è tè*
> *À pena cum'è tè*

('I have the Corsican soul, soaked bright in sun and blue light, encircled by the mountains, a bruised land girdled by the sea. A little like you. A little like you.')

The tune filled his head again and again, the howling of the bagpipes drowning the gentle puttering of his scooter as it turned north away from the coast and took the crooked little D57 road beside the Taravo River.

> *Aghju l'anima corsa*
> *Da i so scogli tinta*
> *Da i venti culpita*
> *E da prumessa finta*
> *Sempre trà more è vita*
> *Eppuru mai vinta*
> *À pena cum'è tè*
> *À pena cum'è tè*

('I have the Corsican soul in the colours of rock, harassed by the winds and empty promises and always wavering but never stifled. A little like you. A little like you.')

He puttered into the modern hamlet of Filitosa, the Place of the Fern, parked the scooter beside the deserted museum and began to walk east along the access road to the ancient site towards the Eastern Platform as the sun rose high above the Central Monument and touched the megalithic stones with shadows. On the top of the hill above the Barcajolo River, among the gnarled groves of olive trees, the stones stood scattered like giant broken dice, the oldest manmade artefacts on all the island: three-thousand-year-old foundations of stone huts, underground chambers and labyrinths lying in ruins; four-thousand-year-old circular *torre*, the Temples of Fire; five-thousand-year-old menhirs, the 'Long Men' statues hewn from ancient rock by Bronze Age hunters and shepherds and carved to protect the land by looking like armed warriors, the noble *Paladini* knights of Charlemagne. There were huge, erect stone phalluses trembling to fertilise the earth. And everywhere the brooding solemnity of the ancient cult of the dead, the heavy memory of burial chambers.

He climbed down the stony hill path beyond the plateau of the Central Monument towards the grassy plain where the five main statue-menhirs stood stern guard over a living herd of browsing cattle, their shadows long in the early light. One of the giant upright stones, carved to resemble a penis with a bulbous head, nuzzled the lower foliage of a huge old olive tree. The tree was said to be twelve hundred years old. They called it the oldest tree in France. In France! *Imbéciles!*

He approached the vast stone phallus and bowed before it and prayed to the Mother Goddess, the Guardian of the Earth.

I have the Corsican soul in the colours of rock. A little like you.

He begged Her to forgive him, to deliver him from his guilt, to release him from his misery, to point a new way. With barely a moment of hesitation his head suddenly filled with the

final verse of the I Muvrini song like a perfumed blessing from
the prehistoric gods:

> *Aghju l'anima corsa*
> *In u terraniu accintu*
> *D'oriente calamita*
> *E ricordu ma'spintu*
> *Da sta voce arighita*
> *Quandu serai scunvintu*
> *À pena cum'è tè*
> *À pena*
> *À pena*
> *À pena*

('I have the Corsican soul, in its Tyrrhenian sea still tugged
towards the East, a memory to retain, a tremulous voice that is
still relevant today. A little like you. A little. A little. A little.')

Tugged towards the East, he thought.

A memory still relevant today.

And then it came to him. Of course: the East. That was
where he must go, like so many Corsicans before him, like his
brother Peppu, like Peppu's old friend Jean Ottavj, the
Corsican owner of the Hotel Royale down by the docks in
Saigon. Like Philippe Franchini, the proprietor of the Hotel
Continental, and the lawyer Peppu had mentioned, and all the
Corsican restaurateurs and barmen who had migrated to
Vietnam like winter birds. That was where he might escape the
vengeance of the dead, in the magic of the East, in the
sanctuary of oriental temples far beyond the reach of angry
Christian spirits.

He would sell his scooter, borrow some money from Peppu,
fly to Vietnam, find sanctuary with Peppu and work there for a
while as a chauffeur or barman. There was always work for a
white man in these places. And slowly he would exorcise his
ghosts in the fragrant shrines of the East.

Legrandu bowed with gratitude before the ancient phallus
statue. He said a prayer in the ancient tongue and turned and

retraced his steps up the steep path to the Central Monument and the track back to the museum and the Twentieth Century.

As the scooter buzzed back home towards Sartène the sun burned hot on his back, lifting the heavy cloud that had hunched his shoulders for so many days. She has healed my soul, thought Legrandu with relief as he rode south across the Col de Santa Giulia and the Rizzanèse river. The Great Mother Goddess had set him free.

In Sartène there was a letter waiting for him: a rich, cream envelope, heavy to the touch, thick and firm.

He opened it.

An invitation. On thick card. Embossed with gold lettering and a scarlet logo. Addressed to him, with his name in fancy lettering in the middle.

It was from La Barrett.

He stared at it, bewildered.

She was inviting him to be a guest at the big *Celebrity* New Year's Eve ball aboard a liner in the South Pacific in December. Him! Inviting him! The South Pacific! Her personal guest! And all expenses paid.

He fingered the thick card. *Weh!* He knew it. He had always known it. The woman was besotted with him. This was the sign of his forgiveness: the Great Mother Goddess had given La Barrett to him. Now at last he would have her. The Corsican way.

'Vietnam?' said his wife nervously. 'But when will you return? How will I live? And the children. Why are you doing this? The children.'

'I should never have married you,' he said. 'You were always a selfish bitch.'

She stared at him with eyes as black as bullets. *À pena cum'è tè*, said her eyes. A little like you.

The Editor came off the overnight Singapore Airlines flight from London and strode through the gleaming canyons of

Changi airport. The best airport in the world, she thought: clean, rational, an airport for the new millennium.

The ninety-degree heat assaulted her like the blast from a wet furnace as she left the air-conditioned airport building but they had sent a Chinese chauffeur to collect her and the air inside the limousine was icy. As they cruised west away from the airport and Changi Jail towards the skyscrapers of the distant city, between the avenues of trees on Tanah Merah and the manicured verges and colourful flowerbeds beyond the sailing club towards Marina Bay, she remembered why she had always loved Singapore. It seemed to her to be the epitome of civilisation, glamour and stylishness. There was never a scrap of litter anywhere, no dogshit in the streets, no beggars, drunken louts, little crime. Here there was none of the wishy-washy liberalism that had so corrupted the West in the last half of the Twentieth Century. Here murderers were rightly hanged, hooligans caned, speeding drivers fined on the spot. Here they had been the first to censor the dangerous free-for-all of the Internet, in 1996. And even the ferocious traffic cops were women. The Editor smiled. And they shopped until they dropped, the Singaporeans. They shopped every day until midnight, carrying bulging plastic bags everywhere they went in the glittering, ice-cold, six-storey malls. Their streets were punctuated by fountains dancing in the sun, their shops and offices by waterfalls at night cascading down tall storeys of spotlit chrome and glass.

Even the bright white sand of the beach on East Coast Parkway had been imported from Malaysia, the palm trees shipped in from Indonesia, the scruffy area around Arab Street and Little India tidied up and sterilised, the shanty shacks of Tanjong Pagar and Chinatown razed to the ground, the mosques, pagodas and temples all carefully rebuilt in loving replica. Even the Raffles Hotel on Beach Road had been refurbished and restored to look exactly as it had in the 1920s, in the heyday of the British Empire.

It was here that you could see the future. It was here that the

Japanese had humiliated the British in 1942 and the power of the white races had been mortally wounded. It was here that the East began. This is the future, she thought as the limousine cruised down Raffles Avenue towards City Hall and the banking district where the huge smoked-glass financial institutions loomed high above the streets as dark and enigmatic as prehistoric megaliths. This is a vibrant Space Age city, she thought: rich, expensive, antiseptic, authoritarian. This is how the world must be run in the future. This is *Celebrity* country, where everything looks as if it has just been unpacked from cellophane, the ultimate golden marriage of the best of East and West in the new millennium. And here they buy more copies of *Celebrity* magazine per head than anywhere else in the world.

They had booked her into the glitzy, Space Age, five-star Marina Mandarin hotel on Raffles Boulevard and she loved it all: the sheer Asian extravagance of it all, the dozens of Malay flunkeys bowing and gesturing, the huge, whispering lift, the vast, twinkling atrium soaring twenty-one storeys high, the sense of importance, the smell of money. This was how she had always been meant to live. Here she was Someone. Here she was a Celebrity.

She switched the TV on to catch the international CNN news and then telephoned Murdoch in Monte Carlo.

'Yo,' he said. 'How was the flight?'

'Sort of up in the air,' she said. 'You know? Up in one of those plane things? And then you fly high up in the sky for about fourteen hours and then you come down again.'

'OK. I got it.'

'What's new?'

'Two hundred more acceptances today, a hundred and eighty yesterday. Some big names, too: Drew Barrymore, Kevin Costner, Barbra Streisand, Mike Tyson.'

'They're all coming?'

'Yeah.'

'Fantastic, Murdoch!'

'And Danny DeVito, Andie MacDowell, Keanu Reeves, Meg Ryan. Some of them seem to be so keen to come that they've accepted more than once. Hugh Grant has accepted about five times!'

'That's great. What's the total now?'

'We've got about eighteen hundred all together, including the celebs' guests. We'll soon be having to turn them down again.'

She considered the possibility. 'If we get more than two thousand we'll just dump the bores at the last minute, junk some of those writers and scientists and politicians. Don't send them their airline tickets yet in case we end up with too many. What about the President?'

'He still can't come, Stella. I'm sorry, but we've tried everything. They're saying the Vice-President might just be able to make it.'

She snorted. 'Bollocks to that. Hire one of his professional lookalikes, one of the impersonators.'

'Yeah. Fine.'

'Good. At least that'll make it look as if the President's there after all.' She was silent for a moment. 'I know,' she said. 'In fact we might hire several lookalikes of all the biggest names who aren't coming. Invite a few doubles: a Michael Jackson if he's not coming himself, a Madonna, a Glenn Close. They'll look good in the pics and nobody will know they're not genuine. It doesn't really matter if the big names themselves aren't all there so long as it looks as if they're there.'

So this is what we've come to, thought Murdoch: what matters now is not reality but virtual reality, not content but image. And we're meant to be journalists, dedicated to facts.

'Is the TV deal all tied up?' she said. 'The live video cameras all over the ship?'

'Yeah.'

'It's all set?'

'As firm as a djintamoonga's droppings.'

'What?'

'Black-footed tree rat. Abo word. And we get fifty percent of all world rights.'

'Entertainment?'

'The band's come across at last and so have two of the singers and all three of the comedians.'

'Food and drink?'

'Yeah. They've agreed the menu you wanted and promised all the vintage champagne and wines you specified.'

Say it, you uptight bitch, he thought. Say it: *Thank you, Murdoch. Well done!*

'So we're nearly there,' she said.

He grunted.

'Any loose ends?'

'No. It's up and running.'

'Good.'

'Like a dingo with diarrhoea.'

'Do me a favour, Murdoch, will you?'

She hesitated. He could hear the television voices in her room in Singapore. At least they sounded human. She could at least thank them, thought Murdoch. She could at least pretend.

'One more thing,' she said. 'My fancy dress costume. Cancel the Boadicea. I've decided to go as Catherine the Great instead.'

'No problem.'

'Anything else?' she said.

'Just two things. The Chief Police Commissioner in Paris says there's nothing he can do about Legrandu.'

'Who?'

'The chauffeur.'

'The murderer. Why not?'

'There really is no evidence against him, he says. And it's tricky politically. The Corsicans are very touchy these days about interference from Paris.'

'That's pathetic.' She thought about it. 'OK, forget it. We've wasted far too much time on the little turd already. And the other thing?'

'This comet.'

'What comet?'

'The one in all the papers.'

'A comet?'

He sighed. 'Jeez, Stella. Don't you read any newspapers at all?'

'Course I do. The diary pages. Gossip. Features.'

And the astrology columns, too, he thought, and the lists of birthdays, and the cartoons, and all the pretty pictures. But not the news. Nothing about the real world.

'It's all over the front pages.'

'For Christ's sake,' she snapped. 'I don't have time to read everything, Murdoch. My God, I've already got to read about a hundred and twenty magazines a week. What about this comet, anyway?'

This woman is amazing, thought Murdoch. This must surely be the first completely illiterate editor in the entire history of journalism.

'There's a comet heading straight towards the Earth,' he said grimly. 'It's about five or ten miles wide and it's coming at us like the clappers at about a hundred thousand miles an hour and they say it's going to come bloody close to the Earth some time between the end of December and the middle of January. Some scientists reckon it might even crash into the Earth.'

The voices on her TV set burbled on in the background.

'So what do you expect me to do about it?' she said. 'It's not going to land on the South Pacific at midnight on New Year's Eve, is it? You're not saying it's going to hit the ship?'

'It doesn't matter what it hits, Stella. If it hits anything at all, anywhere in the world, we're all in deep shit, everyone in the world, from the South Pacific to the North Pole.'

'Why's that?'

'Jeez, Stella, if something that big crashes into the Earth it will go off like a mega-mega-megaton explosion. We could all be blown sky high or drowned in a huge tidal wave.'

'Then there's not much point worrying about it, is there? For God's sake, Murdoch, what the hell am I meant to do about it?'

'We ought at least to be covering the story. Some of the world's greatest scientists are working desperately to see what can be done to divert the thing or blow it up. Shouldn't we be writing about them?'

'Scientists,' she said. 'Bo-ring. Dullsville.'

'Boring? The end of the world? Strewth, Stella: it's the biggest story ever.'

She thought about it.

'I'll think about it,' she said. 'I'll sleep on it. Right now I'm shattered. Jet-lag.'

'The heat,' he said. 'The exhaustion.'

She killed the connection.

She drew the curtains and lay on the hotel bed. Of course she had heard of the comet. They had mentioned it at least two or three times on the TV news. But what could she do about it? Worrying about it was useless. And long before it landed the scientists would have worked out just where it would be coming down. All she had to do was to make sure she was nowhere near. And anyway, the scientists and military were sure to deal with it. They would smash it to pieces with nuclear weapons long before it came anywhere near the Earth.

But at the back of her mind lurked Marian Black-Boyes' warning: 'I can't see anything at all for you after 1999.'

She shivered. The air-conditioning was much too cold.

Late the next morning the limousine wafted her down to the harbour to board the *Celebrity*. The great white ship towered at anchor out in the bay as elegant as a giant swan. Her heart skipped to see it. For the first time she felt a tremble of excitement. It was all going to happen. Everything she had worked so hard for. It was all coming together. Plus no damn chunk of rock from outer space was going to spoil her fun.

As she came on board the Chief Purser met her at the top of the gangway and presented her with a bouquet of flowers. 'Captain Eliades sends his apologies for not greeting you himself,' he said, 'but he is at present tied up with all the port formalities. He asks you, however, to join him in thirty minutes for a drink in the Judy Garland Lounge on Cook Deck and then for lunch in the Escoffier Banqueting Hall.'

Her suite was stunning, a vast luxurious apartment with sweeping views of the Singapore Roads and Sentosa Island and more flowers and a bottle of Dom Perignon 1995 on ice.

This is how I am meant to live, she thought. This is what I am for.

As she entered the Judy Garland Lounge he came towards her, Captain Eliades, a dapper little man with a small, neat beard, twinkling eyes and perfect hands. He was immaculate in his crisp white uniform and blue-and-gold epaulettes.

'Welcome at last, Ms Barrett,' he said in a deep brown voice. 'I have waited so long for this moment.'

He raised her fingers to his lips. His hand was warm. His lips were dry. He looked up at her. His eyes were merry.

She trembled. Her legs felt weak.

It has happened to me at last, after all these years. This is surely the most beautiful man I have ever seen.

In Los Angeles Steve Marlowe slumped onto the stool at his workstation, squirted ketchup all over a Double Jumbo He-Man Hotdog, added mustard, chilli and onion sauce, bit into it, and grunted with pleasure as the juice dribbled down his chins. He wiped his face with the back of his hand, wiped his hand on his T-shirt, swigged at a carton of strawberry milkshake and sighed with satisfaction. He belched, scratched his testicles, glared at Chandler and tugged the keyboard roughly towards him.

<SEARCH LOTTERY> he tapped.

Chandler groaned, moaned and started clanking and

grinding in the depths of his electronic brain. I must get a new machine, thought Marlowe savagely: perhaps I could just afford one of the new ones by paying for it on an instalment plan. Chandler was now taking five minutes to find even the simplest file or byte of information. It seemed almost as though the computer was ageing before his eyes, as though it had become infected with some dreadful Alzheimer virus. Like a tired old man the computer coughed, grunted and dragged itself across the Atlantic to the British computer's access gate.

For more than half an hour Marlowe lurked outside the gate like a mugger, running Chandler's tape so that he would record any activity at the other end as soon as the lottery computer was activated. It was early afternoon in London and he knew that before too long one of the lottery company's staff would return from lunch and log on to the lottery computer.

The first to do so was a guy called Dugdale, his fingers dancing across his keyboard an ocean and a continent away. The client had mentioned Dugdale. He was in and out of the lottery computer all day like a squirrel up a tree. Marlowe hardly dared to breathe.

Dugdale tapped four separate passwords and suddenly Marlowe was at his side and they went into the lottery computer together, almost hand-in-hand.

'Yeah!' shouted Marlowe. 'Yeah yeah yeah!'

For several minutes, as Dugdale browsed around in the lottery computer, Marlowe stayed on-line, not daring to make any movement at all until Dugdale was finished, and then they came out together and Marlowe tiptoed back home unnoticed.

'Yeah!' shouted Marlowe, smacking his fist into the palm of his other hand. 'We done it!'

Chandler lay back wheezing through his sonar peripherals and suddenly flashed up a news agency report on the screen.

'COMET UPDATE' said the screen. 'The comet 1999-04, which some commentators have dubbed the Doomsday Comet, is not nearly as big as was at first reported. Scientists now say that it is no more than five miles wide and that early estimates were wildly inaccurate because of the misleading brightness of the comet when it first appeared in the solar system. A comet that suddenly flares up millions of miles away can appear to be much bigger than it really is, especially if it is emitting large quantities of cyanogen gas.

'They confirm, however, that 1999-04 will come very close to the Earth. Should it hit the Earth all life would become extinct and some religious groups are claiming that 1999-04 is the Doomsday Comet foretold in the Bible, especially since it comes so soon after the great eclipse that is due on 11th August and the Grand Cross of the planets that will form the Sign of the Cross across the solar system on 18th August.

'Should the comet miss the Earth by a safe margin it will provide us all with the most magnificent firework show in history as it streaks across the sky. Comet 1999-04 is heading towards us at about 100,000 miles per hour and is expected to reach the vicinity of the Earth at the end of December or beginning of January.

'A minority of space scientists are still optimistic that if the comet does appear to threaten the Earth the military will be able to deflect it with laser beams, particle beams or with two or three nuclear explosions out in space. The United Nations in New York yesterday held an urgent Security Council meeting to co-ordinate a global defence strategy.'

Marlowe bit his fingernails.

This was getting scary. This was just like something out of all those old space comics. It was just like that sci-fi movie *Meteor* with Sean Connery and Natalie Wood. And who said it couldn't happen? Sci-fi had an uncanny knack of coming true.

He stabbed again at Chandler's SEARCH button. The computer moaned, muttered and wheezed back into action.

<WAIT...> said Chandler.

Marlowe waited.

<WAIT…>

Marlowe bit his knuckles.

<WAIT…>

Tonight, thought Marlowe savagely. This very night. Tonight I am ordering the latest new-generation computer and damn the expense. Chandler will have to go.

Chandler groaned.

The screen flickered briefly. <MALFUNCTION> it said. <CORRUPT DISK>

What if Chandler really had picked up a virus? Perhaps some new virus that no one could have protected him against? In that case it wasn't Chandler's fault at all that he'd been behaving so strangely.

Marlowe called up Chandler's anti-virus software and ran the checks for all the best-known computer infections, from Aids and Armageddon to Nuke and Year 2000, more than sixteen hundred of them. The software ran for nearly ten minutes and suddenly splattered a black window across the screen.

<ALERT ALERT ALERT> it said <NEW WHITE HOUSE VIRUS IDENTIFIED>

White House virus? What the hell was that?

<GOTCHA YOU BASTARD> said the screen <WHOEVER YOU ARE>

Ah shit!

<YOU FUCK AROUND WITH THE PRESIDENTS COMPUTER AND WE FUCK AROUND WITH YOURS>

A White House virus. The CIA. The FBI. They had tracked him down at last.

Maybe there was still just time…

He hammered out an anti-virus firewall code on Chandler's keyboard but already the screen was fading and an unhealthy green fluorescent glow was spreading across the blue.

Ah shit! Too late!

<THATS IT BIG BOY> said the screen <NOW ALL

YOUR FILES ARE FUCKED>

Too late!

<YOU CAN SAY GOODBYE TO YOUR COMPUTER TOO ITS FUCKED AS WELL> said the screen <HAVE A NICE DAY>

Chandler gave a high-pitched whine and died of a hard-disk attack in front of his eyes, his screen suddenly dark with the fading of the light.

Chandler! Chandler! The bastards!

Marlowe pounded the keyboard. All his files. Gone. And he hadn't backed them up for at least a month. Why hadn't he backed them up? He knew he should back them up. It was the first lesson you learn about computers. Even kids back up their files all the time. A whole month's work, lost. And Chandler murdered.

The dead computer sat on the workstation looking smaller somehow. Already it was going cold.

Marlowe wept. It was the bastards in Washington! They must have planted invisible electronic bacteria around the Internet access port of the White House computer. And Chandler. After all the years together. To end like this.

The front-lobby intercom buzzed. He jumped. He wiped his eyes and lurched over to the remote control camera panel beside the door. Its screen showed a squat, angry, red-faced man in his mid-forties standing in the lobby and glaring at the camera.

'Anyone there?' he growled at the camera. 'Marlowe? You there, you nerd faggot? I know you there, you asshole bandit. I found your address. I come ta get ya, Marlowe. Micky Schweitzer. From Long Beach. You bin messin' with ma wife, boy. You cost me five million bucks, you motherfucking shirt-lifter. I come ta cut ya balls off.'

O Mommy! thought Marlowe. A sharp pain burned in his chest. He gasped. He shrank back from the screen and pressed the automatic electronic locks.

O Mommy!

'You got any balls there, Marlowe?' bellowed Schweitzer. 'You better, boy, cos otherwise I'm goin' ta cut your dick off and shove it up your ass. You like that, faggot? You there, you nancy turd-denter? I know you there, you goddam chocolate tunneller. I can smell you shittin yaself. I'm comin' up, boy.'

Marlowe's chest stabbed with pain again. He staggered with terror across the room to the telephone. He had almost forgotten how to use it. Who needed a telephone when you had the Internet? But now Chandler was dead and he needed the telephone bad.

Emergency: 1-1-1. That was it. You just press the buttons, 1-1-1.

'Yeah. Copshop.'

'Police?' he quavered.

'Sure.'

'Thank God for that. Police. Come quick, police. There's a murderer down in the lobby come to kill me.'

The cop sighed. 'You think you're the only one, sweetheart?' he said. 'This is LA, baby: everyone's got a killer down in the lobby. Now let's do this nice and slow. Name?'

Chandler! I'm sorry. I'm so sorry. I just didn't realise.

It took three months for Nguyen Thi Chu to have herself transferred from Tây Ninh to the university in Saigon. The government spy now seemed only too keen to be rid of her, perhaps because he knew he no longer frightened her. He seemed smaller nowadays and she noticed for the first time flecks of dandruff in his hair, a stoop about his shoulders. Nothing much could frighten her any more. The worst thing that could possibly happen had happened already. Quang Linh was dead.

She had faced the government spy after one of her lectures. 'It was you who prevented my letters reaching my son,' she said. 'I know it.'

He had looked uneasy. His pointed ears looked ridiculous.

How could she ever have been afraid of him? He was only a
little man with silly ears.

'Why?' she said.

'Your letters were bad for morale,' he muttered.

'Liar.'

'They would have diverted your son from his duty.'

'How can you say such things?'

'Your relationship with your son was unhealthy.'

'Unhealthy? For a mother to love her son?'

'It was unpatriotic.'

She had stared at him with contempt. 'You disgust me,' she
said.

And he had looked away.

There was only one terror left that she needed to face and
overcome. On the way to Saigon she would stop off at Ben
Duoc and see the Cu Chi tunnels again and exorcise her
ghosts.

She packed her few possessions – the black pyjamas, the
checked scarf, the peasant hat – and strapped the knife again
around her leg, and said goodbye to her judo instructor and
two of her history department colleagues. Then she took the
bus towards Go Dau Ha on the highway south towards Saigon
and some sort of future and understanding, down the highway
they had always known as Route 1, where nine-year-old Kim
Phuc, completely naked, arms thrown wide in agony, came
running and screaming at the AP cameraman to escape the
Saigon Skyriders' napalm in 1972. It had become the most
famous photograph ever taken during the American war. And
yet, despite that trauma, Kim Phuc had later chosen to live in
North America.

At Cu Chi the bus stopped and Chu disembarked where the
road headed away towards the museum and the tunnels, her
heart pounding, and followed a group of American tourists and
their Vietnamese guide into the jungle. Her heart beat faster.
Her hands were wet with sweat. The jungle all around her was

alive with memories of those terrible days and nights living underground for weeks on end eating rats and rotten rice cakes. The sun was shining but just three metres beneath her feet she knew the stifling heat and darkness, the airless claustrophobia that made you want to scream. She remembered the black pyjamas wet against the skin, the dank stench of soil, rotting vegetation, human sweat and faeces. The smoke leaking acrid from the underground kitchens through the decoy smoke channels and the camouflaged ventilators, the teargas grenades and choking smoke pellets; the smell of fear. The heavy silent terror underground as the American soldiers patrolled overhead, their boots thudding along the jungle paths just above. The screeching of the metal tracks of the Yankee tanks. The wounded in the tunnels screaming to be killed or given one last breath of real air and a final glimpse of the sky. She recalled the wide white eyes of the black GI as he came up from the lower level through the narrow trapdoor; his shoulders had become jammed and she had rolled over on her belly and reached for her knife and had cut his throat; the noise he made as he died. And a few days later it was Tran Xuan Kai himself lying bloodless in the jungle beside the bomb crater, American-Killer Hero Tran Xuan Kai – but dead all the same. She could hear again the clattering of American helicopters overhead, clattering, clattering, the roar of the B-52 bombers, the crashing explosions like giants tramping across the jungle, the trees bursting with orange fire and napalm.

The guides now were all in their early twenties, far too young even to imagine any of that. To titillate the tourists they were wearing the dark green uniform of the northern Liberation Army – the double-breasted shirt pockets, the peaked cap, the red lapels with a silver star on each – and they lounged between the trees in black Viet Cong hammocks like whores in a brothel waiting for clients. The Americans came at them like Sherman tanks. They were huge: the men tall, fat and sweaty in garish holiday shirts and baseball caps, with long fleshy noses and big flat feet, the women wobbling in front and back and smelling of chemical perfumes and animal fat. Almost all of them carried cameras, as if they were blind, and shouted at each other as if they were deaf, and laughed as raucously as if they had no sense of humour. Who said the Americans had lost the war? she thought bitterly. Here at Cu Chi, the secret sanctuary of so many patriotic Vietnamese heroes, the Americans had taken over again and were behaving once again as if they owned the universe. The arrogant Anglo-Saxons had returned. And Kim Phuc lived in North America among the enemy.

They looked at her in their friendly American way and most of them smiled and nodded. One said 'Hi there', another 'Good to know you', but she hated them. She could not help it. The government said the Americans must be forgiven now. 'We need their dollars,' one of her colleagues had said. 'We need their technology and expertise.' But Chu still hated them, the sight of them, their smell, for what they had done to Vietnam and Tran Xuan Kai. She hated them for the way they still seemed to expect the world to be grateful.

'You Vietnamese?' said one of the American women, podgy, middle-aged, fluffy hair, chewing something, gum perhaps.

Chu nodded.

'Speak English?'

Chu nodded again. She did not trust herself to speak.

'It's so nice we're all friends again,' said the woman, chewing, nodding benignly. 'So nice we've all forgiven each other for all those silly things that happened.'

'They are idiots,' said the young guide suddenly in Vietnamese.

'I hate them,' said Chu.

'You were in the war?'

'Yes. Here. In the tunnels.'

'We salute you,' he said.

'It was our duty.'

'Yes. I do not hate them,' said the guide. 'I am too young to hate them. But I despise them. They understand nothing.'

The American woman gave them both a big smile. 'I just love to hear you people talk in that lovely sing-song way,' she said.

'You stink like an old barrel of fish,' said the guide in Vietnamese, giving her a big smile.

'I just love it,' said the American woman. 'So elegant! So expressive!'

Chu followed them along the path into the trees and thickets, her mind fogged by fear and hatred and the ceaseless chatter of the crickets in the jungle. They had widened the tunnels considerably to allow the fat tourists to wobble through them and she followed a vast American woman in pink stretch pants and gold-framed sunglasses down into one of the underground chambers. It was the wartime hospital, with its floor of pounded earth and the rough wooden operating table impossibly tiny and narrow beneath its stained white sheet, green mosquito-net canopy and bare electric light bulb. Down here brilliant doctors like Vo Hoang Le had fought to save the wounded and the dying. Her eyes were misty. She forced herself into the chamber. They had brought Tran Xuan Kai here but it had been too late. His body had lain on that tiny table and had looked even tinier and they had covered his face with a sheet with holes in it. She had seen men bleeding here, men without arms or legs, without morphine, oxygen or blood transfusions. How terrible it must be to die beneath the earth, buried alive already even before death.

They emerged from the underground hospital, blinking in the brightness, the fat woman in pink stretch pants protesting shrilly, whining at one of the men. They plunged underground again into the conference room she remembered so well. She felt as if she were in a trance. The two rows of wooden benches were still there in the middle of the room, the table covered by a red-and-white checked cloth. At one end of the room the wall was still decorated with the old campaign maps of the area and two flags – on one the Hammer and Sickle, on the other the gold star and red-and-blue stripes of the Liberation Army. Above them there stretched still the red wartime banner lettered in gold: *KHỐNG CÓ GI QUY HON ĐOC LAP TU DO* (RESOLVE TO WIN THE TET OFFENSIVE). On the opposite wall a matching banner read: *QUYẾT TẤM GIÀNH THẮNG LÓI CHIẾN DICH MẪU THẤN* (THERE IS NOTHING MORE PRECIOUS THAN INDEPENDENCE AND FREEDOM).

But was that really true any more? Chu no longer believed it. Life was more precious than independence. Quang Linh was more precious. And independence did not bring freedom. Who now had really won the Tet Offensive? How really free and independent now was free and independent Vietnam? In the end all those slogans and deaths had been pointless.

She followed the tourists to the commander's office, the kitchen and the eating room, where a young girl dressed in black pyjamas served the fat Americans cassava, rice cakes and tea, as if they had not eaten far too much already in their pampered lives. Chu looked at the cassava and rice cakes and felt the bile rising suddenly in her throat. She wanted to vomit.

'Gee, Martha, this is some helluva diet!' said one of the men with a chuckle as he swallowed a tiny cake, and the others laughed. Chu clenched her fists. *We lived on that for months!* She wanted to scream. *Hundreds of brave men died with no more in their bellies than cassava and rat meat and rotten rice and most of them were killed by your fathers and sons and some of them maybe by you.*

One of the American women glanced at her and smiled. 'These cookies of yours are real nice, honey,' she said.

The young guide led them eventually away from the tunnels towards a jungle clearing. He hit a cigarette, leant against a tree and gestured contemptuously towards the food and souvenir stalls where Coke and hamburgers were on sale, along with

Viet Cong souvenirs: the black pyjamas now in monstrous American sizes, the black-and-white scarves and conical straw hats. There were postcards, baseball caps and T-shirts with cartoon characters and slogans: I ♥ VIETNAM and HERE TODAY SAIGON TOMORROW and one with a grinning Vietnamese baby chortling CU CHI CU CHI CU! At one end of the counter there were model helicopters and tanks, toy guns, and cigarette-lighters made out of old M-16 bullets with military letters stencilled around the side and the flint and flame hidden in the nose-cap. And from deep in the jungle there came the chatter of weapons: more American tourists, this time firing old wartime guns at a price of ten dollars a time.

How can our government allow this to happen? Why are we prostituting our pride and dignity here for filthy American dollars? What price did Tran Xuan Kai have to pay, and all those other fallen heroes? Just for this: that bloated American tourists may swagger through the hallowed jungle with their loud voices and cameras and play make-believe with Vietnamese weapons and buy cheap souvenirs stained with Vietnamese blood.

'These are disgusting people,' said the young guide in Vietnamese, flicking his cigarette stub into the jungle. 'I am sometimes ashamed.'

She looked at the Americans as they clustered around the souvenir counter, shrieking and bellowing at each other, waving their credit cards. Then she turned away, vomited into the trees and ran back through the jungle pursued by American voices – '…poor girl…', '…Saigon belly, I guess…' – back past the ticket office and the museum, back to the bus stop on the Saigon highway, knowing now that she would never exorcise the horror of it all, that she would always be haunted by the underground ghosts and demons of Cu Chi.

On the bus to Saigon she stared in silence at the countryside as it slid past beyond the window: the water buffalo in the bright green paddyfields, the peasants in their straw hats bent low over the crop, the bullocks pulling open carts along the highway past the fruit and vegetable stalls beside the road. The tin shacks were strung along on either side of the road like rusty ribbons, chickens scratching and flapping, ducks swaggering beside thatched huts set back shy among the palm trees and the red hibiscus flowers close beside the clean white family tombs. A hundred eager white ducklings jostled each other in a quiet river backwater. A pet monkey hung by one arm in a cage. In an open roadside cemetery a huge black crow squatted like an omen on a white stone gleaming in the sunlight. Lorries belched black smoke along the highway beside the fields of peanuts, papaya, cassava, tall wavy crops of sugar-cane, and coconut groves. They passed peasants carrying sagging poles that bounced up and down with baskets filled with pineapples, carrots, tomatoes, bananas, and they passed ancient dented buses with their roofs piled high with boxes. There were bicycles and motorbikes and scooters carrying as many as three people. As they neared Tân So'n Nhi they overtook a funeral procession – the open lorry covered by a rich red canopy and decorated lavishly with roaring golden lions, black and yellow drapes, fringed banners – the mourners following behind on foot with white bandannas tied around their heads. Right at the back a tiny girl, no more than five or six years old, pedalled furiously as she rode a bicycle taller than herself by squatting so low she was almost perched on the mudguard and the wheels.

This is the real Vietnam, thought Chu. This is what I must cherish and remember, not the tourist traps, not the loud Americans.

The bus struggled into the outskirts of Saigon through Quân Tân Bình along Đuòng Âu Có and Đuòng Lê Đai Hành, edging through lines of traffic denser and noisier than she could remember, inching forward past the racetrack and the hospital towards the Chinese district of Cholon. The streets were jammed with cars, buses, lorries and taxis hooting and

squealing, scooters buzzing, suicidal cyclists tinkling their
bells imperiously, hand-carts, trolleys, cyclo-taxi drivers
pedalling furiously and weaving in every direction. They
charged at each other across the junctions like medieval
knights going into battle, never giving way, careering this way
and that, brushing disaster, hooting, tooting, clanging,
terrorising nervous pedestrians who danced across the streets.
They came from every side, relentlessly, on and on like
locusts, the young girls on their buzzbikes cool with the
arrogance of youth, some with passengers riding side-saddle
behind them as they swooped through the crush while sitting
straight and elegant on their padded seats, their high-heeled
shoes parked perkily on the footrests, their pretty faces calm
as masks beneath sunglasses and smart peaked caps or flowery
hats, their jeans and trousers as costly as sin, their bangles
tinkling, their bracelets jangling, their fingers tucked neat
into gloves of pink or blue pulled high above the elbows so
that no one should ever mistake them for weather-beaten
peasants. These Saigon girls could almost be Americans
themselves.

From the bus terminus behind the bustling Binh Tây
market she hired a cyclo-taxi driver to pedal her along the
wide French boulevards through District 5 along Đu'o'ng
Nguyèn Thi Minh Khai towards the heart of the city and the
university college on Đai Lô Lê Duân Street beside the park,
the pagoda and the zoo, past the old American embassy that
had lain empty for more than twenty years, blackened and
deserted.

The college seemed surprisingly small and shabby after Tây
Ninh University. There was no smart central flagstone square
or powerful statue of Ho Chi Minh, no brilliant splash of
flowers, just an untidy, dirt-covered central courtyard with a
drab, peeling, three-storey concrete block in the centre
surrounded by low lecture rooms with corrugated-iron roofs
and hemmed in by hundreds of bicycles and scooters parked

on every side. A dozen male students were playing football on a bare concrete pitch littered with broken stone and fenced with rusty netting. It was the sort of tawdry college you might expect to find in one of the poorest African countries, she thought bitterly. It was almost as though the war had never been won.

They had found her a room out in the Quân Bình Thanh suburbs across the Đa Kao bridge, beyond the muddy shanty slums, rusty tin shacks and palm trees on the marshy bank of the Rach Thi Nghè canal, and Chu travelled each day by crowded bus into the college and spent each evening exploring the city again on foot, refreshing her memory.

Some things in Saigon had barely changed. The girls still wore the *ao dai*, the elegant blue or pink tunic split to the thigh and worn over white silk pantaloons. The butchers, fruiterers and fortune tellers still sold their wares in the market on Hàm Nghi Boulevard. The gamblers still played dice and cards on the sidewalk and games of noughts and crosses using orange chalk. The little wheeled roadside stalls still sold scraps of food and small bottles of petrol and Ho Chi Minh's own favourite 555 cigarettes.

But some things had changed beyond recognition. There were huge, palatial new skyscraper hotels all over the city where they said that even the cheapest room for one night cost as much as US$400 – the annual wage of the average Vietnamese. The city was stuffed with hundreds of western businessmen riding around in expensive cars and eating in plush new Western restaurants. Everywhere she went the shopkeepers asked for American dollars or credit cards and accepted *dong* reluctantly. In the gentle, leafy square on the junction of Lê Loi Boulevard and Nguyên Huê Boulevard the statue of Bac Hobut gazed from among the fountains with surprise at a fast food café called Planet Saigon and the Queen Bee Karaoke Restaurant. VISIT CHINA, said a notice in the travel agency, BEFORE CHINA VISITS YOU. Anglo-Saxon humour. Everywhere the hoardings and street advertisements were in English: Heineken Beer, Singer Electrical Products, Citizen, National Panasonic, Kenwood. The hotels and restaurants, too, like the Continental and Maxim's, had all reverted to their English names: the Ben Thanh was once again the Rex Hotel; the pink and white Nine Dragons Hotel, the Cuu Long down by the river, was once again the Majestic; the Doc Lap was once again the Caravelle.

Most terrible of all was the contrast between the open, desperate poverty on the street and the luxury just behind the vast glass doors of the shops and hotels. The streets of Saigon were still stiff with beggars. Cripples injured in the American war lay helpless in the steaming tropical gutters outside the air-conditioned luxury hotels. They slept on the sidewalks even at noon and when they awoke they pestered every Western passer-by, offering shoeshines, postcards, T-shirts, sleazy packs of playing cards, the big-eyed children tugging at the tourists' clothes and pleading '*Baba! Baba!*', the hungry stick-like women offering themselves. Desperate cyclo-drivers cruised the sidewalks, slowly following every walking Westerner like pilot fish. 'Hello! Why you want to walk?' they cried in English. 'Is hot. I hungry. I children. Hello! You help me, I help you.' This is capitalism, she thought. This is what the West has taught us.

On Lê Loi she passed a hydrocephalic dwarf squatting on the sidewalk with a huge, swollen head and no arms, his back propped against a lamp post, a tin collecting mug held in his toes. Legless cripples without hands rattled past him along the sidewalk, lying face-down on skateboards and little wheeled trolleys, propelling themselves with their stunted elbows. She stared at a Western couple as they looked away, embarrassed. This is what you have done to us, she thought. This is how you have brought us to our knees.

In her room at night she read a little or listened to music or sometimes switched on the television set. There were fifteen channels now, most of them American, TV signals beamed in from across the Pacific, CNN, CBS, capitalist commercials for expensive consumer goods. She never worked at all now on her book, *The Old Barbarians: the End of the Western Millennium.* It had died along with Quang Linh and its ghost lay buried in a couple of computer disks at the bottom of her suitcase. What a waste of her life all that research and labour had been. She doubted almost everything she had written. Where was the real evidence that the Anglo-Saxon millennium was over? American Anglo-Saxons were everywhere, waving American dollars. And where was the genuine evidence of growing Pacific solidarity and supremacy? The oriental nations were still jostling around the Spratly Islands and one day they would go to war again. And who in any case reads books nowadays? The book is dead as well.

One Saturday night three female colleagues asked her to join them for supper in the city and for the first time in months she treated herself to a trace of lipstick, some perfume between her breasts, and she wore her best dress. They ate in a little café near the river, on Tôn Đúc Thâng – braised duck, fried rice, noodles, crispy seaweed, Chinese mushrooms – and afterwards they wandered through the sweaty night down to the river to stroll in the gardens beside the quay in search of a muggy evening breeze.

On the far south bank of the river huge flashing neon signs were advertising Canon cameras, Hewlett Packard, Toshiba, Fujifilm, Tiger beer, Carlsberg, Hitachi, the vast hoardings towering above the shacks and shanties lining the river and the sampans and barges out on the water. The lights of the big ships in the harbour twinkled on the ripples. From the dockside a rusting blue and white ferry set off optimistically for the far bank, crammed with passengers, top-heavy, listing badly to starboard, narrowly missing a collision with a tug struggling upriver pulling a huge barge piled high with sand. Western music and Western laughter floated off the river from the Café

Boong, by The Hammock, and a row of silent Vietnamese sat outside on benches on the quay listening to the music in the dark. Towards the Floating Hotel a tiny Vietnamese woman was trying to sell herself to a giant Caucasian while her child of four or five years old slipped its hand into his and squeaked '*Baba! Baba!*' and a cyclo-taxi driver followed three feet behind saying 'Hello! I help you, you help me. Hello!'

Chu pointed across the river. 'What's over there on the other bank?'

'You can't go there!' said one of her colleagues, a lecturer in French. 'That's District Four. You must never go there. It's a terrible place, full of crime, brutality and disease. It's where the old reactionaries live, the anti-Communist capitalists and traitors who joined the Americans and opposed the liberation. Today they live like savages.'

'But aren't we all capitalists now?' Chu asked.

The lecturer laughed cruelly. 'Not them. They have nothing.'

They headed instead away from the river, north up Đông Khoi towards the pink cathedral. The child beggars were out in force, scrambling around the Western tourists, pestering them with phrasebooks, guidebooks, pirated photostat copies of *The Quiet American* by Graham Greene. Đông Khoi was decorated on both sides with sparkling necklaces of Western jewellery shops, souvenir stalls and expensive art galleries. A rat scuttled into the gutter and the fragile prostitutes on their scooters buzzed and darted here and there like mosquitoes in the dark.

'Most of the prostitutes are men,' said the French lecturer. 'Transvestites.'

'Everything seems so Western nowadays,' said Chu. 'So American. It is almost as though they won the war.'

'They did,' said the French lecturer. She smiled sadly. 'Come,' she said. 'You have lived too long in Tây Ninh. We will show you.'

'Where are we going?'

'A bar. A disco. Run by Vietnamese. And then you will know the Americans won the war.'

They took her through the back streets beyond the Continental Hotel and the municipal theatre to Thi Sách Street where they could hear from two hundred yards away the raucous disco music pounding out of a bar at the end of the street. Above the entrance to the disco the name suddenly burned itself into her recognition: *Apocalypse Now.*

Chu stared at it. She could hardly believe it. *Apocalypse Now.* A Vietnamese bar named after the violent American film about the war. Outside the bar the walls were stacked with military sandbags. A mural showed US helicopters clattering over the Vietnam jungle. Every wall was plastered with posters from the film and the big overhead fans were attached to green ceiling paintings of upside-down helicopters so that the spinning fans appeared to be the helicopters' rotor blades. Yet the place was packed not only with big, sweaty foreigners but also with dainty, laughing Vietnamese girls brash in short skirts and fishnet stockings and too much make-up. It was almost as though wartime Saigon had returned. Once again, thirty years later, Vietnamese girls were willingly selling themselves for dollars.

A huge, red-faced American loomed over her. 'Hi, babe,' he said. He touched her waist.

'No!' said Chu. She backed away into the street.

'You see?' said the French lecturer.

'This place is owned by Vietnamese?'

'Yes.'

She shook her head, stunned. In that case, she thought, we deserve anything that happens to us.

She pressed her hands over her ears and stumbled away from the place, away from the noise and heat and terrible indignity. She was overcome by a certainty that nothing in which she had ever believed was worth anything any longer, that honour, pride, duty were all pointless, that it no longer mattered what happened to her or to Vietnam. What was the point of being a Heroic Vietnamese Mother? There was nothing left to be heroic about.

'I am going to get drunk,' she said.

She had not been drunk for nearly thirty years, not since that night when they thought that the war was won.

She turned off the street into a small bar on Lê Thánh Tôn. They followed her.

'Chu,' said the French lecturer. 'No, Chu. This is not the way.'

'Go to hell,' she said.

The bar was furnished like a French café, like a relic of ancient Vietnamese history, with polished brass rails, marbled table tops, Gauloises ashtrays, a waiter wearing a white apron. She could have been in Paris. She wished she was in Paris. She had always preferred the French to all the other western races that had ravished Vietnam. The French at least had had some sort of style.

A small, swarthy European man was standing behind the bar.

'You are French?' said Chu.

He frowned. 'Never!' he said. He drew himself up to his full little height. 'I am Corsican, *madame*. My name is Ugo. Ugo Legrandu. At your service.'

As the summer faded and autumn distressed the land with wind and wet, Helga Gröning followed Arthur Lancelot and the New Age travellers across southern England on their hallowed annual pilgrimage around the mystic sites of Ancient Britain.

In Somerset they joined 100,000 hippies and rock fans at the three-day, open-air festival at Glastonbury, which Lancelot told her had been the capital of Alfred the Great's Wessex as well as King Arthur's Avalon. Here, he said, Arthur and Guinevere were buried in the abbey and Christ came as a child with Joseph of Arimathaea and St Joseph brought the Holy

Grail; and here the ley lines of all the isles of Albion gathered together in mystic communion.

In Devon, on the summit of holy Cadbury Hill, where he told her that dragons once danced and that King Arthur's father was called Pendragon, she watched him with increasing uncertainty as he prayed in the rain to the pagan gods. He prayed especially to Taranis, the God of the Comet, the Thunderer whose human sacrificial victims were burned to death, said Lancelot, in huge wicker cages built in the shape of giant wooden men.

In Cornwall on 11 August, on the rugged Atlantic coast at Tintagel, where Lancelot announced that King Arthur had been born beside the pounding of the ocean, he prayed aloud for reincarnation and the transmigration of souls as the Great Eclipse of 1999 spread darkness across the face of the Earth, as the sun died and was born again.

In Hampshire, at Winchester, where Alfred the Great is buried, the weak September sunlight glinted through the stained-glass windows of the great cathedral and across the tombs of kings, splashing them with rainbows. It was then that Lancelot touched her swelling belly and together they prayed to the great Mother Earth and the three Mother Goddesses of the ancient Celts, *Y Mamau*, for the health and safety of the child.

In Essex, at Colchester, which Lancelot swore had been the real site of King Arthur's Camelot, the grey October fogs shrouded the gloomy walls of the Norman castle with damp as the travellers congregated there to celebrate the Celtic feast of Samain, to bid farewell to the dying sun on 2 November, All Souls' Day, the day of the dead.

Through all the months of summer and autumn Helga's belly swelled with the growth of the child. She became round and sleek and looked more beautiful than ever, her eyes shining, her skin glowing, her hair gleaming. She spent her days spinning and weaving and her evenings quietly doing embroidery and learning to play the harp. And sometimes

Lancelot played his Paul Simon CD and especially the poignant song 'St Judy's Comet', the one that made Helga want to cry, the one about diamonds sparkling in your eyes.

As Helga's doubts grew along with the child within her she thought increasingly about Nat Wakonde, remembering the sadness on his face when she had told him that she could not possibly go with him to the New Year's Eve ball.

'Both of you,' he had said. 'I want both of you to come.'

Lancelot had moved away.

She had laughed. 'But I am being then pregnant eight month,' she said. 'They are never allowing me to fly at eight month.'

His eyes had flickered towards her stomach and then he had stared at her with hopelessness. 'Pregnant?' he had said with such sadness. 'Congratulations.' And when he left he had said: 'If you ever need me I will come to you.'

In November Helga's child was born suddenly, prematurely, a boy. It was dead. She wept for days afterwards and Lancelot joined her, mourning more for himself than for the child, since he knew that this must mark the final break between them. He knew that they were spring and autumn and the world was facing winter.

For three weeks afterwards she was pale and withdrawn and somehow even more beautiful than ever, and Lancelot knew that it was time for her to go. He realised at last that she no longer loved him. She had even stopped wearing his shirts and socks. He could not hold her now. They had lost too much.

'I am thinking about this New Year party,' she said eventually. 'The journalist.'

'Yes.'

'I am needing a change. After the baby.'

'Yes.'

'Some sun…'

'You must go.'

'No, no. Us together. Both of we.'

He had hugged her. 'No, you go alone,' he had said. 'You need space. You need a little while away from me.'

She had stared at him. 'I will return,' she said.

'Of course you will,' he lied.

'If the world does not end,' she said.

It will, he thought, and mine is ending now.

'You are the best thing that ever happened to me,' he said, and this time he told the truth.

In Nuku'alofa the big policeman took New Zealand Jim away and locked him up and then a lady policeman kept asking Afu Faletau all sorts of rude questions about her and New Zealand Jim. She even asked her if New Zealand Jim had put his thing inside her. Afu got cross then. Of course he had! Did they think she was too ugly for him? Of course he had put his thing inside her. She wasn't a pikinini! My gracious! Whatever next?

'You go buggeroff,' she told the lady policeman. 'Thassall.'

They never let her see New Zealand Jim again. Instead they drove her to the airport and put her on an airy plane to fly back to Vava'u. On the way to the airport she had stared out of the car window at bigplace Nuku'alofa and realised through her tears that New Zealand Jim was right after all. It was not a nice place at all. It was dusty and dirty, not clean and tidy like Vava'u. There was rubbish in the streets. There were dirty smells, bad drains, old cooking, rotten *kaikai*. The shabby buildings needed paint. Wood was rotting around the windows. Nuku'alofa looked like a town that nobody cared about, a town that nobody loved. Why did the King allow it to look like that? And what about Princess Sophia? Why wasn't she out clearing up the rubbish? Afu had thought all her life that Nuku'alofa would be paradise and now she knew that it wasn't. Perhaps Los Angeles in America was paradise instead because that's where all the angels were. That's what Viliami had said: Los Angeles, the city of angels. She cried then, as she waited for the airy plane at Nuku'alofa airport, because all that was left for her now to dream about was Hollywood and Los Angeles and Hollywood was so far away.

Even the airy plane was not nearly as exciting as she had thought it would be. You just sat in a tube and the sky moved past you outside and then you got out again. It didn't even shrink you smaller, as she had thought it must. When she was up in the air she was just the same size. They even had drinks up there and emptied their bottoms in the back.

When she got home her mother cried and hugged her and her father scolded her and her grannies Salote and Lini were very cross with her. Even Viliami sent her a letter from Hawaii which said she had been very naughty to go off to Nuku'alofa like that with a strange man. But he wasn't a strange man, not New Zealand Jim. He was kind and gentle and looked after her. Nobody understood. They tried to make her say that he had done cruel things to her but she shouted at them and in the end they just sent New Zealand Jim back to New Zealand in the *Ocean Breeze* and they never even gave him time to buy her the sexy stockings he had promised. Afu cried when she was told she would never see him again. At night she ached to remember what he used to do to her, how he touched her there and made her shiver. When Siole tried to touch her there again Afu smacked his face. How had she ever let Siole do it to her, even for a tin of corned beef? Siole was just a pikinini: New Zealand Jim was a man. She wanted to kiss New Zealand Jim's scar and she wanted to rub his funny squishy nose, but nobody understood. They told her never to mention him again. But she loved him still, all right. Inside her head. And he had promised to take her to Hollywood one day.

And millions of miles away the comet came on, through the endless darkness, faster and faster, breathing its icy fire and flicking its tail behind it like a dragon.

Every telescope in the world tracked it as it came.

Even the optimists began to fall silent.

In Rome the Pope announced a Global Day of Prayer.

But the comet came on with a twinkle winking like a gleam in the eye of some ancient pagan god.

'Dear God,' said a famous astronomer. 'We've left it too late.'

And although he had not believed in God for forty years he knelt and began to pray.

CHAPTER 12

The *Celebrity* sailed majestically out of the new deep harbour of Ho Chi Minh City and down the Sai Gon River towards the South China Sea on a drab December morning when the clouds hung as grey as treachery across the Mekong Delta.

Up on the bridge Captain Eliades thought of the editor of *Celebrity* magazine and smiled. Why did everyone say what a dreadful woman she was? She was not dreadful at all. She was a delight: small, delicate, fragrant, with a flirty smile and tiny, perfect breasts. And she looked up at him with eyes that sparkled like the star she was.

Stella.

Stel-la.

Such a pretty name. Just right for her. Fragile. Twinkling. Like starlight.

Why had everyone warned him what a bitch she was? She was nothing of the kind. Yes, of course, she spoke her mind, certainly, but what was wrong with that? She was forceful and straightforward. He liked determination in a woman. Who wanted a woman who was shy and hesitant? It was a delight to find one prepared to look you in the eye. And she wanted him. She had made that very plain. She wanted him very much indeed.

At the mouth of the Sai Gon River the *Celebrity* carved a graceful circular wake to port and headed into the rising sun for the final leg of the long, long voyage from Helsinki to Manila, sailing east into the South China Sea where pirates in ramshackle ships stalked small vessels, raping and killing refugees, and Chinese warships cruised like sharks around the Spratly Islands.

She had left the *Celebrity* reluctantly to catch her flight back to Singapore and London. She had kissed his cheek. Her lips had lingered. She had smelt of *Poison*, his favourite perfume. She had looked at him with that weakness in her eyes. You could always tell.

'Until three weeks, then, madame,' he had said.

'It's going to be fantastic,' she said, and he knew that she was speaking not only of the New Year's Eve Ball. When they met again in the South Pacific he knew that they would become lovers.

Twelve nights after Nguyen Thi Chu met Ugo Legrandu in his brother Peppu's bar on Lê Thánh Tôn in Saigon she moved in with him in the little apartment where he lived alone above the bar. He took her to dinner at the Continental, where they ate fillet of sole and *crème caramel* in Guido's Italian restaurant beneath chandeliers and were entertained by a pianist and a violin. He took her to the Rex, where they ate *Salade Niçoise* in the open air on the sixth-floor rooftop garden among the huge blue polystyrene elephants and listened to the singing birds trilling duets against the syncopated rumble of the city. He took her to the zoo, and the park across the river, and to Maxim's, where they ate braised duck and Chinese mushrooms and drank Tiger beer and watched the folk singers and dancers in glittering silver, green and blue. They went to the Floating

Hotel, where they watched the sampans and drank white wine overlooking the sullen river and gazed at the lights reflected in each other's eyes.

'You are beautiful,' he said. 'Like a lotus blossom.'

It felt so good to be pursued again, she thought, to be wanted, to have a man again, to be treated like a woman rather than an academic, so good no longer to sleep alone. It was so good to speak French again, haltingly at first, then increasingly fluently as the words and memories returned. He was not at all intellectual or clever and that was a relief, and she was flattered to see how much he wanted her and she revelled in his physicality, his urgency, the tautness of his muscles, the sheer male smell of him: the fresh sweat glistening in the thick black hair of his chest, the private odours, the dampness on the sheets. How had she managed to live for so long without lust? She brought out a passion in him that was so violent it astonished her. Sometimes she was disconcerted by the ardour of their lovemaking. Night after night he took her voraciously, almost brutally, as though he too were making up for years of loneliness, and his need of her made her feel more feminine than she had felt for twenty years. She changed her hairstyle and started regularly wearing make-up and perfume, and suddenly she noticed that other men had started looking at her too. How is it always so obvious when a woman has a lover? He was not a great lover – he was far too rough and selfish for that – but he was a man, the first she had had since Quang Linh's father had gone off with the American woman. She had lived alone and loveless all those lonely years in Tây Ninh because her feelings of guilt had led her to send out the wrong messages to men, the guilty fear that by taking a new lover she would be betraying not only Quang Linh but also Tran Xuan Kai. When she was overcome by despair at the waste of Tran Xuan Kai's life, the conviction after all these years that he had died in vain, she consoled herself with the knowledge that at least she had built a monument to him in her heart. So long as she remained faithful to his memory then he had at least left some trace of himself behind. But Saigon was not Tây Ninh. Here, in the teeming city, she felt liberated and camouflaged by the pounding beat of urban life: the constant hum of noise, the buzzing in the streets, shrill voices calling loud, the desperate energy of millions jostling for life. Life was real here, electric. And nobody knew her. Here she could be herself, behave outrageously if she chose, and no one knew or cared. Nobody minded, even at the university, that she was living with a Corsican. Why should they mind? Vietnamese women had been living with Corsicans ever since the French first came to Vietnam 150 years ago.

Sometimes, when the light was dim before dawn or a shadow fell across his face, Ugo reminded her of Quang Linh's father: his strutting stockiness, the cut of his hair, the defiant way he held his head, the blackness of his eyes. Sometimes the resemblance was so strong that when they made love she seemed to be taking revenge for the American woman. Once, afterwards, she lay weeping silently in the darkness, for she had imagined that she had been making illicit love with Quang Linh himself.

'My baby!' she whispered through her tears. 'My love!'

Ugo grunted and turned away in his sleep.

It was not his masculinity alone that kept them together. She had to admit to herself that it was also partly the convenience of living with him right in the centre of Saigon just five blocks away from the university. No longer did she have to struggle on and off the crowded buses for the sweaty journeys to and from the suburbs beyond Đa Kao. Now she could leave home much later every morning and stroll to work at leisure in five or six minutes. And living with Ugo saved her money, too: when they had been together for three weeks she cancelled her rental of the room in the suburbs and moved everything she had into the room above the bar.

'Why have you never married?' she said.

'Because I never found a lotus blossom before.'

She told him too much in those early days. She told him everything: about Tran Xuan Kai and Quang Linh's father and the years in the Cu Chi tunnels. He had been astonished. 'You!' he said. 'In the Viet Cong! I don't believe it.'

'Why?'

'You're so small. So delicate.'

'We were all small. We had to be.'

'Did you ever kill anyone?'

She could still see the black face coming up through the trapdoor in the tunnel, the whiteness of the eyes, the terror in them.

'Yes.'

'An American?'

'GI.'

'With a gun?'

She could still feel his jaw firm under her fingers and the blood spurting hot from his neck. It smelt rich.

'Knife.'

He stared at her with mock horror. 'An Amazon!' he said. 'A murderess. Do you still have the knife?'

'Yes. In my suitcase.'

He laughed. 'Not just a murderess but a cold-blooded, cold-hearted murderess. I'd better sleep with my eyes open from now on.'

There were drawbacks to their love affair. The noise of customers and television in the bar beneath the living room at night was such that she could rarely relax with a book, and except for Ugo's one night off a week it was always well after midnight before he came to bed. But she soon adjusted herself to her new routine. Even the noise itself became a welcome sort of company, reminding her of the fun and fellowship that she had missed for so long. The noise reminded her that for the first time in twenty years she was no longer lonely.

But as the weeks went by her happiness began to fade. He stopped taking her out to fancy restaurants and his roughness in bed began to frighten her. Constantly he demanded sex, even though he started disappearing from the bar for an hour or two in the evenings and came to bed smelling of other women. Sometimes he glared at her with angry eyes and sometimes in his passion he hurt her, sometimes deliberately, biting or bruising her. She had known it could not last for ever and she knew that soon she would have to leave him. But not yet. For week after week she postponed the decision, reluctant to move back into some tiny room miles out in the suburbs and frightened too of his reaction. There was in him a violence that disturbed her.

And then in December he told her that he had been invited to take a guest to a fabulous all-expenses-paid New Year's Eve party on a liner in the South Pacific, near Tonga. Even the air fares would be paid. Tonga. The South Pacific. How could she refuse?

'Can you get time off from the university?'

'Yes. I think so.'

'Good. We fly to Singapore on the twenty-ninth of December to join a flight to Sydney. It is fancy dress. I shall go as Napoleon Bonaparte.'

'And me?'

He thought about it. He laughed. 'You could go as a Viet Cong terrorist,' he said. 'You could wear the straw hat and the black pyjamas and the knife that killed the American GI.'

Patrick Kelly was sitting at his new desk outside The Editor's door when she came into the office after her trip to Singapore and Saigon. Across the corridor his old office, still stained by evidence of the letter-bomb from Corsica, had been reallocated to the company lawyer, who sat there cowering behind a pile of documents while Kelly sat outside in the corridor exposed to every passer-by as punishment for his insubordination. The Editor's latest chauffeur trotted along behind her, weighed down with boxes, shopping bags and a vast bouquet. Since Legrandu's departure two more chauffeurs had been sacked, one for impertinence and one for being thirty seconds late.

Kelly stood as The Editor approached his desk. One of his regular duties now was to stand whenever she passed.

'Happy, Kelly?' she said.

'Yes, Stella, thank you,' he stammered. 'Very happy, Stella, thank you. Brilliant.'

'I'm sorry to hear it,' she said.

She swept on into her office and he could hear her shouting at the chauffeur. 'Not there, you moron! Over there!'

The chauffeur emerged from her office and rolled his eyes at Kelly.

'Kelly!' she yelled.

He scuttled into her office.

She was waving a sheet of paper at him. 'What the hell is this?'

'It's a list, like,' said Kelly nervously. 'Last-minute refusals, regrets, blah-blah-blah.'

She glared at him. 'What do you mean, refusals? There must be more than a hundred names here. What the hell's going on? You told me two weeks ago that the guest list was finalised.'

Kelly twitched. He rubbed his nose. 'It's like a lot of the guests are nervous about this comet, the danger, end of the world, dah-dee-dah.'

'They're cancelling because of that? What danger, for God's sake? The Americans keep saying they can handle it. They've got enough nuclear weapons to blow the thing up a hundred times. What's wrong with these wimps?'

'It's mainly Americans who are like backing off. Some of them are saying they'd rather be with the children or friends and family. Most of them reckon it's not the time to be away from home.'

'What wankers. How many?'

'A hundred and twenty-eight so far.'

'So far? You mean there might be more?'

'There's still three weeks to go. There could be more cancellations as the date gets closer.'

'I'll sue the buggers!' She raised her voice. 'Murdoch!' she yelled. 'MURDOCH!'

Murdoch sauntered into her office.

'G'day, Stella. Good cruise?'

She glared at him. 'Cruise? I was working. Someone has to. These cancellations. Kelly tells me hundreds of people are backing off at the last minute.'

'Not hundreds, Stella, just over one hundred.'

'So what are you going to do about it?'

'There's the back-up list.'

'All those bloody writers and scientists?'

'And some politicians.'

'I don't want bloody writers and politicians!' she bellowed. 'Doesn't anyone ever listen?'

'Well, there are still a few C-list actors and models.'

'Bloody hell, Murdoch. C-list? This isn't a C-list party. This is A-list. Five star. Shit!'

'What, now? Here?'

'What?'

'Nothing. No worries.'

'I wish to Christ you'd stop saying that. What do you mean, no worries? There's a hundred and twenty-eight sodding worries and probably more to come. If there are gaps at the tables I'm holding you personally responsible, Murdoch. *Capeesh?*'

He shrugged. 'There won't be any gaps. No probs. We'll easily round up a couple of hundred last-minute guests. And why don't we take more of the staff?'

She looked startled. 'The staff? I'm not taking the bloody staff. Idle bastards. The only staff who are coming with me are you and Wakonde and that's only because I need a couple of gofers on the ship. This is meant to be a celebrity party, Murdoch. Glitz. Glamour. Why would I want to take along a bunch of down-at-heel, lazy, no-hoper hacks who would just slop around in the sun guzzling my gourmet delicacies and swilling my champagne? Can you imagine me having to admit to Tom Cruise or Madonna that Kelly's my secretary? Do me a favour, Murdoch. Just you and Wakonde, that's all. The others stay here, and if they're not here at their desks working on New Year's Day when I phone from the ship to check them out then they'll be out on their necks. You tell them that. *Capeesh?* And tell Ponsonby I want to see her piece on Millennium Comet Fashions and Hairdos before close of play tonight. Now bugger off, both of you.'

Kelly headed for the door.

'Just one thing, Stella,' said Murdoch. 'That rise you promised…'

She waved him away. 'Not now, Murdoch.'

'The company car…'

'Not now!' she bellowed. 'Now bugger off!'

Murdoch shrugged and sauntered out of her office. He would not give her the satisfaction of seeing that he was angry.

Kelly followed him along the corridor into Murdoch's office. 'The bitch!' he said. 'So now we're not even invited to the party. After all the work we've done, so we're not. Cow.'

'That's not all, mate,' said Murdoch. 'The lawyer says she's trying to cut our wages as well as our holidays and she's even refusing to pay Nat any exes for all the time he spent in England chasing Salman Rushdie.'

'What a bitch!'

'Just because he never managed to track the bugger down. He spent two weeks looking for him all over England but Rushdie lies as low as a dachshund's bollocks. Nat spent hundreds of pounds chasing after the bloke and still she won't pay his exes. And now Dupont in accounts tells me she's started helping herself to our pension fund to pay for her New Year's Eve fancy dress and some expensive new jewellery to go with it.'

'I thought she was going as Joan of Arc.'

'She changed her mind again.'

Kelly was distraught. 'Jesus, Tony,' he said. 'She can't steal our pensions. That's what Maxwell did.'

'Too right, mate. Perhaps we should push her off the boat as well.' His face lit up. 'Hey, that's not a bad idea. We could feed her to the sharks in the South Pacific.'

'But she can't take our pensions, can she?'

'She bloody well can. She says they're over-funded and the company can take a contributions holiday and she can do what she likes with the money.'

'We ought to complain to Molloy. The trustees, the pension company, blah-blah-blah.'

'Waste of time. Molloy's terrified of her. You know that. He lets her get away with murder.'

Nat Wakonde came suddenly into Murdoch's office. He was breathless. He looked manic. He seemed to have been running a marathon. He closed the door behind him. 'My God!' he gasped. 'Have you heard the latest? The story in *Private Eye*? About Dirk Molloy and The Editor?'

Murdoch sat up. 'They shagging?'

'Brilliant,' said Kelly.

Nat could barely contain himself. 'Friend's just phoned from London,' he said excitedly. 'It's in today's new *Private Eye*.'

'Bloody hell! She's shagging him! I knew it!'

'Brilliant!'

'Molloy!' said Murdoch. 'The Holy Ghost! The Born-Again Christian! And The Editor!'

'No, no,' said Nat. 'It says Molloy's her father.'

Murdoch gazed at him, speechless.

'Molloy's The Editor's father.'

'Bloody hell!' said Kelly.

'She's his illegitimate daughter.'

Murdoch gaped at him.

'Stone me!' said Murdoch.

'Brilliant!' said Kelly. 'The bitch.'

'They've dug up her birth certificate,' said Nat, 'and there it is: Father, Dirk Molloy.'

'Bugger me!' said Murdoch. 'Has she seen it yet?'

'No, she never reads the *Eye*. No glossy pictures. They're faxing the piece to me at home.'

'Fuck me! Could it be a different Molloy?'

'No, they've checked it all out,' said Nat. 'Places, dates. It's the same one, all right. She's a bastard.'

'You can say that again, mate. Hellfire, she'll go spare if she ever finds out about the story.'

'Who's going to tell her?' said Nat. 'I've got to go. See you.' He reached the door and turned back. 'By the way,' he said, 'they're moving poor old Iain Campbell into a nuthouse this afternoon.'

'Poor sod. An asylum?'

'A genuine funny farm.'

Murdoch shook his head. 'Poor bugger. Poor bloody Iain.'

'I'd watch it, if I were you,' said Nat. 'It's an occupational hazard. All her deputy editors end up being carried out by the guys in the white coats. See you.'

He left in a hurry.

'Well, stone me!' said Murdoch. 'Molloy's daughter! No wonder he gave her the top job. No wonder she does what she likes and the poor bugger's terrified of her. She could blackmail him from Cap d'Antibes to Christmas. She's got Molloy stitched up as tight as a Jewish cock.'

'After all we've done,' said Kelly. 'Bloody Brit bitch!'

Murdoch patted his shoulder. 'Never mind, sport,' he said. 'Here's a nice Brit story to cheer you up. No worries. This guy Bruce goes into a pub with his pet crocodile, see, and he says to the barman "I'll have a beer and the croc'll have a large Brit", so the barman gives him a beer and pulls a dead Brit from the freezer and throws him to the croc. Bruce sinks the beer and the croc swallows the Pom. "Right", says Bruce, "same again", and he has another beer and the croc has another Pom and

Bruce keeps repeating the order until he's had five beers and the croc's had five Brits.

'Then he tries to order a sixth round but the barman says "Heck, mate, I'm awful sorry, but I've run clean out of Poms for the croc. Would he fancy a dwarf instead? Or a couple of pygmies?"

' "Hell, no," says Bruce, "not a dwarf or a pygmy, for Christ's sake. The croc goes completely bonkers once he starts on shorts." '

Kelly started laughing.

'Of course when they tell that one in England,' said Murdoch, 'the croc usually gets to eat a Paddy.'

The Afrikaaner Day of the Vow on 16 December 1999 passed unnoticed in South Africa except for a few staunch Boer communities far out on the veld. There they honoured their Voortrekker ancestors surreptitiously with prayers and *braiivleis* barbecues without attracting the wrath of the newly elected, all-black government, the first South African government in history without even one white minister. All the white Uncle Toms have gone at last, thought van der Merwe bitterly, swept out of power and crushed by the kaffirs, all those treacherous bastards like de Klerk who betrayed the legacy of the Voortrekkers and sold out their own people to the kaffirs. In Pretoria now on 16 December they celebrated instead an African Day of Reconciliation and the vast granite Voortrekker monument was deserted. Only the ghosts of a hundred thousand dead still gathered there unseen to sing silent hymns and bellow unheard the Afrikaaner anthem *'Die Stem'* as the ray of sunlight in the centre of the monument shone exactly at noon as always on 16 December, through a hole in the roof, and lit up the cenotaph with its patriotic exhortation *Ons vir jou, Suid Afrika* – 'We For You, South Africa'. In the cities and *dorps* all over the land even the Afrikaans Reformed churches were empty. It was a Thursday, and the drums of battle that once deafened the Zulus were silent.

Van der Merwe caught his breath. He gasped. The pain was fiendish now, knives hourly sharpening themselves against his guts. Instead of kneeling he sat unmoving on the *stoep* of the farmhouse and gazed across his land towards Mozambique, worshipping in his heart and smelling history in the sweet Transvaal air. Soon he, too, would be counted among the great dead Boer heroes. In fifteen days he would make a demonstration of Afrikaaner patriotism that would astonish the world and remind it that here was still a great unconquered people.

Labuschagne came out to the farm on 20 December to collect him for the flights to Jo'burg, Perth, Sydney and some unpronounceable place in Tonga.

'Sorry it's so soon, man,' said Labuschagne, 'but we need to give ourselves a few days in Tonga to work out how to get on board the ship. It should be easy enough to bribe a member of the crew but we need to have plenty of time.'

'And the bomb?'

'It's gone ahead, weeks ago. In three separate, unconnected pieces, in steel packages lined with lead to fool the security X-rays. They've gone by sea. Much better that way. Security checks are much slacker at sea than they are in the air, and they've gone to Tonga via Indonesia and Papua New Guinea. They never bother much there about checking goods in transit. And as for Tonga, security there is a joke. Don't worry about it.'

'Three pieces? How…'

'Don't worry about it, man. I've been taught by the experts. It's easy when you know how. Even high school physics textbooks nowadays tell you how to do it. I'll put it together when we get on board the ship in Tonga. And the bomb's amazingly small. You only need three kilos of plutonium. It's about the size of a rugby ball, even smaller. It's amazing.'

Van der Merwe tidied up all his outstanding business affairs, settled all his bills and added a codicil to his will, leaving small legacies to Moses Wakonde and the woman Miriam that were big enough to protect them from starvation but not so generous that he could be accused of sentimentality. He said no goodbyes. He did not want to arouse suspicion. He telephoned Zechariah, Rebekha and Reuben for one last conversation with each of them but they all seemed vague or preoccupied and the conversations were stilted. They had nothing left to offer him. His own children. They did not care whether he lived or died and yet he was doing it all for them. He was going to his martyrdom so that they might live with heads held high. He did not telephone either Saul or Ruth. He had vowed many years ago never to speak to either of them again.

He told Leah, Wakonde and the woman Miriam that he was going away for medical treatment for a couple of weeks. Leah stared at him, nodded and turned her eyes back to the television. His own sister. The woman he had taken in and protected all her years of widowhood. Truly the Lord had tested him through the plague of his family.

Wakonde could not look at him, fearing the eyes of a dying man, and the woman Miriam wiped her eyes when he told her, as though she knew she would never see him again. Her tears made him uncomfortable. How could he have aroused such strange affection in a kaffir woman? It was not decent. Hephzibah would not approve.

Van der Merwe spent an hour of his last morning at the farm, before Labuschagne arrived, staring out across his memories, across the bluegums and the fever trees and the huge black granite *kopje* behind the house. Then he took one last long look at the house, where he and Hephzibah had been so happy, and Labuschagne touched his arm and he turned away and shuffled towards the truck and Labuschagne drove them to the airport at Nelspruit to catch the flight to Jo'burg and then to Perth and Sydney. Van der Merwe was dreading the long journey across two oceans and a continent but he had the stronger painkillers now and from Jo'burg onwards

Labuschagne treated them to first class seats all the way to ease
the discomfort. The Volksraad could well afford it now: most of
Kruger's gold lay still unspent in hiding places in the bush,
unable to find a home in any bank, useless except in tiny,
discreet amounts.

Labuschagne flew with a forged passport, calling himself
Swart. Van der Merwe grimaced. Nice joke, that. Swart: 'black'
in Afrikaans. He himself flew on his own passport. Why not?
He was not coming back. And when it was all over he wanted
the whole world to know who he had been. He had no need
of anonymity.

'The Oud Baas sends his blessing,' said Labuschagne.

'You've seen him? In prison?'

Labuschagne grunted. 'I'm not that stupid. No, he sent a
coded message. Through Fanie.'

'How are they? Bezuidenhout? Pienaar?'

'Bearing up. What would you expect? They're soldiers.'

'And the message?'

' "Tell the old lion he will wear his wounds like medals," he
said.'

'The Oud Baas called me the old lion?'

'*Ja*, so.'

Van der Merwe twitched his shoulders. So now he was
rehabilitated. Once the Oud Baas had tried to leave him out
but now they all needed him. Now van der Merwe carried all
their hopes alone.

'Wounds like medals,' said van der Merwe.

Labuschagne nodded. 'They will hang him but he will
never flinch. He will sing "*Die Stem*" as they take him to the
gallows. When they put the rope around his neck he will look
them in the eyes.'

Van der Merwe looked up. 'We never flinch,' he said. 'Not
our generation. We fight to the death.'

'The kaffirs will hang them all in the end,' said Labuschagne.
'Now that Mandela has gone the days of reconciliation are
over. And then there will be war.'

★★★

When they left Jo'burg at last, soaring into the black skies above the goldfields to begin the long journey towards the date line and the new millennium, van der Merwe took with him several copies of Leah's sinful magazine *Celebrity* to read in the air. He leafed through them with disgust. They were filth. Abomination. They represented everything he hated. They showed white women with black men and they revelled in all sorts of foulness, blasphemy, softness, self-indulgence, materialism, sin. They turned mere humans into icons and worshipped false idols. One of their idols was even called Madonna. What blasphemy! But he forced himself to read them as the aircraft thundered out across the Indian Ocean, the pain in his gut throbbing in time with the giant engines, for the first rule of any battle is to know and hate your enemy.

The telephone trilled on Nat Wakonde's desk. He tapped the rest of the sentence onto the keyboard and snatched at the receiver.

'Yes?'

There was a brief hesitation and in that moment he knew even before she spoke that it was her.

'I am here,' she said.

The sound of her voice trembled in his stomach.

'Helga?'

'Yes.'

'Helga! Where are you?'

'Here. In Monaco.' Her voice was as beautiful as he remembered. 'I am just arriving, *ja*.'

'Have you got somewhere to stay?'

'Not yet.'

'And you're coming to the ball? On New Year's Eve?'

'If you are wanting me.'

If you are wanting me. Is the Pope Catholic?

'Where are you?'

'The Hermitage.'

Of course. She would be. Poor little rich girl.

'That's just across the port from us,' he said. 'Not far. Do you know the Café de Paris just around the corner from you? Next to the casino?'

'I am finding it, sure.'

'I'll see you there in fifteen minutes. We'll have lunch. Leave your luggage at the Hermitage.'

'The Café de Paris.'

'Yes. Fifteen minutes.' He hesitated. 'Helga?'

'*Ja*?'

'It's wonderful to…well, you know.'

'In fifteen minutes,' she said. 'And you are better not being late.'

He could not take his eyes off her. She was dressed not in her usual hippy clothes but in a simple summer frock and sandals that made her look so young he thought he might be arrested. They sat near a window among mahogany and brass and he caressed her with his eyes. He gazed at her as she sat opposite him on a banquette. She had grown her hair and it trailed long and soft across her shoulders. Her eyes were luminous. Her little nose was perfect, glinting with the small silver stud. Her mouth was luscious.

She blushed. 'You must not be staring,' she said.

'You are the loveliest woman I have ever seen,' he said. 'Will you marry me?'

'Stop stupiding,' she said, 'and feed me. I am starving.'

He let her order. He did not notice what they ate. The food was excellent but to him it was tasteless. He had no appetite. His stomach was tense with anticipation. He bought a bottle of white wine but had no need of alcohol. He already felt euphoric without it. His heart felt like a feather and his head seemed to float. She had come. For him. She was coming to the ball. He would have no trouble at all in persuading The Editor to let her have an invitation. The Editor was desperate for more celebrities and Helga was famous all over the world. The

Editor would be delighted. They would be together at last, for days, perhaps for weeks, maybe for ever. He did not dare to ask about Lancelot. He did not want to risk spoiling the moment.

She ate with gusto, relishing her meal, and he gazed at her with delight. Even the way she ate, the shape and movement of her jawbones, the crumb on her lip, made him shiver.

'Were you finding your Mr Rushdie?' she said. 'In England?'

'Yes.'

'So. And the information you were wanting?'

'Yes. But in the end I never wrote the article.'

She looked up sharply. 'And why?'

Nat stared at her. 'I decided it was none of our damned business what he does in private.'

She nodded with approval. 'And your magazine? *Celebrity*?'

He shrugged. 'I told them I couldn't find him anywhere.'

'That was brave.'

'You taught me that there are some things in my trade that are unacceptable.'

She leaned across the table and touched his hand. 'I am glad,' she said. 'So glad. I am being correct about you, *ja*. You are a man of good.'

He kissed her fingers.

'I am proud of you,' she said.

He wanted to freeze this moment for ever: her happy face across the table, the crisp pink napkins, the glitter of silver and crystal, the gleam of brass and mahogany, the chattering of the other diners, the passers-by glancing at them through the windows, the sunlight outside bright on the rich colours of the flowers in the gardens and glinting on the fountains of the Place du Casino. And the pride in her eyes. The feeling that he belonged to her, that he had been vindicated. You are a man of good. He prayed that she would always think so.

'What are you going to wear for the fancy dress ball?' he said. 'We'd better think of something quickly. We're due to fly out to Sydney in four days' time.'

'I am decide already. I am being an Greek goddess.'

Of course. A goddess. What else?

'Which one? Aphrodite? Diana?'

'Gaia. The Mother of Earth.'

The patron saint of the travellers and the Greens.

He took her hand. 'You don't know how much this means to me,' he said.

'Oh, *ja*, but I do,' she said. 'I am knowing too well.' She nodded. 'But I am coming with you only with one agreement, *ja*. You must be understanding this. I will not sleep with you.'

And then he realised suddenly with a shock that she was no longer pregnant. He stared at her stomach. She must have had the baby already. Prematurely.

'The baby,' he said. 'Where's the baby?'

She started to weep, and as he left his chair and sat beside her on the banquette and put his arms around her he knew that she was the only woman that he would ever truly love.

A waiter approached with a beautiful lace handkerchief, handed it in silence to Nat and turned away. The other customers and waiters ignored them. This was Monaco. In Monaco pretty girls are always crying in the arms of embarrassed young men.

As Nat held her close and she wept silently into his neck he knew that she would never leave him now.

Marlowe's new computer was delivered by an electronics wizard with mad hair and the air of a man who was running a dating agency.

'Ain't she beautiful?' said the wizard.

'He,' said Marlowe.

The wizard scratched his ear. 'Uh, sure. Whatever. He.'

'Bogart.'

The wizard grinned. 'Yeah, they told me back at the ranch. Great! Marlowe, Bogart. Cool.'

The machine was a joy to look at: slim, two-tone grey, elegant, understated, immensely powerful. And immensely expensive. But who cared about that? Marlowe and Bogart were about to win the British lottery and he'd never need to work for money again.

'We've matched your voices,' said the wizard, punching the air with his forefinger, 'and we've programmed in all your personal details and codes, all your software and macros. He'll understand anything you tell him. Here, Bogart: this is Steve.'

'Hi there,' said the computer in Humphrey Bogart's gravelly voice. 'How ya doin', Steve?'

The wizard did a little dance of delight. He chuckled. 'Great, hey? Tell him to do something.'

'Take a fax,' said Marlowe.

'Sure thing,' said Bogart. 'Hit me.'

'Send a fax to Bill Warren. Say "Look, Bill, I'm sorry about the old computer but I've got a great new one that won't fuck up again. Please call me. I'd like to discuss the *Celebrity* ball." End message.'

'Check,' said Bogart.

A header appeared on the screen above the message with Marlowe's name and Warren's Internet address and the screen fizzed briefly as the fax disappeared into cyberspace. Five seconds later Bogart flashed onto the screen an acknowledgement of receipt by Warren's computer in Santa Barbara.

'Is that neat, or what?' said the wizard, grinning and rubbing his hands together.

'Sure is,' said Marlowe.

'Try something else. Download a movie.'

'Right. Bogart: get me *Apocalypse Now*.'

'Sure.'

Five seconds later a message flashed on-screen: *APOC-ALYPSE NOW* FILED/$10 PAID.

'Jeez, that was fast,' said Marlowe. 'Wow! OK, let's see the big helicopter scene. Robert Duvall. The choppers going in to zap the jungle village.'

Bogart's screen blossomed with a sudden sky filled with helicopters clattering above the Vietnamese palm trees, the loudspeakers pounding with Wagner, *The Ride of the Valkyries.*

'Oh boy!' said Marlowe.

He touched Bogart's screen. He stroked the glass. This baby was something else. This baby was the ultimate orgasm.

'You want this on the big movie screen?' asked Bogart.

'No. No. I'll watch it later. Quit.'

The screen went blank, the loudspeakers falling silent.

'Try something else!' chortled the wizard, squeezing his hands together, like a pimp offering his sister.

Marlowe thought.

'I know,' he said. 'Print the seventh from last chapter of Raymond Chandler's last novel.'

Bogart hesitated for a moment, searching the libraries of the Internet, and then flashed up the title *PLAYBACK (1958)*. The printer began to hum and six pages slid out of it in six seconds:

22

IT is like a sudden scream in the night, but there is no sound. Almost always at night, because the dark hours are the hours of danger. But it has happened to me also in broad daylight – that strange, clarified moment when I suddenly know something I have no reason for knowing…'

'Oh boy!' said Marlowe. 'Mega!'

The wizard was almost tap-dancing. 'Give him something really difficult to do,' he chortled. The wizard seemed to be about to come in his pants.

'Ah, hell,' said Marlowe excitedly. 'Uh – I know – list the winners of the ten biggest prizes in the most recent Chinese national lottery.'

Bogart barely hesitated. Another sheet of paper slid from the printer.

'My God!' said Marlowe. 'It's all in Chinese.'

'Of course,' said the wizard.

'He speaks Chinese?'

'Sure does.'

' ほゆグざ,' said Bogart.

'Chinese!'

'And Japanese!' said the wizard. He was bouncing about on the balls of his feet. 'And Russian! And Turkish! And anything you can think of. This is the greatest PC in the world. This is the god of all computers.' He nudged Marlowe with excitement. 'Go on, try the VR.'

'How do I do that?'

'Just tell him. Just tell him to take you wherever you like on VR. Go on, try it. Where d'you wanna try?'

Marlowe thought.

'Paris,' he said. 'Paris, France. The Left Bank. The Quai St Michel.'

'Tell him. Tell Bogey.'

The computer sat on the workstation as enigmatic as Aladdin's genie.

'Go to VR,' said Marlowe. 'The Quai St Michel in Paris.'

'Sure thing,' said Bogart, closing all the curtains in the apartment. For a moment there was complete darkness and then Marlowe became aware that all around him shapes were gradually emerging from the darkness like ghosts after midnight. He could hear the hooting of car horns and the traffic in the Place St Michel and in front of him the slapping of the Seine against the old stone, the artists' paintings clattering in the breeze against the riverside railings and to his right, beyond the Petit Pont, the huge, majestic, looming shape of Notre-Dame.

'Oh wow,' whispered Marlowe. 'Magic. Oh boy. Magic.'

'It's nothing,' growled Bogart.

After the wizard had left Marlowe played for hours with Bogart, calling up scene after scene all over the world: Times Square in New York, a canalside street in Amsterdam where once he had had a German sailor, the foyer of the Hilton in Saigon, Trafalgar Square in London, the pyramids in Egypt.

Some places were still not yet connected to the Internet, so Bogart failed to conjure up Mount Everest or the pampas in Argentina or the Great Wall of China. But wherever the Internet had spread its tentacles Bogart recreated each place in such vivid detail around Marlowe that he could barely believe that these scenes were not real but merely virtual reality, just electronic ghosts. In Egypt he could smell the foul breath of a camel, in Trafalgar Square he could hear the evening cry of a cockney newspaper seller. It was like owning a magic carpet, he thought. Now he would never need to leave his apartment again. Now he was master of the universe. How had he managed so long with only poor old Chandler for company? Bogart was beautiful. Bogart was brilliant.

'Gee, thanks,' grunted Bogart.

And on Saturday night, when they made the next draw in the British lottery, Marlowe and Bogart were going to win millions of dollars when the numbers 37, 38, 39, 40, 42 and 44 came up and no one else had a winning ticket.

'Where are we gonna retire?' asked Marlowe.

'How about Casablanca?' said Bogart.

Eventually Bill Warren came on the line after weeks of sulking because of Chandler's mistake about the Limey astrologer.

<So you're not coming to the Celebrity Ball?> said Warren.

<nix>

<Shame. Could be fun>

<i don travl good>

He wasn't going anywhere ever again. What was the point? What was there outside that you couldn't have here?

<I'm going in fancy dress as an old-time highwayman> said Warren <with a black mask like the Lone Ranger>

<cool>

<I'm leaving on Tuesday>

<have a grate time>

<I'll let you know how it goes. When I get back. :-) If we're all still here by then!>

Not a bad guy, Warren, after all. If we're all still here by then! The comet. A joker right up to the end.

Marlowe knew that not everyone was still joking about the comet. The government and the Pentagon were playing down the dangers but some scientists and newsmen were becoming increasingly shrill in their warnings. The thing was still millions of miles away in space but rocketing towards the Earth on a route that was alarming even the experts.

'Get me the latest reports on the comet,' said Marlowe.

'Check,' said Bogart.

The screen sat blank for three seconds and then was splashed with a vast scrolling menu of international items about the comet.

'Most comets that come dangerously close and enter our atmosphere are small enough to burn up quite safely before they hit the planet,' said one of the items, 'like the football-sized one that roared bright blue over Western Australia in May 1995 as it crashed through the sound barrier, reaching an estimated speed of 670,000 mph at a height of about twelve miles and shaking buildings before it disintegrated. Others could do a great deal of damage if they came too close. Halley's Comet, for instance, is only fourteen kilometres wide – nine miles – but it could still cause huge devastation if it hit the earth. Even an asteroid no more than one mile wide would create a ten-million-megaton explosion and would kill a quarter of the human race. If it landed in the Pacific it would cause a vast wave, three miles high, that would sweep around the globe and destroy every city on the edge of the ocean from Los Angeles to Sydney to Tokyo.'

A wave three miles high! thought Marlowe. Even Robert Duvall would have trouble surfing that one!

He shivered. It wasn't funny. It wasn't at all funny any more. He scrolled anxiously through the menu, finding another item.

'Some heavenly bodies do survive long enough to plunge into the Earth, leaving big craters,' it said, 'like the one sixty metres wide that exploded over Siberia in 1908 and devastated the forests of Tunguska, or the one that hit the Earth in the fifth century and plunged Western civilisation back into the Dark Ages, or the one that wiped out Mycenean civilisation with "rocks from the sky" in about 1100 BC, or the one that caused Noah's Flood in about 9600 BC. Indeed, astrophysicists and fossil experts now believe that crashing comets have destroyed as many as twenty civilisations in the last 600 million years.'

Twenty civilisations, thought Marlowe. Ever since the dawn of history, time and again, numerous civilisations suddenly destroyed by huge intruders from outer space.

He surfed on nervously through item after item: picking out articles, letters, discussion groups, frenzied warnings, official denials. Suddenly he wondered whether everyone had been far too complacent for too long. He felt frightened and threatened for the first time since they had put Mickey Schweitzer in jail. Mickey Schweitzer was safely out of the way but now this thing was coming straight at the Earth and the world just seemed to be sitting waiting for it, holding its breath, waiting for the three-mile-high wave.

Marlowe scrolled on through the menu of hundreds of items and clicked at random onto an article from a British magazine. He stared at it with mounting apprehension.

'Mathematicians have calculated that each of us runs a 10,000-1 chance that the Earth will be hit by some awesome heavenly body during our lifetime,' said the article, 'and the distinguished Australian astronomer Dr Duncan Steel has estimated that each of us is twice as likely to be killed by a heavenly body as we are to die in an airplane crash.'

Twice as likely as an air crash! And there are air crashes every day. Marlowe gazed at the article on the screen. He bit his knuckles.

'Some day a comet or asteroid may suddenly come out of the sky to extinguish all life and maybe even obliterate the Earth itself,' said the article. 'Not this week. Not tomorrow. But one day. Maybe soon. As Dr Steel says in his book *Rogue*

Asteroids and Doomsday Comets: "It is not a matter of *if* an asteroid or comet will hit the Earth with cataclysmic consequences, it is merely a matter of *when*".'

'I'm scared,' said Marlowe aloud. 'They're not gonna be able to stop it.'

'Don't worry, baby,' said Bogart. 'I'll take good care of you.'

The young woman left the hospital in Venice at last on 27 December, limping on crutches to the ambulance.

'A miracle,' said the doctor. 'I never thought she would survive.'

On the same day, in Corsica, in Sartène, the armed police brought in from Ajaccio surrounded Ugo Legrandu's house and called through loud-hailers for him to come out.

His wife emerged alone, her hands held wide, her black dress clouded white with grains of flour.

'Where is he?' shouted the police chief. 'Where is the bastard?'

'He has gone to Saigon,' she said.

On the Tongan island of Vava'u in December it began to rain almost every day. Afu Faletau stared out mournfully at the deluge. My gracious! Soon it would be the hurricane season again. The hatches were battened down on the few yachts still moored in the Port of Refuge and the rain pelted down for weeks on the coral reef, the grey lagoon, the drooping palm trees, the canoes pulled up on the tired beaches. The rain lashed down on the hot tin roofs of Neiafu and the Paradise International Hotel and the Stowaway Village and the Tufumolou Guest House and silenced the squawking of the parrots in the thick jungles on the slopes of Mount Talau and the squeaking of the fruit bats and the *kark-kark-kark* of the herons. It rained for most of Advent and all through Christmas Eve and Christmas Day and Boxing Day. It rained fit to satisfy old Noah. The Wesleyan church in Neiafu was full of puddles on Christmas Day and the rain thundered like drumsticks on the tin roof as they sang 'Silent Night' and 'We Three Kings of Orient Are' although Afu could see only one King of Orient Are in church and he was sitting up at the front as usual, though of course he was so huge that he was at least the size of Three Kings even if he was in fact only One King.

On the Monday, Tuesday and Wednesday after Christmas, Afu squatted on the back step and stared hopelessly out at the back yard and chatted mournfully to Grandpapa Salesi, who must have been terribly damp underneath all those puddles. They had all given her some lovely Christmas presents but Afu was still unhappy. She missed New Zealand Jim. And she was bored. Afu had never been so bored in all her life.

The big white ship *Celebrity* sailed, tall and elegant, into the Port of Refuge on Wednesday 29 December, and anchored out in the bay along with several other cruise liners that had suddenly arrived at Vava'u. Airy planes kept flying in from Nuku'alofa, Fiji and Samoa and the bay was busier than Afu had ever seen it. When the rain stopped for a couple of hours she wandered down to the harbour and sat on a wall and watched all the activity, the little boats coming and going to and from the liners, passengers going on board in between the squalls of rain, barges carrying supplies, the tug bustling about importantly. There seemed to be some special excitement in the air, as though something important was about to happen. Why were there so many airy planes in the sky and so many big ships in the harbour? Some of the ships were like floating mountains. They were painted all sorts of colours – white, pink, yellow, purple – and they flew all sorts of coloured flags. Where had they all come from? Where were they all going?

'It's nearly New Year's Eve, Afu, that's why,' her father had told her.

New Year's Eve? 'She like Adamaneve?'

Her father's eyes glistened. 'It's on Friday night,' he said.

Sometimes she worried about her father. Sometimes he said things that made no sense at all.

She sat on the wall beside the harbour and smiled at passers-by and watched all the busy activity and swung her long, slender legs, tinkling the silver ankle chain she wore. Her long black hair hung straight and gleaming down her back, crowned by a scarlet hibiscus flower. Her skin was the colour of pale fudge. A red-faced white woman in one of the little boats tripped and fell down. Afu laughed, wrinkling her pert little nose. Her eyes glistened. Her teeth gleamed white. Her lips were wide and soft.

'You Tongan?' said the sailor.

She looked up. He was young, good-looking, fit. From one of the northern islands, perhaps Fiji, or maybe a Filipino.

She nodded.

'You're beautiful,' he said.

She nodded.

He sat beside her on the wall. 'I'm Miguel,' he said. 'What's your name?'

'Me callim Afu.'

He chuckled. 'You talk kinda cute,' he said. He pointed out towards the elegant white liner. 'I'm on that ship out there. The *Celebrity*. The best ship ever built. Brand new.'

She stared at it. It did look beautiful. So big and white and beautiful.

'*Ceberty*,' she said.

'*Celebrity*.'

'*Celebry*.'

He patted her arm. His fingers were hot. 'Have you ever been on a big liner, Afu?' he said.

She shook her head.

'Would you like to come on board and see it?'

She looked at him. He was very handsome. She liked his neat white uniform, with the gold badge and the smart white cap. She liked his smile. It made his eyes crinkle. His eyes were very bright and very black.

'I'll show you around if you like before we sail tomorrow.'

They had told her never to go off with a man again. Not

after New Zealand Jim. They had told her that some men were horrible and would do her harm. 'Men only want one thing,' her mother had told her.

'Jus onefella thing?' Afu had asked with surprise. 'For me they are wanting touch three thing, four thing.'

Her mother had smacked her then. Sometimes she thought her mother was mad.

'On Friday night there's going to be a huge New Year's Eve party on board the *Celebrity*,' said Miguel, 'with famous people from all over the world. They say Michael Jackson's coming. Liz Taylor. The American President. Even the Pope.'

She looked at him again. He grinned. His eyes twinkled. He was not much older than she was. He looked strong and firm. His teeth were white. How could he harm her? He was nice.

'Where you go sail?' she said.

'First the international date line, then Western Samoa. Then America.'

'You go belong America?'

'Sure.'

She gasped. 'You go belong Hollywood?'

He laughed. 'Sure, why not?'

She hesitated and then jumped down off the wall.

'I come then,' she said. 'I go first place belong me then by an by I come boat belong you.' She laughed. Who cared what her mother and father thought? She was not a pikinini any more. She was twenty. She could do what she liked. She could go off with anyone she liked. She was twenty now. She skipped up and down with excitement. Her eyes glittered. 'You know Hhugh Grrant?' she said.

'Who?'

'No who. Hhhhugh!'

'Oh, him. Yeah. Sure. Hugh Grant.'

'You know? Him bigfella Hhugh Grrant?'

'No sweat.'

'My gracious!' She did a little dance. 'Hhugh Grrant Hhugh Grrant!' she sang.

Miguel smiled. 'Yeah. He's coming on board tomorrow as well. For the big party. He's on the passenger list.'

She stared at him and sat down again suddenly as though her knees had given way.

'Oh my gracious!' she said. 'Oh my goodness gracious me plenty too much!'

A huge black cloud settled on Mount Talau. Thunder rolled down the hillside and it began to rain again. She ran for home.

'Tomorrow!' called Miguel. 'Tomorrow morning! Here. At ten o'clock.'

'Hhugh Grrant,' she panted as she ran for home. Hhhhugh Grrrant! HHUGH GRRANT!

Six million miles away the comet hurtled on through space towards the fragile little planet hanging lonely in the blackest emptiness with its little silver moon. Its destination was blue and green with life and draped with thin white wisps of cloud like a virgin on her wedding night. The comet came on now at more than a hundred thousand miles an hour, skimming the solar system at two-and-a-half-million miles a day, surfing the galaxy at seventeen million miles a week. It sang in silence through the void, dancing with joy past tiny unknown asteroids and massive empty spaces, exuberant with destiny, trailing two thousand miles behind it a brilliant multi-coloured tail like a peacock falling in the solar wind. The small blue-green planet tugged it ever closer, flirting with it, hugging it in towards itself like an unborn life demanding to be fertilised. This time they would surely meet. This time, after all those long millennia, after all those endless icy journeyings through space, after all those times that they had failed to meet their destiny. It had taken so long, so many million years, from when the planet was still boiling and when the monsters had walked its surface and when they built the pyramids and Stonehenge. It had nearly happened over and over again, closer and closer every thousand years, and when the Child was born at the inn two thousand years ago and the three great kings had come by camel from out of the East.

This time.

This time for sure.

In Washington and Moscow, in Paris and Beijing, in London and in Brussels, they watched it come, watching it all the way as it danced in with jubilation towards them like a frozen promise, like a bullet from a billion years ago.

'Shit!' said the President. 'We're gonna hafta nuke the bastard!'

PART
THREE

CHAPTER 13

The *Celebrity* sailed out of the Port of Refuge and north from Vava'u towards Samoa and the international date line. Six thousand fathoms deep beneath its keel there brooded the massive underwater hollows of the Tonga Trench, a 35,000 foot liquid valley vast enough to swallow Mount Everest, a blind and secret midnight place where undiscovered prehistoric monsters have survived a million years of changes and catastrophes.

As the sun went down across the South Pacific on the final evening of the Twentieth Century the *Celebrity* flirted with the new millennium, lurking a mile west of the date line at latitude 16°S, longitude 172°31′W. The sky towards Fiji melted into the ocean, gold and pink and scarlet, touching a distant wisp of cloud vermilion. Tomorrow should be a glorious day, thought Murdoch as he leaned over the port rail on the boat deck. Red sky at night, Ned Kelly's delight. Tomorrow? Glorious? Who said there was going to be any tomorrow at all?

He gazed towards the darkness creeping in from the east

across the massive ocean stretching, uninterrupted by land, for seven thousand miles to South America and the coast of Peru. The sky was still too bright to glimpse the comet yet. In an hour or so it would become quite clear in the velvet night, a small, bright sparkle sharpening by the hour as it came towards the Earth at 106,000 miles an hour.

An eerie silence haunted the *Celebrity* as two thousand passengers and over eight hundred crew tried to forget the comet or huddled nervously in their cabins watching the non-stop TV news bulletins and speculation beamed from around the globe. Some were telephoning friends or relatives around the world.

The rumours were feverish. The USA and Russia were both said to be co-ordinating plans to blow the comet up with nuclear explosions when it finally came close enough to target it properly, perhaps an hour or so before the expected impact at about one in the morning. Or they were going to blast a rocket off from Cape Kennedy to nudge the intruder onto a different course. And the Pope, they said, was praying in the Vatican. Big deal, thought Murdoch. The old aboriginal legends told of the Devil Rock that once fell from the sky and here was another that was not going to be stopped by some old guy in a dress muttering mumbo-jumbo in Rome. Beyond the row of lifeboats suspended above the rail on the boat deck he could see a couple of dozen other ships strung out on either side of the *Celebrity* along the international date line, all waiting for the new millennium. According to the TV bulletins there were hundreds of vessels loitering all along the two-thousand-mile eastward bulge of the date line between Samoa and New Zealand, where the first light of the year 2000 was waiting to be born across the Pitt and Chatham islands. Chatham and Pitt, thought Murdoch: both Englishmen, the father and the son, both prime ministers when the world was still the playground of the Anglo-Saxons. Where are the Brits now, he thought, when we really need them?

On board all these ships there must be half-a-million people, he thought, and he and The Editor had been arrogant enough to think that they alone were smart enough to be the first to welcome the new millennium by meeting it on the date line. What skites!

He turned to face the west again, towards the last red sliver of the setting sun, towards the distant coast of Australia, where he had been born far too many years ago. *That's where I should be tonight. In Oz. In Northern Queensland. Near Cairns. The Daintree River. There in the ancient untouched rainforest. Not here. What the hell are we all doing here when the world is about to end?*

But where else should we be at the end of the world, those of us who have no home and no one waiting for us? What could be better than a final song and dance and 'Auld Lang Syne' before the lights go out?

Two decks down, on Nelson Deck, The Editor was lying naked in a vast pink bath awash with bubbles in the bathroom of her suite, sipping a steamy glass of champagne and humming 'All the Nice Girls Love a Sailor'.

She felt wonderful. Marian Black-Boyes was dead. A sudden heart attack. The astrologer who had told her that she could see no future for her at all after 1999. But now it was Marian Black-Boyes who was dead instead. That was why she hadn't been able to see anything after 1999! The Editor sniggered. Some astrologer!

She sipped her champagne and twiddled the taps with her toes. She was not at all nervous about this blasted comet, either. Not now. When it came within range, at one or two o'clock in the morning, the Americans would shoot it down. Of course they would. That's what their nuclear warheads were for. What was there to be nervous about? Even if it did somehow hit the Earth it wasn't going to land in the South Pacific. The scientists estimated that if it did come down it would land thousands of miles away, near Los Angeles. So what was there to be worried about?

The ball was going to be a huge success, she was sure of that.

And afterwards, as the first daylight of the third millennium began to creep across the globe, she was going to take the little Greek skipper to bed and screw him until he whimpered.

She slid her thighs against each other in the soapy water. She shivered. Goose-pimples tiptoed across her small soapy breasts. Stavros Eliades was the most beautiful man she had ever seen and at dawn she was going to have him.

She glanced through the open door of the bathroom into the huge cabin. Her fancy dress costume lay spread out on the double bed. She smiled. Her costume would wow them all. All those famous celebrities would gasp when they saw her.

She was going as someone more famous than any of them, more famous even than Madonna. She was going as the Virgin Mary.

Two decks beneath The Editor's suite, on Drake Deck, in a cabin labelled MR & MRS HUGH GRANT, a TV newscaster was reading the headlines, his voice blaring urgently about the comet. Nguyen Thi Chu listened nervously as she slipped into her black Viet Cong pyjamas. Ugo bellowed with laughter when he saw her wearing them. She would put the fear of God into all the Americans at the ball, he said. *Mon Dieu!* A Viet Cong gook at the millennium ball! The Americans would all faint!

The newscaster was blaring on and on about the comet. Chu was apprehensive. Could it be true? The end of the world? Ugo kept saying it was rubbish. Ugo was convinced that the Americans would blow the thing up. The Americans. Always the Americans. Did the world have no other heroes? Even the decks of this ship were named mostly after Anglo-Saxons: Cook, Nelson, Drake, Magellan.

Ugo was standing in front of the full-length mirror, his stocky legs braced apart, admiring himself in his Napoleon Bonaparte costume: the bicorn hat, the high-collared, red and gold coat, the white gold-braided breeches, the gold-handled sword and the gold-tasselled leather boots. He preened himself, turning this way and that in the mirror. *La Barrett will never be able to resist me in this. Tonight at last I shall astonish her with my virility.*

He looks ridiculous, thought Chu: short, fat and pompous. He strutted, like Napoleon himself. One day, when she really wanted to hurt him, she would tell him the truth: that even though Napoleon was Corsican himself he came to despise the Corsicans so much that when he was Emperor of France and they tried to fight for their independence he burned Corsican houses and executed at least one Corsican a day. Ugo would go berserk if he ever found out.

Chu slipped past him in her black pyjamas in search of her knife. He smacked her buttock as she passed. '*Très* sexy, *chérie!*'

She slapped his hand away.

He grabbed her again.

She pushed him away.

Would he never leave her alone? He never stopped pestering her. He was always patting her, squeezing, fingering her, as though she were a vegetable on a market stall. And he chased other women. She knew it. Sometimes when he returned from the bar in Saigon in the early hours he smelled of scents that were not hers. Deep in her heart she had stopped trusting him. How had he managed to have them invited to this extraordinary ball? And why was the name Hugh Grant on their invitation card? When they had come on board the Filipino master-at-arms had challenged them at the top of the gangway.

'Hugh Grant?' he had said.

Ugo had shown his passport. 'Ugo Legrandu,' he had said. '*Voilà!* Hugh Grant. It is the same. In French.'

Most disturbing of all, there was also about Ugo a hidden violence that alarmed her. Sometimes when he was having her she felt that he was stabbing her to death.

He reached for his Venetian carnival mask and fitted it onto his face. Beneath the Napoleonic bicorn hat the sinister, beaky nose pointed silver at her like a threat. His eyes glittered through the holes. He leered.

She shuddered. 'Do you have to wear that horrible thing?'

'*Weh!* It is tradition. All the best New Year parties are masquerades until midnight.'

Soon she would leave him. Soon. She must. How could she have given herself to a man like this after Tran Xuan Kai?

'And now the rest of the news,' said the TV newscaster. 'Vietnam.'

Chu glanced at the screen. A map of the South China Sea. A fat red circle around the Spratly Islands.

'In Hanoi the Vietnamese government has accused the United States of deliberately encouraging confrontations between Vietnam and the Philippines in south-east Asia's long-running dispute of sovereignty over the Spratly Islands, which are also claimed by China. Hanoi alleges that the USA is cynically manipulating the Spratly dispute so as to sabotage south-east Asian plans for increasing co-operation between the nations of the Pacific. The Vietnamese also claim that American agents disguised as Filipino fishermen have built provocative structures on some of the Spratly islands and were responsible for a skirmish with the Vietnamese navy earlier this year in which a young Vietnamese sailor was killed.'

'Quang Linh!' said Chu.

Her knees buckled.

She sat down suddenly on the edge of the bed.

'Quang Linh,' she said.

'*Quoi?*'

'*Mon fils,*' she said.

She started to weep.

'My son.'

Two decks further down, on Magellan Deck, where The Editor had eventually agreed irritably to allow most of the *Celebrity* magazine staff to huddle into cramped inner cabins with neither windows nor portholes, Helga Gröning and Nat Wakonde were putting on their fancy dress costumes in his cabin. She was still refusing to sleep with him, even after a week together.

'What does it matter,' said Nat, 'if the world is about to end?'

Men! Why could they never understand? She had slept too easily too often with men she had not loved. This time she wanted it to be different.

The silver stud glittered like starlight in her nostril. Nat wanted to kiss it. Her lips were like velvet. He had never seen eyes so blue. He wanted to make them flicker.

'I love you,' he said.

'*Ja*. I am seeing this. I think this is so, *ja*, but I am needing time.'

But time was so short. What if the Americans failed to deal with the comet? What a waste it would be to die without ever loving her.

She touched his hand. He looked so sad. 'Poor Nat,' she said. She kissed the side of his mouth gently.

She gazed at him fondly. He was so sweet, so vulnerable. And so black. So very black. Her father would have a fit if he ever discovered that she had given herself to a man so very black. Her Nazi grandfather would be screaming in hell with rage as well as pain.

She touched Nat's cheek and smiled. Her fingers were so very pale against his skin.

She nodded.

'So you are right,' she said. '*Ja*, very good. I will sleep with you tonight, *ja*, after midnight.'

'Ah, yes,' he said. He kissed her fingers. 'Ah, yes.'

'Me and you lying together,' she said, 'for waiting the end of the world.'

It cannot be true, he thought. Not now. Please no – not now.

He watched her as she changed into her fancy dress, reaching for the white gown, the vivid green cloak, the leather leggings, the brown sandals. He glimpsed her body in the mirror. She was perfect, her breasts as smooth and white as the secret cream-of-tartar fruit of the baobab tree.

'Oh, no,' he said. 'Your gown's all torn.'

She caught his eye in the mirror. '*Ja*, this is correct. Gaia is also torn, the Mother Earth, for being raped by the Mankind ever since the starting of Time.'

She looked so small, so earnest. He wanted to hold her.

'I am dressing this way in protests for all these places where men are raping the Earth like Nazis.'

He stood behind her, placed his hands on her shoulders, and kissed the back of her neck. 'I am never going to let you go,' he said.

She stared at his reflection. Her eyes were huge. 'I am thinking this is true, but for us maybe it is now too late.'

He kissed the top of her head. 'Never,' he said.

He smiled at her reflection and turned away and started to put on his own fancy dress costume: the white feathered armlets and leggings, the leopard-skin skirt and stole, the head-dress, the oxhide shield, the short assegai.

She turned and laughed. 'You are looking so fierce!' she said. 'Who do you be?'

He shook the shield at her and did a little war dance. 'Shaka,' he said. 'The King of the Zulus. They called him the Black Napoleon.'

On Magellan Deck, too, Hendrik van der Merwe lay in pain on his single bunk beneath the little porthole just above the waterline. The agony in his stomach was now beyond under-standing. Even when he swallowed the pills there were knives in his guts and the old lion wound on his leg throbbed like a tribal drum. But tonight, at last, all his suffering would be over. And he would take two thousand sinners with him into eternity to deliver at the foot of the Lord. Tonight he would be in Paradise with Hephzibah.

He had no fancy dress. 'Just wear your usual stuff,' Labuschagne had said. 'Your bush jacket, the *velskoene*, your bush hat, and tell them you're President Kruger.'

How right that would be, thought van der Merwe, to leave

this valley of tears in the guise of the greatest Boer hero of them all. Tonight too in Paradise he would meet Kruger himself.

The old knapsack holding the bomb was still propped in the corner. Labuschagne had carried it on board for him. He would never have managed it himself. It was far too heavy. Labuschagne had organised everything. It had been ridiculously easy to get an invitation to the ball. In that pisshole of a *dorp* Nuku'alofa some Irishman called Kelly had approached them in the bar of the hotel and had given them two invitations for free. 'We're like a bit short of guests at the last minute,' he had said. They had brought the bomb on board in three separate pieces and no one had suspected a thing. Nothing suspicious had shown up on the security X-rays when they came aboard. Why should it? One of the crew had brought the most important piece onto the ship in the steel, lead-lined case via the crew's gangway, where they body-searched the crew only when they left the ship but not when they came on board.

Labuschagne had put the bomb together in van der Merwe's cabin in less than an hour and before he had left the ship Labuschagne had gripped van der Merwe's hand with both of his. 'You're a great man, Hendrik. We shall not forget. Your name will be engraved on the monuments of Afrikaaner martyrs.'

And then perhaps the family will all be proud of me at last: Zechariah, Rebekha, Reuben. I have always done it all for the family, for their future, and maybe now they will understand how much I love them.

'The Lord will reward me,' said van der Merwe. 'Praised be the name of the Lord. *Ons vir jou, Suid-Afrika!*'

When Labuschagne had gone and van der Merwe was left alone with the steady hum of the ship's giant engines he lay on his bunk and wept for the first time in forty years.

In the deepest depths of the ship, just above the keel, in the tiny windowless cabin that Miguel shared with Raul, Silvestre and

Luis, three other members of the crew, Afu Faletau hugged herself and laughed aloud.

'My gracious!' she said. 'Thassall.'

Hhugh Grrant was on board! Hhugh Grrant was here, on this bigbigbigfella ship! Miguel had even found out which was Hhugh Grrant's cabin. And tonight she was going to find Hhugh Grrant and then he would take her to Hollywood.

She hugged herself again.

'Come here, you,' said Raul, the horrid one with the bunk near the door. Raul was ugly on the inside and the outside.

He threw back his sheet. He was naked.

'Come on, then, moron,' he said. 'Suck it.'

In Los Angeles it was just after 10 p.m. on the previous day. Marlowe was up early, watching the TV programmes about the comet and using his sleek new computer to patrol the comet bulletin boards on the Internet. What was the point of sleeping now? If they failed to shoot the comet down he wanted to be there, watching it, standing at his window facing west and watching the giant tidal wave surging in across the Channel Islands and drowning Hollywood and Huntington Park and Long Beach and the whole coast from Santa Barbara down to San Diego. If they failed to shoot the comet down nothing at all would matter any more, not even the lottery disaster.

Marlowe was still bitter about the lottery. Afterwards he had raged at the client.

<U TOLD ME THE NOS WERE PICKT BY COMPUTER> he flamed.

<i thort they were>

<U ASSOLE THEY USE NUMBERD BALLS INSTED>

<i no but i thort the computer picked them>

<ASSOLE THE FUCKIN THINGS R PICKT BY GRAVITY>

The jackpot had been won instead by some old man in Scotland who collected nearly $20 million. $20 million!

Marlowe was still sore about it. But what the hell? Nothing at all would matter any more, not even $20 million, if they failed to shoot the comet down.

He heaved himself out of his seat, sweating like Niagara, and waddled from room to room, wheezing, switching on all the four TV sets in his apartment. Then he fixed himself a small snack: a Jumboburger with fries and ketchup followed by a peanut butter and banana sandwich, a king-size pizza, a tub of chocolate chip ice cream and a quart of raspberry milkshake. With a heavy sigh he then settled himself down at the work-station in front of Bogart.

'Hi there,' said Bogart, sensing his presence with the electronic eye. 'How ya doin'?'

It still felt strange to work without a keyboard and to do everything just by voice. It was just like when he gave up smoking: what do you do with your hands?

'Let's go to VR,' wheezed Marlowe. 'The *Celebrity* ball.'

'OK, baby,' said Bogart, and the lights died, the shutters came down across the windows and one entire wall blossomed with colour as it showed two dozen screens and two dozen different scenes on board the *Celebrity* six thousand miles away in the South Pacific.

'Screen three,' said Marlowe, 'the boat deck. And let's go to full VR.'

'Sure thing, kid,' growled Bogart.

Marlowe was surrounded by the shadowy VR images of lifeboats hanging above the *Celebrity*'s boat deck. A dark figure was leaning over the rail in front of him and beyond his silhouette the sky was fading fast. Out on the ocean a line of vessels rode the Pacific swell, their lights twinkling. A gentle breeze ruffled Marlowe's hair.

Magic, he thought. Sheer magic. He could even smell the sea.

Bogart was brilliant. Bogart was going to be his last and greatest love.

'Play it, Bogey,' said Marlowe. 'Play it.'

★★★

And as the final sunset crept across the globe, the final shadow leaking west like ink across the oceans and the continents, the comet came dancing in from between the stars like a bride, its head framed in a joyous halo of light, its elegant train streaming three thousand miles behind it in the darkness of the universe. As it hurtled through space towards its destiny a quarter of the sky before it was filled with the graceful curves and colours of the beautiful blue-green planet it had passed so many times before, the fragile living planet that meandered lazily across the darkness, its glistening colours gleaming with life, its white cap glowing against the blackness. Above it the planet's little moon hung like a silver Christmas bauble.

The comet hurtled on, 109,241 miles an hour, a half-a-million miles to go until the first midnight of the last night of the old millennium.

Yes. This time. At last.

This time.

At 7.30 p.m. the guests aboard the *Celebrity* began to gather in the vast, lavishly decorated Nureyev Ballroom on Cook Deck, where the orchestra was playing tunes from *South Pacific* as the ship rode gently on the swell. As the guests arrived in their fancy dress they were filmed by remote-control cameras and greeted by a red-coated toastmaster who bellowed their names red-faced across the room. Beside him stood The Editor, Captain Eliades and the tiny Filipino chairman of the shipping line, who was dressed in sumptuous silks as a Chinese emperor, and beyond them sixty stewards disguised as Roman slaves moved through the throng with silver trays, sparkling flutes of pink champagne and canapés of prawns, asparagus, smoked salmon, caviar. In Los Angeles the distant ghost of Marlowe moved among them too in Virtual Reality, invisible and silent, slavering at the tempting trays of snacks.

Outside the entrance to the ballroom, beyond the coloured central lobby fountains, Murdoch and Caroline Ponsonby were standing by to see that everything went smoothly.

'I like your frock, mate,' said Murdoch, who was wearing a natty white suit, two-tone 1940s co-respondent shoes and a white fedora hat perched on the back of his deep black head. 'Let me guess. Elizabeth I?'

'Queen Elizabeth I, thank you very much. But you can call me Bess. And who are you meant to be? A gangster? *The Godfather*?'

'Certainly not! I'm Sammy Davis Junior.'

'Who?'

'Sammy Davis Junior.'

'Never heard of him.'

'What?'

'Never heard of him.'

'Come off it, Caro! Strewth! Sammy Davis Junior. The singer. Hollywood entertainer.'

'Never heard of him.'

'But he was huge! Famous all over the world. The celebrities' celebrity. Black genius, crippled, one eye – just like me.'

'Nope. Never heard of him.'

'Jeez, Caroline! Friend of Frank Sinatra, Dean Martin, that lot.'

'Dean who?'

'Rack off! What's wrong with all you kids these days? You don't know anything.'

Across the lobby, beyond the milling crowd, he spotted The Editor receiving the guests.

'Jesus!' said Murdoch. 'Look at her costume! Look who she's come as!'

The Editor was wearing golden sandals, a long, sumptuous gown of cobalt blue, a nun's white silk head-dress and across her breasts a bodice encrusted with jewels and glittering with thousands of sequins depicting the bloody head of Christ wearing a crown of thorns. Above The Editor's head there floated a golden hologram halo.

'Christ!' said Murdoch.

'No,' said Caroline, 'His Mother. The Virgin Mary. And it's a Verucci, too. The gown. A Verucci Madonna! It must have cost her a fortune.'

'I wouldn't bank on it.'

'The woman must have gone completely bonkers.'

'I reckon *Private Eye* were right,' said Murdoch. 'She must be Molloy's daughter: the daughter of the Holy Ghost. No wonder she got the job.'

Beside The Editor Captain Eliades looked almost drab in his normal crisp white uniform.

'The poor little skipper looks gutted,' said Murdoch. 'Poor little bastard. He looks as embarrassed as a croc with a bandicoot gnawing its goolies.'

'As a what?'

'Ethnic marsupial rat.'

'I reckon she's got the hots for the captain,' said Caroline. 'She won't leave the poor little blighter alone.'

'Well, we know what she's having for breakfast, then. Poked skipper.'

The Editor was greeting the guests with a regal air as they shuffled past in line in their fancy dress costumes: an Elvis, a Churchill, a Marie Antoinette, a witch and a wizard, a hippy, a punk rocker, a couple of fat, half-naked men wearing babies' bonnets and sucking comforters and wearing nappies pinned around their waists.

'There's Pascale and Paddy,' said Caroline.

Kelly was wearing a little green tunic with a pointed green cap and pointed green shoes, Pascale a girly hat and a flurry of pink tulle, frills and flounces.

'They look bloody stupid, too,' said Murdoch. 'OK, Pascale, let me guess. You're Little Bo Peep.'

'No.'

'Little Miss Muffet?'

Pascale giggled. 'You are so stupid.'

'OK, then, mate. Fair do's. Who are you meant to be, then?'

'The Duchess of York,' said Pascale.

They gazed at her frills and flounces, the ludicrous hat.

'Brilliant,' said Murdoch. 'Dead ringer.' He looked at Kelly. 'OK, Paddy, I'll buy it. So who are you, then, sport? Some sort of flaming fairy? A gnome? An elf? Naughty Little Noddy?'

'I'm your lucky leprechaun,' said Kelly. He waved a plastic four-leaf clover. 'I'm one of the Little People, so I am.'

'Right!' said the Duchess of York. 'Now let's all get pissed.'

The guests came swarming past, up the sweeping staircase from their cabins on the lower decks: a clown, a ballerina, a tramp, an athlete, a monk, a nun. Some looked frightened, perhaps nervous of the comet. Others were over-hearty, laughing too loudly. Several were drunk. A Hitler went past and was hissed by a rabbi. A Batman held hands with a bathing beauty. A Roman senator passed by with a veiled concubine. A crusader gripped the elbow of a nervous Arab belly dancer. A highwayman wearing a black mask came past with Cinderella.

In Los Angeles Marlowe stared as the highwayman passed the TV camera. That must be Bill Warren. Of course. He was armed with a pair of ancient flintlock pistols. The highwayman approached the Barrett woman, gave a little bow, and passed on into the ballroom. She showed no sign of recognition. 'I want to destroy her,' Warren had said, 'and then I'm going to kill her.'

'There's Hugh Grant!' said Caroline excitedly.

'Where?'

'There. And Tom Cruise.'

In Los Angeles Marlowe's head swivelled. Tom Cruise. Tonight. Tom Cruise.

'There. The one dressed as an astronaut,' said Caroline.

'Take him,' said Marlowe to Bogart. 'That one. The astronaut. Download his image. I want him.'

'Sure, baby,' said Bogart. 'No problem.'

The computer's remote camera locked on to the astronaut's image, froze it, converted it to hologram and dragged it back down the Internet to download onto hard disk.

A message flashed up on Bogart's main screen: ASTRO-NAUT FILED.

'Is it really Hugh Grant?' enquired the Duchess of York.

'Where?'

'There. The pirate.'

'No.'

'Yes.'

'No, that's the lookalike we hired.'

'But there's Liz Taylor. I think.'

'And Madonna.'

'No!'

'Really?'

'Looks like her.'

'Maybe.'

'And Paul Newman. Isn't it?'

'Brilliant.'

'No.'

'Maybe.'

'Isn't that the Pope?'

'My God, wait 'til he sees The Editor's dressed as his boss's old mum. He'll hit the Sistine Chapel ceiling.'

'Never. That's not the Pope.'

'That's someone just *dressed* as the Pope.'

'The real Pope's praying in the Vatican, so he is.'

'I hope to God he is.'

The TV cameras tracked the guests as they pressed past in their hundreds: an undertaker with a black top hat; a Marilyn Monroe; a Viet Cong peasant wearing black pyjamas; a little Napoleon wearing a sinister carnival mask; a pretty Polynesian girl with a flower in her hair.

The Napoleon nodded at Murdoch and raised his hand. 'Happy New Year,' he said in a thick French accent. '*Weh!*'

'I know that voice,' said Murdoch.

'Charles Aznavour?'

'No.'

'Prince Rainier.'

'No.'

'Prince Albert, then. Chirac. Johnny Halliday.'

'No. No.'

'Search me,' said Caroline.

They came on up the staircase like a living tableau from Madame Tussaud's: a Mickey Mouse, a Superman, a Wizard of Oz, all the famous fantasies of a dying century.

'There are an awful lot of people I don't recognise at all,' said Caroline.

'A couple of hundred like cried off at the last minute,' said Kelly. 'We had to hand out a lot of like last-minute invites in Tonga to fill the empty tables.'

They came on up the staircase, all the pirates and witches and tramps and nuns and clowns.

'The Editor's going to go potty: dozens of them are smoking.'

'Good idea,' said Murdoch. He offered her a cheroot. 'Fancy a drag?'

'You wouldn't dare. Not in front of her.'

'Watch me, darling.' He lit a cheroot and blew a grey smoke ring that hovered across the lobby towards The Editor.

'She'll go spare.'

Murdoch grinned. 'So what? It's the end of the world. Who cares? And anyway, it's part of my fancy dress. Sammy Davis Junior smoked like a crateful of kippers.'

'Wow! Is that the King of Tonga?'

'Cripes! He's huge! What's he come as?'

'Australia.'

'Hey! And isn't that the American President over there? With those heavies?'

'I bloody well hope not!' said Murdoch. 'He's meant to be back in Washington blasting the bollocks out of this bloody comet. Bugger me – isn't that Michael Jackson?'

'Nah. Not white enough.'

They came on and on, up the wide staircase and past the Roman slaves and into the ballroom like lions into the arena to hear their famous names bellowed across the floor: 'Mr Tom Cruise and Mrs Cruise'; 'Miss Julia Roberts'; 'Mr Jack Nicholson'; 'Miss Jodie Foster'; 'Mr and Mrs Elton John.'

'Shit a brick!' said Murdoch suddenly. 'Mrs Elton John? Elton John was divorced years ago. And that isn't him.'

'No!'

'Gatecrashers!'

'That doesn't look much like Tom Cruise, either,' said the Duchess of York.

'Or Jodie Foster.'

'Or Julia Roberts.'

'Or Jack Nicholson. They're all imposters!'

'Gatecrashers!' said Murdoch. 'Shit, Stella's going to hit the fan.'

'Well, I very much hope the fan hits her back,' said Caroline.

A World War I pilot came past with his arm around the waist of a nurse. A bearded artist in a beret was escorting a famous model. A Buddhist monk in saffron robes was chatting to an American cowboy. A Dutch girl with plaits and clogs was clumping up the stairs beside a Dracula.

'There's Meg Ryan! Over there.'

'No!'

'And Hugh Grant again! As a Red Indian chief!'

'No racism, please!' said Murdoch. 'An Amerindian chief.'

'But Hugh Grant's gone in already.'

'That one was a lookalike.'

'It's another Hugh Grant, then!'

'Oh, goody!' said Caroline. 'Maybe we get one each.'

In the queue in the doorway to the ballroom the pretty Polynesian girl with the flower in her hair was elbowing her way past the Viet Cong woman in the black pyjamas and was tugging at the sleeve of the Napoleon with the carnival mask.

'Hhugh Grrant?' she said.

Napoleon stared at her. She was very pretty.

'You bigfella Hhugh Grrant?' she said.

'How did you know?'

'I come you cabin, thassall. I follow.'

TheViet Cong woman gave her a glassy gaze. Her mind was elsewhere. She was thinking of her dead son and the American President who had killed him.

'I want come you for Hollywood,' said Afu.

Napoleon glanced at theViet Cong woman. She seemed to be in a daze.

'Later,' he whispered. 'Ten-thirty o'clock. Top deck. Boat deck.'

'Ten dirty clock,' said Afu, nodding seriously.

Napoleon squeezed her arm and turned away, taking the Viet Cong woman's elbow and leading her forward to meet The Editor.

'And here's Nat,' said Murdoch across the lobby, beyond the fountains, 'and his German sheila. Helga Thing. Jeez, but she's gorgeous, the lucky bastard.'

'I think I'm falling in love again,' said Kelly. 'This is my lucky leprechaun night for sure.'

'Wankers!' said the Duchess of York.

'I am Gaia,' said Helga. 'The Mother Earth.'

'Course you are, sweetheart,' said Murdoch.

'She's been raped, you see,' said Nat.

'That doesn't surprise me at all,' said Murdoch. 'You're a Tree-hugger. No probs.'

'I am the bleeding Earth,' she said. 'I am the Mother of the Age of Aquarius.'

'Whatever turns you on, sweetheart. No worries.'

From the ballroom there came yet another bellow from the toastmaster – 'Mr and Mrs Hugh Grant!' – and the little Napoleon with the mask advanced with the woman in the black pyjamas and kissedThe Editor's hand.Then he whispered in her ear. She started back, disconcerted.

That's not Hugh Grant, thought Murdoch. No way. And that's not his wife, either.

'And you?' said Nat.'Who are you meant to be? Mafia, is it?'

'Certainly not. I'm Sammy Davis Junior.'

'Who?'

'Sammy who?'

'So who was Sammy Davis Senior, then?' said Kelly.

'Go fuck yourself,' said Sammy Davis Junior.

A camera flashed. It was one of the official photographers.

'God, I hate New Year's Eve,' said Potter.

Down in his little cabin on Magellan Deck Hendrik van der Merwe lay breathing heavily on his bunk. His eyes were closed, his face pale. He was sweating. The pain now seemed to have become the whole universe. His body was a galaxy of agonies. His mind was a black hole. The bomb sat ticking silently in the knapsack, waiting for midnight.

And the comet, 400,000 miles away, began to feel the warm embrace of the beautiful blue planet, the tug of gravity that hugged it like a lover. The planet seemed to swell by the minute, its blues, greens and browns defining into recognisable shapes, lights twinkling in the shadows as the twilight moved across the globe. The moon winked silver in the darkness. The comet hurtled on towards it, throwing behind it a glittering spray of sparks, 100,000 miles an hour and now just four small hours away from home.

Not long now.

Not long.

At last.

At 8.30 p.m. The Editor led her guests in to dinner in the huge Escoffier Banqueting Hall where the orchestra began to play a medley of the two thousand most popular tunes of the Twentieth Century. Two hundred heavy tables gleamed in the light of two thousand candlesticks; the light glittered off cut glass, silver cutlery and flickered across the festive decorations of red and green and gold. In the centre of the hall there stood a massive iced cake decorated with the *Celebrity* magazine logo and two thousand burning candles. Scarlet banners stretched above the stage – WELCOME TO THE THIRD

MILLENNIUM: 2000 GREETINGS TO THE YEAR 2000 –
and the ceiling was draped with two thousand rich silk
streamers and two thousand balloons. Beside each place setting
a gift-wrapped present nestled beneath a tiny Christmas tree:
two thousand digital clocks all showing 20.32, all surfing
silently towards midnight. And in front of each place, on a little
silver holder, there stood the menu for a ten-course feast, one
course for every century of the old millennium:

CELEBRITY MILLENNIUM BANQUET
SS Celebrity, International Date Line, South Pacific
Friday 31 December 1999

Oyster Tagliatelle with Beluga Caviare
Stolichnaya Blue Label Vodka
Pâté de Foie Gras en Brioche
Château d'Yquem 1899
Salad of Maine Lobster with Truffle Butter Sauce
Le Montrachet 1985
Fillet of Roast Seabass with a Herb Crust
Corton Charlemagne 1990
Poulet de Bresse with Morels
Château Haut Brion 1989
Champagne Sorbet
Lamb's Kidneys en Papillotte Glazed with Port and
Rosemary
Domaine de la Romanée Conti 1985
Fillet of Venison with Juniper Berries
L'Hermitage 1990
Reblochon with Oatcakes
Château Latour 1982
Tulip of Tropical Fruit with Vanilla Ice Cream
Louis Roederer Crystal 1995

The US President's lookalike led The Editor into the
banqueting hall through an avenue of applauding guests,

photographed all the way by snappers scuttling backwards in front of them. She did not even think of the comet. She felt magnificent. She looked magnificent too in her stunning Verucci creation: the shimmering blue gown, the white silk head-dress, the sequinned bodice glittering with the head of Christ. The golden holographic halo hovered like magic above her head. This was it, at the climax of all her plans, her night of glory. Tonight was the greatest night of her life. Tonight she was as famous as any of them.

She clung to her escort's arm and smiled and smiled on every side. She felt invincible. In the receiving line in the ballroom before dinner even the odd little Napoleon in the carnival mask had found her irresistible. He had kissed her hand and whispered in her ear. 'You were right to invite me tonight, *chérie*,' he had said. 'I have wanted you for many years.'

A French voice. Somehow familiar. Where had she heard that voice before?

There were thick black hairs on the back of his hand.

He had touched her like a lover. 'Later, *mon petit choux. Weh!* Later I will come to you, and we will be alone at last.'

She knew that voice. *Weh!* From Nice? Monte Carlo?

'Until midnight,' he had said and had strutted on into the ballroom with the dozy-looking oriental woman in the strange black pyjamas who looked as if she was on drugs.

The Editor was flattered. A mysterious admirer. Her pulse throbbed. How good it was to be desired again. Love had always seemed to her to be a mirage, ever since David had left her in 1989 and she had let him take the child. Since then she had always managed quite well enough with gigolos.

With the President's double she climbed the short red-carpeted flight of steps up to the top table, followed by the eight most famous guests of all: the princess, the actor, the TV personality, the pop star, the model, the footballer, the chef, the hairdresser – EIGHT LIVING LEGENDS she had called them in *Celebrity* – as the cameras flashed and the orchestra played 'There's No Business Like Show Business'. The Editor turned and surveyed the crowded room. The golden halo hovered above her head. She smiled and smiled and knew that this was the crowning moment of her life.

The archbishop said grace in Latin before they sat to eat and two thousand chairs rumbled like thunder. Ugo Legrandu and Nguyen Thi Chu found themselves at a table close to the dais with a famous actress, a soccer star, a TV presenter, a couturier and their partners. Legrandu was facing away from the top table and removed his mask. The actress, sitting beside him, peered at the name card in front of his place.

'I guess you have the wrong table, honey,' she said, with eyes like lasers. 'It says Hugh Grant on the card.'

'I regret Monsieur Grant is at another table,' said Legrandu. 'There has been a mistaking.'

Her lips drooped with disappointment. 'Gee, but...'

'I am Ugo Legrandu, madame.' He bowed and kissed her hand.

'French?'

'Corsican.'

'Is that in Africa?'

'*Non, non, madame*. Is an island in the Mediterránée.'

'Is that why you're dressed as Lord Nelson?'

'*Non, non, madame*. I am the great Emperor Napoleon.'

She giggled. 'Isn't that what all the lunatics say? I guess I should know you but...'

'I am very famous in Corsica,' he said. 'I am Corsican terrorist.'

Across the table Chu was sitting motionless between the TV presenter, who was dressed as a baseball player, and the footballer, who was rigged out as a Chinese coolie. She recognised neither of them, nor any of the others at her table. Her mind was numb. Voices came to her as though from a great distance, echoing like the inside of a seashell. Why was Ugo kissing that American prostitute's hand? He was always flirting with other women.

Quang Linh, betrayed and murdered by an American President, not by Filipino fishermen at all. Just like my darling Tran Xuan Kai, murdered by Lyndon Johnson.

'You must be Yoko Ono,' said the soccer player.

She looked at him without understanding. She shook her head distractedly.

And then she saw the American President sitting up at the top table, no more than thirty metres away, laughing with a famous comedienne. He was laughing with empty eyes, huge gleaming teeth. Like an animal.

How can the American President be here and laughing, when he betrayed Quang Linh and now Quang Linh is dead?

At the humblest table of all, so far from the dais that The Editor was barely recognisable as she sat beneath her halo on the distant platform, the staff of *Celebrity* magazine sat just inside the door beside the hall's starboard entrance. Murdoch tipped his fedora onto the back of his head and raised his glass. 'Bums up!' he said. 'To absent friends. Bill Warren, Iain Campbell.'

'Yes!'

'Poor old Iain.'

'Poor sod.'

They drank.

'Well, bugger me!' said Murdoch, a big white smile leaking across his big black face. 'We've done it! Against all the odds and despite the old bitch.'

'We've done it!'

'Brilliant.'

'Who's like missing over there?' said Kelly. He nodded at the empty seat between Caroline and Pascale, wobbling his pointy green leprechaun's cap.

Caroline read the name on the place card.

'H. van der Mer-wee,' she said. 'Who's he?'

'One of the last-minute fillers we rounded up in Tonga to make up the numbers,' said Murdoch.

'It's pronounced Merva,' said Nat. 'What a coincidence. I

knew an H. van der Merwe back in South Africa, when I was a kid. Owns a farm where my uncle works in Eastern Transvaal.'

'Where in bejabers name is he, then?' said Kelly.

'Having a Mer-wee in the dunny, I 'spect,' said Murdoch. 'Come on, team. Brace yourselves. Pass the bottle. Time to get stuck into the grog.'

Unnoticed on the floor beyond the table a faded old khaki knapsack sagged against the bulkhead. It was scuffed and stained, the leather straps tired and worn. Like me, thought van der Merwe an hour earlier when he asked his cabin steward to carry it up to his table in the banqueting hall; scuffed and stained, like me. Stencilled in fading black across the front of the knapsack were the letters K R U G E R.

The loudspeakers rumbled around the hall with a roll of drums, a trumpet fanfare and then the stentorian voice of the toastmaster bellowing: 'YOUR MAJESTIES, YOUR ROYAL HIGHNESS, YOUR GRACE, YOUR EXCELLENCIES, MY LORDS, LADIES AND GENTLEMEN: PRAY SILENCE FOR YOUR DISTINGUISHED CELEBRITY HOSTESS, THE EDITOR OF *CELEBRITY* MAGAZINE, MS STELLA BARRETT.'

The Editor rose from her place at the top table on the distant platform to a gathering ripple of applause: a tiny, fragile, deep blue figure shimmering with sequins and crowned with a halo of golden light, so far away, so small, so vulnerable, assaulted by flashlights and TV cameras.

'Christ, here we go,' said Murdoch. 'The major ego-trip.'

The Editor's voice was soft and sweet in the loudspeakers, almost humble.

'Here comes the Sermon on the Mount,' said Murdoch.

'And then we get like the Last Supper,' quipped Kelly.

'Dear friends,' said The Editor.

'Fuck me!' said Murdoch.

'I'm not going to make a speech,' she said. 'I just want to welcome you all to the best New Year's Eve party in all the world tonight, the first New Year's Eve party of the new millennium.'

Applause rippled around the room.

'At midnight, in just over three-and-a-quarter hours, our clever captain here, Captain Eliades, promises me that because of his awfully clever computer we will be sailing exactly on the international date line so that we will be the very first party in all the world to enter the year 2000.'

The applause began to swell across the room.

'Plus: as for this silly little comet,' she said, 'it doesn't frighten me and I'm quite sure it doesn't frighten you, either.' She simpered towards the President's lookalike as he sat grinning on her right. 'My distinguished guest here tells me that the Pentagon has just fired three nuclear missiles that will intercept the comet thousands of miles out in space in about two and a half hours, at eleven seventeen our time.'

The applause now was deafening. She turned and applauded the President's double, who stood and grinned and waved and sat again. At some of the tables men were standing, clapping. Some of the women looked tearful.

The Editor gave her sweetest smile. 'So there's nothing to worry about,' she said. 'Enjoy the banquet and then I suggest that soon after eleven o'clock, before the fancy dress parade, we should all go up on deck to watch the nuclear fireworks. My friend here tells me that it should be quite spectacular. But please, please wear your dark glasses when you watch the explosions. Although they will be thousands of miles away they could still be dangerous to your sight.'

The whole room rose to its feet, cheering, clapping, whistling, shouting, even the *Celebrity* staff table by the door, and The Editor stood demure on the platform, simpering. One table suddenly started singing 'For They Are Jolly Good Fellows' and The Editor pulled the President's lookalike to his feet and they stood with their fingers locked and hands held high above their heads as the whole hall swelled with a chorus of roaring voices. Only Murdoch stayed slumped in his seat.

'Isn't it great?' said Caroline.

'Fantastic. Pass the bottle.'

'We're safe, begob.'

'I wouldn't bank on it,' said Murdoch. 'The Yanks will probably miss the bloody thing, no matter how big it is. They bloody nearly missed two huge world wars.'

In Los Angeles Marlowe bellowed at Bogart to flash up the TV screens. Excited newscasters and commentators on every channel were announcing that the White House had just announced that nuclear missiles had been fired to obliterate the comet at 7.17 a.m. Eastern Standard Time.

'It's true!' wheezed Marlowe. He slumped into his seat, gasping. 'I knew they'd nuke it OK. I knew they'd take it out.'

'Cool, baby,' said Bogart.

And somewhere out in cyberspace the ghost of Chandler smiled.

Aboard the *Celebrity* the band launched into a rousing version of 'Happy Days Are Here Again' and the diners clapped and hammered at the tables and stamped in time to the music. On the top table the Eight Living Legends mobbed The Editor and the President's double and hugged and kissed them. Don't they know he's just a lookalike, thought Murdoch, or do they just not care what's real any more and what's false?

The medieval princess sitting beside Ugo Legrandu grabbed his face in both hands and kissed him wetly on the lips. 'I don't care who you are!' she trilled. 'This is your lucky night.' She put her hand between his legs and squeezed.

Chu stared bewildered across the table. Why was Ugo kissing another woman? And right in front of her? He had no shame any more. And why were they all cheering the American President? The murderer. Why were they hugging him? Her eyes misted. Why should he be allowed to live when Quang Linh was dead?

The soccer player grabbed her arms and hugged her so hard

that she could hardly breathe. 'We're safe!' he bellowed. 'We're goddam safe!'

'God bless the Pentagon!' roared the TV presenter. The banqueting hall was an uproar of cheering, stamping and clapping. 'God bless the U. S. of A!'

Tears filled Chu's eyes. *God damn America! I hate them all! God damn all the Anglo-Saxons!*

'Dear God,' said Murdoch at the distant table by the door. He tipped his fedora hat onto the back of his head. 'They love her. Would you believe it? The bastards love her.'

Eventually the pandemonium diminished and the orchestra launched into a medley of bouncy songs from the First World War – 'We're Going To Hang Out the Washing on the Siegfried Line'; 'It's a Long Way to Tipperary' – and the waitresses, all dressed as Vestal Virgins, began to serve the first of the ten courses, the oyster tagliatelle with Beluga caviare. The banqueting hall resounded with a bellow of noise, as though an express train had just escaped from a tunnel. Strangers raised their glasses to each other and laughed. It was going to be a magnificent night, the most fantastic party ever.

There were tears on Helga Gröning's cheeks. Her eyes brimmed. Nat leaned across and touched her hand. 'What is it, darling?' he said. 'What's the matter? The danger's over.'

Tears dribbled silently down her face and Nat watched each one of them, bewitched. He wanted her so much. He ached for her. Tonight, at last.

'Now they are raping the sky with nuclear bombs,' she whispered, dabbing at her nose with the back of her hand. 'I am Gaia, the Earth, and now they are murdering my lover, the sky. They are killing the Spirit of the Age of Aquarius.'

A camera flash assaulted her stained face.

'Nice tits, darling,' said Potter. 'Lovely knockers.'

Deep in the bowels of the ship, in Miguel's empty little cabin, Afu sat on Miguel's bunk and waited for 10.30 when she could go up to the top deck and meet Hugh Grant and go off to

Hollywood. Miguel and all the others were working but he had lent her his watch and she kept staring at the glowing green of the digital display. It said 20:52. For ages. The more she stared at it, the longer it stayed the same. Then it said 20:53 for ages as well. Miguel had said she should wait until there were four 2s on the green display – 22:22 – and then she should take one of the elevators up to the top deck and wait by the little boats hanging next to the rail. She had never been in an elevator before. He had had to show her how to do it. Now she sat in his cabin with the watch in her hand, staring and staring at it.

Hhugh Grrant! She had found him at last.

Chu sat in her straw hat and black pyjamas between the base-ball player and the Chinese coolie amid the raucous clamour of the banqueting hall and stared at the American President as he sat laughing and joking with the famous comedienne at the top table. She hated him. She wanted to kill him. His smile was as wide and empty as the Arizona desert.

'Amazing likeness, isn't it?' said the baseball player.

'Please?' she said.

He gestured towards the top table. 'That lookalike guy over there. The one that looks just like the President. Amazing, eh? They could be twins.'

She stared at the top table.

'That is not the President?'

The baseball player guffawed. 'Hell, no, ma'am. That's his double. The real President's got enough on his plate in Washington just now.'

'This man is someone else?'

'Sure. His lookalike. The guy's a real celebrity now back in the States. Makes millions impersonating the President. Makes more than the President himself, they say.'

She stared at the top table. Not the President, then. Not the murderer himself. Just a carbon copy.

She would have to take revenge on someone else, then. Some other loud American.

She looked at the baseball player.

She could feel the knife strapped hard against her hip.

'My name is Nguyen Thi Chu,' she said.

He chuckled. 'Well, I guessed you weren't Mrs Hugh Grant, like it says. Nice to make your acquaintance.'

'Did you ever go to Vietnam?' she said.

Down in his little cabin on Magellan Deck van der Merwe injected himself shakily with the most powerful painkiller of them all and lay for an eternity in the darkness, breathing heavily, waiting for the pain to ebb. His muscles shrieked for mercy. His limbs were like concrete. His heart thundered like a Zulu drum before battle. This time he would lose the battle, but in the end the Boers would win the war. *Ons vir jou, Suid-Afrika!*

He lay on his bunk and waited for the pain to recede a little. He had to get up to the ball some time before midnight. Somehow. He had to do it. For the Oud Baas. The Volksraad. For the Name of the Lord. The bomb would explode automatically at midnight but they had to know just why they were doomed. They had to understand the justice of their suffering, just as he understood the justice of his own, and to accept their places 'in the lake which burneth with fire and brimstone'. He would stand on the stage and tell them before they died: it was 'eye for eye, tooth for tooth, hand for hand, foot for foot, burning for burning, wound for wound, stripe for stripe'.

Yea, burning for burning, thanks be to God.

At 10.25 p.m., as the Vestal Virgins were flitting between the tables, serving the ninth course, Legrandu fitted the carnival mask to his face again and slipped away from his table. The medieval princess was drunk. Her head-dress was lopsided, her hair dishevelled, her lipstick smeared. 'Come back quick, honey,' she slurped, 'whoever you are. I wannanother kiss, whoever you are.'

He hated drunken women. He despised her.

From the other side of the table Chu stared at him as he went. Where was he going now? The lavatory? Or to meet another woman? Another woman. She knew him so well. He was going to meet another woman.

He left the hall, anonymous behind the mask, and climbed the sweeping central staircase up three decks to the boat deck. Portraits of the famous watched him all the way: Marilyn Monroe, Mike Tyson, David Copperfield, Neil Armstrong, Glenn Close, Eva Peron. On the boat deck itself he breathed deep and fresh in the balmy night and strode along the line of lifeboats hanging high from the davits in the shadows above the rail. The deck was deserted. It moved slightly beneath his feet, trembling with the throb of the engines. Beyond the rail the silhouettes of a dozen ships were strung out in line across the ocean, their lights twinkling in the swell like phosphorescence. Across the waters there came the sounds of distant laughter, music, singing.

He glanced up at the sky. The sharp nose of the mask sliced the darkness. The comet was now quite visible, its head bigger and brighter than the brightest star. Its tail threw a long silver bow across the sky. He laughed. He felt invincible. They were going to destroy the comet. Of course they were. Mankind and men still ruled the universe. The blood pounded in his veins. A small warm breeze tickled the hairs on the back of his neck.

She was waiting for him in a pool of light beneath the funnel. She couldn't be more than nineteen or twenty, he thought. She was perfect. Her light brown skin was as smooth as fudge, her eyes as dark and sparkly as the heavens. Her hair fell long and black all down her back and was crowned with a scarlet tropical flower. Her face was open. She was smiling. Her legs were endless. She was barefoot. A thin silver chain glittered around her ankle. Eternal woman, he thought. This is Eve, the mother and the mistress of us all.

'Hhugh Grrant?' she said. 'Is you?'

Her eyes shimmered. Her teeth glinted in the moonlight.

Why did she think that he was Hugh Grant? Of course: the name-plate outside his cabin door.

'Yes,' he said.

She threw her arms around him. She hugged him. She kissed the corner of his mouth, just under the mask, leaving a small damp mark of possession. She laughed aloud. 'Hhhugh Grrant, Hhhugh Grrant!' she sang. 'I find!'

Her lips were as soft as peaches. Her breasts were as firm as promises against his chest.

'Me Afu,' she said.

Miafu. It sounds like a waterfall tumbling into the jungle. It sounds like a whisper at dawn among the old grey stones of Filitosa.

She laughed. Her laughter was the sound of temple bells, of planets singing in the universe.

'I look you longlong time, Hhugh Grrant, thassall. Why you gotim silly hat en clothe?'

'It is fancy dress.'

His voice was hoarse. He cleared his throat.

'Napoleon,' he said. 'Bonaparte.'

'Bony part?' She giggled. 'You got bony part?'

She looked at his groin. 'Ooooh yes. I think.'

She touched him with her fingers. 'Oooh, yes. Hhugh Grrant! Very bony part.'

He felt the blood draining from his mind, surging through his body. He felt faint.

'You now take off face belong you?'

The mask gazed at her.

'I want see.'

'*Non.* Not yet.'

His tongue was thick. It seemed to fill his mouth. He tried to swallow. His heart was pounding at his throat.

'I want see you Hhugh Grrant face,' she said.

Her eyes were as bright as diamonds.

He wanted to bite her mouth.

Her teeth glistened.

'Hhugh Grrant?' she said. 'We go Hollywood now?'

He gestured at the lifeboat hanging from the davits above the deck. His voice was heavy.

'In there,' he said.

She looked at the lifeboat and giggled. 'Too much small boat for Hollywood,' she said. 'Thassall.'

'In there!' he said roughly.

She put her right foot on the first rung of the small ladder up the side of the lifeboat. Her leg was long and smooth. The ankle chain glittered. She climbed the ladder, her hips swaying. She pulled back the cover and climbed into the lifeboat.

He followed her. His mind was a black hole.

As he reached the top of the ladder her head popped up from under the lifeboat cover.

'Peep-bo!' she whispered.

She started giggling again.

'Boo!' she said.

He fell into the lifeboat after her, grazing his knee, and tugged the mask away from his face. Throwing it down in the lifeboat, he unbuttoned his breeches and pulled her towards him viciously, sliding his hands up her legs, squeezing her thighs, filling his fingers with her, nuzzling her breasts.

In the darkness he could see only the whites of her eyes and the flash of her teeth. She was laughing.

He tore at her skirt. She was laughing still.

She was laughing at him.

He would teach her to laugh at him. He gripped her roughly, forcing himself onto her, pressing his mouth against hers, biting her lips, tasting blood.

'Ahhh, Hhhugh Grrant!' she said. 'Hhhugh Grrant!'

He fumbled between her legs, spreading them, pushing her hard against the bottom of the lifeboat. In his memory he saw the pale teenage English girl in Sagone, whimpering, begging for mercy.

But this one was not afraid.

He bit her neck viciously.

'Ah yes!' she said. 'Yes!'

He drew back.

They were always afraid of him.

Always.

But not this one.

'More more,' she said, pulling him back on top of her. 'Hhhugh Grrant Hhhugh Grrant Hhhugh Grrant.'

He felt himself soften.

'No no!' she said.

She touched him.

'Hhhugh Grrant,' she said.

She touched him again. She stroked him.

'Hhhugh Grrant!' she said.

He felt himself weaken.

She sighed.

He felt himself diminish.

She sighed again.

'Poor Hhhugh Grrant,' she said.

He lay beside her in the darkness on the bottom of the lifeboat. His face burned with shame.

She put her arms about him.

'No mind,' she said. 'Plenty time, Hhugh Grrant. Next time.'

She kissed him as a mother might kiss her child.

He pushed her away.

'Get out!' he said savagely.

'Hhhugh?'

'Go, go! *Pouffiasse!* Get out!'

'Hhhugh?'

'*Va-t-en, garce! Ta gueule!*'

She stroked his hair.

'We go now bigplace Hollywood?' she said.

He rolled over and hit her in the face.

'*Connasse!*' he hissed. '*Radasse!*'

She reeled back into the bottom of the lifeboat.

'Hhugh?' she wailed. 'Hhugh?'

'*Idiote!*' he said. '*Imbécile! Crétine nègre!*'

He swore at her in Corsican, a cascade of foulness dragged

from deep within the ancient frustrations of his race. This moronic whore who had laughed at him, who tempted him, belittled him and threatened his manhood.

He would kill her. Now. Like the whore in Venice. Who would ever know? They had never known then. They would never find her here. Not for days. Kill her now. No woman belittles the manhood of a Corsican.

The blood flamed behind his eyes. Kill the bitch. Kill the sneering black whore.

The blood pounded in his ears and in that pounding he heard the muffled thud of the drum of death and the marching tramp of dead feet, the *squadra d'arozza* come to claim their own — *meurtrier, meurtrier*, the high-pitched, wheedling voices calling *Ugo, Ugo* down from the mountains behind Sartène. *Ugo, Ugo, we have come for you at last.*

He started back in terror, the pounding in his ears, backing away from her in the huddled darkness of the lifeboat, scrabbling at his breeches, fumbling with the fastenings. The creaking of the lifeboat, the clack of the breeze against the cover, sounded like an omen, like the bird of evil, the *maleceddu*, tapping against his tomb.

He crossed himself.

There were horrors in the darkness. Evil stirring. He could suddenly smell the stench of the woman in Venice as her soul crawled away through the filth.

She was here. She had come to claim him at last.

Perdonnu mio Dio, mio Dio perdonnu, Perdonnu mio Dio, Perdonnu pietà.

He crossed himself again.

Perdonnu mio Dio…

In terror he raised the lifeboat cover and she saw his face for the first time in the light from the lamps strung along the boat deck.

She frowned.

'Hhugh Grrant?' she said, bewildered. 'You not Hhugh Grrant. You not.'

Ugo, Ugo whined the keening voices in the dark. *Come, Ugo. Come. It is time.*

He scrambled out of the lifeboat and tumbled in terror down the little ladder and she came deliberately towards him along the deck from the direction of the main staircase, Nguyen Thi Chu, striding purposefully towards him without any hurry, the peasant hat pressed low across her face, the black pyjamas flapping in the breeze, the black-and-white checked scarf around her neck, the sandals slapping quietly against the deck, the knife glinting in the starlight. She looked up once, at Afu's frightened face peering over the edge of the lifeboat, and she looked at Legrandu staggering along the deck, fastening his breeches, dishevelled in his Napoleonic uniform. Without a word she stabbed him twice in the groin, blood spurting from between his legs.

He howled.

Like a wolf. In his pain he could hear himself howl. In his pain he imagined that somewhere on a Corsican mountainside a *mazzere* was dreaming even now of hunting a howling wolf through the forest to its death.

'Napoleon despised the Corsicans,' said Chu in a high-pitched voice. 'He treated them like dogs. He was right.'

He staggered towards the rail for support, clutching his groin, and with a double flick of hand and leg she flipped him over the side of the ship, not even bothering to watch as he fell fifteen storeys screaming into the ocean.

In the second before his body hit the water and the prehistoric ocean monsters smelled his blood and twitched towards him in the deep, he saw in the darkness of his memory the jealous dead carrying his coffin at noon across the Place de la Libération and into the church of Sainte-Marie des Grâces. He heard the *squadra d'arozza* chanting the Mass for the Dead, their white knuckles clutching the silver handles, their bones clicking and rattling the chains on the wall beside the great door, the groaning penitential chains of the *Catenacciu*.

Chu looked up again at Afu in the lifeboat and walked

towards her, wiping the blade against the black pyjamas, leaving a scarlet wound on the cloth.

Afu screamed.

Chu scrambled towards her up the ladder into the darkness of the lifeboat, like all those ladders in the tunnels of Cu Chi, like so often before. The face in front of her was black in the darkness, the eyes rolling white in the night like the eyes of the black GI in the tunnel so long ago.

Chu lunged with the knife at the rolling eyes and slashed once across the neck, slicing the windpipe with one blow, blood gushing just like the GI.

She laughed. *God bless America! God bless the U. S. of A.*

The GI was dead already beside her in the lifeboat.

Chu lay down beside the GI and listened to the body gurgling, bleeding and farting in the darkness of the tunnel.

When the GI's body was still at last she cut her own wrists and as the blood crept warm and sticky down her fingers she lay in the darkness and waited for the black mist to wrap behind her eyes and for Tran Xuan Kai and Quang Linh to come and fetch her home to join the ancestors.

Just after eleven o'clock the diners began to surge excitedly out of the banqueting hall and up the stairways onto the boat deck to witness the murder of the comet. Most of them were wearing sunglasses to guard their eyes against the sudden flash of the explosions and they crammed into every available space and stared up at the sky.

The comet's head was huge and bright now, its light rivalling the gleam of the moon. Its tail sparkled across thousands of miles in the darkness, trailing behind it across Fiji and the Coral Sea and the Queensland coast of Australia.

Loudspeakers along the deck boomed with a CNN broadcast filling the minutes with speculation.

At 11.16 a great silence fell across the globe: in the darkness of the deep Pacific islands, the icy wastes of Siberia, the massive outback spaces of Australia, in the evening twilight of Calcutta and the paddyfields of Vietnam, in the sultry afternoons of Madagascar and the Middle East, in the golden blaze of noon in Lagos and Tangier, in the ageing mornings of Brazil and Greenland, in the dawning of the great Americas. The peoples of the Earth gazed up in wonder at the sky and held their breath.

For a moment even the global Babel of the airwaves fell silent. A thousand languages all seemed inadequate. Words were unnecessary once again, just as they had been in the very beginning.

Nat Wakonde stood in the jostling crowd on the boat deck with his arm around Helga. The smell of her hair bewitched him. It smelled of apples. *Tonight. Please God. Tonight.*

Murdoch, squeezed between a pirate, a Druid priest and a Mickey Mouse, realised to his surprise that he was holding Caroline's hand. Their hands were sweating.

Kelly stood beside them, silent. He began to whisper the Hail Mary.

Stella Barrett was up on the bridge with Captain Eliades, his officers and her Eight Living Legends, watching the comet through powerful binoculars with filtered lenses, her face bathed in the green glow of the radar console. Her face was a portrait of delight. The banquet had been a triumph. And now they were going to have the most spectacular firework display in history. She looked across at the skipper and smiled. She licked the corners of her lips.

In Los Angeles, Marlowe was watching the comet on TV. His heart was pounding.

'Cool it, baby,' said Bogey.

'Jeez, I'm all stressed out.'

'No sweat,' said Bogey. 'Relax. Be happy.'

Only van der Merwe was unable to watch the comet. Down in his little cabin on Magellan Deck he was lying semi-conscious on the floor of his bathroom. In the depths of his helplessness he realised now that he was never going to make it up to the banqueting hall. He was far too weak. The painkillers had dulled even his resolution. It could not be long now, surely. And what did it really matter if he did not make his speech of denunciation? The bomb would still go off at midnight, wherever the steward had left it.

He pressed his stubbly cheek against the cool tiles of the bathroom floor. It was good here. He could sleep.

He could hear a Go-Away bird chattering beyond the bluegums and cedrilla trees.

He could smell the early morning, the pine and gum, damp grass, dust, animal hides, warm elephant dung.

He could hear Hephzibah scolding him for not dying in bed.

'Christ Almighty!' said a voice at the edge of the crowd on the boat deck. 'There's blood dripping from the lifeboat.'

In the silence that fell like a shroud at 11.16 the tension was pierced by Helga's shrill voice.

'This is being against God law, *ja*,' she cried.

Her voice was like a siren.

Nat squeezed her hand.

'This universe is being too beautiful for desecration with nuclear weapons, *ja*,' she shouted.

'Shut up, you stupid German cow,' yelled someone.

'Sssh!'

'For God's sake!'

'Why are you all being afraid to be dying?' she shouted. 'We all must be dying but not the world. We must not be killing the world. We should be leaving the comet alone. The comet is coming from God.'

In the seconds just before 11.17 the blackness of the sky beside the distant silver comet flared suddenly three times, three flashes winking like amber traffic lights in the darkness.

'There they are!'

'That's it!'

'They got it, bejaysus!'

A roar went up from the ship.

'Hey! Hey!'

'Wowee!'

'Whooo-ha!'

But the comet came on, unblinking, its tail streaming like a victory salute.

There was a terrible silence.

Aboard the *Celebrity* a man shouted.

Kelly crossed himself and began to recite the Lord's Prayer.

A woman wailed.

'Dear God!'

'Ah, Jeez!'

'They missed it!'

'This is good,' shouted Helga. 'The God is good.'

All over the boat deck people fell to their knees and began to pray.

A keening noise could be heard from beside one of the lifeboats.

Someone started sobbing.

Someone started screaming.

'They missed it!' boomed the CNN commentator. 'Dear Lord, they missed it. The thing's still coming.'

Nat wrapped his arms around Helga and hugged her close. He pressed his nose into her hair.

'They missed it,' he whispered.

'I am glad,' she said. She smiled at him. 'I am not being afraid to be dying.'

He pressed his face against hers. 'Come with me now, my love,' he whispered. 'Come with me now.'

Murdoch squeezed Caroline's hand.

'Ah, shit!' he said.

She started crying and buried her face in his chest.

Up on the bridge Stella Barrett removed the binoculars from her eyes. She stared at her guests. She stared at Captain Eliades.

'But they've got thousands of nuclear warheads,' she said. 'Why did they fire only three?'

The skipper ground his teeth together. 'Perhaps they were over-confident. Or worried about the fallout. Pollution.'

'But the party,' she said. 'What about the party?'

'The party's over, you stupid bloody woman,' said the princess.

In Los Angeles, Marlowe was sitting in virtual reality at the debris-scattered *Celebrity* staff table in the deserted ballroom aboard the *Celebrity,* but he was also watching the comet on TV as it danced between the flashes of nuclear light. The table in the banqueting hall was littered with dirty plates, glasses and napkins. An ashtray overflowed with dead cigarette butts and grey filth. He shuddered. How could people abuse their bodies like that?

A scuffed khaki knapsack lay against the bulkhead beside the table. Across the front of it the name K R U G E R was stencilled in fading black letters.

The Hubble Space Telescope had locked onto the comet firmly already and was tracking it all the way as it came on towards the Earth with a glorious resolution, its beauty bright and sharp.

It really is beautiful, thought Marlowe. Its head was sleek and silver, its tail flowing like a sailor's hair.

He shivered.

There was something noble, too, about its inevitability. You might as well defy the will of God.

Marlowe tugged his T-shirt off, gasping with the effort, and struggled to reach his sneakers.

'Gimme Tom Cruise,' he wheezed. 'The astronaut.'

'Sure thing, baby,' said Bogart, retrieving the captured image from the VR memory.

'And Sly Stallone.'

A good name, that, Stallone: stallion. Italian.

Marlowe removed his pants. The sweat was dribbling down his face.

'And Michael Douglas. And that Filipino kid. The one with the big dick.'

'Check.'

And then when he had had them all he was going to have the biggest pig-out ever in the history of the world as he watched the comet go down on Los Angeles.

From the north-west, high above the islands of Tuvalu, Kiribati and Nauru, there came a sudden split-second flash across the sky that sliced the darkness and splashed the comet with pure white light.

'Lasers!' cried the CNN commentator. 'They're using lasers!'

Another flash zapped across the sky, nudging the comet.

A third.

A fourth.

The comet seemed to falter for a second, hanging in space, and then it seemed to dance with the moon.

Then it skittered away towards the south-east, high above Niue and the Cook Islands towards Pitcairn and Easter, skipping across the outer ionosphere like a child's stone skimming a pond.

'My God, they've done it!'

'Lasers!'

'Brilliant!'

'Lasers!'

'Oh God! Thank God! Thank you, God!'

A roar went up from every ship stretched out along the date line, a huge animal sound like a million lions bellowing at the moon. Applause swept across the boat deck of the *Celebrity*, a vast torrent of sound like wind whirling through the heart of a firestorm.

The comet seemed to acknowledge the applause as it went, surfing across the upper atmosphere as elegant and graceful as a ballet dancer.

'The world is saved!' croaked the CNN announcer. 'The Pentagon has just confirmed that the comet has been edged off course away from the Earth. Already it is heading back out to space.'

The comet swayed in the solar breeze, flicking its tail across the South Pacific and the islands of South America, dancing and spiralling away across the blue and gold towards the outer darkness.

'My God!' said the CNN announcer. 'Newsflash. The Pentagon has just announced that it was not the USA that fired the lasers. It was China. Some secret new high-powered laser beams. The lasers were fired by the Chinese!'

Murdoch hugged Caroline Ponsonby. His fedora fell off and was trampled in the crush. Her Tudor ruff dug painfully sharp into his neck. He did not care. She clung to him as though she would never let him go.

'The Chinks!' he said. 'Strewth! Welcome to the Pacific millennium. Fuck me!'

'Any time you like,' she said. She hugged him hard. 'I thought you'd never ask.'

Up on the bridge The Editor glared at the princess. 'So the party's over, is it?' she snarled. 'Get a life, Princess. Arrogant bitch!'

On VR in Los Angeles Marlowe was rising naked from the empty *Celebrity* table in the deserted banqueting hall aboard the *Celebrity* and was about to molest the image of Tom Cruise when Kelly came into the hall and sat at the table. He removed his green, pointed cap and wiped his brow.

'Aw, hell,' said Marlowe. 'This ain't the real Tom Cruise. This is just another goddam lookalike.'

The highwayman followed Kelly into the banqueting hall.

He was carrying the flintlock pistol.

'Paddy,' he said.

Kelly looked up.

'Paddy, it's me,' said the highwayman. He raised his mask.

'Jaysus!' said Kelly. 'Bill Warren. My God, what are you doing here?'

'I'm trying to find The Editor, the bitch.'

'I think she's like up on the bridge, so she is. But –'

The knapsack leaning against the bulkhead beside the table exploded with a mighty roar that blew a hole in the bulkhead and sent tables and chairs flying across the banqueting hall.

Kelly was hurled across the room.

Warren was catapulted through the door.

The explosion roared across the Internet, deafening Marlowe.

'Jeee-sus!' said Marlowe.

A pain seared his chest. Sweat poured down his face.

He staggered away from the image of Tom Cruise, clutching his chest.

The heart attack hit him with a searing spasm of pain. His head jolted back ferociously, cracking his skull against the floor. His legs jerked uncontrollably, kicking like a heifer in an abattoir. His fist smashed down on the EXIT button.

'So long,' said Bogey. 'Have a nice day.'

The computer played a little tune and its screen went black.

As Marlowe died an ambulance siren howled along the freeway in the dark.

'An explosion in the banqueting hall, Captain,' said one of the officers when Captain Eliades telephoned the bridge.

'Emergency procedures.'

'Hardly anyone in there, thank God. Most people up on deck.'

'Any hurt?'

'Two dead. Two men.'

'Who?'

'Don't know yet about one of them. There's not much of him left. But the other is an Irishman. Kelly.'

'Irish, eh? The IRA. The bastard. What about the vessel?'

'Not too bad. Damaged bulkheads, a big hole in the deck, blackened ceiling. Luckily it was only a timing device, just a detonator.'

'Master-at-Arms.'

'Sir!'

'Cordon the hall off. There may be another bomb.'

'Sir!'

'Evacuate the deck. Three decks. Above and below. How the hell did the bomb get on board?'

Captain Eliades swore. 'An Irishman, eh? The bastard. I suppose he was planting the thing when it went off. The Irish bastard.'

Hendrik van der Merwe heard the muffled explosion as he lay semi-conscious on the floor of the bathroom beside his cabin. His brain felt muzzy. Why was it only a muffled explosion? Where was the nuclear holocaust? Or was he dead already?

The pain was returning, probing the deepest recesses of his body like a rat investigating the sewers. He lay in the darkness listening to the rasping of his breathing, listening to the relentless pounding of his heart. On and on and on it went. Pounding pounding pounding. Would it never stop?

His heart beat on and on and on, relentlessly.

Helga and Nat lay together in their cabin on Magellan Deck. They were still not lovers. They held each other like old friends.

'Poor Paddy,' said Nat. 'What a way to die. How can they all just carry on as though nothing had happened? How can they all carry on dancing?'

She cradled his head against her breast, against the little blue tattoo of the dove of peace.

'He was such a nice man,' said Nat. 'So kind. And gentle.

How can they just go on as though nothing has happened? How can they even think that he was responsible for it?'

He lay against her breast like a child. She held him close. She stroked his hair. It was thick and wiry, springy under her fingers. He smelled of wood smoke.

I could love this man, she thought.

They lay together in silence for long minutes, as though they would never now run out of time, as though they had for ever.

He traced his fingers across her lips.

'I'm going to resign,' he said. 'I'm not staying after this.'

'And what will you be doing?'

'I'm going to go back home,' he said. 'South Africa. They need people like me.'

He brushed her hair away from her temple.

'Come with me,' he said.

She kissed his fingers.

'First we make wonderful love, *ja*?' she said. 'And then I say yes.'

On the bridge the Greek First Officer watched the dawn come up over Western Samoa.

Down below they were still carousing throughout the ship, still singing, dancing, drinking, boasting, fornicating. Down there it was like the last days of Pompeii. The whole ship was throbbing with relief and optimism. Who cared about the bomb and the two dead terrorists? It served them right. Even the skipper was behaving like a teenager. Half an hour ago the Second Officer had spotted the skipper kissing the woman Barrett in a corner of the library. She seemed to have lost her white head-dress and halo.

The First Officer dared not tell the skipper the truth. Not yet.

Someone had obviously been tampering with the computer. That was the only possible explanation. Some joker had hacked into it across the Internet and had altered the navigation settings.

He checked the navigation record again. There was no doubt about it.

At midnight the *Celebrity* had not been just a few yards to the west of the international date line after all. At midnight, because of computer error, it had been just a few yards to the east of the date line.

This morning was not the 1 January at all.

It was still yesterday.

It was still the 31 December 1999.

The *Celebrity* was going to be the very last place in all the world to enter the new millennium.

Half a million miles away the comet sang as it danced away into space, leaving the pretty little blue-green planet behind yet again. It tossed its head as it went, flicking its tail like a gossamer dragon, heading back across the universe across a billion miles of yet another millennium, back the way it had been so many times before.

Next time.

For sure.

Next time.

ACKNOWLEDGEMENTS

I am especially grateful to Brian MacArthur of *The Times* for making it possible for me to research this book in South Africa, Corsica, Vietnam, Singapore, and Australia and to sample the joys of a modern cruise liner between Bermuda and Boston.

I am also grateful to Singapore Airlines and New World Hotels for their generous assistance in Vietnam, to the Marina Mandarin Hotel and the Singapore Tourist Promotion Board for their generous hospitality in Singapore, and to Austravel for their generous hospitality in the southern hemisphere.

I must thank Emma Heald for her expert advice about the various diplomatic and political conflicts over the Spratly Islands in the South China Sea; Anthony Baring for allowing me to ransack his knowledge of computers and for introducing me to the mysteries of the Internet; Thu Stern for advice about Vietnamese names and words; the Corsican musical group I Muvrini for the words of their haunting songs '*À Voce Rivolta*', '*À Tè Corsica*' and '*À Pena Cum'è Tè*' (© 1991 AGFB); Hamish Hamilton for permission to quote from *Playback* by Raymond Chandler; Leslie

Thomas for help with research on Tonga; and James Leith and Auberon Waugh for choosing the food and wines for the ten-course millennium banquet described in Chapter 13.

I would also like to acknowledge with gratitude my debt to the following authors' books:

T.V. Bulpin, *Lost Trails of the Transvaal* (Printpak Books, 1989)

Dorothy Carrington, *Granite Island: A Portrait of Corsica* (Penguin, 1984)

Dorothy Carrington, *The Dream-Hunters of Corsica* (Weidenfeld & Nicolson, 1995)

Bob Cotton and Richard Oliver, *The Cyberspace Lexicon* (Phaidon, 1994)

John Dyson, *The South Seas Dream* (Heinemann, 1982)

John Fisher, *Paul Kruger: His Life and Times* (Secker & Warburg, 1974)

Fodor's South Pacific (Fodor's Travel Publications, 1991)

G. N. Garmonsway's translation of *The Anglo-Saxon Chronicle*

Graham Hancock, *Fingerprints of the Gods* (Heinemann, 1995)

John Hogue, *Nostradamus: The New Revelations* (Element Books, 1994)

Peter Hunter Blair, *Introduction to Anglo-Saxon England* (Cambridge University Press, 1977)

Tony Koenderman, Jan Langen and André Viljoen, *Van der Merwe: 100 stories* (Lorton Publications, 1975)

Ed Krol, *The Whole Internet Catalog and User's Guide* (O'Reilly & Associates Inc, 1992)

Peter Lorie, *The Millennium Planner* (Boxtree, 1995)

H. R. Loyn, *Anglo-Saxon England and the Norman Conquest* (Longman, 1991)

A. T. Mann, *Millennium Prophecies: Predictions for the Year 2000* (Element Books, 1992)

Tom Mangold and John Penycate, *The Tunnels of Cu Chi* (Hodder and Stoughton, 1985)

Claire Nevill, *White River Remembered* (Natal Witness Printing and Publishing Co)

Suzanne Romaine, *Pidgin and Creole Languages* (Longman, 1988)

Duncan Steel, *Rogue Asteroids and Doomsday Comets* (John Wiley, 1995)

Sir Frank Stenton, Oxford History of *Anglo-Saxon England* (OUP, 1971)

Paul Theroux, *The Happy Isles of Oceania* (Hamish Hamilton, 1992)

Rita van Dyk, *Eastern Transvaal Travel Guide* (1993)

Richard West, *War and Peace in Vietnam* (Sinclair-Stevenson, 1995)

Other bestselling Warner titles available by mail:

☐ Quite Ugly One Morning	Christopher Brookmyre	£6.99
☐ Country of the Blind	Christopher Brookmyre	£6.99

The prices shown above are correct at time of going to press, however the publishers reserve the right to increase prices on covers from those previously advertised, without further notice.

WARNER BOOKS

WARNER BOOKS
Cash Sales Department, P.O. Box 11, Falmouth, Cornwall, TR10 9EN
Tel: +44 (0) 1326 372400, Fax: +44 (0) 1326 374888
Email: books@barni.avel.co.uk.

POST AND PACKING:
Payments can be made as follows: cheque, postal order (payable to Warner Books) or by credit cards. Do not send cash or currency.
All U.K. Orders   **FREE OF CHARGE**
E.E.C. & Overseas   25% of order value

Name (Block Letters) _____

Address_____

_____

Post/zip code:_____

☐ Please keep me in touch with future Warner publications

☐ I enclose my remittance £_____

☐ I wish to pay by Visa/Access/Mastercard/Eurocard

Card Expiry Date

_____